Praise for C...

'...nthralling and wonderfully r... ... with gorgeous ...racters, this is perfect to cu... ... wit... and get lost in'
Katie Ffo...

'A moving, sweeping sag... of l..e and loss'
Dinah Jeff...ies

'Thoroughly engross...g'
Julian Fello...es

'Enthralling... ensnares us in an ... ...ghtening circle of love and despair, secrets an... f...giveness'
Joanna Luml..

Caroline Montague won her first National Poetry competition at 10 years old and from that moment dreamed of being a writer. After juggling motherhood with modelling assignments, she founded an Interior Design Company working on many projects in the UK and abroad. Her second marriage to the widowed Conroy Harrowby brought four stepchildren into her life, giving her a wider audience for her imaginative bedtime stories. As a family they all live at the Harrowby ancestral home, Burnt Norton, which famously inspired T S Eliot to write the first of his *Four Quartets*. At last Caroline has the time to fulfil her dream of becoming a full-time author.

A PARIS SECRET

Caroline Montague

ORION

An Orion paperback

First published in Great Britain in 2019 by Orion Fiction
This paperback edition published in 2020 by Orion Fiction,
an imprint of The Orion Publishing Group Ltd
Carmelite House, 50 Victoria Embankment
London EC4Y 0DZ

An Hachette UK Company

1 3 5 7 9 10 8 6 4 2

A CIP catalogue record for this book is
available from the British Library.

ISBN 978 1 4091 8082 1

Typeset at The Spartan Press Ltd,
Lymington, Hants

Printed in Great Britain by Clays Ltd,
Elocograf S.p.A.

www.orionbooks.co.uk

To David Watson MBE with gratitude and thanks

Prologue

To the casual observer, the woman who sat on her own in the corner of the Belle Époque tea house on the Rue de Rivoli, in the first *arrondissement* of Paris, was typical of the many regulars of a certain age who populated Café Angelina. You may have suspected that she would have ordered hot chocolate, or the famous Mont Blanc *patisserie*, but when she chose a glass of Krug Grande Cuvée, you would soon realise this woman was out of the ordinary. If you looked closely you would see the arched, sweeping eyebrows, the thick silver hair that framed her face in soft waves. Her slim fingers could so easily have belonged to a pianist and her cheekbones were high above the delicate curve of her chin. Her gaze, though not as keen as it had once been, still had the power to mesmerise. Her suit, blue wool crêpe, worn with a cream silk shirt, was clearly chosen to match the colour of her eyes. The jacket itself was intriguing, for though not of the latest fashion – nipped in at the waist and decorated with large shell buttons – it harked back to an earlier more glamorous age. To the discerning eye, it was quite probably Schiaparelli. Certainly, the woman at the table was not to be easily dismissed.

When her glass was empty, a waiter emerged at her side. 'Would Madame like some more champagne?'

'Thank you, Armand,' she said, in a low voice that held a hint of laughter. 'Champagne would of course be my preference, but I believe I should wait for my guest.'

'Of course,' he replied, deftly removing the glass, but as he slipped away he smiled. For all her great age, Madame was still quite a lady.

When he had gone, the woman pulled a scrapbook from her crocodile bag, and put it on the table in front of her. She smoothed the fabric cover, her fingers lightly touching the letters inscribed there. '*Sophie Bernot*'. Her hands shook a little as she turned the pages, and then she stopped, a frown creasing her brow. To the outward eye, the thick grey paper held nothing but a faded diagram, curled at the edges, but to the elderly woman it clearly meant everything.

She leant back in the chair, her eyelids closing, remembering the day in 1942 when it all started.

'Sophie Bernot.' The name hung in the air.

The child's eyes flicked open.

'The school prize for the most outstanding project has been awarded to you.'

The child glanced round the assembly hall, aware that everyone was watching her. Her face coloured pink, but there was a feeling of exhilaration in her heart. How hard she had worked for this.

The headmistress's hand was outstretched towards her, and her warm voice rang through the hall.

'Come to the front, Sophie.'

The nine-year-old rose to her feet and walked along the aisle and up the four steps to the podium. She smoothed one of her tightly braided plaits, trying to anchor it to the side of her head.

'Tell us about your project and why you chose it.'

Sophie took the diagram from the headmistress and held it up for everyone to see. She lifted the layer of tissue paper to reveal a diagram of the human heart.

'I chose the heart,' she said, her voice getting stronger as her courage increased, 'because we all have one, and I feel we should know how it works. Like every other organ or tissue in your body, it needs oxygen-rich blood to survive. Blood is supplied to the heart by its own complex system, so without the heart pumping for us day and night the organs and tissues will die, meaning of course that we will die!'

There was a titter around the assembly.

'And one day I'll be a heart surgeon and I promise that I will save people's lives.'

The assembly were listening to her now, their interest roused. A girl wanting to be a surgeon, it was unheard of.

For the next few minutes, she pointed to the valves and arteries depicted in different brightly coloured crayons, and explained their uses. When she had finished, she let the tissue paper fall and looked up at her audience. There was silence in the room and then clapping.

Madame stepped forward and gave her a small silver cup, a bar of chocolate and a book token. Afterwards she caught up with her in the corridor.

'I feel sure you will break the ground for many women in this country, Sophie, and I will do everything in my power to help you.'

Sophie looked up at the headmistress, her young face glowing with intensity. 'Thank you, *madame*, I truly meant my promise. I will mend faulty hearts.'

Madame patted her on the back. 'I know you are longing to tell your brother, so run along home now, but be back bright as a pin in the morning.'

3

After dissecting the chocolate into minute sections with her penknife and sharing it with her class, Sophie ran down the streets, her plaits flying, her long, thin legs quickly covering the ground. She was longing to tell Max, her beloved older brother, and in a few minutes she would see him. At twenty, he was the first Bernot to go university; she would be the second. He would be at home working on his final exam piece, a treatise on sixteenth-century Palladian architecture. She would show him her precious diagram, his face would light up and he would hug her and tell her she was the cleverest girl in the world. She would give him the last square of chocolate.

She entered the Renault factory gates where Hans, the German guard, was standing with his gun propped against his shoulder. '*Guten Tag*, Hans,' she said.

His face softened and he smiled. '*Guten Tag*, Fraulein Sophie.' She didn't hate the Germans, not Hans at any rate. Papa, of course, felt differently. He was the factory manager and had to answer to the German officer in command.

'*Merde*, when will this end?' he had yelled, only a few days before. 'It's bad enough making trucks for their bloody war machine, without having to report back to Daimler-Benz. Every key position is now held by the Boches and I have them crawling over my production lines all hours of the day. Do you know, that makes me a bloody collaborator, and as for Monsieur Renault, one day he will be strung up by his neck, of that I am sure, and with my luck I'll follow.'

At this he had banged his fist on the dinner table and her mother had gasped, her handsome face turning quite pale. 'Cyrille, don't say such things, not in front of Sophie.'

'It's fine Maman, Papa's just cross.'

She had seen her father wince as her mother's leg shot out beneath the table.

4

'I'll give you something to be cross about,' she had hissed, getting up to clear the plates. 'Saying things like that in front of your child!'

Sophie was brought back to the present when Hans called after her. 'Did you win, Sophie?' he asked, sweeping off his cap, his tight blonde curls glinting in the winter sun. She held up the cup.

'*Gut gemacht!*' he saluted, smiling broadly.

Sophie walked briskly through the compound – her mother had always told her not to run, past factory units and housing for the workers, past the bridge to the Île Seguin where the main factory was located, past the German guards. When she reached the small cul-de-sac of terraced cottages where senior management were housed, she opened the gate to number five and turned the key in the lock. She couldn't wait to tell her brother, he had always believed that she would get the prize. She paused for a moment on the doormat, the sunlight slanting through the coloured glass planes. Everything was just as she had left it three hours before, her mother's upright piano was open in the sitting room, the dinner table was covered with the lacy cloth made by a deaf woman several years before, and the Turkish rug was still covering the threadbare patch in the carpet. She picked the letters from the floor and placed them on the hall table then she ran upstairs. Hurtling along the corridor, she opened her brother's door...

What she had seen would define the rest of her life, but as Sophie sat at her table in Café Angelina sixty-six years later, she still couldn't bear to think of it.

A woman at the next table was extolling the virtues of her grandchildren in a loud voice, but she didn't hear her. After all these years *that* door was a barrier she couldn't breach.

Sophie coughed. She could feel her heart pounding in her chest. Her hands were shaking.

She turned the page in the scrapbook. Why after all this time was her father's fury still so real, and her banishment so painful?

She could see her younger self, hanging onto her mother's arm, tears streaming down her face.

'Maman, please don't make me go to Grand-mère Yvette, what have I done?' she had begged. 'Please, I want to be with you and Papa and Max.'

'It is nothing you have done, *ma chérie*, just a misunderstanding between Papa and your brother,' her mother had replied, hugging her tight. 'And you'll be back at the weekend. Grand-mère will be thrilled to have you stay.'

'But you haven't seen my diagram, I won the prize, and *Madame* said I could be a surgeon when I grow up.'

Her mother had taken the diagram and examined it closely. 'My clever, beautiful daughter. I will pin it to the wall by the fireplace, so I can look at it every day.'

'What about Max?'

'Sophie, *ma chérie*, one day I will explain, but now you will have to trust me.'

But she hadn't explained. Three days later Sophie was woken by her grandmother.

'They are coming, Sophie,' she said, shaking her violently. 'The leaflets they dropped from the sky are true, the bombs are coming.'

She bundled her out of the house and down the road towards the safety of the Métro, but not before Sophie had seen night turn to day as flares lit up the streets around her. They were nearing the entrance when the bombing started. The noise was deafening.

'Hurry up, child.' Yvette's voice trembled as she looked up

at the sky. She pushed her down the steps to join the crowd jammed onto the platform. 'We'll be safe down here.'

'But Grand-mère, what about Maman and Papa?'

'They'll be fine, *ma petite*,' she replied, the expression on her face suggesting otherwise.

Sophie sat on a woollen blanket beside her grandmother and pulled her knees to her chest. She stared at her watch, the little green hands luminous in the darkness, but tonight it didn't bring her comfort even though Max had given it to her. It made the minutes go too slowly and the explosions, great thundering bursts of noise, last for ever. Then they stopped and there was quiet in the tunnel, until another wave of bombing shook the ground. As the dust fell like rain mothers nursed their babies, old women clutched their rosaries and veterans of the Great War muttered oaths, remembering past misery.

'Please,' Sophie prayed, rocking to and fro, 'please let this stop.' But her prayers went unanswered, and as the hands of her watch moved inexorably round, she believed the end would come and they would be incarcerated for ever in the claustrophobic tunnel. She would never say goodbye to Max and her parents; she would never get out.

By three o'clock a hush had descended on the Métro station, but Sophie was wide awake. Her stomach was churning, and she wanted her mother. She looked across at her grandmother who was snoring.

'Grand-mère,' she prodded her gently. 'Grand-mère,' she tried again, but when her grandmother only grunted, rolling away from her, Sophie inched her way towards the exit, shivering despite her thick coat. She found the warden smoking a cigarette.

'I need to find my parents.'

He glanced along the platform. 'They'll be here, somewhere.' He inclined his head at the sea of sleeping humanity.

'No, not here, out there.'

'Sorry *mademoiselle*, but you can't leave until the all-clear has sounded – the English are not finished with us yet.' He drew the smoke into his lungs and the end burned orange.

'Has the Renault factory been hit?'

He rolled his eyes. 'What do you think? They're making lorries for the Boches.' He stamped the cigarette beneath his foot.

Sophie felt the dread deep in her gut. 'But my father runs the factory.'

'It seems *les Anglais* have forgotten we are on their side.'

Sophie climbed back over the sleeping bodies and slumped against her grandmother, trying not to cry.

At dawn, the occupants of the shelter came into the light. Children blinked, rubbing grimy fists across their eyes. Adults stared into the distance, where a pall of smoke hung over the Renault factory. The birds had stopped singing and an eerie silence hung in the air, broken only by the wailing of distant fire engines. Sophie's teeth started to chatter. 'I have to find Maman and Papa,' she said, breaking free of her grandmother. 'Follow me, Grand-mère.' But before her grandmother had time to reply, she was gone, running down the street, conscious only of the panic in her heart, entirely oblivious to her grandmother's cries.

By the time she came to the factory gates, her lungs were bursting in her chest. But there were no gates, and no Hans to greet her, only a tangle of twisted metal. She skirted the newly formed craters and the smoking ruins. Her eyes were smarting, she could hardly breathe, but she needed her parents, her house, Max. The roads intersecting the compound had gone; she was confused. Where were the worker's apartments and the little *épicerie* on the corner where her mother queued with her ration books to buy their provisions?

A fireman was sifting through the rubble, throwing aside bricks and jagged shards of glass.

'What has happened to the houses?' she begged.

'You shouldn't be here.' The man turned his soot-covered face towards her. 'This is no place for a child.'

'Please, *monsieur*, where are the houses?'

'Go home *petite*,' he reached out his arm.

She skipped sideways. 'But one of them is my home,' she cried.

She found the cul-de-sac beyond the gutted bridge to the island. Workmen were lifting a beam from a pile of masonry. She stared, unable to comprehend the chaos in front of her. Number two, where Monsieur and Madame Dutoit lived with their three little boys, had gone completely; number one also. And then she saw it: her house. A bed was upended in the remains of the kitchen, it still had a bedcover on it – Max's bedcover – and his painting of Mont Blanc was in the sink. The small upright piano her mother polished every day was wedged beneath a door. Tables, chairs, her mother's apron were scattered in the ruins.

'Maman, Papa, Max, where are you?' she cried, her voice strange in her ears.

Her grandmother panted down the street towards her. 'Sophie, come away,' she said, her own voice cracking with grief.

A workman approached them, shaking his head. 'So many bombs. You could have touched the planes they were flying so low. Nothing is left, the factory on the island has gone, the apartments – so many dead.' He spat on the ground. 'The only warning we received were a few damned leaflets! In all my years, I've never seen such a thing.'

Sophie dived forward, past her grandmother and the workmen. She scrambled over the rubble, fell, picked herself up. 'Maman,' she screamed. 'Maman.' There was no reply.

A workman grabbed her. 'You have to come away, little girl. It's dangerous.'

'No, no, no,' she screamed in reply, beating at his chest as she tried to get away. And then she saw it pinned to the wall by the fireplace: her diagram, fluttering in the breeze.

Chapter One

Sophie Bernot hurried along the corridor of the *Faculté de médicine de Paris*. She glanced at her watch, biting her lip in concern. It was five past nine. On this most important of days, Professor Manon had waylaid her, and now she was late. She ran down the stairs and along the dark and narrow basement passage, her stomach churning as she pushed open the laboratory door.

'*Bonjour* Mademoiselle Bernot, did something or somebody keep you?'

The professor in charge of anatomy lessons stood at the head of a group of students by a granite stone slab. His dark, bushy eyebrows were pulled together in a frown.

'*Pardon*, Professor.'

'You will not be late again,' he said, looking down at her from his great height. 'I risked my reputation to ensure you gained a place. Do not disappoint me. Ah, here comes our body, make way.'

Sophie could feel her cheeks burning and was grateful that all eyes had now turned to the two porters who wheeled the cadaver in on a trolley. The students watched the attendants deftly switch the body onto the stone slab.

'Now, *mes enfants*,' it was the professor's little joke. 'You will gather round the slab and you will listen and watch. Mademoiselle Bernot, if you feel a little faint you will retire quietly, but you are not to disturb the others.'

Sophie lifted her head so that their eyes met. 'I will not be the one to faint, I assure you, Professor.' As the only female student doctor in the hospital she would prove that she was capable.

The porters left, and the class waited.

'Miss Bernot, you may remove the blanket.'

Sophie held her breath. It would be her first glimpse of the body on the slab. Would it be a man or a woman, or even a child? She had seen death before, of course. In the war, it had been all around her. For a second the image of an arm sticking through the rubble at Boulogne-Billancourt broke into her thoughts.

She pulled back the blanket, exposing a young woman with red hair and freckled skin. There was something blatant about the pubic hair that sprung between her white thighs, something brutally stark about the pale lips and staring eyes.

'We shall give her a name – Clara,' the professor said, his voice becoming gentle. 'Not her real name of course, but we will have one moment of silence for the human being she was, and we will treat her with respect.' There was a murmur through the class and then silence as each pupil said their own prayers for Clara.

Sophie looked at the girl and felt infinitely sad. Where did she come from? Did somebody love her, were her relatives grieving a life unlived?

'We will learn more about Clara as the days go by,' the professor continued. 'From her body, we will learn how she died and why. We will learn what she ate yesterday and what social group she came from. The body can tell us everything. Monsieur Thibault, you will go first.'

He passed the scalpel to a young man with dark, unruly hair and dark eyes. The professor then drew his finger in a line from above the girl's chest, down to the abdomen. 'Now Georges, make your cut.'

Though Sophie knew that Clara was beyond pain, she still winced as the blade went in between her breastbone, opening skin, flesh and muscle. As Francois Petout, a tall gangly boy with blonde hair, watched the blade go in, his legs buckled, his formerly ruddy face turned green and he slumped to the floor. She would always remember the thud, the students crowding around him.

'Give him air and a few moments to recover,' the professor advised. 'There will always be one.' He caught Sophie's eye with just a hint of a smile.

Over the next few days, the students came to know Clara. She had been a prostitute and, from the damage to her lungs and the telltale stains on her fingers, she had been a heavy smoker. Frostbite suggested that Clara had been homeless at the time of her death. Slowly the scattered clues gave them a picture of Clara's life. It had been hard and brutal and for Sophie the more she knew, the more difficult it became to remain detached.

As they left the laboratory for the last time, Georges ambled towards her.

'It affected you, didn't it?' he asked, his hands pushed into the pocket of his slightly grubby white coat.

'Yes,' she replied, smiling into his kind brown eyes. 'I imagine I will become used to it, but I will always remember the first time.'

Chapter Two

Sebastian Ogilvie was on his way to the office of Blackheath Holdings Limited when he stopped to look up at the sky. It was a fine morning at the end of May – just the sort of weather for a climb, he grinned, not, of course, that there were any mountains in Mayfair.

He ignored the fluttering of nerves in his stomach and strode on down Bruton Street, his father's briefcase wedged beneath his arm. The dark brown leather was a little battered, the gilding on the family crest faded, but inside the compartment were his ideas for a brand new residential square in Kensington. If the senior partners agreed with his proposals, he would be the leading property developer on the project, from the initial planning stage, right through to completion. It would be quite an undertaking for a twenty-three-year-old, only two years out of university. But then of course, everything had been changed by the war. With so many dead, and a generation of survivors altered by their experiences, there were unlimited opportunities for young men with ideas and ambition.

His father had been one of the casualties. The Honourable Jasper Ogilvie had been forty-four when the war started, and as a major in 11th Hussars, he had come through Egypt unscathed. It was later in the battle to regain France that he was injured at Courseulles-sur-mer in Normandy. His survival was a miracle, his body protected by the two officers who died beside him. He never spoke of Courseulles or his two friends, and the only time he regained some of his former *joie de vivre* was when he was rock climbing with his son. His death six years later came as no real surprise to anyone, but at least it was peaceful; his wife Liliane had found him in his chair beneath his favourite tree in the garden. A copy of the bible lay open in his lap.

Sebastian took a lift to the fifth floor, greeted the girl on reception with a cheerful wave and walked down the plush, carpeted corridor. He stopped outside the boardroom, straightened his tie and knocked on the door.

The three senior partners were waiting for him.

'Good morning, Sebastian.' It was Peter Hamilton, the most dynamic of the partners, forty-five with dark hair streaked with grey and a smile that was said to melt many a female heart.

'I believe you have found an architect for the Cloisters.'

Sebastian cleared his throat. 'Yes, sir, I have. Well at least I am pretty convinced Marcus Donadieu is the one.'

'And why is that?' It was another partner now, Sir Humphrey Gifford, who delighted in intimidating the younger members of his practice, but he was also known to have the keenest eye.

'Because sir, though I have only met him once, I have seen his work, and I find it remarkable. He combines integrity with innovation. I know you wish the square to be in the eighteenth-century style, but Marcus will make it fresh and inspiring.' He took some documents from the briefcase and handed them to Sir Humphrey, who first scrutinised the photographs of the existing bombed-out site, and then the new designs. He passed them to the gentleman on his right.

Andrew Lovell was the oldest partner; a short, dapper man in a pinstripe suit with a carnation in his buttonhole and sparse grey hair. It was his capital that had taken Blackheath Holdings from a small enterprise directly after the war, to the sizeable company it had become. 'I say we get Sebastian to bring this Marcus fellow back to England,' he said, leafing through the plans. 'I've done my homework and his development schemes in Paris and Rouen are excellent. He is also young enough to believe that small projects are still exciting, and his fees should be affordable. As you know I'm not keen on that modernist stuff, and the last office block Denys Lasdun designed for us cost a fortune.' A look passed between the other two partners before Peter Hamilton tapped the plans now lying on the polished mahogany table.

'It seems, Sebastian, you have our vote of confidence. Bring Marcus to England and let's see what he can do.'

'I may have to travel to Paris in order to secure his services, sir, he is a very busy man.'

'So you wish us to take your word for it?' Sir Humphrey enquired with just the suggestion of a twinkle in his eye.

'Yes sir, I think perhaps I do,' Sebastian countered with a wry smile.

'And you will see your mother in Burgundy?'

'If that is agreeable to the partners, Sir Humphrey.'

There was a murmur round the table.

'I suggest you take a week's holiday afterwards. Go and climb one of those mountains you talk so much of, but don't forget to bring back a bottle of my favourite burgundy!'

Outside the boardroom, Sebastian punched his fist in the air.

'Well done, Mr Ogilvie,' Cheryl the receptionist breathed, blushing a deep pink. 'I knew you'd do well.'

'Thank you, Cheryl, that's very kind.'

Sebastian hurtled down the stairs into an office on the first floor.

'I've got it Robert, they're sending me to Paris to fetch him.' The words came out in a rush.

A man with dark hair, and the first hint of lines at the corners of his eyes, looked up from the figures he was working on.

'I assume you are talking about Marcus Donadieu?'

'You know I am.'

'I had no doubt you would impress the boss.'

'Not just one, Robert, all three were there to grill me.'

Robert Marston got up from his desk and clapped his friend on the back. 'Well done. I'm delighted for you. I suggest we have a drink later to celebrate.' He grinned. 'But I have to ask *my* boss, you know what she is like.'

Sebastian did know. Giulietta Marston was Italian, beautiful and feisty. Although her husband had been a Spitfire pilot and a member of Special Operations Executive, he was happy to be ruled by her.

'When you have obtained permission,' Sebastian chuckled. 'Let's go to the Dog and Duck in Soho.'

Robert laughed. 'I am sure I can wangle an hour or two if I promise to put the children to bed.'

As Sebastian left the office he smiled. It was Robert who had recommended him for the position at Blackheath Holdings, and who had also prepped him for his interview. They had become great friends at Oxford. Robert had been in his last year, retraining after the war, while he had been in his first, but though Robert was seven years older they still had a lot in common. Both their mothers were foreign and had returned to their family estates at some point in their lives. Both fathers were dead and they each had one sister whom they adored. Robert would probably return to Italy to run his estate when his mother retired, just as one day Sebastian would take the reins at their estate in France. For a moment he thought of his home.

Le Chateau de Villienne lay above the small village of Pommard in Burgundy. It was built of pale cream stone with large sash windows that bathed the interiors in light. The roof was deeply pitched, with four dormer windows punctuating the grey slate tiles. The central pediment contained yet another window, small and circular, particularly enticing for an adventurous child. His grandmother had always scolded him.

'Sebastian, *mon cherie*, do not lean out so far, come down immediately or you will fall.' How he loved the aristocratic old woman who had remained at the chateau throughout the war, defying the Germans, protecting her precious vineyards with deceit and guile. In fact, Marie-Claire de Villienne's family had managed to stay alive through many tempestuous times. They had retained their heads during the Reign of Terror of 1793, a fact that aggrieved Marie-Claire. 'They took our titles but refrained from taking our lives,' she had said with a sniff, and Sebastian's mother had raised her eyes heavenwards. '*Maman*, you should not feel insulted, your ancestors survived!'

In the nineteenth century two wings either side of the house had been removed, and three decorative balconies added. Despite its still generous size, the house felt intimate and cosy, the rooms full of furniture, porcelain and paintings acquired by *la famille Villienne* over the centuries. The facade was covered in a wisteria that in early summer was a mass of purple blooms. His father would cut it back every February, wobbling on the decrepit ladder, despite his wife's objections.

'I may have a gammy leg,' he had stressed, 'but if I can climb the Matterhorn, I can certainly climb a ladder.'

It was no wonder Sebastian liked climbing; it was in the family's genes. As soon as he could walk, his father had taken him to the granite massif of the Morvan. It was the perfect place to learn. Sebastian remembered his father's patience when teaching him how to belay the ropes and his joy when Sebastian scaled the largest face. They had done so much together, and his death had left an empty place in his heart.

Sebastian was putting his clothes into the suitcase when the telephone rang. It was Robert Marston. 'Permission granted,' he said.

Sebastian's eyes lit up. 'Give me fifteen minutes to finish packing and I'll be there.'

After adding his walking boots, his maps, compass and his father's silver whistle to the case, he snapped the catches, and headed out of his flat in Marylebone. Nineteen minutes later he walked into the Dog and Duck in Soho.

Robert Marston watched Sebastian come in and chuckled to himself. His friend's coat was done up on the wrong buttons, and his floppy fair hair hung over his eyes. He looked so devilishly handsome that everyone watched him as he entered the room.

'What's your order?' Sebastian asked, grinning at Robert.

'Whisky please.'

Sebastian sauntered over to the bar, oblivious to the attention of males and females alike.

Perhaps, Robert thought without envy as Sebastian placed the order, it was this lack of vanity, combined with his sheer vitality, that had first impressed him in Oxford. He was a tonic after the mayhem of the war. He looked up as Sebastian flung himself down in his chair, slopping half the contents of his beer over the table.

'Oops,' he grinned, 'sorry old chap.'

Robert smiled. When he was with Sebastian, the killing and the chaos was a thing of the past. There was something so refreshing about him that brought only positivity.

'So did you get a grilling from the wife?' Sebastian asked, mopping the mess with a cloth.

'I did,' he replied, thinking of Giulietta standing in the hallway, her amber eyes flashing at him.

'So you go out, huh, and leave me to look after the babies?'

'If you really mind, I won't go.'

She had glared at him for a moment then she had started to laugh, pulling his face towards her and kissing him on the lips.

'You still do it to me with those puppy eyes of yours. Go on, but not too long, I don't want that blond boy taking all of your time.'

Chapter Three

Two days after Sebastian's meetings with the senior partners, he was sitting opposite Marcus Donadieu in his favourite restaurant, Au Pied de Cochon, in Rue Coquillière. It was his father who had first taken him as a treat before the war had started. They had feasted like kings on filet mignon and *fraises des bois*, the small wild strawberries that he had dreamt of when living in England during the war.

Sebastian gestured to a waiter, and an elderly man hurried over.

'Ah Monsieur Jaubert, it is you, is it not? It is so good to see you. I hope you are keeping well? You probably don't remember me, Sebastian Ogilvie?'

The waiter peered at Sebastian, and tapped his forehead, his wrinkled face wreathed with smiles.

'Is it really you, Monsieur Ogilvie?' he drew out the last syllable. 'Last time I saw you, you were a child.'

'One and the same, *monsieur*.'

'It is a pleasure to see you again, and your father, how is he? Such a good man.'

'Sadly he is no longer with us.'

'*Je suis malheureux*. So many fine men gone.'

Sebastian nodded. 'I am afraid so, but I'm here now with my friend and colleague Monsieur Donadieu.'

'Welcome,' he turned to Marcus. 'I hope you will enjoy our superb cuisine. I can recommend trotter of the pig, it is the favourite recipe of our Président.'

Marcus visibly winced. 'If you will forgive me, I will examine the menu first.'

While Marcus looked through the menu, Sebastian cast his eye round the restaurant. The mirrored walls and art-deco columns were just as he remembered them. The long, red leather banquettes were filled with men and women who talked and laughed with an air of sophistication that suggested they were used to luxury. Waiters hurried back and forth to the kitchens, carrying silver platters with domed covers. Expensive bottles of wine were brought to the tables, dishes were changed, courses were served; the same atmosphere had been preserved. As a cover was removed from a filet of beef at the table next to him, and the delicious aroma wafted through the air, Sebastian remembered another smell, his first encounter with black pudding at his uncle's gloomy mansion in the Lancashire moorlands, where he was sent in '39.

'Have you never seen a sausage, boy?' his uncle had glowered down the long table. 'You will eat every last mouthful, there's going to be a war, people will starve.'

Sebastian had eaten everything on his plate, but he could never look at black pudding without thinking of his uncle. Older than his father by a year, and crippled with polio, he seemed to take his resentment out on his nephew.

It was actually a welcome relief when term finally started at the Catholic boarding school in Yorkshire.

He was jolted back to the present when Marcus put down the menu.

'I would choose the *sole meunière*,' he said, looking a little bashful. 'But it is very expensive.'

'The firm are paying, and in any event I have been told to entertain you well.'

Their orders came – filet mignon for Sebastian and the sole for Marcus.

'Sometime in the future I would like my own practice, Donadieu and Frère,' Marcus mused once the waiter had finished filleting his fish and his plate was in front of him.

'You have a brother?'

'I don't actually,' Marcus grinned. 'But somehow it sounds more professional.'

'No family?'

Marcus's eyes clouded. 'My parents are both dead.'

'I'm sorry.'

'In these times everyone has lost someone, but I have much to be grateful for. I'm alive and a little successful. How many can boast that they are happy with their work?'

'And your name, Donadieu?'

Marcus sighed. 'Given to God, a good name, no?'

Sebastian could sense the young man's sadness. He looked at him, his expression questioning.

'One day I will explain.' Marcus tapped his slim fingers together in a spire. 'But Sebastian, I can tell you that our worlds are very different: you come from a rich, privileged background, and I come from nowhere at all.'

Sebastian was about to protest when Marcus stopped him.

'You are unlike so many of the rich, arrogant young men that I have met. I would very much like to work with you.'

'Presumably you work for any client that can afford you?'

Marcus pushed his tortoiseshell glasses back on his nose. 'Actually no, if I do not get on with a client, they are passed on to one of the other architects in the practice. My firm know that

23

I dislike working for people who are not *sympathique*. I get a little anxious. You see, Sebastian, my designs come from within, without passion there is no art. You must think I am a pedant.'

Sebastian shook his head. 'Integrity is everything.'

'Well then, we have this in common, and I have heard that you also like to climb. I have done my homework you see.'

'A legacy from my father,' Sebastian confirmed.

For the next half hour the two men discussed various walks they had done or hoped to do, and cliff faces they would like to attempt.

'If you are going to Chamonix you should walk up to glacier d'Argentière. It takes a couple of hours, but it's worth it, the views are extraordinary. And of course the Mer de Glace.' He put his elbows on the table and leant forward, his dark eyes earnest. 'I remember my father telling me that one day there would be a cable car right up to the top of the Aiguille du Midi. At the time I didn't believe it possible, but he was right, Sebastian, and it's going to be the highest in the world. Soon I suppose there will be more cable cars, more people on the mountains. Maybe I'm selfish, but I believe they should be left to those who wish to climb them.'

Sebastian smiled. 'I think it's called progress.'

'We seem to manage to destroy so much in this world. I would like the mountains to be left alone.'

'To a long and happy collaboration.' Sebastian shook Marcus's hand as they left the restaurant. 'I feel sure the project in Chelsea will be the first of many.'

Marcus grinned at his new friend. 'To success and to finishing my backlog of work here!'

'To climbing Mont Blanc.'

'One day, Sebastian Ogilvie, you will do it, and I would very much like to come with you.'

Chapter Four

Sophie Bernot glanced at Max's painting of the Mont Blanc massif that hung in the tiny sitting room of her grandmother's flat in the Latin Quarter of Paris. She had rescued it from the ruins of her parent's house in Boulogne-Billancourt. It was all she had left of her brother. She hugged her grandmother, slung her rucksack over her shoulder and headed for the door.

'Be careful, Sophie,' the old lady said, concern showing on her lined face. 'I worry; you know that I do.'

'Of course I will, Grand-mère, it's only a walk.'

'But you have your boots, and they mean one thing: a mountain.'

Sophie laughed. 'You have eyes in the back of your head, Grand-mère, but I love you. I will be careful.'

Sophie was humming as she walked to the Métro. Medical school was exhausting and exacting; though it was all she had ever wanted, she needed this break more than anything.

But it wasn't to be an ordinary holiday, it was a pilgrimage to a mountain path above Chamonix – to the exact spot where Max set up his portable easel that summer, so long ago. They had all been there, Maman, Papa and Sophie, and while Max painted, and her parents slept in the shade, she had made a chain of flowers from the abundant buttercups that grew in the rough grass.

'I would give you diamonds, but these will have to do,' she had proclaimed hanging them around her brother's neck.

'A king can have diamonds,' he had laughed. 'But I have something far more precious.'

Then she had leant over his shoulder, congratulated him on his painting and he had put his brush aside and picked her up, hugging her tight. 'But I am not as bright as my little sister. One day we will have a doctor in the family, how clever is that!'

Since the bombing of the Renault factory, Sophie had searched for her brother, prayed to the Virgin Mary that he was alive and that one day he would walk through the door. But she knew she was fooling herself. Max had died in the ruins beside her parents. Now she would say goodbye to him for ever and move on with her life. She hoped she would at last know some peace.

As the train sped through the tunnels, she thought back over the last three years. Getting into medical school had been easy, staying there was different. She had known from the start that eighty per cent of her peers would be gone by the end of the year.

When her first-year exams had approached, she had studied night and day. Her textbooks on the physiology and pharmacology of the circulatory, respiratory, neurological and renal systems were dog-eared from working. She had researched the latest papers on heart disease, cancer, neurology, pathology, bacteriology virology and immunology. The list went on. As she had watched the failed students pack up their bags, her regret had been tinged with relief. She knew only too well that her survival had relied on hard work and self-discipline.

In the third year she had started her clinical years. Though the afternoons were spent in lectures, she spent the mornings on the wards. Every three months she had moved to another department. She took blood, wrote up the notes, followed the doctors on their rounds. She was involved in every aspect of medicine, but the path she had chosen many years before was still clear. One day she would become a heart surgeon, she would achieve her dream and fulfil her childhood promise.

After taking the overnight train from Paris to Saint-Gervais-les-Bains-Le Fayet, Sophie changed onto the narrow-gauge railway in the direction of Chamonix and Argentière. As she looked up at the snow-covered peaks, sadness threatened to overwhelm her. An image of her brother pushed to the front her mind. He had been sitting in the seat opposite reading aloud, his face flushed with excitement.

'"I cannot otherwise convey to you an image of this body of ice, broken into irregular ridges and deep chasms than by comparing it to waves instantaneously frozen in the midst of a violent storm." This was written by an eighteenth-century traveller, William Coxe, about the Mer de Glace, the largest of the Mont Blanc glaciers,' Max had said, taking her small hand in his own. 'Can you imagine an Englishman coming all this way? No trains, no proper transport.' His dark eyes had been shining as he leant towards her. 'Today there are trains to get here, and cable cars, but then ...' He had stopped talking and gazed from the window towards the seracs, the stark ice teeth where the glacier broke up and became a stream. 'What must he have thought when he first saw all of this? Tomorrow, we shall walk a little way up the mountain together.'

'But I want to climb like you, high over the valley with boots and ice axes and crampons.'

'One day when you are bigger I promise we shall, but Sophie, you are still only seven!'

Sophie remembered her indignation as Max had tweaked her ear.

'I can do it,' she had stated, pulling away from him. 'I'll show you that I can.' Now all these years later she still had the same determination, but her naivety had gone.

At the sound of the piercing whistle that heralded their approach to Argentière, Sophie's thoughts returned abruptly to the present. She pulled her rucksack from the overhead locker and helped an elderly Frenchwoman onto the platform with her suitcase.

'Please could you point me in the direction of the Auberge les Gentianes,' she asked the porter.

'Straight on, *mademoiselle*, it is a kilometre at the most.'

'Thank you, *monsieur*.'

She was walking down the road when a taxi sped past. A man was glancing through the window towards her, a magnetic smile lighting his face. For an instant Sophie paused, their eyes met, then the taxi was gone, and she was alone on the empty road. She kicked at a pebble, blushing deeply and strode on. She would not have fantasies about strange men in remote places, however good-looking they were.

She was nearing her destination when she remembered the last words Max had said to her. Her face crumpled. 'Oh Max,' she sighed, wondering whether it was the wind that was making her eyes so wet.

She had reached the *auberge* and was hovering in the reception area, breathing in the familiar smells of wood smoke and floor polish, when a thought occurred to her. If she registered using her full name, the owner may well remember her visit all those years before. Bernot was unusual for these parts, and the last thing she wanted was to be recognised. She couldn't bear to answer any questions about her family, to hear the sympathy in their voices, it was still too painful. It would be so much easier to be a stranger, totally anonymous.

When the girl at the desk was taking her details and asked her name, she looked her straight in the eye.

'Sophie,' she said. 'Just Sophie.'

It was dawn and as Sophie stood at the window, vast shadows shifted and moved across the mountains. She dressed quickly and went down to the pine wood dining room. The six tables were laid with checked red and white cloths and in the corner of the room a fire simmered in a cast-iron stove. It was cosy and intimate, in complete contrast to the changing landscape outside. A waitress with a frilled apron and blonde plaits took her order and Sophie smiled to herself; Heidi had walked from the pages of her favourite children's book. When her breakfast arrived, brioche and a cup of steaming hot chocolate, she thought of her grandmother.

'You will stay in a proper hotel,' she had insisted, pushing a roll of francs into her hand. When Sophie had protested she had kissed her on the forehead. 'One day you will afford to pay for yourself and it will be only the best, *mon petit chou*, but for now you will humour your old grandmother.' She had paused for a moment, her dark eyes scrutinising Sophie. 'Why not go to the Auberge les Gentianes? You may bury a few ghosts.'

Sophie had finished the last brioche in the small wicker basket, when she returned to her room. A glimmer of sun was beginning to show on the mountaintops, but she still needed to be prepared. She put on her red-belted jacket and took her water bottle, gloves and a large bar of Lindt chocolate, stowing them all in her rucksack. After hanging her whistle around her neck she went down to the reception desk.

She found the walkers' book, wrote down the route she would take, and signed with a flourish. Lacing up her boots, she headed outside.

*

Sebastian had set his alarm clock and was in the dining room by seven. On the table beside him, an empty plate caught his eye.

Someone was keen, he thought, frowning in annoyance. This was quickly followed by a sheepish grin. His thoughts were childish, it was not a competition. He was here because he loved walking, not because he needed to be first up the mountain. He was signing his name in the walkers' book, when he noticed a signature above his in bold, black ink, 'Sophie'. He looked at the route she was taking, intrigued. So this young woman was heading towards the viewpoint at the bottom of the glacier d'Argentière. Well so would he.

But of course he was premature to assume she was young; she was probably one of those robust, middle-aged British women who strode up the mountains as if they were walking in the Chilterns.

Sebastian took a quick look at his map and set off for the village. He crossed the bridge over the stream, went past the church with the pointed spire and headed down a small lane bordered with alpine chalets. Where the lane ended and the forest began, he followed a path into the lower slopes of the mountain. The sun was rising as the path wound upwards, shadows flickering through the trees. After forty minutes of hard walking he was out of the woods and the village was far below him. He wanted to take a break, but it had become a matter of pride. He threw his head back and strode on, invigorated by the mountain air and the extraordinary beauty surrounding him. Either side of the path, the scrubby grass was filled with alpine flowers. He could hear the stones crunching beneath his boots and a stream tumbling down the mountain. Then he heard another sound, a female voice.

'So you are trying to catch me?' the girl called in French. She was standing on a boulder, her hands planted on her hips as she stared at him.

Sebastian was caught off guard. 'No, I mean, of course not.'

'Really? I have seen you stride after me. I think you are following me.'

Sebastian came nearer. The girl, for she was young, was looking down at him. She was not particularly tall, but she had dark hair that hung down her back in a glossy sheet and a heart-shaped face. Her bright red jacket couldn't disguise her slim figure or long legs.

'I admit I saw your name in the book.'

'Ah, the walkers' book.' She jumped down and Sebastian put out his hand. 'Sebastian Ogilvie.'

The girl hesitated. 'Sophie, but that of course you already know.' She surveyed him for a moment, her clear blue eyes assessing him. 'I was actually intending to walk alone.'

'My apologies, I shall wait here while you go on.' He sat down on the boulder.

The girl started to laugh and the sound was infectious, like the water flowing down the mountain, gurgling and bright. Sebastian wanted to know her better.

'You have to be English.' She was biting her lip as she surveyed him. 'The French find it difficult to apologise.'

Sebastian was finding it hard to concentrate. 'My father was English,' he admitted at last. 'I didn't know it was so obvious.'

'It would now be rude if I didn't invite you to join me,' the girl looked at him and smiled. Sebastian noticed there was a tiny gap between her two front teeth.

'Besides,' she continued putting her head on one side. 'I have never known an Englishman before.'

'Well in that case, it is time you did.' Sebastian jumped to his feet and fell into step beside her. When they had to climb over rocks, she skipped up like a gazelle. By the time they reached the bare upper slopes, Sebastian was captivated by Sophie.

*

They had walked for two hours when the path came to an end and they were out in the open. They stopped for a moment, dazzled by the huge river of craggy ice that curled in suspended animation down the mountainside. The Argentière glacier occupied their entire vision. 'It's huge,' Sophie gasped her eyes round with excitement. 'And so...' She looked for the words. 'So still and yet I believe it is moving. My brother said it was like a frozen sea.'

'Glaciers are never still,' Sebastian confirmed. 'Like a flowing river, the centre moves faster than the sides. I am not sure about the Argentière, but I know the Mer de Glace moves about one centimetre a day.'

'And what else do you know about mountains, Sebastian?'

'A little,' he admitted, as they stood alone on the grass promontory. Then he told her of his childhood expeditions, learning to rock climb with his father outside the village of Lormes, in the Morvan National Park, and later the clubs he belonged to when at school in England during the war.

'I remember the rock faces seemed enormous at the time. My mother didn't like it of course – too dangerous, but she insisted I learnt the proper skills. During National Service, climbing was encouraged. I love it, Sophie.' He looked at her, his face lit up with inner passion. 'It's difficult to describe.'

'Try,' she said, watching him.

He grinned. 'You are at one with nature, tied by a rope to your companions, pushing yourself beyond your own physical and mental limits. That rope is a sacred bond between you and your partners. Sorry,' he grimaced. 'I get carried away.'

'Don't stop. I'd like to know more, Sebastian.'

'Really?' He felt a rush of happiness and found himself revealing things he had never revealed before.

Sophie told him of her dream to become a surgeon. 'I come from a family who had little,' she finished. 'But we worked hard.

I didn't have many opportunities, but I had people around me who believed in me. And that is worth more than money and possessions. So I was rich in a different way. I know it is a man's world, but I will prove that a woman can do better than a man.'

'I have no doubt that you will,' Sebastian replied. For a while they were silent, taking in their surroundings, until they retraced their steps into the forest.

'Despite the fact that it is summer, I could do with a hot chocolate and an even hotter bath,' Sophie announced, picking her way down the wooded slopes. 'In Paris we have to share the bathroom with all the other apartments. Here there are two bathrooms in my corridor alone. I can stay in the water for as long as I wish. What a luxury.' She looked back at him, a mischievous grin on her face.

'We?' Sebastian enquired, suddenly worried she might be married.

'I live with my grandmother.'

Sebastian hoped his delight didn't show on his face.

'You are grinning, Sebastian,' Sophie observed.

Sophie had poured a copious amount of home-made geranium bath salts into the large enamelled bath and was now immersed, her dark hair tied on top of her head, the water coming nearly to her chin. This was not what she planned, she mused, not what she had planned at all. Sebastian was obviously the man she had seen in the taxi, his smile had caused her to take a second look. Now she had agreed to have dinner with him in the cosy dining room, and she was alarmed at the possible consequences. But she was protected by her anonymity; no one had recognised her as the little girl who had stayed with her family years before, there were no unwanted questions or awkward explanations. For a brief period Sophie Bernot did not exist.

She drank the last of her chocolate and got out, rubbing

herself over with the towel until her skin glowed pink. She put on her only dress, floral silk with small pearl buttons and let down her hair. It wouldn't do to have an affair with a man, not now when she was nearing the next set of exams. She couldn't let herself be distracted.

'No,' she said looking at herself in the mirror. 'Absolutely not.'

Sebastian shaved, put on his jacket and went downstairs. He was nervous, and he wasn't sure why. There had been many girlfriends in the past, one of them serious, and to his dismay he had broken the girl's heart, but he had never felt this heady, intoxicating excitement. There was something about the tiny gap in her teeth that made him want to smile. She wasn't exactly beautiful, her nose tilted a little and there was a small mole on her cheek, but he had wanted to run his fingers down the contours of her face, touch the tip of her nose.

He laughed. What on earth was he thinking about, Sophie was a nineteen-year-old medical student, living in Paris with her grandmother. He continued down the stairs.

He stopped at the door to the dining room. Sophie was sitting at a small table studying the menu, a strand of hair had fallen over her forehead and she brushed it away. There was a look of fierce concentration on her face as if this decision was the most important in the world. She seemed to sense his presence and she looked up. Their eyes met and Sebastian knew it was too late to worry about where she lived, or an old grandmother. He had already lost his heart.

They were the first in the dining room and the last to leave. Sebastian told her about his job in London and Sophie revealed more about her ambitions. 'I want to be a pioneer in the field of surgery,' she had said leaning forward in her chair, her eyes shining. 'There is so much that will happen in the future. One day soon they will find a way to give you a new heart. Extraordinary, is it not? Someone else's heart will beat in your body.' She put her hand across the table and touched his shirt. 'Right there.' She laughed and shook her head. '*Excusez-moi*, I also get carried away.' But she didn't need to apologise because Sebastian wanted to catch hold of her hand, hold it against his chest and never let it go.

Over coffee, she asked about his family.

'I think you would like them, Sophie,' he said, mentioning briefly the members of his family, including the colonel who lived in the village.

'Tell me more.' She leant her elbows on the table and cupped her face in her hands.

For a moment Sebastian was reticent, his life sounded affluent by comparison.

'It's all right,' Sophie grinned cheekily. 'You don't have to be ashamed of being rich.'

Sebastian chuckled; Sophie was bewitchingly perceptive, and he realised he wanted to open up to her. He relaxed and allowed his mind to return to Pommard.

'Well at first glance, my grandmother, Marie-Claire, can seem intimidating – grey hair, piercing grey eyes. She doesn't suffer fools gladly but beneath the formidable exterior, she is the most generous person I know. Adeline, the housekeeper, jostles with Grand-mère for power. She came to the house, first as a nanny to Gillienne, and then to me. She is now cook and housekeeper, and woe betide anyone who crosses her. And Maman is ...' he leant back in his chair and smiled as he contemplated his mother. 'She is wonderful, a little vague at times, but focussed when she wants to be, and charming. Then there is Gillie. My sister is eight years older than me and very protective. She would probably kill anyone who tried to hurt me.'

'I'm scared of her already.'

'So you should be. But she would admire you, Sophie, pushing the boundaries for women.'

Sophie's face was animated. 'My mother always encouraged me. She told me that if women can work, they can vote. She said I should never be afraid of taking on the men.'

Sebastian laughed. 'In recent years our house and vineyard in Pommard has been run by women, and very successfully! So you see I am surrounded by strong women.'

'And what about the colonel, you have left him out.'

'Ah, the colonel.' Sebastian's eyes were twinkling. 'For a start I am sure he is secretly in love with my grandmother. He has a typical military bearing with a moustache and a slight limp from the war. But the colonel is not entirely as he seems. He used to write rather racy novels under a pseudonym. They were the kind you read with a torch at school when lights are out.'

Sophie looked perplexed and Sebastian grinned. 'So Matron wouldn't discover them.' He started to laugh. 'The colonel's writing definitely enlightened me.'

'Really?'

Sophie was looking at him, her head on one side, and Sebastian drained his glass of wine.

They were so engrossed in each other that they were unaware of the middle-aged couple on the next table who barely spoke to each other, or the two noisy young children on another table who were exasperating their tired-looking parents.

'Do you realise,' Sophie giggled, when the restaurant was empty and Heidi was clearing tables around them, 'it's midnight and well past my bedtime.'

'I hadn't noticed,' Sebastian admitted.

'I certainly need my sleep. It's not good to hike in the mountains when you are tired.' When Sophie stared through the hotel window into the darkness outside, Sebastian sensed a change in her.

'What is it?' he asked.

She was silent for a moment as if making up her mind, then

she drew in her breath. 'There is another reason I came here, Sebastian. My family were killed in '42. A bomb was dropped on the Renault factory. The employees' accommodation was within the factory gates.'

The light had gone out of her eyes, and for an instant Sebastian wanted to hold her, make her laugh again.

'That's awful.'

'They never found my brother's body, only my parents.' She shook her head as if trying to get rid of the memory. 'So you see I have come here to say goodbye.'

'Why here?' he asked, instantly regretting his words. 'Forgive me, I didn't mean to pry.'

Sophie brushed aside his apology. 'Because we came here as a family a year before the war started: Maman, Papa and my brother.' She looked up at Sebastian, her eyes sombre, the teasing gone. 'I don't usually speak about this.' She rubbed her forehead with the palm of her hand. 'Before I leave on Thursday, I will take the cable car and walk to the spot where we had our picnic. Perhaps I will at last be able to say goodbye to them.'

'Would you like me to come with you?' Sebastian asked, before checking himself. 'Sorry, I am being presumptuous, you'll want to be on your own.'

Sophie was silent for a moment. 'No, I think I would like that,' she said.

They were about to go to their rooms, when she kissed him lightly on the cheek.

'I am envious of your wonderful family,' she said, holding onto his arm. 'It is only me and my grandmother at home.'

As Sebastian lay in bed that night, he thought of her words. Beneath her capable, determined exterior there was a deep sadness to Sophie. He wanted to protect her, take away her loneliness – and yes, he realised with a jolt, he wanted to love her if she would let him.

The following morning Sebastian was up before Sophie. Despite the crisp linen sheets and woollen blankets, he hadn't slept at all.

He placed himself at a table opposite the door and when she didn't arrive for breakfast, the fresh croissants were no longer appetising – clearly Sophie had changed her mind. She had left without him, and who could blame her. He was about to leave the table when Sophie came into the dining room and sank down into the chair next to him.

'Ugh,' she said holding her head. 'How much wine did we drink last night?'

'Only a bottle,' he smiled, his relief palpable.

'Did I drink half?'

'You did, but that's not very much.'

'My head hurts, and I shall probably die,' she groaned. 'You see, it does not cost a lot to make me drunk.'

Sebastian started to laugh. 'I like girls who are inexpensive to run.'

She looked up at him. 'But you won't be running me, *mon cher* Sebastian.'

Sebastian's disappointment was like a physical blow.

'Don't look so wounded,' she laughed, taking hold of his hand. 'Has anyone ever told you, you have very nice eyes.'

When Sebastian had recovered his equilibrium, they finished breakfast, and after collecting their things they met downstairs in the lobby. Each armed with a long walking stick and a packed lunch made by the *auberge*, they took the short bus ride to Les Praz, and bought two tickets for the cable car up to Flégère. As Sophie stepped into the sunshine, she shaded her eyes and looked towards the vast expanse of the Mont Blanc massif on the other side of the valley. Sebastian followed her gaze. The view of the snow-topped peaks was humbling. The sides of the Aiguille du Midi were razor-sharp and craggy, but like its name would suggest, it rose like a needle into the sky. There were other formidable peaks, but the highest, the dome of Mont Blanc itself, dominated the rest. It drew Sebastian like a magnet. One day he would stand on that slightly curved dome.

They walked in single file along the narrow path that skirted the mountainside, stopping occasionally to look at the infinite landscape of sparkling summits. At first spindly fir trees grew either side of them, their trunks formed and bent by the wind, but they gradually petered out and it was just the path and rocks with thousands of feet of mountainside below them. Sophie was making good progress, until she stopped suddenly and turned back to Sebastian.

'It's disappeared,' she gasped, her face drained of colour.

Sebastian came up beside her and sure enough the narrow path had tumbled down the mountainside, leaving a length of loose scree to scrabble across before the track resumed.

'My father taught me that if you ever feel nervous, you should look into the hillside. Put your stick into your outside hand and keep your eyes away from the edge,' he advised her. 'Now let me go first.'

'I'm not nervous,' she retorted, as Sebastian scrambled past, but as a million tiny fragments of shale slithered beneath Sebastian's feet before descending down the mountain with an alarming clatter, she covered her ears and turned her face to the hillside.

'Come on, it's your turn,' he encouraged, putting out his hand. When Sophie slipped, he caught her.

'I've got you,' he said, holding onto her, feeling her shivering with fear.

'You can let go now,' she said reaching the path, her colour returning. 'It wasn't so bad.'

When the path widened a little, Sophie's confidence grew. 'Quite easy when you get the hang of it,' she pronounced.

Sebastian tried to stop himself smiling. There was a vulnerable side to the girl and he found it appealing.

A short while later he took out his map. 'Once we get around this shoulder, it will be easier,' he assured her. They had just navigated the bend, when Sophie cried out in delight. 'This is it, Sebastian, the exact spot my brother set up his easel.'

They sat down in the rough grass and Sophie pulled a tiny guidebook from her pocket. 'This is a wild orchid,' she cried, pointing to a small purple spire with darker spots in the throat, 'and this,' she was looking at a pale blue flower, 'I think it's a campanula. Imagine, Sebastian, this delicate little plant has to survive in winter beneath several feet of snow.'

Sebastian was watching her, transfixed; she was like an excited child, curious about everything.

'Thank you for coming with me,' she said at last, her eyes bright. 'It means a lot.'

He was about to reply when she pulled the rucksack off her back.

'And now Sebastian, *jai faim*. We shall have lunch.'

Sophie had finished her baguette and was tucking into a large piece of chocolate when her expression changed.

'It's strange, when I came here with my family the altitude didn't worry me at all. Perhaps we get more apprehensive as we get older, perhaps life makes us fearful, not that I was frightened of course.'

'You have had a lot to contend with Sophie,' Sebastian said, resisting the urge to pull her into his arms and kiss the smudge of chocolate that remained on her upper lip.

She sighed. 'Do you know there is not a day goes by that I don't miss my family. My mother was an incredible woman, in some ways she was ahead of her time – while other wives stayed at home, she did all the bookkeeping for the factory, but she also encouraged Max and me to follow our dreams.'

'She would have been so proud of you,' Sebastian confirmed.

Sophie brushed her hand across her eyes and looked at him. 'I think she would.' She smiled suddenly. 'She was also old-fashioned. Papa had brought her a pair of hiking trousers, but Maman refused to wear them. She strode up the mountains in her heavy pleated skirt. She was completely unafraid, unlike me just now.' She giggled suddenly. 'You see, I have actually admitted my fear. Now that is a first.'

Later they were relaxing in the sunshine. Sebastian had made a pillow of his coat and Sophie was beside him. He could see the rise and fall of her chest, her profile. He could hear her soft breathing. For a moment he fantasised about making love to her, undoing the small shell buttons on her blouse, kissing her neck, her breasts.

'Do you ever feel that you are outside your body?' she asked, turning to face him. 'I mean, you are looking down at yourself from above.'

Sebastian wanted to laugh because at this moment he felt totally present in his body.

'Not really,' he said. 'I think that may be more of a girl thing.'

'No, no absolutely not,' Sophie was sitting up now. 'My brother often made the same observation.'

'I wish I had met him.'

'You would have liked him, Sebastian, everyone did. He was warm, generous and so kind.'

'If he was like you...'

'No, he was far more artistic. Sometimes I am convinced he can't be dead because I would know it. At other times...'

She looked away but not before Sebastian had seen tears in

her eyes. Sebastian was no longer thinking of her brother; his only wish was to look after her and take away her pain.

She turned back, her shoulders drooping. 'I have his landscape of Mont Blanc in my flat. I found it in the ruins. It is the only thing I have left of him.'

There was a pause before she spoke again. 'Perhaps one day I shall show you his painting.' She looked at her watch and jumped to her feet. 'We need to get going if we are to catch the last cable car down.'

The distant peaks had turned to a dazzling terracotta pink when Sebastian and Sophie trudged up the lane to the *auberge*. Sophie stopped and threw her arms wide. 'Have you ever seen anything more beautiful?' she asked.

Sebastian was watching Sophie as well as the view.

'No,' he replied.

'You have to forgive me if I'm a little forthright,' Sophie stated as they had a drink in the chalet's intimate sitting room.

'I like your honesty, it's refreshing.'

'Staying in Paris throughout the war taught me to say what I think today, because tomorrow I might not be able to say it at all.' She leant forward, her hands clasped around her knees. 'Unless you have actually lived through it, you would find it hard to understand.'

Sebastian nodded in acknowledgement. 'Hearing the news second hand was frustrating. Everyone sent me letters, but I spent four years worrying about my family.'

'Why did they send you away?'

'Papa thought I'd be safer stuck in the wilds of the English countryside. At the time he was probably right, but I would rather have been in the thick of it.' Sebastian filled up Sophie's glass of wine. 'Was it awful when the Germans marched into Paris?'

Sophie looked at him. 'It may sound extraordinary, but to

42

an eight-year-old child it was exciting. I remember it so well, June fourteenth, I was awake because Maman and Papa were arguing in the next room. Many families from our area had already fled into the countryside. We watched them go, their possessions tied onto carts. They took their pets, their mattresses, anything they could carry. It was utter chaos, a mass exodus. We stayed behind because Papa had to run the factory, and we had nowhere else to go. Max and I had strict instructions to remain indoors that day, but of course we didn't. We crept from the house and went into the centre of Paris just as thousands of German soldiers entered the Place de la Concorde, row upon row. Aeroplanes flew overhead, and we didn't know if they would drop their bombs. The city trembled, and that was not just the earth moving beneath the tanks, it was the trembling of hearts.'

She fixed her blue eyes on Sebastian. 'There were military bands, banners everywhere, but the Parisians were quiet – I remember that – and resentful, but I was too young to care. The shops were shuttered and locked. Old ladies were weeping, but I saw only these young men in smart uniforms with shiny buttons striding along in the sunshine. They were smiling at us because they were the conquerors. A Swastika flag was hoisted on the Arc de Triomphe. The crowds were too frightened to rebel. But Max wasn't frightened. "I am going to take it down," he yelled. "We will not allow the tomb of our unknown warrior to be defiled." They took it down anyway, the Germans that is, and put one on the Eiffel Tower instead! We never told Papa we had gone, he would have thrashed us.'

She picked up her glass and looked at Sebastian over the rim.

'I learnt later that German planes on strafing runs killed thousands of weary travellers. They were shot as they walked through the countryside, searching for somewhere safe to go. That is when I understood what was really happening.'

Sebastian sighed, the image she had painted vivid in his mind.

'It sounds terrible, all of it, but I wish I had been there. Though I listened to every broadcast on the wireless, read every newspaper I could, the nearest I got to the actual war was watching the bombing of Hull from an upstairs window at school.'

Once again Sebastian and Sophie had supper together in the dining room, but neither was particularly hungry. Sophie asked Sebastian about his job, his life in London, his degree at Oxford, everything. It was as if she was building a picture of him that she could carry in her head.

'Why property development?' she asked.

'You go first, Sophie. You have chosen an extraordinary path and I am in awe of you. I want to know everything about you.'

'Really?' She put her head on one side, dimples showing in her cheeks. She drew in her breath. 'From when I was a very young child, I wanted to know how our bodies, this miracle of design, worked. Later, I realised I wanted to spend the rest of my life learning how to heal people. I know it won't be easy, but I believe it is my destiny.' She took his hand and turned it over, tracing the lines that ran across his palm. 'I am going to be a surgeon, Sebastian, so there is little time for distraction. You have to understand there is no place in my life for serious relationships. I have a difficult road ahead and need to be focussed.' Her face was solemn, and Sebastian's heart sank. She was trying to tell him something, and he didn't want to hear it because his feelings for Sophie were growing by the minute.

'Your turn now,' she said, letting go of his hand.

Sebastian thought for a moment. All his hopes had been dashed, but he wouldn't give himself away.

'I am lucky enough to have had a privileged upbringing, but I am in a tiny minority. In every city in the world, there are poor areas, slums where housing is overcrowded with poor sanitation, no electricity. I want to build housing not just for the rich but for the poor. I want everyone to have the opportunity to live in decent surroundings. The firm I work for mainly builds for the affluent, and I would be lying if I said I did not love working with architects on grand schemes. When I pass a beautiful building, I stop and look at it, I take it all in, remembering it for the future. You probably think that is foolish.'

'Of course not. Why should I?'

Sebastian smiled, his eyes never leaving her face. 'But we are also doing housing projects for lower income families and these excite me too. I am not trying to be Haussmann,' he laughed, talking of the man responsible for rebuilding areas of Paris under Napoleon III. 'I don't want to be criticised like him either, but I would like to make a difference in some way. Sorry, have I bored you?' he asked.

Sophie smiled at him. 'You could never bore me, Sebastian. We are a little the same, you and I, we both want to make it possible for people to have better lives. That is good is it not?'

Sebastian put his hand over hers. 'It is very good, Sophie.'

Later when their puddings remained untouched on their plates, Sophie drew in her breath and looked at Sebastian. 'This is our last night. After that I may never see you again.' She put her hand on his arm, ran her fingers along the soft flesh on the inside of his wrist. 'That makes me sad.' She paused for a moment, biting her lip. She had spoken the truth. She couldn't bear the thought of never seeing Sebastian again. She drained her glass of wine, feeling her inhibitions slide away. 'Come to my room,' she whispered at last, her cheeks flushing.

Sebastian looked across at her, suddenly embarrassed. Their eyes met and with a flicker of recognition, the question was answered.

Sophie smiled shyly, and Sebastian picked up her hand and kissed her fingers.

Sophie stood in front of the cheval mirror in her cosy bedroom and put her head on one side, surveying herself critically. She had a good figure, small firm breasts, and a narrow waist. As she looked at the dark triangle of hair between her legs, she felt a wave of longing.

She put on her dressing gown and was standing by the fireplace when Sebastian entered the room. She had turned down the oil lamp, and as the light flickered and ebbed she looked vulnerable and incredibly young. He noticed her mouth trembling and was overwhelmed by his feelings. He took her in his arms and for a moment they stood together. Sebastian could feel the warmth of her body through the thin silk, he could smell her scent, delicate and floral. He inhaled deeply and lifted her face until she was looking into his eyes.

'Are you sure?'

She nodded, her dark eyes shining. '*Oui*, Sebastian, I am.'

He untied the belt, slipping the gown from her shoulders until she was naked. Then he gazed at her, savouring the moment, wanting it to last for ever. Lowering his head, he kissed the hollow at the base of her neck, feeling the soft texture of her skin. He stroked the contour of her breasts with his fingers, tracing her nipple until it rose and hardened.

'You are so beautiful,' he breathed into her hair. He kissed her mouth and as her lips parted beneath his, he forgot everything except the woman in his arms.

Dawn filtered through the curtains and Sophie opened her eyes. As she remembered the joy of the night before, she watched Sebastian's face, relaxed in sleep. She traced his jaw, his lips, her fingers light as a butterfly. 'I think I am falling in love with you,' she whispered softly, overcome by the intimacy of being so close to another human being and the growing feeling of tenderness towards him. She whispered the words again, marvelling at her confession but knowing he couldn't hear.

Later that morning they went for a last walk up the hill, before Sophie had to catch her train.

'I don't want to let you go,' Sebastian said, as they stood together, looking down at the village below. Sophie rested her head against his chest.

'It has been a magical few days,' she murmured.

'The best of my life,' Sebastian agreed.

She turned her face up to meet his and he kissed her gently.

For a moment all the unhappiness of the past years disappeared. Sophie was elated, freed by her love. She had never felt more alive. She wound her arms around his neck, feeling all rational thought slip away.

They wandered back to the *auberge* together. Sophie could feel the sun on her cheeks. She could see Sebastian's handsome face looking down at her with that quizzical look in his eyes.

'What?' she laughed.

'You are the most intriguing and extraordinary woman I have ever met,' he said. 'Everything about you is truly unique.'

'I will take that as a compliment,' she giggled, squeezing his hand.

They ordered baguettes from the *auberge* and ate them sitting on the wall. Cowbells jangled in the meadows above them, and the sound of singing came from the little church nearby. 'I shall imprint all of this in my memory,' she said, leaning against him. Sebastian put his arm around her shoulders.

'We will make more beautiful memories,' Sebastian promised, his voice intense. 'I can come back from London most weekends.'

Sophie felt the first stirring of unease. This was going too fast, what had she got herself into?

'I must get my things.' She jumped off the wall. 'It's getting late and the train is due at three.'

'I am missing you already,' he laughed.

'I'll be down in a moment, and you can walk me to the station,' she glanced at her watch. 'Actually, there's no time, could you bear to order me a taxi?'

As she ran upstairs to the bedroom, she could feel the first bubble of panic build in her chest. She couldn't give in to these feelings for Sebastian. They would become all-consuming and if she wanted to fulfil her dream, every ounce of her energy must be channelled into her work. Falling in love was simply not an option. She mustn't allow Sebastian to derail her future.

Sebastian found her in her bedroom.

'Are you all right?' he asked, seeing her frenziedly pulling her clothes from the drawer and tossing them into a rucksack.

'No, Sebastian,' she yelled. 'I'm not! Don't you see, I can't get involved with you or anyone else. This is not your fault, it is mine. I'm training to be a surgeon for heaven's sake.'

'But I wouldn't hold you back,' Sebastian stammered.

Sophie wasn't listening. 'Do you know how long it takes, Sebastian? Twelve years. I can't afford to be distracted. It has been a constant struggle. I have worked all hours of the day and night to be better than anyone else.'

'But what about us?'

'Us? There is no us. Why is it that the moment you go to bed with a man they expect you to give up your independence? I'm sorry, but I can't.' She threw her rucksack over the shoulder and ran down the stairs.

'I just want to see you, not change you,' Sebastian mumbled, but Sophie didn't hear.

She was already in the waiting taxi when he came outside.

She rolled down the window, 'Forgive me,' she said, tears blinding her eyes.

'I love you,' he whispered to the wind as the taxi drew away. When Sophie looked back, Sebastian was still standing in the road, staring after her.

Chapter Five

Early the following morning Sebastian bought two packets of Gauloises cigarettes from the station kiosk and waited for his train. He was numb with misery. Sophie had come into his life like an explosion and she had gone just as quickly. He didn't know where she lived, or the hospital where she studied. He realised with a jolt he didn't even know her surname.

Three changes and several hours later, his mother was at the station in Beaune to pick him up.

'*Mon cheri*,' she exclaimed, taking his face in her hands, looking at him closely. 'You are usually so alive from the mountains, what on earth has happened?'

'I'd rather not talk about it, Maman.'

'Fair enough,' she said, linking her arm through his. 'But don't for one moment think that Adeline will leave you alone.' They walked back down the platform, Liliane glancing occasionally at her son. 'Your grandmother is so excited to see you,' she said, at last. 'She has had flu, and you are just the tonic she needs.'

As the old Peugeot wound through the country lanes, Sebastian couldn't keep his heartache from his mother. 'She's called Sophie,' he began.

Three miles after leaving Beaune, Liliane turned off the road and drove through a pillared entrance into a long avenue of lime trees. She parked the car, and listened quietly while her son finished speaking.

'So you see,' he said, coming to the end of his tale, 'it's obvious that she wants nothing to do with me, and I thought there was a chance we could have a future.' He stared through the window. 'Oh I don't know Maman, it's all such a muddle.'

Liliane put her hand on her son's arm. 'It seems this girl has her life mapped out and she wants no distractions. *Mon cheri*, you will not change her mind. Take my advice, do not chase her. It may be difficult, but one thing is for certain, in time you will fall in love again.'

Sebastian stepped from the car and inhaled deeply, his senses assaulted by the smell of jasmine and honeysuckle. Soon it would be the lime trees' turn to flower and their intoxicating scent would fill the air.

As he opened the gate for his mother into the courtyard at the front of the house, she squeezed his hand. 'You know who will also be pleased to see you?'

He nodded, 'I believe I do.'

'Coco and Louis have been waiting all day! Your sister of course isn't here.'

As she spoke, the door opened, and two black Labradors bounded across the gravel towards them. Sebastian leant down and ruffled their heads. How good it was to see them, to be back at home with his family. He looked up to see an elegant white-haired lady surveying him from the top of the flight of stone steps. His heart lifted and he bounded up, taking them two at a time, before enfolding her in his arms. She seemed smaller somehow, more delicate. 'You look tremendous,' he pronounced.

'Humph,' she said. '*Ne me mens pas*, don't lie to me.'

'Would I ever?'

'Yes, you would, Sebastian, all the time. Now change and come down for dinner; I'm hungry and we can't keep Adeline waiting.'

The dogs followed him up the wide polished staircase to the first-floor landing. He opened the full-length casements and leant over the small balcony.

Below him the box hedging stood out against the white gravel. The only sound was the gentle splash of water and occasional birdsong. How soothing it was to his rattled senses, how wonderfully familiar. As he watched the swallows dip and dive over the ancient fountain, he realised he mustn't let his recent disappointment destroy his precious time with his grandmother. He must enjoy every moment, because despite her indomitable will, she couldn't last for ever.

He looked at his watch, he had better get a move on, or she would give him one of her memorable reprimands. He picked up his bag and continued to his room at the top of the house. Again nothing had changed, the dappled grey rocking horse remained in front of the small circular window, the toy farmyard was there, the knitted quilt Adeline had made for him was folded at the bottom of the wooden bed. His stuffed toys, abandoned years before, seemed to blink at him reassuringly, and the lead soldiers remained in perpetual battle on top of his school trunk.

He changed and was about to go downstairs when he saw a note from his sister on the chest of drawers. He opened the envelope.

My dearest little brother, she had written.

He smiled softly. Gillie's letter was there at just the right moment. He closed his eyes and her face was in front of him, eccentric, outspoken Gillie. She was tall with fair skin and dark brown hair from the Ogilvie side of the family. Her stunning clear green eyes came from her paternal grandmother. She was eight years older than Sebastian, and in the initial war years, while he was in England, she was nursing in Paris. But it didn't stop her writing to him, short coded letters because of the censorship. In 1942 she had returned to Burgundy, nursing in

Beaune until the conflict ended. She was at the same hospital all these years later. Sebastian turned on his bedside lamp and continued to read.

I'm so sad not to be there at home with you, but it's not every day you get asked to Rome by an attractive man. He is a little older actually – thirteen years older, but he is extremely intelligent and charming. He's a politician, but I mustn't tell you more! He came to see the vineyard last summer and bought several cases of wine. Grand-mère, of course, immediately invited him to dinner, and I admit he made a big impression. He has been pursuing me ever since, bombarding me with flowers and lovely presents. It's nice for a change to be taken out for expensive dinners in Paris. I'm not sure what he sees in me, but he does appear keen and it's a wonderful feeling to be wooed.

I hope when I see you there will be something more to report.

The new camera you gave me for Christmas is hanging around my neck as I head to the airport. I look like a tourist but for the next week I will behave like one and take hundreds of photographs. Love to you.

Gillie

Sebastian folded the letter. As always his sister's enthusiasm had leapt from the page. Thank goodness one of them was happy, he thought, putting it back in the envelope; it made his own misery a little easier to bear. He glanced in the mirror and ran a hand through his hair. Hopefully his grandmother would approve, he thought, going down the stairs to find her.

'So Sebastian,' she said as they sat down in the small panelled dining room. 'Are you conquering the world?'

'I hope so.'

'Throughout history your ancestors were conquerors.'

'You have told me, Grand-mère ... several times.'

He winked at his mother and she lifted her glass and smiled. His mother was still beautiful, he thought, looking at her. Tall, slim, with a few streaks of silver threading through her abundant hair. She had the Villienne patrician nose, but it suited her and balanced her high cheekbones. He had the Ogilvie features, but he believed he had some of his mother's and grandmother's spirit. He must try and live up to it now.

'Your mother tells me you have employed a French architect.' Marie-Claire was peering at him over her delicate metal-rimmed spectacles. 'Very sensible. *Les Anglais* do not have our style. If I remember correctly for a residential square in Chelsea, *non*?'

Sebastian nodded.

She picked up her glass and drank slowly, savouring the contents. 'Despite the war, '42 was a good year for Chateau Villienne, and I managed to keep this from the Boches.' Her eyes were glinting wickedly. 'Now it is your boss Sir Humphrey Griffin who would steal my wine and not the Germans. Take back a bottle of course but tell him he should pay for it.'

'Gifford, Grand-mère, Sir Humphrey Gifford. And he's been very good to me.'

'What is the difference, he still wants something for nothing,' she tutted, but she was smiling.

Over the next hour as Adeline brought in *crème vichyssoise* followed by *filet de boeuf* then a *tarte tatin* – Sebastian's favourite upside-down pastry, filled with caramelised fruit – he told his grandmother about Marcus and the plans, and about his meeting with the directors of Blackheath Holdings. He did not mention Sophie. When it was obvious that she was tired, he stood up. 'Forgive me Grand-mère, I am flagging, will you be cross if I go to bed?'

'The young have no stamina,' she laughed. 'Liliane, it is all your fault, you have been too soft with your son.'

After thanking Adeline for her superb cuisine, and expertly dodging her questions, he escorted his grandmother to her room. 'Sleep well, Grand-mère,' he said letting go of her hands, shocked by the transparency of her skin and the tiny bones, fragile as the wings of a bird.

The following morning he rose early. Adeline was sweeping the stone flags in the hallway when he came downstairs.

'Your grandmother tells me you have been jilted.' She was leaning on her brush, her dark eyes scrutinising him.

Sebastian laughed, he couldn't avoid her questions any longer. 'It seems there are no secrets here, Adeline.'

'From me, never. Start at the beginning.'

When Sebastian had retold the story again, she picked a hair pin from the floor and pushed it back into her abundant silver hair.

'If you ask my opinion, this Sophie baggage will come running back to you. You may be a little scrawny, but you are handsome nonetheless, and you are certainly quite a catch.'

'Thank you Adeline,' he grinned. 'I can always rely on your support.'

'I have made you breakfast. You'll have it in the kitchen like old times.'

Sebastian followed her down the passage, remembering the countless occasions he had eaten with his father at Adeline's kitchen table.

'*Assieds-toi*,' she commanded, putting a fluffy omelette in front of him.

'My favourite,' he said.

'Of course. Your father's too,' she grinned. 'Nothing like Adeline's cooking to mend a broken heart.'

As Sebastian layered Adeline's strawberry conserve onto a piece of toast, he smiled. The world may change around her, but Adeline's character would always be the same. She was older and a little larger, but she was still a rock he could rely on.

It wasn't until he was drinking his coffee in the library afterwards, the dogs at his feet, that he allowed himself to think of Sophie.

It wasn't just her looks that attracted him, but the combination of her vulnerability and intelligence and also her humour. He remembered Sophie lying on her side in bed, her arm thrown over his chest as she gazed at him. 'You are a dark horse, *non*?'

'It depends what you mean.'

She had smiled, her blue eyes elongating. 'I mean that you have a sensitive soul.'

He had laughed then, '*Moi*? Never.' But of course she was right – however successful he became, there was always the little boy inside him, telling him that he could do better, be stronger.

'That is why you do so well,' she continued. 'You have something to prove!'

At the time he had been amazed. She had looked into the depths of his being, she understood him where others had failed. He smiled, remembering what had happened afterwards.

'So,' she had said, running her hands over his stomach, an impudent grin on her face, 'now you can prove to me how you can do it again.'

Sebastian had been at home a day when his mother came into the library, where he was trying with little success to read a book on modern architecture. He put it down with relief.

'Can I take the car, Maman?'

'You are going to see your uncle.' It wasn't a question.

Sebastian nodded.

'Well you should. You seem wound up like a coil. He'll put you right, he always does.'

'I'm fine Maman, I want to see him that's all.'

His mother turned her grey eyes on him. 'Of course. May I come with you?'

They left after an early lunch and at just before three they could see the village of Vézelay perched on the hilltop above them. They entered through a medieval archway in the ancient walls, and as the car crawled slowly upwards into the tiny, narrow streets, Sebastian could feel the tension slipping away from him. They stopped at La Basilique Sainte-Marie-Madeleine and climbed from the car just as Pierre de Villienne came down the steps towards them.

'Divine providence,' he laughed, 'or possibly your telephone call earlier, Liliane.'

He rested his hand on top of Sebastian's head. 'Welcome, my son,' then he turned to his sister, his face creasing into a gentle smile.

'Pierre,' she said. 'I probably shouldn't call you that, because you are an abbot, but you are still my brother, and still the most elegant monk I know.'

'You may call me what you like, my dearest.'

'But I can't hug you?'

'Probably not here in the square,' Pierre stepped away from her and laughed. 'I am a priest after all.'

'Oh well, I shall console myself with a cup of tea with Sister Teresa. I'll leave you two together.' Liliane patted her son on the arm and set off across the cobblestones towards the centre of the village.

'She has never really got over my decision,' the abbot murmured, and as Sebastian stood in the June sunshine with his uncle, watching her go, he wondered what had driven this tall man with black hair – now threaded with silver – and piercing blue eyes, to give up his home, the estate, all his worldly possessions in order to devote his life to the service of God.

When Liliane had disappeared from view, the abbot turned to his nephew. 'Come, young man, let's go inside.'

They walked into the narthex, the antechamber of the abbey, and Sebastian paused while he acclimatised to the subdued light. Moving on through the central portal, they came into the main body of the church where Romanesque arches enclosed the sunlit nave and soaring piers with sculptured capitals had once revealed bible stories and legends to illiterate medieval worshippers. The basilica had been pillaged, burnt, sacked and yet each time it had risen again, more beautiful than the last.

'Extraordinary, isn't it?' His uncle was watching him.

Sebastian nodded.

'I sense that you have come here not for the beauty of my church, but for some counsel?'

Sebastian looked into his uncle's eyes. 'Both. Your counsel is always welcome, but I am hoping the abbey will restore my equilibrium.'

'The builders of long ago designed our church so that the pilgrims who came here experienced a journey, both physical and spiritual, from darkness to light.'

'Am I a pilgrim, Uncle?'

'We are all God's pilgrims if we wish to be. Do you see how the light is captured and distributed in the different spaces of the building, so that the journey starts in the subdued light of the entrance porch, through to a final flood of light in the choir. But enough of my ramblings, tell me what troubles you?'

As Sebastian looked at his uncle standing before him in his simple white robes, he was humbled. 'It's silly really,' he started, 'insignificant.'

'Nothing is insignificant.' The abbot shook his head and smiled. 'Everyone has a story, Sebastian.'

Sebastian drew in his breath. 'I met a woman who changed my life,' he admitted. 'And now, Uncle, I have no way of finding her, and more importantly, she doesn't want to be found.'

'I see,' Pierre said. 'I know this may not be what you wish to hear, but perhaps you should put your trust in God.' His eyes settled on the sculptures filling the area between the portal and the top of the arch. 'Do you see, Sebastian, Christ is welcoming mankind into his arms. In times of need you could try turning to him. He will give you comfort.'

Though Sebastian didn't have his uncle's conviction, he was moved by the half-standing figure of Christ.

'It is our wish that you should feel nearer to God in this church, but he is everywhere,' the abbot said at last. 'Go to the gardens on the south side of the abbey, overlooking the valley, there you will find peace. And one more thing, my dearest nephew, and I say this as a man and not as a priest: life may look bleak at the moment, but I can assure you the pain will soften in time.'

As Sebastian walked down the dusty, white lane, past a small manor house with silver-grey shutters and cream rendered walls, he pondered on the abbot's wistful expression.

He continued down the lane, beyond the crumbling remains of an old twelfth-century refectory to arrive at the gardens of a chateau that had long since disappeared, and leant over the stone parapet. Gazing out over the valley to the undulating landscape of multicoloured fields that rose gently to the dark outline of the Morvan hills, he knew why his uncle had sent him. It was an unchanging scene. It had been the same for a thousand years and would stay that way long after he had gone. He was a drop in the ocean of time, and it was up to him to live that small moment to the full.

When the Abbot of Vézelay returned to his church, he knelt in front of the tomb of Mary Magdalene. According to popular belief, her remains had rested there until torched by the Hugenots in the sixteenth century. Whether this was true or not didn't matter, she was the first example of a penitent. He was also a penitent. A shadow of a smile crossed his face. He was not innocent in the ways of love.

When he rose to his feet, he crossed himself. It was true, his pain had lessened with the years, but the memories remained. As he wandered down the dusty lane to the gardens on the south side of the abbey he could see his nephew, a silhouette in the distance, gazing out over the valley below. 'Let us hope he is enjoying the beauty of nature,' he murmured, 'and hopefully it will bring him peace.'

Chapter Six

The Clinical Sciences library was normally Sophie's favourite place for revising. She loved the weight of the large medical tomes, some new, some old, but all full of fascinating diagrams. She enjoyed being amongst thousands of books, inhaling the smell particular to a library. On this day she was poring over the text, her brow furrowed in concentration, but her mind kept wandering. '*Understanding the mutual relationship between the liver and the heart is important for both hepatologists and cardiologists,*' she read, but the information would not sink in. Instead all she could focus on was the confusion on Sebastian's face when she had left him, the hurt in his eyes. She gritted her teeth and read the text again. Finally, she gave up. She had to get outside.

She was leaning against the wall smoking a cigarette when Georges found her. He had remained her best friend at medical school since the very first day.

'You seem distracted. Could it be that you are still thinking about the young Englishman you told me about?'

'I don't know any English men.'

'Perhaps this will jog your memory – chiselled jawline, blonde hair? You met him in Chamonix?'

'Sebastian is half-English,' she muttered. 'And as to thinking about him, of course I wasn't. You are as bad as Grand-mère, the moment I told her about him, she wanted to plan a wedding.'

He grinned and shrugged his shoulders. 'If you'd like to chat, you know where I am.' He kissed her cheek and headed off, whistling a tune.

As she watched his retreating back, she sighed. Her confusion would cease, she was sure of it. It was merely a phase.

'Don't go, Georges,' she called after him. 'I haven't seen you properly for days.'

He turned around. 'So you want me at last?' he grinned.

She punched him lightly on the shoulder. 'Grand-mère has instructed me to invite you for supper on Saturday. She is planning her famous *boeuf bourguignon* and I have promised to go shopping for her.'

'Well then, we'll go to the market together.'

Early the following Saturday, they picked their way through the busy market stalls in Place Maubert. Sophie headed first to a flower stall, and after examining every bloom she purchased a small blue campanula in a zinc pot.

When they returned to the flat, their baskets were filled to the brim with vegetables, meat, two bottles of wine purchased by Georges, and the plant.

After thanking Georges for the wine, her grandmother tore back the bloody paper and prodded the meat.

'Brisket hung properly,' she beamed. 'Even the worst cuts were a luxury during the war.' She sighed suddenly, the joy leaving her face, and Sophie put her hand on her arm.

'You did as well as you could under the circumstances, Grand-mère.'

The old woman's eyes focussed as she turned back to Georges.

'Take my granddaughter to a café or the park. I can never get her head out of her books. Supper will be ready at seven.'

Georges nudged Sophie. 'Come on, my serious little friend, we have the whole day together!'

They were passing the entrance to the Métro when Sophie hesitated.

'What is it Sophie, you look as if you have seen a ghost?' Georges questioned.

'My grandmother's face just now ... she looked so wretched. I imagine she was remembering the day when we returned to the bombed out houses at Boulogne-Billancourt, the moment when she knew that her son was dead. I want to go there, Georges, to the old Renault factory – would you come with me?'

'Of course I will,' he replied.

As they climbed the stairs at Pont de Sèvres and came out into the sunshine, Georges took her hand. 'Are you all right?'

'I haven't been here since that night. It will be difficult.'

'Well, I am here at your side. You can do it.'

She grimaced. 'With you, my dearest friend, perhaps I can.'

There was a man on the gate of the compound, a young Frenchman with lank hair. He nodded at them, a surly expression on his face and Sophie remembered long-dead Hans, his wife and two little girls growing up in Germany without a father.

They wandered in silence, past the buildings and the workers' houses, until they came to the empty shell of her house. Ten years later it was still awaiting restoration. Georges picked up a tiny piece of coloured glass in the patch of garden at the front and handed it to Sophie. She turned it over, and in her imagination, she was once again standing in the hallway, the sunlight filtering through the glass door panel. Her mother's Sevres plates, seconds from the factory nearby, were proudly displayed on the dresser, her piano was open. In that exquisite moment of anticipation, Sophie had known her life was going to change.

It had changed, but not in the way she had imagined. She had lost everything.

'Life hasn't been too kind to you, has it, *ma cherie*?' Georges murmured, putting his arm around her shoulder.

Sophie leant against him. 'There has been so much regret and sadness, I sometimes forget what it is like to enjoy myself.'

'Do you want to talk about it?'

'For years I've locked it away because it is easier. Everyone has their own tragedy of course, you lost your brother. It feels indulgent to talk about mine.'

'I didn't lose my mother, father and my brother in a bombing raid, Sophie. Tell me please.'

'Really?' she looked at him.

He nodded, and his eyes were full of compassion.

Sophie sighed. 'For weeks I shut myself into my room, I wouldn't speak. I could hear the world going on outside my window, but I didn't want to be part of it. All I could think about, all I could see, were my family buried in the ruins of my house.' She looked at Georges, her face bleak. 'The memory of the destruction here at Boulogne-Billancourt haunted me night and day. I had nightmares, I woke up screaming. I even refused to go to school. Poor Grand-mère was sick with worry. In the end *Madame*, the headmistress, came to the flat where we lived. She talked to me for hours, made me realise I had to go on. "We have such faith in you Sophie," she said. "You are a child now but one day you will be a woman who can make a difference. You made a promise to me that day, so please come back." I returned to school, Georges, determined to be better than anyone. I was driven, I still am.'

As she described the night in March when the bombs came, her voice shook, then she told him about Max.

'We did everything together, despite the age difference. Painting, football. We used to play in the park; I wasn't much of an opponent, but he was so patient. He used to play Maman's piano and we sang together. He had such a beautiful voice. He was in the church choir and every Sunday Maman and I would go to watch him. Occasionally he would wink at me and I would giggle. Maman would poke me, but she was smiling too. I miss him so much, Georges.' Her voice broke and she buried her face in his shoulder.

'*Ma pauvre petite* Sophie,' he murmured. 'Remember, you always have a brother in me.'

Sophie allowed herself to be led away. When they reached the entrance to the compound she gazed past Georges to the Meudon hills on the other side of the river.

'Maman used to take me there,' she whispered. 'A long time ago.'

They had returned to the Latin Quarter and were passing their favourite café, when Georges pulled her into the entrance.

'You deserve lunch and at least two glasses of wine,' he laughed. 'If, of course, you can face Victor?'

Sophie laughed, all the anxiety leaving her face. 'I adore Victor though I would never tell him so.'

At that moment a middle-aged man with cheeks like polished apples, wearing a striped apron, opened the glass door.

'Sophie, the most beautiful young woman in Paris.'

'You are a terrible flirt.'

Georges laughed. 'You see, Victor, she has a heart of stone.'

She made a face at both of them.

After they had ordered their favourite lunch of *oeufs en cocotte* and half a carafe of wine, Victor produced a small plate of home-made sweet pastries. 'Complimentary,' he beamed. Sophie jumped up and kissed him. 'You see, I am not made of stone.'

Victor chuckled and walked away, his hands placed on his heart. After they had finished lunch and had paid the bill, they cut through the cobbled side streets to the Jardin des Plantes.

The gardens, first established in 1635 as a royal park, were one of their favourite haunts. The National History Museum was housed there. Today Georges dragged her down the dusty chalk paths, past the zoology museum, the Marinarium de Concarneau and the anthropology museum, to the maze. 'Come on, it will be good for you,' he said, and for the next half hour they ran along paths hiding from each other, acting like children.

When Sophie finally caught up with Georges, she was flushed and panting. She grabbed his arm. 'Can we sit?' she begged. They climbed up to the Gloriette de Buffon, a delicate ironwork folly on top of a small mound, and sank onto one of the benches. Sophie closed her eyes.

'That was fun,' she murmured.

'It is good for you to have fun, *ma petite*,' he replied.

Chapter Seven

The exams started towards the beginning of September, but Sophie's confidence had dwindled. In the past she never had a problem revising and could retain information with almost photographic accuracy, but now facts kept slipping away. Although she gained a pass she was disappointed she had not attained a distinction. She tried to work even harder but was constantly exhausted. One morning in the middle of July, she was in the mortuary dissecting the spleen of a middle-aged man who had recently died, when the room spun in front of her. She put down her knife and clutched the marble slab. The embalming fluid was strong, a mixture of glycerine, ethyl alcohol and phenol, but it had never affected her before.

'Is something the matter, Sophie?' It was Professor Manon. 'Perhaps you need some air?'

'*Merci*, Professor.' Sophie fled the mortuary and into the lavatory, where she was violently sick.

That was pathetic, she chided herself walking back down the long corridor. She was in the hospital canteen when Georges sat down opposite her.

'Are you feeling better now?' he asked.

'Not really,' Sophie muttered, pushing around the food on her plate without eating a bite. When Georges took the lid off a plate of sweetbreads, Sophie felt the bile rise in her throat. She screwed up her face and looked away.

'Have you been tired lately, *ma cherie*?' Georges asked.

'Why?'

'You look a little pale.'

'I suppose I have. It's the revision, it has been catching up on me. I was in the library until midnight.'

'And you are feeling nauseous?'

'Occasionally, it is most strange.'

'Have you thought about the possibility that the fatigue is for another reason?'

'Georges, you are being obscure.'

Georges leant across the table and touched her hand. 'Has it crossed your mind that you could be pregnant?' he said quietly, his eyes never leaving her face.

'Don't be ridiculous,' Sophie gasped, but even as she said the words, she knew they might be true.

As she walked home that night she was filled with horror. Her life was over, or at least her medical life. She had now damaged her chances of fulfilling her promise to be a surgeon. Everything she had worked for would be lost. She kicked at a puddle and cursed as the water splashed her stockings. How could she have been so careless; she was training to be a doctor for heaven's sake. She knew the hospital board rules.

That night Sophie lay in bed, her mind in turmoil. She considered her choices over and over again. Having a termination was one of them. But she had seen too many girls admitted to hospital with their insides destroyed in some backstreet practice. The lasting misery inflicted on them had made her seethe with anger and frustration. It was out of the question. Another alternative was to raise the child in Paris, but as a medical student this would be impossible. Her only family was an aging grandmother, and though she would have gladly looked after her baby, she was eighty years old and fragile. All her strength had been sapped by the war, and all her resources had been used trying to keep them both alive.

As she tossed and turned, she knew in her heart that she couldn't give up her career and everything she had worked for, neither could she look after a child. It was unthinkable. Hard work had made her childish dream of fixing people's hearts attainable. She couldn't give up now.

She got up and went to the kitchen. As the water dribbled into the chipped sink, she could feel the tears slip down her face. Although it would break her heart, she would have to give the baby up for adoption. Her child deserved a loving and secure home, one that she could not offer. It was the only thing she could do.

'Are you all right?' It was her grandmother's voice.

'I'm fine Grand-mère, just getting a glass of water.' But she wasn't fine. The look on her brother's face that terrible day floated before her eyes. She would never again be responsible for so much pain. She leant against the sink, her body shaking, before returning to bed for a few hours of troubled sleep.

The following evening she was eating supper, blanquette de veau, with her grandmother to celebrate her first day shadowing Professor Manon. It was a day she'd been working towards for years, and she had survived it.

She put down her fork and looked at her grandmother. The old women was clutching at her chest as she tried to catch her breath. Blood-tinged phlegm was dribbling from her mouth.

'Grand-mère, I want you to do something for me,' she said as calmly as she could, when the coughing had subsided. 'I want you to tell me the day you were born and the year.'

Her grandmother looked confused. 'I don't remember, Sophie.'

A pulse beat in Sophie's temple. From her training Sophie

believed she was suffering from a pulmonary embolism – a blood clot had formed in her grandmother's leg and had travelled through the veins and heart to her lungs. Without treatment she would undoubtedly die. Not only could the embolism permanently damage the affected lung, but starved of oxygen, other organs would be harmed. She fought to keep control of her emotions. Her grandmother couldn't die, it was inconceivable, Sophie loved her too much.

'Grand-mère, you must lie on the floor, while I call for an ambulance.' Yvette nodded slowly and allowed herself to be led from the table and helped onto the rug, where Sophie put her in the recovery position and raised her head onto a pillow. Only then did she hurtle down the two flights of stairs to the phone box. Two hours later her grandmother was in the same ward Sophie had been working in earlier.

'You are aware of the severity,' the doctor on duty looked at her, his manner sympathetic.

'What do you mean?' Sophie asked, knowing full well the answer.

'We have put your grandmother on blood thinners, the anti-coagulant injections should stop the clot getting bigger, but I am convinced there is another reason for the breathlessness. I am so sorry, I think you need to prepare yourself for the worst.'

'You mean cancer?'

'I am afraid I do. I believe your grandmother has a tumour in her lungs.'

Sophie felt the world tipping upside down. Her vital, energetic grandmother was slipping away.

For the next two weeks Sophie rushed between the wards or lecture halls to her grandmother's side. As she sat by her bed, listening to her shallow breathing, she mourned the woman she had once been. She had always been petite, but wiry and strong. Sophie knew she had sacrificed everything for her. After the tragedy at Boulogne-Billancourt, she had worked all hours so that she could put clothes on Sophie's back. When Sophie couldn't sleep, her belly grumbling with hunger, she had forgone her meagre rations so that Sophie could eat. When cold had chilled her to the bone, her grandmother had taken an axe to the furniture in order to provide fuel for the fire.

'The Boches, they take everything,' she had stormed. 'But they will not take my pride.'

Sophie remembered her grandmother's wrath in 1943, when she had returned home with her schoolfriend Luke, pushing a dark green bicycle.

'Where did you get that?' she had demanded.

They had both looked at the ground.

'*Merde*, you stole it from a German soldier, didn't you? I heard you plotting but I never believed you would carry it through.'

'Sorry, Grand-mère,' Sophie had whispered.

'Sorry? You will be shot if you are caught,' her grandmother had stormed. 'Luke, you will get rid of it, do you understand? What would your parents say?' But the two children had kept it, hiding it in the shed at Luke's house, cycling through the streets of Paris when her grandmother's back was turned. It was only after the occupation had ended that she told Sophie how proud she had been.

For the next two months Sophie established a pattern of coping with the side effects of her pregnancy, her medical studies, and rushing every evening to the hospital. Her grandmother had remained bed-ridden, but with a strength of will that amazed the doctors, she asked to be moved to the chair in the afternoons and was able, with the aid of a nurse, to potter to the bathroom.

'I need to go home now,' she announced to the doctor each morning. 'I am quite well enough for my own bed.' At last in late September, the doctor in charge succumbed to her persistent nagging. She would be discharged, on the condition that she was cared for by her granddaughter.

'Of course, it goes without saying,' Sophie agreed with the doctor, knowing that she would do it gladly. It would be her chance to repay her beloved grandmother in some small way for everything she had done.

Now for the difficult part: she had to obtain permission from Professor Manon to take time off from her studies to look after her grandmother, whilst giving him no reason to suspect she was pregnant.

He was wearing a new bow-tie when she went into his office. Today it was dark blue with yellow spots.

'So you expect me to give you a sabbatical?' he looked at her over his desk, his expression stern.

'*Oui*, Professor. I understand it is not regular, but my grand-mother does not have long to live.'

'It is not regular at all,' he said, but then his face softened. 'Your marks have been exemplary, Mademoiselle Bernot, and despite my reservations you have proved an extremely capable student. We will be happy to hold your place, but you will have to retake the modules from this year.'

'*Merci*, Professor.' Sophie wanted to hug him but realised this would be one step too far. When the door had closed on his office she ran down the stairs and out of the hospital, to find Georges who was waiting for her in a café nearby.

'He didn't notice a thing,' she said, her face a picture of relief as she sank into the chair beside him. 'And, thank the Lord, I'll be able to continue with my studies afterwards.'

Sophie took her grandmother home. From then on, she under-took all her daily care. It was not a chore to wash and dress her and she enjoyed finding new recipes to tempt her dwindling appetite. It gave her more pleasure than she could have imagined to spend this valuable time with her. She treasured the late afternoons reading to Yvette and together they rediscovered books Sophie had loved as a child. Georges came regularly, cheering them both up with his humour, making them laugh. He also kept an eye on Sophie's health during her pregnancy.

'Good practice for my next stint in obstetrics,' he said checking Sophie's blood pressure and the foetal heartbeat.

It wasn't long before her stomach swelled and she could no longer hide her condition from her grandmother.

She was trying to get her grandmother to eat some soup, when Yvette waved away the spoon.

'I don't feel like eating, *cherie*, we need to have a talk. I still have eyes and your waistline is increasing daily. If I am not mistaken there is a new life in there, Sophie.'

Sophie looked down at the curve of her stomach and sighed. 'You are right, of course. I fell pregnant in Chamonix.'

Her grandmother drew in her breath. 'So this is the Englishman's child?'

Sophie nodded. 'But I didn't want to concern you, Grand-mère. Your condition...'

'Of course I am concerned,' she said. 'But you do me a far greater disservice keeping these matters to yourself. I noticed your bosom increasing in size weeks ago and now you have bought a new floaty dress. Then Georges came into the sitting room with a stethoscope hanging round his neck! Do you think I am deaf and blind? Please Sophie, credit it me with some wisdom.' She pushed away the tray and looked up at Sophie.

'My beloved child, you and I both know that my time on this earth is limited, and I need to be sure that it is spent wisely. We should be discussing this now.'

'You will get well again,' Sophie argued.

'And we both know that is not possible.' Yvette patted the

bedcover. 'So have you decided what to do when your baby arrives? It is mid-October,' she started adding on her fingers. 'So you must be four and a half months pregnant.'

Sophie sank down onto the side of the bed and put her head in her hands. 'Oh Grand-mère, I try not to think of it, I try to pretend it's not happening, but my body tells me otherwise. Every day that goes by, I wonder what the future will bring. I don't know what to do?'

'Have you thought of finding this Sebastian? He sounds an honourable man, I am sure he would marry you.'

'Even if he wanted to, his family would never accept me. Anyway I can't, Grand-mère.'

'And why not?'

'He lives in London; my life is here. I will not leave the hospital, not now when I have come this far, nor will I leave you, Grand-mère.'

Yvette tutted. 'Leave me? That is nonsense child, but what about asking him for financial help, he is the father after all?'

'No, I will never do that. I sent him away and I won't go begging now that I am pregnant.'

Her grandmother sighed, shaking her head. 'At this moment you are not thinking rationally. I would suggest you wait until the baby is in your arms. Only then will you know what is right.'

Chapter Eight

Six months after Sebastian had met the young French architect, Marcus Donadieu, in Paris, the drainage and the foundations for the new square in Kensington were already underway. The architectural drawings had exceeded even the partners at Blackheath Holdings' high expectations, and despite the few limitations imposed by Kensington Council, the planning had been achieved with relative ease.

Sebastian was working late in the office when the call came. Cheryl popped her head round his door.

'You are burning the midnight oil.' He smiled at the receptionist. 'You should have left ages ago.'

Cheryl blushed. 'I stayed on because your sister Gillie telephoned while you were in your meeting on the Mayfair project. Do you want me to call her back and put her through?'

'Yes, that would be grand, thank you. Then go home and have a lovely evening.'

He picked up the call to his sister, and her voice crackled through the fuzzy line.

'I am coming to London for a few days, I need cheering up,' she shouted. 'Firstly can I stay with you, but more importantly, will you have time to spend with me?'

'Yes to both your requests. Is it your French politician, *ma cherie*?'

'I have just found out that my politician is in fact still married.'

'The shit,' Sebastian exclaimed. 'Sorry shouldn't swear, but that really is off the mark.'

'You can swear darling and I will too. He is a horrid shit and I could kill him.'

'Perhaps we should arrange for him to disappear,' Sebastian laughed. 'At any rate, the least I can do is to give you a good time in London. I will put together a plan.'

'As long as it doesn't involve any *suitable* men!'

That night Sebastian had his pre-arranged drink with Robert Marston.

'My sister is coming to stay and needs some distraction. Will you both come with us to the theatre next Thursday?'

Robert looked at his diary. 'Giulietta fills in my evening engagements,' he grinned. 'Yes, we are free apparently, as long as we can get a babysitter.'

'I have managed to reserve four tickets for the new Agatha Christie play, *The Mousetrap*. It's opening on the 25th at the Ambassadors. What do you think?'

'We would love to. It will be great to see Gillie again, and we will do our best to distract her. Is it an affair of the heart?'

'Poor Gillie found out her latest beau was still married. I think she was hoping this would be the one. She is desperate to have children, and she is beginning to panic.'

'Well I'm panicking for another reason. Giulietta is pregnant again.'

'What? So soon?' Sebastian laughed 'Congratulations old chap.'

Robert looked sheepish. 'A bit too soon. It wasn't actually planned.' He picked up his pint. 'All her fault of course!'

'Of course,' Sebastian replied.

'You are coming back for supper by the way. It's an order from above, but only if you fancy some good Italian pasta?'

As Robert opened the door to the small mews house, two small children hurtled along the passage and clutched at his legs.

'Papa, Papa,' they yelled and he picked each one up in turn. He was putting Genevra, the younger of the two daughters, down when he heard his wife call from the kitchen.

'Roberto, is that you?'

'I believe so,' he grinned at Sebastian.

As Giulietta emerged untying the apron from around her waist, Sebastian could see the gentle swell of her stomach beneath. Even in pregnancy she was stunning. Her hair, which she brushed impatiently from her flushed face, fell in a glossy titian sweep down her back. A few damp strands stubbornly remained on her smooth brow. Her eyes were the most unusual colour of gold flecked with grey. She fixed them on her husband and leaned over to kiss him on the lips.

As Sebastian watched them together, it was easy to see how Robert's natural charisma had made him stand out in the war. He could also see why Robert, against all his better instincts, had fallen in love with his radio operator. 'I can't tell you much,' he had confided to Sebastian one evening at their usual pub, 'but golly I was blown away when I first saw her. It was in Cairo, where the head of operations in Italy was based at that time. As she walked down the passage towards me I nearly fell over. I knew I was being unprofessional, but I couldn't help myself, she was a bolt from the blue. Of course, it took months to convince her that I was anything but a stupid schoolboy.'

'But you did,' Sebastian had smiled.

'I believe I finally did,' Robert had agreed. But Sebastian knew that Robert was anything but a stupid schoolboy. Rumour had it, he had trained and armed a group of partisans near Arezzo in central Italy and he had nearly died in the subsequent sorties against the German occupiers. His friend had been a hero in his time.

While Robert lingered with his wife, Sebastian's mind returned to Sophie. She too had been a bolt from the blue, but the difference was, Sophie had left him. All that remained was the hurt, still raw after all these months. He could see her eyes laughing up at him and her full mouth with small white teeth. He could remember the concentration on her face when she talked, two small furrows appearing on her forehead, and her beautiful fingers fiddling with a strand of dark hair. But of course, she had never loved him, never looked at him the way Giulietta looked at Robert.

The evening was filled with warmth and laughter, and Giulietta's delicious Italian cooking. When it was time to leave, Giulietta hugged him.

'Stop thinking of that silly little French girl; it is her loss not yours,' she exclaimed.

'Not sure about that,' Sebastian grinned ruefully.

'If I wasn't attached to this man,' Giulietta prodded Robert in the ribs, 'I would be after you.'

'You behave yourself,' Robert scolded with a smile.

Giulietta made a face at her husband and left the two men together.

'Goodnight,' Robert said, clasping Sebastian's hand.

'*Bonsoir, mon ami,*' Sebastian replied.

As Sebastian walked home across the park, he wondered if he would ever get over Sophie. He remembered his foolish trip to Paris in search for her. His only lead had been her description of the library with a narrow walkway on the second level and wrought-iron steps. He had visited every library in every medical school in central Paris. By the time he reached his final destination at the Rue de l'École de Medecine, he believed his efforts were for nothing, but as soon as he opened the heavy wooden doors, he knew this was the room she had described; this was where Sophie spent her days. He had paused for a moment, gazing at the bookcases that stretched as far as the eye could see. Assuming the air of a student, he had wandered in past the librarian, noticing the glass cases displaying priceless manuscripts, leading to the desks where students had studied for centuries. Afterwards he had waited in the central hallway trying to curb his impatience, hoping that Sophie would come this way.

At six o'clock precisely, Sophie had wafted down the wide, elegant staircase, wearing a loose floaty dress sprigged with flowers. A canvas bag hung from her shoulder and she was looking at her watch. He was about to emerge from his hiding place behind a marble pillar, when a young man with dark curly hair had run towards her.

'Georges, thank goodness you are on time,' she had laughed, flinging her arms around him and holding him tight.

'Sophie *cherie*, would I ever be late for the woman I love.'

Sebastian melted into the background, all hope fading. Sophie had a lover and clearly belonged to someone else.

It was not until he had boarded the train bound for Dijon later that evening that he had got his emotions under control. What a fool he had been. He vowed never to speak of Sophie again.

A week after having dinner with Robert and Giulietta, his sister arrived at his flat, in time for a drink before dinner.

She took off her beret, shaking out her dark hair.

'My journey was so tedious,' she complained. 'A woman in my carriage insisted on lecturing me all the way from Dover on the impending catastrophe in London.'

'And what was that?'

'Smog,' Gillie said, following him into the sitting room and taking off her cream belted coat. 'All she talked about was campaigning for a restriction on the burning of coal, apparently it is polluting the atmosphere. After that I need a stiff drink.'

Sebastian mixed his sister a strong martini. 'There's something in what she says,' he said grimly. 'But I admit I am one of the culprits.'

Gillie laughed, seeing the fire burning merrily in the grate. 'Well you need a fire, it is freezing.'

Sebastian looked at his sister for a moment, appraising her. 'It's funny; in England you seem French, and in France you seem English.'

'You are saying I don't belong anywhere,' she teased.

While Sebastian reheated a chicken and vegetable casserole left by his housekeeper, Gillie had a bath. Sebastian could hear her humming as he laid the table. She seemed to have remained relatively unscathed from her encounter with the politician, or she was putting on a good show, he thought, putting bread rolls into the oven.

'I never believed my little brother would manage on his own, let alone prepare something as good as this.' Gillie put down her fork, a smile on her face. 'But I can't help wondering – were you the cook?'

Sebastian shook his head and laughed. 'You know me too well – the wonderful Irene calls these her one stop wonders, meaning everything is in a single pot. I am still a hopeless bachelor!'

Gillie smiled at her brother. 'Never hopeless,' she looked around the open-plan room with admiration, 'I can see my little brother has an array of talents.'

*

They had three days together. On the first morning, Gillie went with him to look at a site in Upper Brooke Street. Robert joined them.

'Hello Gillie,' he said, kissing her cheek. 'Good to see you again. So what do you think of one of our latest projects? The men are working on the roof and the windows have just been finished. We need to get it watertight before Christmas.'

Gillie looked up at the smart Georgian-style house, emerging from the ruins of a bomb site. 'It's lovely of course,' she said. 'But what happened to the people living there? I hope they weren't...' Her voice trailed off.

'No, thankfully they were away at the time,' Sebastian confirmed. 'But Robert has left out one rather important detail, Gillie; it is where he lived as a child.'

'My mother had sold the lease in '37,' Robert interjected, 'but the project is still close to my heart.'

'I'm sure it is,' Gillie murmured, remembering the terror of the bombing raids in France during the war.

When Sebastian had given the foreman the wiring specification, they all went off towards the pub for lunch. Gillie linked arms with both men and turned to Robert. 'I hope you are going to buy it back when you have made your fortune,' she quipped.

Chapter Nine

Sophie and her grandmother spent a quiet Christmas together. While Sophie listened to the carols on the wireless recorded at the Sacre Coeur, and studied her medical books, her grandmother knitted, her needles flashing in and out in her haste to finish a small woollen blanket.

The New Year came and went, but Sophie refused to look beyond the birth of her child. 'Let's not speak of it,' she said when Yvette brought up the subject. 'There will be plenty of time.' But she knew that time was running out for her grandmother.

Sophie was clearing away the lunch when she felt the first contraction. She clutched the table, her eyes round with fright. 'I'm only thirty-eight weeks, Grand-mère. It's not right.'

'Nature happens in its own time,' the old woman wheezed. 'Now Sophie, fetch Madame Guerin, she brought your brother into the world.'

'But that was thirty years ago!'

'There is no time to argue; her apartment is above the *boulangerie*. Number five, Rue des Bernardins.'

With no better option Sophie staggered out, clutching onto the stair rail. She found Madame Guerin's flat and knocked on the door. There was no reply. At the second attempt an old woman shouted from the inside. 'Go away. I don't need anything, piss off.'

'Please,' Sophie begged. 'My grandmother, Yvette Bernot, sent me.' She bent double suddenly, crippled with pain. The door opened.

'Why didn't you tell me?' An old woman was standing before her in a grubby floral pinafore and carpet slippers. 'Lord girl, you had better come in.'

'Could you come to my home please,' Sophie panted. 'Grandmère. I can't leave her. She is sick. Please.'

The old woman put her hands around Sophie's distended belly. 'You'll be having a baby on the pavement, if we don't hurry up. Come on then, love.'

Wearing her carpet slippers, the woman followed Sophie until they came to the apartments.

Sophie was at the top of the stairs when her waters broke; she staggered into the flat and collapsed on the floor. She woke to find herself stripped to the waist, the old woman peering between her legs. Her grandmother was directing operations from the chair.

'Towels are in that cupboard there, Ruth, and we have an electric kettle, so you won't need to boil the water on the stove.'

The woman got up and shuffled about the room. Sophie felt powerless in her body as the contractions took over. With each rising surge she gritted her teeth and grimaced in agony until the pain subsided only to begin again.

When Sophie screamed, the old woman glared at her.

'*Alors*! I didn't take you for a coward,' she admonished.

'I'm not a coward,' Sophie panted.

'Well then, prove it to me. You are at least four centimetres dilated – but don't get excited, you may be in for a long night!'

'Excited,' Sophie groaned. '*Merde*, why should I get excited?'

83

It was one o'clock in the morning and still no baby had arrived. Her grandmother looked on anxiously.

At three o'clock on February 28th, the old woman finally cut the umbilical cord, cleaned the baby and wrapped it into one of the towels. She placed the infant into Sophie's outstretched arms.

'It was worth it, you see,' she said smiling. 'A beautiful baby boy.'

As Sophie looked into the child's face, at the small, perfect nose, the rosebud mouth, she was unprepared for the rush of emotion. 'Thank you,' she whispered. 'He's beautiful. I'm sorry if I was a little rude; my training as a doctor has made me apprehensive.'

'You are not the first mother to curse me,' the old lady said, looking very pleased with herself. 'A doctor, eh? Well I can tell you this for nought, I can deliver a baby better than any doctor.' She surveyed her handiwork. 'You have two of the neatest stitches in the world.'

Madame Guerin stayed for an hour and there was an atmosphere of celebration in the small flat.

'I'll come again tomorrow,' she said as she was leaving. 'Put him to your breast every time he's hungry. You'll know when that is!' she grinned, showing nicotine-stained teeth, and hobbled to the door.

'Have you a name?' she asked, turning around.

'*Oui*,' Sophie replied. '*Il s'appelle* Alfred, Alfie for short.'

'And a Pisces – a very good sign.'

When the flat was quiet, her grandmother asleep in the next room, Sophie realised she couldn't put it off any longer and she considered her options anew. She had always known it would be difficult to give up her child, but now with Alfie cradled in her arms, she believed it would be impossible. How could she give him away? She looked down at his tiny trusting face, the dark fuzz of hair. This perfect creation was part of her, she had given him life. She glanced across the sitting room. On the windowsill the small plant she had bought in the market still flourished, and she was reminded of the campanulas she had seen with Sebastian high above Chamonix. Would he have stayed with her, she wondered? Would he have willingly been father to his child? Her grandmother had said her decision would become clear when her child was born, but it was not true. She was now more confused than ever. She stroked Alfie's brow; was it her imagination, or was his forehead the same shape as Sebastian's? There was a visceral pain in her chest as she imagined the future without her baby.

Three weeks later, Sophie was resting in the armchair, with Alfie asleep in a cot at her side. She looked up to see her grandmother leaning against the door jamb in her dressing gown. Sophie guided her back to bed.

'It is obvious, Sophie,' she said in a weak but firm voice. 'I have watched you with the child, you can't give him up. Next year you will receive a small salary from the hospital and I have a few savings to tide us over till then.' Yvette started to cough and put her handkerchief to her mouth. 'We will find a young girl to help us and I can keep an eye on her. Instead of always studying in the library, you could bring the books back and work from home.'

Sophie was overwhelmed with love for this tiny, dying woman. She could feel joy bubbling in her chest. 'Are you sure, Grand-mère?'

Her grandmother smiled. 'No, *ma cherie*, but we can give it a try.'

Chapter Ten

Yvette's condition seemed to stabilise, and Sophie was trying to be optimistic. Her grandmother would be well, Sophie could go back to medical school and keep her son.

'Take Alfie for a walk', Yvette instructed on a blustery April afternoon. 'The child needs some air.'

'You don't mind me leaving you, Grand-mère?'

'Stop treating me like an invalid,' she smiled.

Sophie was pushing Alfie's pram through the park when it started to rain. She ran back home, the wheels trampling the fallen blossom.

'So, that was a bit of an adventure wasn't it,' she laughed, pulling the pram up the steps and kissing his chubby fist. 'Your very first rain. Shall we tell your great-grandmother about it?'

Unlocking the door, she put Alfie in his cot and took off her shoes. Padding across the bare boards she felt a twinge of alarm. There was a quietness to the flat; something didn't feel right at all. 'Grand-mère,' Sophie called. There was no response. Panic built in her chest. She rushed down the passageway and opened the door.

Yvette was lying on the floor.

'Sorry, *ma petite*,' she gasped, her eyes open, her lips tinged blue.

'I shouldn't have left you, this is my fault,' Sophie cried, feelings of guilt crushing her as she knelt beside her grandmother. She felt her pulse. 'We need to get you to the hospital, Grand-mère.'

'No Sophie, not this time,' she whispered. 'I tried, I really did, but God has other plans.'

'Please,' she begged. 'They will make you better, Grand-mère.'

Her grandmother was fighting for breath. 'I mean it Sophie, I don't want to go to hospital, I want to be in my own home till the end.'

'But—'

'No buts, it's time.' Yvette squeezed her hand with all the strength she could muster. 'Do you understand, Sophie?'

Sophie was sobbing. 'Since Maman and Papa died you are everything. Alfie and I need you.'

Her grandmother lifted her head. 'Sophie *ma cherie*, that is about you, not about me.' She paused, fighting for air. 'Do you want this to be my life? Unable to breathe, always in pain?'

Sophie slowly shook her head, tears stinging at her eyes.

'Well then, if you feel unable to treat me yourself, you may fetch that nice Doctor Fleury, but please, there will be no hospital.'

Sophie struggled to lift her grandmother into the bed before grabbing Alfie. She hurtled down the stairs, clutching her child in one arm, the bannister rail in the other and ran out into the rain. By the time she arrived at the surgery Alfie was bawling with anger, his little face spattered with rain.

'Please,' she begged, running into the reception. 'I must see Doctor Fleury.'

'Go back home, my dear,' the receptionist instructed Sophie. 'I will get the doctor to come to you just as soon as he has finished with his patient.'

By the time Doctor Fleury arrived at the apartment, Alfie had been fed, changed and was gurgling in his cot.

Sophie took the doctor through to her grandmother's room and left them alone.

'I have made your grandmother as comfortable as I could,' Doctor Fleury advised, finding her in the sitting room afterwards. 'She has a few days at the most, Sophie. You are a doctor, you understand.'

Sophie nodded, a dull ache in her heart. 'Of course I do. It's just...' She turned away.

Doctor Fleury put his hand on her arm. 'I know it's very different with your own family.' He took a bottle from his bag. 'I am leaving you with this. You must administer it to your grandmother and increase the dose as you wish. It will certainly take away the discomfort and with a large dose she will slip quietly away.'

'What are you saying, Doctor?'

'I am saying nothing, but it is your judgement to decide.'

When he had gone Sophie stared at the bottle of morphine. She went to her grandmother, her face composed.

'It seems you will live for ever, Grand-mère.'

Chapter Eleven

Sophie was in the churchyard standing by the freshly dug grave, holding Alfie in her arms, when Georges hurried along the path towards her.

'I'm so glad you're here,' she said, then paused, a lump building in her throat. 'I thought you would be late, and we would be on our own with Monseigneur Martin and the two old dears who are already in the pew.'

'Would I ever?' he smiled.

'Oh Georges.' Sophie looked at him, tears streaming down her face, and he gathered her into his arms, Alfie wedged between them.

'I know, *ma cherie*, I know,' he murmured, kissing her forehead. As Alfie started to whimper, he led them into the church.

'Thank you, Georges,' she whispered.

'I couldn't let you do this without me,' Georges replied. 'This is what best friends are for.'

Madame Bernot's death had not rocked the world, but it had rocked Sophie's. When Georges arrived at the apartment a week later to find her still in her nightdress at three o'clock in the afternoon, he threw the curtains wide and opened the window.

'Sophie, my darling, we need to talk, but first you need to dress.'

'Now?' Sophie looked at him, her eyes dull.

'Now.'

'You are not going to lecture me?'

'Not a lecture but a discussion.' Georges went to Sophie. 'I didn't tell you at the funeral, but the professor has been asking after your grandmother. I couldn't lie. He knows she is dead.'

Sophie's face paled. 'I see.'

'I'm here to help you with your decision.'

Sophie went to the cot and picked up her son. 'It's too soon, Georges,' she said, cradling Alfie in her arms. 'I can't think about it now, not yet.'

'But my darling girl, you will have to. Your sabbatical is coming to an end and if you don't return you will lose your place.'

Sophie kissed Alfie's head and turned away. 'But Georges...'

'I said you were hoping to come back in the next couple of weeks.'

Tears slipped down Sophie's cheeks. 'You know what you are asking me?'

Georges nodded dully. 'I can't begin to imagine how hard this is, but surely you are not contemplating resigning from the course. Do you want give up your dreams? You now need to consider your future, Alfie's future, you need to think what is best for your son.'

That night, Alfie was hot and restless, he wouldn't settle. He wouldn't take his milk. Sophie wheeled him up and down the cobbled street outside. By four o'clock in the morning she was exhausted and Alfie was still crying.

She took him back into the flat and put him down in the cot where he finally fell asleep. Sophie slumped in the chair. She had lost her grandmother and she was overwhelmed with grief. It was as if she was submerged in a mire and she couldn't climb out. The energy that had propelled her through medical school had gone, but she had to make up her mind. Georges was right, she really had to come to a decision.

Georges returned the next morning to find Sophie pacing the small sitting room, with Alfie coughing and grizzling in her arms.

'Alfie is sick, Georges.' Sophie's voice was rising. 'I need to take him to the doctor.'

Georges strode across the floor and took Alfie from her. 'It's cold outside, fetch another blanket and we'll go together,' he said.

An hour later Sophie returned to the apartment with Alfie, Georges and a large bottle of medicine. Her purse was several francs lighter. Alfie was yelling, his little face purple with anger, and while George averted his eyes, Sophie put him to her breast. He started to feed at last.

'This time it is simply a throat infection,' she stated, her voice filled with despair. 'It can be cured with a dose of antibiotics, but what if he were really sick? What would I do. I can't afford his care.'

'If I had the money I would help, but we both know that is not the answer.'

Sophie looked at him, her face bleak. 'I feel so inadequate, Georges. I am useless, I can't even care for my own son.'

'Don't say that. You are the most amazing woman I know, and you have done brilliantly, but at this moment looking after a child may not be right for you or Alfie.'

'You are saying I should let him go?'

'I believe your son should be with someone who has the time and the money to nurture him, to give him the life that at the moment you cannot. We both know that as a female surgeon you are already fighting the odds – as a single mother it would be impossible.'

Sophie put Alfie in his cot and went into the small kitchen. As she filled the kettle with water and turned the switch to boil, she thought only of the words she was about to say, and of the crushing and momentous decision that would rip her in two. She was shivering uncontrollably as she returned to the sitting room with a coffee for them both.

Georges took the cups and she sank onto the sofa.

'I have thought about it night and day for months, and you are right. I can't do both, and perhaps through my work, I can make up for all of this. One night of foolishness and look at the havoc it has caused. This dear beautiful boy is the one to suffer.'

'He doesn't have to suffer, Sophie.' George said, sitting down beside her.

Sophie looked at him, her eyes blurred with tears. 'I am going to give him to his father's family. There he will have love and security and grow up with everything he needs. He will have a big family around him, away from all this.' She looked around the shabby sitting room, her eyes closing in on the patch of damp in the corner of the room. 'He might even have a dog,' she smiled ruefully. 'I always wanted a dog.' She set down the cup and put her head in her hands.

'I can't bear it, Georges, but I think it is the right decision. I want the best for Alfie. I don't want him growing up in Paris with a struggling single mother, ostracised from society. I want him to have everything that I did not.' She looked up at him. 'And even if I did give up my dreams of becoming a surgeon, I would never find a respectable job.'

'My poor Sophie,' Georges took her hand. 'Perhaps you will be able to see him in the future.'

'If I give him up now it has to be a total break. It would hurt me too much to see him and would only confuse Alfie. No, if I do this I must leave them alone to bring Alfie up as they see fit. I believe this is the only decision for my son.'

Chapter Twelve

That weekend, Georges borrowed his father's battered old Citroën, and they began the long drive to Pommard. Sophie was in the back, with the baby in a wicker bassinet beside her. To the outside world they could have been a family going on an outing, she thought, touching Alfie's head. They could have been setting out for a wonderful day. Instead she was about to give her child away. Once again, her tears flowed. When she started to sob, Georges pulled the car to the side of the road and squeezed himself into the back beside her. He put his arms around her. 'I am so sorry,' he soothed when at last she had calmed a little. 'I know this is a terrible decision to have to make – but you are doing the right thing for Alfie, I know it.'

They were nearing their destination and Georges navigated the car around the large church at the centre of the village and continued up a lane. When they reached a pair of tall stone pillars at the beginning of a drive, Sophie clutched Georges's arm.

'That's it, I am sure of it,' she whispered. Georges drove slowly up the tree-lined avenue. He opened the door for Sophie and she stepped from the car.

As she reached an elaborate gate, Sophie started to shake. Georges held her by the shoulders.

'I can't face meeting his mother and grandmother,' Sophie uttered, her teeth chattering. 'Perhaps I could leave him with the colonel. He is like a father to Sebastian.'

Georges drove back to the square and parked the car. Directly behind the war memorial was a small stone house, with a wrought-iron porch. Sophie knew without doubt it belonged to the colonel.

She lifted Alfie from the crib. 'You will have a good life,' she whispered, 'a very excellent life.' She breathed in his scent one last time and laid his head against her shoulder. In her other hand she carried the crib containing Alfie's blanket, his rabbit, a bottle of milk and three tins of milk formula.

Georges opened the gate for her. She stepped through. As she walked across the cobbled courtyard, past the stone well, heading to the back door, she thought the pain in her chest would explode. She could hardly see, her vision blurred by her tears. She was nearly at the door when it opened.

'May I help you?'

An old man was standing there – the colonel, just as Sebastian had described.

'*Oui*,' she stammered. 'May I come inside?'

'It would be helpful to know your name,' the old man queried, a little perplexed.

'Sophie,' she replied, and holding Alfie closer still, she stepped into the house.

Georges stopped the car outside Sophie's flat later that evening. It was raining heavily. They sat in silence, staring through the windscreen as the wipers swept to and fro.

'I expect you want to be alone?' Georges said at last, turning off the engine.

Sophie nodded. 'Thank you for understanding me, Georges.' Her hand was on the door when she turned around and leant towards him. 'You are the dearest of men, my best friend.' She hugged him and stepped from the car.

She hauled herself up the stairs to the apartment and opened the door. The flat looked the same: the worn velvet sofa, the desk, Max's painting on the wall, but the crib had gone, the rabbit she had bought Alfie, the blue blanket knitted by her grandmother, and so had her son. She took a little boot from her pocket, Alfie's boot, and put it to her lips. She could see the imprint left by his tiny foot, smell him in the wool. She would never be with her son on his birthday, never see his first steps. His first word wouldn't be 'Maman'.

She went down the narrow passage and into her room, slumping down on her bed. She could imagine her grandmother's words. 'You think at this moment that your life is over, but it will go on and your pain will lessen. You will never forget him, my love, but you will learn to live with the loss. As we both know, life is like that. You are a strong girl, a good girl, and one day in the future you will be happy again.'

Chapter Thirteen

Sebastian was getting ready for work, when Irene the house-keeper knocked on his bedroom door.

'It's your sister on the telephone, Mr Sebastian,' she said, wiping her hands on her overall. 'And it sounds important.'

Gillie never rang at this time in the morning unless it was serious. He hurried into the sitting room, tucking in his shirt tails as he went.

'Sebastian, you need to come home immediately.'

'What's wrong? It's not Grand-mère?'

'No darling, she is fine, but you still need to come home and I can't disclose anything on the telephone.'

'I'll ask the partners if I can take a couple of days off. I'll leave first thing in the morning.'

'Good, just let me know when you'll arrive.'

Sebastian arrived at Beaune Station to find Adeline's husband, Jean, waiting for him. As he opened the car door he avoided Sebastian's eye.

'What's wrong Jean? I'm getting worried.'

'I am not aware of anything, Monsieur Sebastian, but there is no death in the house, that I will tell you.'

Sebastian shook his head; something was going on.

The car stopped on the gravel and Sebastian ran up the front steps, his heart pounding.

His mother was waiting for him, her expression inscrutable. 'I think you had better come upstairs.'

Sebastian followed her into the spare bedroom and heaved a sigh of relief as his grandmother came towards him. Gillie had spoken the truth on the telephone – she appeared to be in good health.

Then, quickly scanning the room, his eyes landed on his sister leaning over a small crib.

The next hour would remain forever printed on Sebastian's brain. First he had stared at the crib. Then he heard a small cry that quickly increased in tempo until it became a howling scream. After glancing at Sebastian, his sister had plucked a small angry baby from the crib and calmed it lovingly with a bottle of milk.

Sebastian looked at the baby and then at his sister. 'Gillie, why didn't you tell me sooner? I had no idea, I would have supported you no matter the circumstance.'

Gillie laughed. 'Don't be ridiculous, this is nothing to do with me. This is your son, dear brother.'

Sebastian's face blanched, he hesitated for a moment as the information sank in. 'It's not possible, it can't be,' he whispered at last.

'I am afraid it is entirely possible, Sebastian. You know how these things work.'

'But how and who brought him here?'

'Sophie, the girl you talked about. She is the mother.'

'Sophie.' Sebastian said her name softly. She had come to him with his son, their child.

'Where is she, Maman?' he asked.

His mother came towards him. She raised her hand and gently brushed the hair from his brow. 'My darling, she is not here. We didn't even see her; she left the baby with the colonel, asking him to bring the child to us. She did leave you this letter.'

Stunned, he took the letter from his mother and walked from the room.

Her bold handwriting took him back to that day when he had first seen it in the walkers' book.

May 15th 1953

Dear Sebastian,

By now you will have met Alfie. He is nearly three months old, born on the last day of February – I am told that is a lucky day. I am leaving him with you not because I want to, but because he will have a far better life. The family you described to me on those glorious days in the mountains are all I could wish for our son. I can assure you my decision has not been easy, but it is done with a clear head. I love him with all my heart, but I realise I could never give him the future he deserves. I have every faith that you will be a good father, and you will give him all the things that I could never provide. Please don't attempt to find me. However harsh this must seem, it is the best for everyone concerned, particularly Alfie.

Always,
Sophie

Gillie found Sebastian hunched on the bed with his head in his hands. She sat down beside him. 'I can't do this,' he mumbled, passing her the letter.

She read it quickly. 'It's not a question of can't. The child, Alfie, is here. He is not a parcel that we can return.'

'I work in London, it's mad. She has to take him back. I don't even know if it's my child! I saw Sophie in Paris with another man.'

Gillie patted his back. 'He is the replica of you as a baby, Sebastian. A little darker, but he's yours, I know it.'

Sebastian sat up. 'I don't want him,' he declared.

Gillie looked at her brother and something snapped inside her. He was eight years younger and the world was ahead of him. He could click his fingers and a hundred women would run to him. He would never experience the misery of seeing his friends getting married, with little prospects himself. 'Oh, for goodness sake, Sebastian, stop feeling sorry for yourself. If you were foolish enough to get yourself into this situation then you have to take the consequences. Adeline would relish bringing up yet another generation in this house, and I shall help you look after him.'

'You have your own life to lead.'

'And what life is that, Sebastian? Don't you see? I want to do this. I would like nothing better than to have children of my own, but I don't have a boyfriend, let alone a husband and I am thirty-two years old! I would love to care for my nephew.'

They went back into the nursery together. Sebastian watched as Gillie scooped the baby into her arms. 'Alfie,' she whispered, kissing the top of his head, 'your papa would give you back, but I'll look after you, I promise.'

Before Sebastian had time to move, Gillie had thrust the baby towards him. He tried to step backwards, but the baby was already in his arms.

As he looked into the small face, something shifted inside him. The child with the tiny tilted nose and solemn eyes that were gazing up at him, was his son, his responsibility now. 'Do you realise what you are suggesting, Gillie – this is not one of your Labradors.'

She started to laugh. 'No, my little brother, he is not.'

*

Later, when Adeline had taken the baby and settled him, Gillie, Sebastian, their mother and grandmother had a drink together in the salon.

'I think a plan should be put in place,' Marie-Claire observed, putting down her glass. 'I suggest the child stays here. Gillie can oversee his care during the week and you, Sebastian, return at the weekends.'

Sebastian interrupted. 'No, Grand-mère, he should come to London.'

'But this is a far better place to bring up a child,' Marie-Claire insisted. 'I imagine that would be the mother's wish.'

'The mother,' Sebastian said, his voice rising a fraction, 'has relinquished all responsibility for her son. His future is now up to us to decide.'

Gillie interrupted. 'I agree with Sebastian, that woman has just abandoned her son.'

The conversation went round in circles, until at last they came to a solution.

'Are we agreed then?' his grandmother said. 'Alfie will stay with us while you sort your life out in London, Sebastian. When you feel it appropriate, he will come to you. Gillienne, don't make faces, I am sure your brother would be more than grateful if you joined him. You can nurse in London if you wish and it would do you good to have a change. You never go anywhere these days except for the hospital.'

'I went to Rome. That is not exactly around the corner.'

Her grandmother sniffed. 'And look what happened in Rome?'

'It didn't turn out well,' Gillie admitted. 'But I was unaware that Marcel was still married.'

'You should never trust a politician!' her grandmother replied.

Sebastian was helping Gillie to another glass of wine when a gong announcing dinner echoed through the hall. Liliane stood up. 'I think Sebastian has had enough surprises for the day; at least he can rely on Adeline's cooking.'

After dinner, Gillie was making her way upstairs when she saw the small ribbon of light beneath the nursery door. Her brother was standing over the cot watching his sleeping child. There was a look of awe on his face and of something else: pride. Would he rise to the challenge? she wondered. Would he be a good father to Alfie? She knew the answer: Sebastian would be a brilliant father. She bit her lip. Everything had been easy for her brother, and now he had been given the one thing she had wanted most in life. She was happy for him of course, but she was also a little jealous. As the angelic younger child, he had been pampered by both his father and mother. In contrast she had been awkward and shy and, in her opinion, plain. Now she made up for this by being eccentric.

There had been a number of men in her life, including the recent politician, but only one who ever really meant anything to her. He had been *un résistant* during the war, and though their time together was brief, Étienne had made her feel beautiful, feminine and so very alive. But he would never return. She would never see his face remade in that of a small child.

She remembered the first time she had seen him, literally bumped into him. She had finished her night shift at the American Hospital and was hurrying to the house she shared with several other nurses. Her mind was still on her last patient when the man emerged from the shadows. His mind, she would learn later, was bent on getting to the safe house as quickly as possible.

'*Merde*,' he had sworn. 'Why don't you look where you are going?'

'I could say the same for you,' she had replied tartly.

Seconds later he had pulled her into his arms, kissing her firmly on the mouth. When she struggled, he held her tight and whispered in her ear, 'Please, you need to be quiet, and pretend you are enjoying it.'

She was about to strike him when she saw a German soldier walking towards them.

She froze.

'It is after curfew, you know the penalties.' The soldier was standing in front of them. Even in the gloom she could see the sharp cheekbones and prominent nose over thin lips.

'I have been on nights Capitain, and my fiancée never gets to see me.'

Gillie adjusted her starched cap and smiled at the soldier.

'On your way both of you, if I see you again…'

When they were out of earshot, the man at her side had laughed. 'My apologies. I am not in the habit of kissing strange women, necessity of course.'

'Of course,' she had stuttered, feeling at once deflated.

It was as if he sensed her confusion. 'Am I allowed to know the name of the woman with the nice lips?'

Gillie had felt herself blushing.

'*Je m'appelle* Gillie Ogilvie.'

'Well, Gillie Ogilvie, I hope we will meet again.'

'I hope so too.' The words were out before she could stop them. She could feel her cheeks redden.

'And your name?'

'Étienne.'

Then he was gone, running into the darkness.

It would be two weeks before she saw him again. She was in a civilian ward, dressing an ulcerated leg on an old man, when a pair of scuffed shoes attached to trousers with frayed turn-ups, came into her line of vision.

'It's not visiting hours,' she said without looking up. 'Can't you see the sign?'

There was silence, then a laugh that she recognised immediately.

'Well then, I will go.'

'It's you.' She looked up into mischievous brown eyes, and her heart lifted.

'It seems so, Mademoiselle Gillie.'

Gillie smiled. The man in front of her was shambolic to say the least. His unruly dark hair tumbled over his forehead and she longed to reach out and pull it from his eyes.

'You will get me into trouble if you are caught.'

'I am often the cause of trouble, but I think you will find I am worth it.'

No man had ever said anything like that to Gillie before.

'You must still go,' she had laughed. 'But meet me after my shift, before curfew. Do you know the café in the Rue Chauveau?'

Étienne laughed. 'It is one of the only places in Paris where you can still get a good glass of wine.'

The café was just around the corner from the hospital and when she arrived Étienne was waiting for her. She had hurried in, conscious of inquisitive glances from the men. Few German soldiers frequented the café, and Étienne's appearance suggested that it was better this way. As one glass turned into three, she learnt that he was a member of the Maquis, intent on freeing his country from the German oppressor. 'I believe I can trust you, Gillie,' he had said, running his finger round his glass, 'but if you betray me, I will be forced to kill you.'

'I would never do that,' she had reassured him, and he had laughed, his open mouth revealing two gold crowns.

Étienne was unlike anyone she had ever met before. One moment he was wary, like a hunted animal, the next, the tension would disappear from his face and his wiry body would relax and he was whispering terms of endearment. When he arranged to meet her and he didn't turn up, she learnt not to rely on him. She also learnt not to question him.

'It is better you do not know, *ma cherie*,' he had said.

'But I worry.'

'Then we should not see each other.' His chin had set in a firm line and for a moment he was a stranger. Then he had laughed, and his face had softened once more.

Lifting her chin he had looked deep in her eyes. 'You have to accept that I can't tell you my movements, otherwise...' He shrugged his shoulders.

'I understand, of course I do,' she replied.

'I thought you would,' he said. Then he had taken her hand and he had run his thumb along the inside of her palm, until a thrill went down her spine and she forgot her fear.

With Étienne, Gillie had felt beautiful. He told her that her eyes were the colour of emeralds and her hair was like silk. Their lovemaking had been tender and intense but necessarily hurried and at times strained. From the beginning Gillie had realised the danger. Her sense told her to walk away, but her heart said otherwise.

When a few months into their relationship Étienne disappeared without warning, Gillie forced herself to be positive. A week later all optimism had gone. She found his comrade Geraud in their usual bar.

'Étienne, he has not come home,' she whispered, leaning towards him.

Geraud glanced at a table in the corner where two men were deep in conversation.

'Abwehr,' he mouthed and Gillie fell silent, her hands clasped beneath the table to stop them shaking. When they had gone, she followed Geraud outside.

He spoke in a fierce whisper. 'You should be more careful.'

'But Étienne – where is he, please tell me?'

'We assume he has been taken,' he had mumbled.

'Assume?'

'We don't know for sure.'

'Fresnes?' she urged. 'Is he there?'

'Sorry *mademoiselle*, I can't tell you any more.'

Gillie had stumbled back to the flat and had leant against the door.

Étienne had told her what happened at Fresnes, the prison south of Paris where the captured *résistants* were taken. Behind the severe walls, prisoners were brutally tortured and when they were no longer of any use to their captors, they were shot. Throwing herself on the bed, Gillie had buried her head in the pillow trying to block the images of her lover in the hands of the Gestapo, but to no avail. She could imagine Étienne tied to a chair, she could hear his screams as his nails were ripped from their beds, and burning cigarettes were pushed into his sensitive flesh. 'No,' she had cried. 'No no no.' But her cries wouldn't help her lover for he would be dead either way.

For months afterwards she had tried in vain to get information, but she had always drawn a blank. Perhaps it was fear that made many of Étienne's former comrades deny any knowledge of Étienne's disappearance; perhaps they had their own secrets. Whatever it was, she returned home to Pommard traumatised and frustrated, with no answers. She had continued with her enquiries, and though the anxiety dimmed with the years, she vowed she would never give up until she had found out the truth.

Chapter Fourteen

In June 1953, while the coronation of the young Queen Elizabeth was taking place in England, a christening was being planned at the Chateau de Villienne. The Abbot of Vézelay had been asked to officiate. Though the gathering wouldn't be unduly large, the guests would come, not only from the estate, but from Pommard and the surrounding villages. Three days before the event, Marie-Claire produced the Villienne robe from a trunk at the bottom of her bed. It was washed and pressed, along with a little silk bonnet that had been in the family for two hundred and fifty years. In the chapel adjacent to the house, the pews were polished, the black and white marble floor was swept. Liliane cut flowers from the herbaceous border to the indignation of Jean, who had tended the gardens for the last thirty years.

'She, that is *madame*, is robbing my garden,' he grumbled to Adeline, running his hand over the stubble on his chin. 'How am I meant to keep any colour in the beds, if she goes on taking it?'

Adeline had laughed. 'Don't look so miserable, Jean, you are as happy as any of us to have the little boy. It's a very special occasion.'

Wine was brought up from the cellars and food prepared.

Adeline's eyes were like a hawk, detecting anyone who dared to steal her culinary creations.

Sebastian, who had taken the week off work, was constantly in the firing line.

'Hands off my *patisserie*, young man. I can still chase you around the kitchen with my broom.'

Sixty-eight miles away in Vézelay, Pierre de Villienne was packing his small suitcase, a frown creasing his forehead. He hadn't been home for a year, though of course he didn't think of it as home any more. Home was the austere room in the monastery, where the only adornment was a painting of Our Lady hanging on the wall. He snapped the catches and went down the stone staircase to the refectory. Sunlight slanted through the high windows, gently illuminating the thirty monks who ate in silence below. He gave his blessing to the assembled company, and ten minutes later he was in his car and rattling down the hill.

There was something about his bright red Citroën DS19 cabriolet with cream folding top that made him reconnect with the outside world. It was his only indulgence. Despite his holy orders and the occasional pursed lips of the ecclesiastical hierarchy, he was proud of it. He started to whistle, and as the wind blew in his face, for a brief while he was free.

It wasn't until he was nearing Pommard that he could feel the nostalgia building in his chest. He drove faster, trying to bury the long-ago memories of his friends marching off to war, and of Fleur. He had been going to renounce his vows for her, marry her and take over the estate. How different it all would have been.

As he passed the war memorial the years melted away, and he was once again in the hell and chaos of the battlefields of France. The year was 1914, and as a recently ordained priest, he had volunteered as a stretcher bearer, leaving his former life as the aristocratic Pierre de Villienne behind. During the following months, he had stepped over the bloated bodies of the dead to give the last rites to those barely alive. He had celebrated mass in the newly dug trenches with men who only a short while later would be slaughtered like lambs. He had been sent from one battleground to the next, closing his mind to the horror, blotting out the images of young men tangled in the cruel wire, friends, brothers, lying next to each other in death.

His belief, though tested, remained firm, until February 1915, when Fleur had come into his life. She was an English volunteer with the French Flag Nursing Corps. He had seen her first at the casualty clearing station, near Ypres. The hospital was the largest tent amongst the vast sea of beige canvas. Pierre had just delivered six wounded soldiers from the front line, and was about to climb into the ambulance when a nurse ran towards him.

'Please, come quickly,' she had said pulling at his sleeve. 'There is not much time.' He had followed her into the tent.

'The priest has come to talk to you,' she had said in passable French, stopping at a bed and running her fingers across a young man's brow. Then she had looked up at Pierre and their eyes had met, and amidst the misery and suffering, he had felt her compassion.

'Don't leave me,' Michel had begged.

'Well then, I'm here,' she had soothed, 'always.'

As Pierre came closer, he had seen Michel's condition. Blood seeped through the bandages covering his stomach, and one leg had gone above the knee, skin, muscle and bone protruding from the gaping hole. He was beyond hope.

Fleur held the boy's hand while he gave God's blessing. She had soothed him, occasionally bending to put a soaked bandage to his parched mouth, and as the light faded from his eyes she had kissed his lips.

'He's gone,' she had said, her grey eyes filling with tears. 'What is this all about, Father?' For the first time he had no answer.

During the following days, her eyes had become the beacon he sought in the madness, her calm voice his inspiration.

'I'm angry, Father,' she had said, lifting the blanket over yet another boy's eyes. 'It's the mass slaughter of innocent lambs.'

'God would say we have to fight for a just cause.'

'And you think this is just?'

Though Fleur never failed the men in her care, her anger had mounted. After another morning of carnage, when the tent was filled with the stench of death, she had caught hold of his arm. 'So priest, what does your God say now?' As he looked at the chaos around him, his belief in divine mercy began slipping away. His decision to give his life to a God who didn't look after his flock seemed wrong.

When on a fine early spring morning, he had walked with Fleur away from the trenches and the battlefield, into a parallel world of apple orchards and farmhouses, as yet untouched by the ravages of war, Fleur told him why she had volunteered.

'After my brother was killed, I was compelled to leave England; I had to do something to help these young men.'

She was speaking slowly, wrinkling her nose as she tried not to cry, and Pierre wanted to comfort her.

She looked up at him and for a brief moment he longed to put out his hand and touch her skin. He looked away, ashamed.

'I am filled with admiration; you are a very brave young woman.'

'Probably a little reckless,' she said, her face relaxing, and Pierre noticed the dimples in her cheeks and the way her lips curved when she smiled. He could feel the colour rise in his face.

'Forgive me, was I staring?'

'There is nothing to forgive,' she said. 'I'm glad that you look at me. I just wish you were not a priest.' She shook her head. 'I'm sorry, I should not have said that.'

'Neither us should be having these thoughts,' he murmured.

Fleur had sighed and plucked at a strand of grass. 'Would you like to know why I have a French name?'

Pierre had smiled. 'I think you are going to tell me anyway.'

'My grandmother was French, so I belong here, you see.' She had gazed at him, her lips parted, and Pierre had pulled his eyes away and had tried to think of something, anything, to take his mind off the beautiful girl beside him.

'So Fleur,' he said at last. 'I shall tell you how I came to take my vows.'

As they sat on the steps of a disused barn amongst the poppies and wild flowers, he had told Fleur how his life had been mapped out for him. He had inherited an estate, hectares of vineyards making the famous Pommard *rouge*, and one of the prettiest houses in Burgundy, but always at the back of his mind God was calling him. As time went on, his responsibilities to the estate and his family became secondary to his responsibility to God. He told her of the day he had found his mother in the study of their home. 'I have something to tell you,' he had said.

'And what is that?' she had asked, looking up from the letter she was writing. It was then that he broke his mother's heart.

They were in Belgium near Ypres when Fleur came to his tent. He would always remember the date. The nineteenth of April 1915. He was reading by the light of a small oil lamp when he saw her illuminated in the entrance.

'It's me,' she had said. 'Do you mind, I couldn't sleep.'

'You shouldn't be here.'

'Are you going to tell Matron?'

Before he had time to stop her, she had sat down on the camp bed beside him and pulled a flask from her pocket. 'Armagnac,' she had announced taking a draught. 'It helps obliterate all this.'

They were silent for a moment, listening to the thump of shells dropping in the distance. She passed the flask to Pierre and he drank deeply. As he gave it back to her, he noticed the dark smudges beneath her eyes.

'Perhaps you should ask for leave?'

'Why?' she asked, running a hand through her auburn hair, 'do I look tired?'

'A little perhaps.'

'But I couldn't, not with all this going on, and don't say it, please. I knew the danger when I came here, but you are in far greater danger.'

'I'm a man.'

'And I am a woman – so what?'

Pierre smiled. 'And a fierce one.'

'Do you get frightened?' she asked at last.

'Of course,' he replied. 'I would be lying if I said otherwise.'

She started to say something and stopped. She swore softly and leant against him. 'Why are you a priest, it's not fair.'

At that moment Pierre wished he was an ordinary man, far from the trenches.

'You are making me doubt myself,' he murmured. 'I have feelings for you, Fleur, you must know this, but they are wrong.'

'No, they are not.'

Pierre smiled. 'Oh little Fleur,' he whispered, lifting a strand of hair from her neck, and stroking the soft, pale skin. When she sighed and lifted her chin so that it was inches away from his own, he had pulled her into his arms and kissed her.

He drew away. 'No. This must stop. I can't, Fleur, however much I would like to.'

She stood up, her eyes never leaving his face.

'I want you, Pierre de Villienne. Not as a priest but as a man.' In the dim light she had unbuttoned her blouse and stepped out of her skirt. All the while her eyes were fixed on him. He knew she was waiting for him to stop her, but he could only watch as she had taken off her silken camisole edged with lace and slipped out of her pants until she was naked and the moon had touched her body with silver.

Three days later, on the twenty-second of April 1915, at the Second Battle of Ypres, Pierre had been repaid for his sins.

Unwittingly he could see her face, her clear green eyes and auburn hair. 'Dear God,' he groaned, remembering the scene that awaited him at the field hospital. Soldiers were staggering into the tent, blinded by gas. They were knocking over trolleys, falling into beds. Their faces were purple as they tried to breathe. Fleur was amongst them, her beautiful eyes no longer green, but red with blood.

The memories still had the power to destroy him after all these years.

He turned into the drive. He mustn't think of it; this was his great nephew's christening, not his time to grieve.

The following morning, Alfred de Villienne Ogilvie was baptised by the Abbot of Vézelay. Once again in charge of his emotions, Pierre placed a white linen cloth on Alfie's head and gave the godfather, Robert Marston, a candle. As the service neared the end, and the candle flickered and glowed in the dim light, Pierre made the sign of the cross on the child's forehead.

'*Vade in pace et Dominus sit tecum. Amen.*'

His smile was beneficent as Alfie was handed back to his father. Gillie then carried him back to the house and the party began.

That evening Marie-Claire was the perfect hostess, presiding over dinner for thirty with grace and charm. She was in sparkling form, the colonel sitting on her right, Pierre on her left.

'Ah, my beautiful son, it is just like old times,' she said, indicating Pierre's plain suit and white shirt. 'How I love to see you without the dress.'

'Maman, you are so irreverent,' Pierre smiled.

'Just because you are a priest doesn't mean your mother has to treat you like one.' She raised her hand and touched his cheek and they smiled, understanding each other perfectly.

She flirted with the colonel, who basked in the warmth of her smile.

'Have you written any more books recently?' she asked, her face a picture of innocence.

'No, Marie-Claire, I am too old to be climbing trees in search of the lesser spotted woodpecker.'

'I found two of your books in my grandson's bedroom, and I am sure they had nothing to do with woodpeckers.'

The colonel's eyes were twinkling. 'How did you know they were by me?'

'I have always known, my dear Aramis. I didn't believe you could make a living writing about birds of the feathered kind.'

Gillie was sitting next to Robert and after the second glass of wine found herself talking to him about Étienne.

'It's the not knowing that is the worst. After he disappeared I spoke to some of his friends, any of the *résistants* I had met. I hit a brick wall. When the National Resistance Council was formed, I begged them to help me, but it was chaos, people were disappearing every day, they couldn't waste their time with me.'

Robert nodded. 'Confidentially, when I was no longer fit to fly, I worked in intelligence. In '43 I was dropped into Italy to train the partisans. We lost many good men and at the end, events happened so fast.'

'Oh I don't blame anyone Robert, it was just frustrating.'

'Did you try the civil registration office?'

She nodded. 'And the police. I still ring them occasionally, but no one has been able to shed any light on his disappearance. So many of the Maquis just vanished into thin air.'

'Believe me, I know how important it is to find out the truth, however distasteful.' Robert brought down his glass with a thump, and as the wine threatened to spill, Gillie shivered involuntarily, wondering what had happened to Robert during those last charged days of the Italian campaign.

'Thank you, Robert, it's good to talk to someone who truly understands.'

'If you ever want any help,' he said, the angst disappearing from his face, 'you know where I am.'

They were distracted when Pierre tapped his knife against his glass and everyone turned towards him.

'I would like to propose a toast to my great nephew, Alfie.' He raised his champagne flute, and everyone followed suit, charging their glasses to the child asleep in the nursery upstairs. As Sebastian looked around the room at his family and friends, he was filled with emotion. Whatever hurt and disappointment he had felt on that beautiful June day, when Sophie had left him, she had given him an irreplaceable gift – she had given him their son.

Pierre stayed three days at the Chateau. He took long walks with the dogs, read in the old library, and spent hours with his mother, Marie-Claire.

On the Thursday morning he stood in the hall with his family around him. He took Alfie from Sebastian's arms and held him above him like a small aeroplane, making Alfie gurgle with delight.

'You will grow into a fine young man,' he said. But as he held the soft warm infant against his chest, he couldn't help mourning the life that had passed him by.

He was climbing into his car when Liliane ran after him.

'Please Pierre, will you come for a walk before you leave?'

'Of course,' he replied, grateful for the distraction, but as he looked into his beloved sister's face, he realised she too had painful memories and her request was born out of a need to talk to him, not as a priest but as her brother. He remembered her grief when her husband and his best friend Jasper had died in '46, shortly after the Second World War ended. She had never really got over him.

As they walked through the vineyards behind Pommard he linked his arm through hers.

'I think I know what is troubling you,' he said, pausing at the top of the hill and looking back through the lines of grapes that stretched as far as the eye could see, some of them their own, others from different houses, different labels.

Liliane brushed the hair from her face. 'Of course you do, you could always read my mind.'

'You are my little sister Liliane, and we have always been close. My vocation has not changed that.'

Liliane sighed. 'I still miss Jasper so much, and it seems to get worse. You obviously have the church and I have my wonderful children and Maman of course but...' She faltered. 'Why after all these years?'

Pierre took her hand, remembering the time when Jasper had been his best friend and not Liliane's husband, and the future was ahead of them. 'Sometimes life isn't fair and it's not for us to reason why.'

'I wish I had your strength,' she sighed.

'My dearest sister, I miss him too. Do you remember when I first brought Jasper here? You were only sixteen, and I was in my second year reading theology. You were pretty precocious. "Are you going to be a priest too?" you demanded.'

'I remember his reply,' Liliane smiled. 'No, *mademoiselle*, but as the second son, that is what my father would like, but God certainly would not.'

'And you said,' Pierre was laughing, 'well I believe God has had a lucky escape.'

'I can't believe I was so cheeky.'

'You always were, but this time I could see you were smitten. He was a good man, Liliane – all the time we spent together, those climbing expeditions on our university vacations, the fun we had. That is of course until you married him and curtailed some of our adventures!'

'Did I?'

'A few, but I was delighted when my sister married my best friend.'

'You still managed to do some climbing afterwards.'

'It was his passion. I had to keep an eye on him for you!'

Liliane laughed out loud. 'Now that isn't true.' She squeezed her brother's arm. 'But of one thing I am sure, Pierre, you have always been there for me and I am grateful. I will love you my dearest brother till my last breath.'

Pierre was nearing the monastery when he stopped the car. He adored his sister, but how little she knew of his life. Why hadn't he told her about Fleur, he wondered. He had had the opportunity so many times, but something had always held him back. Perhaps because she had always looked up to him and it would somehow break the spell. Ah, human vanity. He smiled softly and gazed across the fields, but he didn't really see the landscape. He could only see Fleur's face. He had known love, and in the end, it had almost broken his spirit, his will to live. But he *had* lived. He had returned to the church, burying himself in his work, always trying to stem his pain. He had climbed the ecclesiastic ladder, and in the end he had found his way back to God.

Chapter Fifteen

1955

When Alfie had gone from her life, Sophie had found every day a torment. It was as if a fog had wrapped itself tightly around her brain, isolating her from the real world. In spite of this enveloping depression, she had forced herself to go on. As the months and then the first year had passed, the fog began to lift. She had thrown herself back into her medical course with an almost fanatical energy that even Professor Manon commented upon.

'Mademoiselle Bernot, it is one thing to study, it is another to make yourself ill,' he had observed.

Finally Georges had taken her in hand. 'I know what this is about,' he had said, drawing her aside at the end of a lecture. 'But you must stop punishing yourself, *ma cherie.*'

'How can I, when I miss him every moment of the day,' she declared, leaning against him.

'Of course you do.' Georges had lifted her chin, so she had to look at him. 'But giving Alfie up was the right decision. At the time it was the only decision.'

'You're right, you are always right,' she had said, her tone weary.

'I am afraid, Sophie; at this moment I am. You must remember the reasons for letting him go.'

Sophie had stiffened and drawn away. 'Of course I remember them,' she snapped. 'We have been through them enough times, but you can't possibly understand how it feels to be a mother and not hold your son. It is just so hard living without him.' Her tone had softened as her head came to rest against Georges's chest.

'I'm sorry, that was mean. Forgive me?'

'You could never be mean my love, just a little angry at the world, but trust me I do understand. I only have to look at the pain in your eyes.' He had taken her hand. 'Try to take each day as it comes. You will never forget Alfie, but time has a way of healing. It has only been a year and I am sure it will get easier.'

The second year had dawned without her son. Sophie had somehow managed to get through a half-hearted new year's celebration with Georges and Francois. As the spring leaves began to unfurl, Sophie had started taking long solitary walks through the city, sometimes through the Latin Quarter, at other times crossing the Seine to wander through the wide avenues and boulevards. As she walked past buildings built in different periods and styles, she had felt a strange connection to Sebastian. She observed the architecture through Sebastian's eyes. Once she had taken Paris for granted; now she noticed it for the beautiful city that it was. There had been moments when she had wanted to write to him, beg his forgiveness, but she had vowed never to contact Sebastian or his family again. Eighteen months after leaving her son in Pommard, she had broken that vow. She had finally plucked up the courage to compose a letter to his sister Gillienne. There would be no harm in asking for occasional news about her son, she reasoned, as she folded the letter into the envelope. She ran to the Bureau de Poste and put it into the box before she could change her mind. As she returned to her apartment, she wondered if Gillie would respond or just throw the letter away.

It would be three months before she received a reply. Sophie was entering the flat one evening when she found an envelope on the doormat. Scooping it up, she scanned the postmark and held it to her chest. At last the letter she had been waiting for. She tore it open, her fingers fumbling with the paper. Would she be rebuffed; would this be a curt denial? As she drew out the letter a black and white photograph fell into her hand. An infant was standing on the steps of the Chateau de Villienne, a toy rabbit in his hand. He was looking into the camera, his eyes bright with life and laughter. Sophie touched the photograph, stroked the chubby arms clad in a silk smocked shirt, the little shorts. 'Alfie,' she whispered holding the photo to her lips. 'My little boy.'

Dear Sophie,

I admit I was somewhat surprised to receive your letter. I know it has taken me a while to respond, but as far as we were concerned, when you left your son in our care, you gave up your entitlement to know about his life.

After serious consideration I felt it would be unfair to ignore it. I must stress that while I will give you occasional updates as to his progress, it will be no more than that.

Alfie is well, and as you can see from the photograph, he is happy. He is a charming little chap; strong-willed and quite capable of having a tantrum, but he has brought joy into our lives.

As you requested I will keep this from Sebastian, but if he ever finds out and asks me to stop, I will obviously bow to his wishes. For the time being at any rate, I will keep you informed of his progress.

  Yours faithfully
  Gillienne Ogilvie

Sophie learnt one thing from the photograph: there could be no denying Alfie's happiness. She had done the right thing.

In time she started to socialise again, and though her son was never far from her mind, she allowed herself to live. With Georges and Francois Petout, the lanky blond who had remained their friend since he had fainted in their first anatomy lesson, they visited the bars and cafés of Paris. They drank alongside poets, artists, musicians and writers. They went to night clubs and jazz clubs. When Francois decided he was a nascent communist, they even joined in political gatherings. They were in a liberated, humming city and along with most Parisians, they were determined to have fun. It seemed the medical students could party all night and be on the wards first thing in the morning. They frequented the cellars below the Vieux Colombier, and the vaulted subterranean arches of the Caveau de la Huchette. It was in this atmosphere of smoke, alcohol and social tolerance that many of the famous black jazz players honed their skills. During the war jazz had become embedded in the French psyche as a symbol of freedom and resistance, and ten years later it was as popular as it had ever been. Playing the saxophone was Georges's third passion in life, after Sophie and medicine. When Bob Wilbur and Sidney Bechet invited him onto the stage at the Vieux Colombier, it was the highlight of his student years! But it wasn't only Georges who had a passion for jazz. Sophie knew every Louis Armstrong melody and would sing along whenever the opportunity presented itself. If the musician was in Paris she would find out where he was playing, and they would go.

'It's part of our education,' she would say to the boys.

One morning they emerged from the jazz club and went straight to the hospital. The boys disappeared one way, while Sophie went the other to change. She bumped straight into Professor Manon.

'It seems as usual you will be on time for my class, Mademoiselle Bernot, but where are Monsieur Thibault and Monsieur Petout?'

'They are assisting in ward seven,' she assured him.

The professor had looked at her, his eyebrows raised.

'I hope *la petite dégustation* in the Vieux Colombier aided your beauty sleep?'

Sophie blushed a deep pink.

She found Georges and Francois in a side ward with an intravenous drip attached to their arms.

'Restorative fluids are the best thing for a hangover,' Francois muttered, grinning sheepishly.

She kicked his leg, and he looked affronted, his blond hair falling over his sleepy eyes.

'If the professor finds you, you'll need more than restorative fluids,' she urged.

She was sitting at the bar of the Vieux Columbier on a muggy mid-September evening when a stranger with untidy dark hair and a sardonic smile pulled out the stool beside her. She noticed his green eyes and the shadow of stubble on his chin. His battered leather flight jacket was slung over his shoulder. He put his martini down on the bar.

'You like Miles Davis?' he asked.

'Don't you?' she smiled.

'"Oh Lady Be Good". The rhythm really gets to you,' he said with a grin. 'Your feet are tapping.'

Sophie looked down at her feet and started to laugh. 'My friend Georges is on the sax.'

'Your boyfriend?'

She shook her head. 'Best friend in the world.'

'And are you a Good Lady?' he asked.

Over another dry martini, Sophie learnt that Todd Dexter

was a thirty-five-year-old American journalist who had recently arrived in Paris. He wrote a regular column for both *Life* magazine and *The New Yorker*.

'I love this beautiful city,' he drawled, 'it casts its spell over you, catches you unawares.'

'*C'est vrai*, it's true now,' she replied. 'But you obviously weren't here during the war.'

He looked at her then, his eyes challenging. 'France wasn't the only country to be occupied, but actually you are wrong.' He offered no other explanation.

'Of course there were other countries, but not...' She paused, thinking of the humiliation the French had suffered, the atmosphere of defeat. 'I think this is rather a serious conversation for a first drink,' she continued.

'So you want there to be other drinks?' he enquired.

'*Mais oui*,' she smiled.

The following day Sophie found Todd waiting for her after her morning class.

'*Bonjour*, Mademoiselle Bernot. Does coffee count as a drink?'

She smiled. 'I imagine it does,' she said.

They walked down the street together and stopped at Le Chat Noir.

'So,' he stated, after ordering *deux cafés noisettes* from a waiter in a striped jersey. 'A woman doctor in 1950s Paris, that is a most unusual profession.'

'Are you interviewing me for one of your periodicals?'

Todd laughed, and there were creases around his eyes that suggested he liked to be happy.

'You know Sophie, I think that is a great idea. There would be a picture of your pretty face on the front, in a white coat with your stethoscope. *Time* magazine would love it. I can see the strapline now. "Beautiful Young Girl Breaking Ground for all Women in France."'

Sophie giggled, and the half hour flew by before he walked her back to the hospital.

'Do you want me to come again?' he asked, kissing her cheek. Sophie liked the smell of his aftershave, spice with a warm hint of musk.

'I'd like that very much,' she said.

They got into the habit of having lunch together before she returned to the wards. If she was on night duty, it could be breakfast the following morning.

'My little doctor,' he said, over croissants and strong black coffee, his eyes tinged with humour.

'Are you mocking me?' she asked.

'Would I dare?' he quipped, paying the bill. 'But unfortunately today I have a deadline to meet, so I will have to run.'

Over the following weeks she gathered that his editorial pieces alternated between gritty realism and upbeat social commentary.

'The Algerians should be allowed their independence,' he protested to Sophie. 'They are second-class citizens in their own country. I hate racism and bigotry and it continues today. Haven't we learnt anything from the last war?'

Moments later he was telling her about the new Dior *atelier* at 30 Avenue Montaigne, before he diverted to the fall of French Indochina. Sophie soon became intrigued by his quick mind.

It wasn't long before he called her his Audrey Hepburn having persuaded her to go a re-showing of *Roman Holiday* at the Cinéma du Panthéon. When Todd realised Sophie had never been to the opera, he booked seats for *La Bohème* at the Opéra Comique, in Place Boïeldieu.

It was Todd's birthday and as they stepped out of the taxi he said, 'It will be my treat to see the expressions on your pretty face,' and Sophie did not disappoint him. Even before the performance started, she was captivated by the elaborate neo-baroque building. When the heavy velvet curtains opened, she leant forward in her seat, totally enthralled by Puccini's overture. It was only when Rudolfo and Mimi sang their arias that she allowed the tears to stream unchecked down her face.

As they were leaving the foyer Sophie was quiet.

'Is everything all right?' Todd asked, putting his arm around her shoulder.

'I have never heard anything so sublime,' she murmured. 'Thank you, Todd.'

Her reaction was the only birthday present he needed. '*The Magic Flute* next,' he said.

They browsed in Todd's favourite bookshop, Le Mistral, at 37 Rue de la Bucherie in the fifth *arrondissement*. He bought her a first edition copy of the novel, *The Old Man and the Sea*.

'Hemingway used to frequent another bookstore called Shakespeare and Company,' he said, handing her the novel wrapped in brown paper. 'It closed in 1941. Many great authors gathered there to discuss literature, Hemingway amongst them. I believe you will love this book, it is filled with symbolism that I know you will understand.'

Todd never patronised her; he treated her as an equal and she was flattered and more than a little enchanted.

Despite her increasing workload she continued to see Todd regularly. He was exciting and unpredictable but the gut wrench-ing, all-consuming passion she had felt for Sebastian was absent. It was the perfect antidote to a broken heart.

'I'd like to take you away,' he said, 'to somewhere you've never been.'

'And do I want to come?' she asked flirtatiously.

'I think you do,' he replied.

Two weeks later when the conkers littered the ground in the

Bois de Boulogne, Todd collected Sophie from her apartment. It was her mid-term break and as they drove out of Paris in his borrowed Delahaye convertible, he told Sophie of their destination. They were heading to the ferry at La Pallice next to La Rochelle.

'I'm kinda sure that Île de Ré will appeal to you, Sophie. It's not Monte Carlo, I'm afraid, but my budget won't run to that.'

'Do I look as if I play at the tables?'

He ruffled her short, newly cut hair and laughed. 'A classy lady like you may love roulette, but it's my guess you'll like this better. It's simple and charming with quaint villages and long sandy beaches, but it has a rather gruesome past. I stayed on the island when I did an editorial for *The New Yorker* on the unfortunate occupants of the prison.'

'That sounds romantic!'

He threw his head back and laughed. 'That is not where we are staying,' he assured her.

As they drove through the French countryside towards La Rochelle, the top down, the wind blowing in their faces, Todd asked Sophie questions about her childhood. Her response was cautious, redirecting the conversation to his life in America.

'With two brothers, and a single mom, it was fairly chaotic,' he said grinning. 'But she did her best and I hope I haven't turned out too bad.'

'Your father?'

'He left when I was five. I've never seen him again.'

'I'm sorry.'

'Don't be, I had a good childhood.'

They waited for the ferry at La Pallice and Todd told her about the island and its rich history. When it docked at Sablanceaux, he drove the car down the ramp and negotiated his way through the busy little port to their final destination. Entering through a pair of pillars, he parked in the shade of lime trees within a high perimeter wall. He took out their luggage and together they walked down the path.

'It is absolutely perfect,' Sophie declared.

The house, now an occasional *chambre d'hote*, was built around a courtyard, with long green shutters and white painted walls. The roses were still flowering, and an abundance of geraniums still spilled from grey stone pots. The owner, a Madame Calas, came hurrying towards them. She was wearing a spotted silk shirt that stretched across her expansive bosom, and a tight blue skirt. She clapped her hands in excitement. 'Welcome to La Baronnie, Monsieur Todd. You have returned. I hope you will enjoy my beautiful house once more. Do come this way.'

They followed her through the black and white marble tiled hall and up the stairs, to a spacious panelled bedroom at the front. It was painted a pale powder blue and furnished with a large canopied bed. She threw the shutters open wide and turned to Todd. 'You must show *mademoiselle* our unique island. We are only five minutes from the Quai and the lighthouse of Saint-Martin and the fortifications, you must take her to the salt marshes and—'

Todd interrupted her.

'Thank you, *madame*.'

'Ahhh of course, you must wish to unpack, I will leave you alone.'

Todd winked discreetly at Sophie. 'And will you be cooking one of your delicious meals for us tonight?'

'*Mais oui*. For you *monsieur*, anything. *Sept heures et demie*, as usual in the small dining room. We have one other guest, but he always dines alone.'

She left them, bustling from the room. At the door she turned. '*Mademoiselle*, I love your hair. The new style, and with your heart-shaped face, so charming.'

'*Merci*,' Sophie replied, patting her hair, both flattered and a little amused.

When the door closed behind her, Todd took Sophie in his arms.

'So, *ma petite*,' he drawled. 'What now?'

'Your accent is appalling,' she said, a smile on her face. 'I think before anything I should teach you better French.'

'*Le leçon de Francais*,' he smiled, undoing the buttons on her shirt one by one.

Sophie drew backwards. 'Sorry Todd, it's just that...'

Todd lifted her chin and looked into her eyes. 'I won't let you get pregnant, if that's what you're concerned about.'

'Oh Todd, that's part of it, but it's more than that. I wanted to come away with you and I had thought about the consequences, but now... I don't think I should be here.' She shook her head as if confirming what she felt.

'Do you want to go home?'

'No...' Sophie's lip trembled. 'Actually, I don't know.'

'Are you afraid this is a casual fling?'

Sophie sank onto the silk counterpane and looked up at him. 'Well is it?'

'Trust me young lady, I would not take you to my favourite island in France if this meant nothing. And you Sophie, what do you feel?'

'I don't think I'm looking for love, and certainly not marriage, there is no time in my life for that, but...' She folded the counterpane in her fingers. 'Oh, I am in such a muddle, Todd.'

'Has someone hurt you, Sophie?' Todd sat down beside her and stroked her hair.

Sophie thought for a moment. Sebastian hadn't hurt her; she had inflicted the pain, but she was still suffering.

'Put it like this: I have a chequered past and I can't revisit the anguish.'

'Well then, we will take it slowly, my little Sophie.'

Over the next few days Sophie and Todd explored the island. They cycled through the forest between Phare des Baleines and Les Portes-en-Ré, they went from one village to the next. At night Sophie went to sleep in Todd's arms in the canopied bed, with the sounds of the waves whispering through the open window. Todd kept his promise to take things slowly and as the days passed, Sophie's resolve was crumbling.

'Do you realise how pretty you are?' Todd asked on their penultimate day as they had a picnic in a sheltered sand dune overlooking the sea.

Sophie smiled. 'Is that what you say to every girl you take away on holiday?'

'I've told you already,' he grinned, running his hand down her arm. 'I am not in the habit of spending my hard-earned cash on just any girl. Secondly, it's the truth.'

As she looked at Todd, his arms now golden from the sun, her heart turned over. He was handsome – of that there was no doubt. She loved his finely chiselled face and his dimpled chin. His lean muscled body made her long for him, but it was more than that; he was amusing and knowledgeable. She felt safe in his company.

After braving the sea for a refreshing swim, they walked back to the house, pushing their bicycles, their towels wrapped around their waists. They washed and changed, listening to an eclectic collection of records in the salon, before dining in the court-yard by candlelight on scallops and oysters and other delicacies cooked by Madame Calas.

As the fountain played in the background, Sophie stroked Todd's hand.

'I have never admitted this before.' She paused to pick up her glass of wine.

'What, Sophie?'

'Something happened once…'

Todd could see that Sophie was about to tell him something important. He smiled encouragingly.

'You see, I did something awful – something that I didn't understand the consequences of fully.'

'I can't imagine you doing anything awful, Sophie.'

'Oh I did, trust me. I didn't mean to, but I betrayed someone close to me. I'm sorry I can't say any more.'

Todd picked up her hand and kissed it. 'I shan't pry; one day perhaps, you will tell me the rest.'

Sophie bit her lip and looked him in the eye, grateful for his integrity and sensitivity. 'Tonight, if you want me…' her voice trailed off.

'Of course I want you, Sophie. It's been hell keeping away from you. In fact,' there was a grin on his handsome face, 'I am not sure how much longer I would have lasted.'

That night, as Sophie gave herself to Todd, she realised that despite her best intentions, her feelings were growing for this man. Perhaps, finally, she could open her heart.

On the last day, they went to the fishing port at La Flotte, with its rich merchants houses with creamy painted walls and terracotta roofs. They had lunch in a small restaurant on the quayside overlooking the boats and ate fish, caught fresh that morning.

'Thank you, Todd,' Sophie murmured as the seagulls circled above them and the sun warmed her face. 'This has been very special.'

'Thank you for coming, *ma petite docteur*. It's been fun.'

'Just fun?' Sophie queried, a little hurt.

'Much more,' he replied, tapping the tip of her nose. 'Now you mustn't distract me because I need to pay the bill if we are to get to the ferry in time.'

They had left Île de Ré behind them and were in the car heading back to Paris when Sophie turned off the wireless.

'I have told you everything about me, Todd, but you have been quiet about the war.'

Todd glanced at her, his expression changing. 'What's there to tell? It was a hideous time, millions of young men died, but if you're really interested, I was a reconnaissance photographer flying P-38 Lightnings. I covered the Normandy beachhead landings.'

'I didn't know,' Sophie murmured.

'I watched many of our young men mown down by German machine guns as they waded through the water. It was pretty bad and I don't really talk about it.'

'I'm so sorry.'

'Yeah well…' He brightened suddenly. 'Only a few days later I photographed the V bomber site at Renescure near Saint-Omer. We were flying as low as fifty feet. Oh boy did the adrenaline pump, but the photographs were crucial to the Allies.'

Sophie stroked his arm.

'Then it was Korea, so you see, Sophie, I've done my bit.'

'I never thought for a moment that you hadn't,' she protested.

'At least the planes were unarmed.'

'So you had no guns?'

'Nothing at all.' Todd put his foot on the accelerator and as the car shot forward, Sophie lapsed into silence.

They reached Rue de Bièvre and Todd turned off the engine outside number twenty-two. Sophie leant towards him.

'Are you going to come in?' she asked.

'Sorry, *ma cherie*, I have to go back to New York in the morning. There's a lot to do before I leave.'

'You'll be back soon?' When he didn't answer, there was a sinking feeling in her stomach. She moved away from him. 'Todd, are you trying to tell me something?'

Todd looked at her and the laughter had gone from his face. 'Sophie, something's come up.'

'Are you saying it's over?'

'Of course I'm not, there are just things I have to do. I'll write as soon as I get there, I promise.'

'Did you find out about these things before or after you slept with me?' she said bitterly. She pulled her suitcase from the back seat and jumped from the car, running beneath the stone archway to the front door.

When the car had disappeared down the road, Sophie could feel tears of shame burning down her cheeks. She had allowed herself to have feelings for Todd, and she knew from bitter experience this brought suffering and pain. As she climbed the stone stairs and unlocked the door, she vowed she would never let it happen again.

Chapter Sixteen

Marcus came out of the *boulangerie* on the corner of the Rue Beauvoisine and strolled down the street. It was mild for November and he was wearing the lightest cashmere jersey and dark blue slacks. He was carrying cheese from the *épicerie* in one hand, and a loaf of delicious French bread in the other. He paused outside a large medieval building, reflecting on his good fortune. He still found it hard to believe that he was the owner of the first-floor apartment in the courtyard beyond. He whistled to himself as he strolled beneath the archway, taking a moment to contemplate the architecture.

The exposed beams on the exterior walls had faded to a light silver-grey and the lime-based render between the beams was painted cream. His apartment had three sash windows that rose from floor to ceiling, each with its own wrought-iron balcony. He had added a splash of colour to the otherwise serene exterior with window boxes filled with geraniums in the summer and deep claret dahlias in the autumn months. The charming apartment was Marcus's haven of peace and tranquillity. It had become his solace, helping him to heal from the tragedy in his life. Never a day passed without giving thanks to the man who had made it possible.

He remembered his first day in Rouen. The war had ended

and the Parisian firm of architects he worked for had sent him to compile a detailed study of the damage, not only to the cathedral but to the housing and factories. When he stepped off the train, he had been struck with a powerful sense of despair. The shelled and scorched buildings in the medieval city struck a chord in his heart. Windows and doors were gone. Walls that had stood firm for a thousand years had collapsed, leaving masonry like jagged teeth challenging the space where there should have been order. It was a brutal reminder of war.

As he walked through the ruined streets, he vowed not only to complete the study, but to help restore Rouen to its former beauty. He had set about his task with energy and commitment and within six months he had compiled a list of every building and the scale of damage. On the strength of his report, a branch office was opened in Rouen, with Marcus leading the design team. He was only twenty-four.

Within five years his reputation was growing, and the restoration was continuing apace. It was his idea to throw off the yoke of misery gained during the war, choosing different colours for the render on the half-timbered houses. Some were painted blue, some terracotta pink, until the Rouen streets were glowing with colour.

One summer evening after finishing work he had returned to his favourite haunt in Rouen, a café on the corner of Rue Martainville. It was here that he would read the newspaper, eat a baguette or simply chat with other customers.

'Monsieur le Architecte.'

He looked up to find a gentleman in front of him. The man had thick silver hair, and he wore a white carnation in his buttonhole. His brown eyes were smiling at him.

Marcus looked puzzled.

'Marcus – it is you, isn't it? Good, may I sit down?' The older man drew out a chair.

Marcus inclined his head. '*Oui monsieur*, but it seems you are already seated.'

The older man laughed. 'You must consider me rude, but old men like me are allowed that prerogative.'

Marcus didn't challenge him and the man grinned, his eyes dancing.

'I am here to thank you for the fine job you are doing in our wonderful city.'

Marcus was taken aback.

'No, don't look concerned, young man. You see, I am also an architect – retired now, of course, but I enquired about you. It seems you are gaining quite a reputation. You start at dawn each morning and finish late, always ending the day at this café.'

Now it was Marcus's turn to laugh. 'A creature of habit, I'm afraid.'

'Well habit or not, I hope you will break it to have dinner with an old man? Charles Donadieu at your service.'

Monsieur Donadieu turned out to be a well-known architect and huge admirer of Le Corbusier. Like his more famous colleague, he had dedicated much of his life to providing housing and better living conditions for the poorer residents of crowded cities. He took him to La Couronne, the oldest *auberge* in Rouen. It was where the rich and famous dined, but it came with a price tag to match.

'I am rather dull,' Charles confided over dinner, 'I always wanted to be like Corbusier, but unfortunately I did not have not his vision. How I wish I had designed the Unite´d'Habitation in Marseille. I am not jealous of course – well maybe a little.' He had smiled wryly at this – a gentle smile and Marcus immediately liked his manner. 'Have you seen his designs for La Cité Radieuse, the radiant city. If it is ever built, it will be a village within a city, with indoor shops, a hotel, even a preschool and gym. I hope it comes to fruition. I tell you young man, Corbusier is a genius. It must inspire you?'

Marcus looked at him and grinned. 'Actually no. Corbusier likes sweeping away the old; I like restoring it.'

Charles laughed completely unperturbed. 'I like that too, Marcus, and I am moved by everything you are doing here, but have you read his book, *Vers une Architecture*? I am sure that a young man like you would agree with his philosophy.'

Marcus coughed, as he gathered his thoughts. If he was honest his opinion may sound rude, but he believed he should tell the truth to this man. 'I have read it, but it didn't inspire me. Now you will probably wish you hadn't taken me out to dinner.'

'Hardly.'

For two hours the men chatted and laughed and drank good claret.

After Charles had paid the bill, they strode through the market square and stopped at the small memorial garden, built to mark the place where Joan of Arc was burnt at the stake.

'I come here often,' Marcus admitted to Charles. 'Stupid really, but I like to pray for her. Of course, after five hundred years, it won't do her any good, but she was badly wronged.'

'A young girl betrayed by her king,' Charles mused. 'It doesn't seem right, does it? I wish the world were a kinder place.'

Marcus looked at Charles. 'It seems you are an idealist like me.'

'I was once. I'd still like to change things, but now it is up to young men like you.'

'I believe I should put you right. I am twenty-eight, not that young.'

Charles laughed. 'When you are my age it is. I'm old and tired, Marcus, but I'd like to see you changing the world.'

From that day Charles became his mentor. He guided Marcus and encouraged him; he became a sounding board for ideas. He helped him to grow in stature and confidence, teaching him about interior design as well as external.

'You see, Marcus, this room is not just about functionality; it is about beauty.' He showed him how to create areas for the eye to stop and appreciate before moving on. 'Group those objects on the table, Marcus, those chairs by the window, even the pictures on the wall. We want you to linger, not pass on by.' They became constant companions: the older man always immaculate, wearing a suit, a bow tie and a button hole; Marcus dressed in trousers and a modern jacket, his dark curls tumbling almost to his collar.

Marcus learnt to cook and to drive a car, and when Charles insisted on adopting him as his son, Marcus finally agreed.

'I want you to take my name,' Charles said. 'One day you will understand.' For the first time in years Marcus was happy, and he grew to love Charles. It shook him to his very core when his mentor and the man who had become a father to him was taken from him, just three short years later. It was only months after Charles's first diagnosis of cancer.

After the funeral Marcus had found himself in a firm of Rouen solicitors, sitting on a hard chair in a stuffy, panelled room, amongst a handful of Charles's family, wondering why he was there. When a large gift was bequeathed to him, Charles's nephew, a man with thin lips and receding hair, drew him aside.

'We'll fight you for this, you little faggot.'

Marcus reeled with embarrassment and rushed from the room. But as he stood in the dimly lit corridor, he realised that Charles's family hadn't been there for him when he was dying. They hadn't read to him, cooked for him or loved him. They were there for the money.

But there would be no fight; as the adopted son of Charles Donadieu, he was his legal heir.

Afterwards the solicitor gave him a side letter written in Charles' beautiful scripted hand.

My dear Marcus,

I hope you will forgive me, but I have taken the liberty of putting down a deposit on a beautiful apartment off the Rue Beauvoisine. You do not have to take it of course, but knowing you as I do, I believe it will suit you well. It has given me so much pleasure to think of you there, arranging your furniture and possessions, living there, reading your books, designing beautiful buildings. There is a second bedroom with plenty of light that I thought might be your studio. The exterior needs a little decoration, but I believe it structurally sound.

You will now understand why I wished to adopt you. Apart from being the son that I never had, there were the legal issues. You must feel no guilt, for it is my money to do with as I wish. I can now die content knowing that you are well provided for.

Live well dearest boy and whatever demons continue to plague you, try to let them go.

Always,
Charles

Marcus patted his inside pocket where the letter remained and went up the oak staircase to his front door. He unlocked it and went inside. The interior was light and airy, with pale sofas and armchairs on the polished boards. Persian rugs, cushions and paintings added bright splashes of colour to the otherwise cool palette. He stood in front of the paintings, his head on one side as he studied them. He had purchased them with Charles, always arguing and laughing over the final decision.

'No, Marcus, the road is better, believe me. You should have the road.'

'Why would I want to look at a road all day, Charles? I like the seascape; those waves are so well painted.'

Now the beach and the road hung on the wall beside each other, grouped together just as Charles had suggested.

Marcus put the bread in the kitchen and opened the fridge and took out a bottle of wine. He was doing just as Charles wanted, he was living well. He had a good job doing what he loved, he had a beautiful apartment and friends, but there was something lacking in his life. He was lonely; he longed for someone to share it with.

He put the glass down and put a record on the gramophone. As the music washed over him he remembered another time, another place and the sound of a child's voice.

Chapter Seventeen

1958

Alfie Ogilvie was feeding the peacocks when he heard his great-grandmother calling him. It was favourite occupation when he arrived home from school.

He looked up, a smile crossing his chubby face and ran towards her. He put his arms around her legs. 'Mémé G,' he laughed.

'Alfie, you will pull me to the floor! I am extremely old, and you have to be careful.'

'But you are young! Not like Madame Bernard.'

Marie-Claire laughed out loud. Madame Bernard was the grumpy postmistress, who must be thirty years younger than herself.

'And you are flattering me – that is a new word for you, Alfie; it means you say nice things that are not necessarily true.'

'Flattering,' he rolled the word around on his tongue and smiled once more. 'Papa says fibbing is bad.'

'And you, child, are impossible.'

They walked up the stairs towards the house, Alfie's hand held firmly in her own. There was some truth in her great-grandchild's words. Marie-Claire felt younger than she had in years. Alfie had brought joy to the Chateau de Villienne. His charming innocence had brought the house alive. His made-up name for her was just another example, 'Mémé G'. No one else would dare call her that and get away with it. He reminded her of her own son Pierre, not in his colouring or looks, but in his personality. Pierre had been a sunny, charming child – that is, of course, until he started withdrawing from life and had turned to God.

She would never forget the day he told her he was entering the church. It was two years before the Great War started and he was just eighteen. Everything she had hoped for, dreamed of, had instantly turned to dust. She had always gone to church and she had believed in God, but not one who took young men away from their families, who stole their hearts and minds.

'Please, Pierre,' she had begged, and he had smiled in that engaging way he had. 'Maman, I have to, you know that. God has called me.'

'Called you? What about the estate, your obligations here?'

'I am so sorry Maman, but my obligations are now to God.'

She had known then not to argue, and she had watched him pack his bags with a heavy heart.

'Will you come back?' she had asked.

'How could I keep away?' he had replied. Little did she know then that the Great War would take so many young men away from the village. The memorial by the church was testament to those who had died.

Marie-Claire was having a cup of tea at the kitchen table while Alfie ate his supper. Adeline was plucking a duck on the door-step nearby.

'It's not Mimi, is it?' he called, anxiously.

Adeline turned around and laughed. 'No, *mon chéri*, it is not.'

'I couldn't bear it if we ate Mimi.'

'We would never do that.'

Satisfied that his favourite duck was not for the pot, he returned to his food.

'Nor Myrtle?' he piped up a moment later.

'Now, why would we eat a scraggy old moorhen?' Adeline put the duck down and came into the kitchen, wiping her feathery hands on her apron.

'You are a funny young man.'

'You understand why we eat the produce from our estate, don't you, Alfie?' Marie-Claire asked.

'Yes, Mémé G. You've told me. If no one ate cows, they wouldn't be here, but when I grow up I am going to have a farm where there are lots of cows and they won't get eaten.'

Adeline and Marie-Claire looked at each other and smiled.

'Papa is coming tonight,' he announced a moment later, his mouth not quite empty. 'It's Friday and I'm so 'cited.'

'I know, *chéri*,' said Adeline, 'and he is having his favourites: asparagus from the garden, followed by duck!'

'*Ex*cited, Alfie,' his great grandmother prompted. 'And finish your mouthful before you speak.'

Alfie ignored her admonishment. 'He is going to take me climbing, Mémé G. He promised at Easter we would go when the weather was better. Look outside, it's sunny now.'

'And where is he taking you?'

'To huge rocks!'

Marie-Claire held her tongue; she would have words when her grandson arrived. Alfie was only five for heaven's sake. What on earth was he thinking of?

'Don't be cross, Mémé G.'

'You are a precocious child, and I'm not cross,' she scolded.

'Your face has gone all pink.'

Marie-Claire couldn't be cross for long, not where Alfie was concerned.

'Can I stay up till Papa comes?' His young voice cut into her thoughts.

'Bath and hair-wash first, then a story with Tante Gillie when she returns from Beaune, and we'll see how tired you are.'

'Hair-wash, Mémé G?'

'Yes, Alfie.'

At six o'clock after the dreaded hair-wash and bath with the young French au pair, Alfie was sitting on the bottom step of the elegant staircase wearing his dressing gown and slippers. He looked up when the door opened and flew into his aunt's arms.

'Tante Gillie,' he exclaimed. 'You're back.'

'I think I am,' she replied, 'unless of course you are seeing a ghost.'

'You're not a ghost,' he giggled. 'Neither is Papa, even when he puts that sheet over his head and makes funny noises.'

She hugged him. 'Who is my little man then?' she asked.

'Me,' he squealed, 'me, me, and Papa will be home soon, and Mémé G says I can stay up until he is here.'

'That's not what I said at all.' His great-grandmother came in and kissed her granddaughter on the cheek. 'I said . . .' She looked at Alfie's expectant face. 'Oh, never mind. Let your aunt go and change and we'll see.'

Gillie threw her coat onto a chair by the fireplace and went upstairs followed by her nephew.

'Did you have fun at work today?' he asked, coming into her room.

'I'm not sure that I would call freezing a verruca off an old man's big toe fun, Alfie.'

'Yuck,' he said screwing up his face and Gillie tapped his bottom.

'You wouldn't think yuck if you had one; it hurts.'

'Sorry, Tante Gillie. Will you always work at the Hospices de Beaune?'

'I only went back when you started at nursery school; I was bored without you.'

'Poor Gillie. But it's the holidays now.'

Gillie had worked at the medieval hospital in Beaune for several years, only having a break when Alfie had arrived. Now she was back again. It was no hardship, and it was no normal hospital. Since the fifteenth century, the masterpiece of gothic design had been a place of sanctuary. Behind the austere façade lay a courtyard with dazzling, glazed roof tiles that shimmered in the sunlight. It had been built to serve the poorest in the community and it hadn't changed in the intervening years. It had been the perfect retreat for Gillie after the loss of Étienne.

Occasionally she took Alfie to see the patients who treated their stay in the hospice as a period of respite and company. She would find him sitting beside one of the many beds in the old 'poor room' chattering to the patients, listening to their stories, making them forget their own infirmities. But the hospital had its own intriguing anecdotes that he would relate to his father.

'Matron told me that old Monsieur Drouhin, who owns the vineyards next door, was a member of the res ... What is it called Papa?'

'Resistance?' Sebastian had prompted.

'Yes, Papa, that's it. Anyway the Germans were going to kill him, but they couldn't find him because he had run down a secret passage from his house to the hospital. And do you know what, Papa?'

'You are about to tell me,' Sebastian had said, smiling at his son.

'The Sisters hid him for four months and at the end of the war he gave them two hectares of his best vineyards to thank them for saving his life. That's a good story isn't it, Papa?'

'It most certainly is,' Sebastian had replied. How Alfie loved stories. Now, he was sitting on his aunt's lap while she read him a French translation of *The Ugly Duckling* for about the tenth time. When his head lolled forward, he jerked it up again and opened his eyes.

'Do you want to go to bed, little one?' Gillie asked.

'No, please Tante Gillie, not before Papa arrives.'

At just past ten, Liliane stopped the car outside the house. Sebastian rushed up the steps and through the front door, followed by the two elderly Labradors.

Alfie hurtled into his father's arms. 'Papa, I have missed you.'

'Me too,' Sebastian hugged his son. 'Me too, my darling little boy.'

They walked through to the study and piled onto the mint green sofa.

'Coco, Louis, get down,' Liliane admonished, pushing the large dogs away from her, but they took no notice.

'Please do your work in France, then you don't have to leave me,' Alfie cried, twining his arms around his father's neck. 'You agree don't you, Tante Gillie?'

'I was working in Paris today,' Sebastian interjected. 'With the nice man that I told you about – the architect Marcus Donadieu.'

'I mean you could work here.'

'You could come to live with me in London,' Sebastian suggested, holding him close.

'I couldn't leave Grand-mère, Gillie and Mémé G. And of course Coco and Louis.'

'I'm glad to know where I stand young man, but I can't leave my firm. I build houses for people who need them.'

'I'll come to London soon Papa, I promise.'

Sebastian looked at Gillie over his son's head and raised his eyebrows. The discussion had been carried on for years. But Alfie was happy at the Chateau de Villienne and the school in Beaune; Sebastian couldn't bear to tear him away. It meant of

145

course that he spent half his life travelling and the other half in the office. Each Thursday, he took the night ferry from Victoria Station to Dover, to reach Paris at 8.55 in the morning. He would spend a few hours in Paris, then onward by train to Beaune. On Sunday evening, the same sleeper train left Gare du Nord Paris at 9.50, to arrive in London in time for work the following day. In order to get this dispensation from his superiors, Sebastian worked late, leaving long after the rest of his associates.

In truth it didn't actually matter. At this moment, Alfie was all he needed in life. He had become his reason for being.

'I've got something for you.' He pulled a box from his overnight bag. 'It's a present from Uncle Robert. We can make it tomorrow if you like.'

Alfie seized the present gleefully. 'Oh Papa, it's a Spitfire.'

'As you know, Uncle Robert flew them in the war.'

'He told me that a German plane shot at him and he had to jump out over the sea. It must have been very scary.'

'You have a good memory, Alfie.'

'Of course.' Alfie looked at his father indignantly. 'I'm not a baby anymore.'

Though Robert Marston wasn't really Alfie's uncle, he was his godfather and Alfie adored him. 'Is he coming to stay soon, with the children?'

'This summer, I promise.'

'All of them, Harvey, Genevra and Marcella?'

'Yes, all of them.'

'They'll have another one soon because Tante Giulietta likes making babies.'

'Really?' Sebastian replied, trying to keep a straight face.

Sebastian took Alfie to bed and tucked him in. He kissed the top of his glossy, dark hair. He smelt of soap and shampoo.

'Sleep well, little one.'

'Sleep well, Papa,' Alfie murmured, putting his arms around his father's neck. 'I love you.'

'And I love you more than anything in the world.'

'More than Coco?'

'Even more than Coco.'

After a Saturday spent at Adeline's kitchen table, the Spitfire had taken shape.

'We'll have to leave it overnight for the glue to set,' Sebastian informed her.

Adeline put her hands on her ample hips. 'You will do no such thing,' she assured him.

'Please,' Alfie begged, and Adeline smiled. 'Go on, the pair of you. You are as bad as each other, making doe eyes at poor Adeline. I want it out of here in time for breakfast and that means you will have to get out of bed, scamp.'

'Are you referring to Alfie or me?' Sebastian was laughing.

'Both of you.'

On Sunday morning, having retrieved the aeroplane from Adeline's kitchen, Alfie and Sebastian settled down to breakfast with Gillie.

'So what are you boys doing today?' she asked.

'We are going to the Morvan to climb, aren't we, Alfie?'

'Yes Papa, yes. I told you, Adeline. I wasn't fibbing.'

Adeline tutted. 'He is too young, Monsieur Sebastian.'

'I was the same age, you must remember Papa taking me?'

'I didn't like it then and I don't like it now.'

'You know I'll take care of him.' Sebastian put on a winning smile but Adeline ignored him. She leant over Alfie. 'You do what your father tells you, you understand?'

Chapter Eighteen

Sebastian parked the car on the side of the road, a mile from the village of Lormes in the Morvan National Park. Alfie jumped out and leant over the metal railings, looking down into the wooded gorge below.

'Are we really going to use ropes?' he asked, turning back to his father, his eyes round with excitement.

Sebastian lifted the kit from the boot and put it into his rucksack. 'We are,' he smiled, ruffling his son's hair.

They walked in single file down the steep path to the bottom of the gorge, stopping occasionally for Sebastian to point out a feature of the landscape, a bird or a flower. The further they went down the path, the denser the vegetation became. Trees towered above them and they could hear water rushing down the hillside.

'Look, Papa,' Alfie squealed, pointing ahead. 'Over there, a waterfall.'

It wasn't exactly a waterfall, but a stream rushing over moss-covered boulders.

'Do we have to wade through it, Papa?'

'There is a footbridge further on down,' Sebastian reassured him.

'I wanted to wade,' Alfie responded, and Sebastian smiled. At his age, he had also believed fear to be a sign of weakness. But there was a set to the child's jaw that reminded him of Sophie. For a moment he could see her pale but determined face as she walked across the narrow mountain ridge beyond La Flégère. He shook his head, banishing the image. He had done with Sophie.

They had crossed the small wooden bridge and had started up the other side when the path petered out. Sebastian went first, climbing over boulders and pushing aside vegetation, then stopping to help his son.

'Phew,' Alfie said, 'it's hot in here, Papa.' He wiped his brow with his small hand.

Sebastian looked at his son. 'You do look a little flushed; perhaps you're coming down with something and we ought to get you home.'

'I'm not coming down with anything,' he stated. 'But it's like a big jungle in here, hot and wet.'

Sebastian laughed, and looked up at the little patch of sky, just visible through the tall trees. 'You are absolutely right, you clever little boy.'

Ten minutes had passed before they reached a clearing where several large rocks rose upwards through the trees. Sebastian paused as the memories flooded back. Like Alfie, he had started on the smallest and easiest face, and as he became more proficient, his father had let him tackle the larger rocks.

'I hope you are not doing this just to please me, Alfie?' Sebastian put his hand on his son's shoulder.

'Of course I'm not.'

'Well then, let's go.'

Sebastian could hear his father's voice. 'So young man, are you ready for this?' and his reply. 'More than ready, Papa.' Now he was doing the same thing with his son – creating new memories. Despite his mother and grandmother's disapproval, he wouldn't wrap Alfie in cotton wool.

He took a hat from his rucksack and gave it to Alfie.

'Put it on.'

'But it's a riding hat, Papa!'

'It may be, but it will protect your head if you fall. When they bring out a special helmet for climbing, you will have it, but until then you will use this, understood?' As Sebastian fastened the strap beneath his chin, he remembered his own kit or lack of it when climbing with his father. Sometimes they had used ropes, but in those days, they were hemp and easily broken. Though no harm had come to them, he wouldn't take chances with his son. After looping a section of rope around Alfie's shoulders and chest to make a simple harness, Sebastian scrambled up the hillside and secured a rope around a boulder at the top. The other end he took down to the bottom and attached it to Alfie's harness with a knot. He grasped it firmly. 'Ready, Alfie?'

Alfie nodded, and Sebastian taught his son how to climb.

'Find a ledge, Alfie, and place the tip of your shoe on the ledge. Don't take your eyes off your foot until it is securely placed and don't lean into the rock.' Alfie was a natural, he swung his leg out, easily finding the footholds in the rock, his face screwed up with determination. Up and down the face he went until his father told him to stop.

'I think we've done enough for one day.'

'Please Papa, a little more.'

'Enough Alfie, I will help you down.'

When Alfie arrived at the bottom, he ran into his father's arms.

'So, clever little man, did you enjoy that?'

'Yes, oh yes, Papa,' he said, his eyes shining. 'When can we go again?'

Sebastian took off his riding hat and ruffled his hair. 'Oh Alfie, sometimes you remind me so much of your mother.'

'Tell me about her, Papa? Please.'

Sebastian held him tight for a moment, remembering the first morning he had come across Sophie, standing on a boulder, her face smiling down at him.

'Well,' he said, 'I met her in the mountains and she was training to be a doctor. She was so full of life, enthusiastic and determined, she was just like you.'

'I wish I could meet her, Papa.'

'Just remember that she loved you so very much, but she had to study, and she wanted the best for her little boy.'

Chapter Nineteen

Alfie's Ascension Day school holiday in May was a significant occasion, and as a treat, Gillie had taken him to the circus in Bois de Boulogne. They were on their way back to the Métro when the idea came to her.

'Would you like to see where I worked during the war?' she asked. 'It's not far from here?'

'Oh yes please, Tante Gillie,' he replied, anxious to prolong the day's excitement.

'Come on then,' she smiled, aware of a fluttering in her chest.

They took a bus to Neuilly-sur-Seine and walked the short distance to the hospital. In the lobby the atmosphere was calm, the tension of war long gone, but as Gillie went down the corridor with Alfie trotting beside her, the years melted away. It was here that Étienne had come into her life, this very ward where the *resistant* had trespassed all those years before. It was here that she had fallen in love. When she sensed Alfie was losing interest, she leant down so that their faces were level.

'The house where I lived was next to a café. Shall we see if it is still there?'

'Do they serve ice cream in the café?'

'I am sure they will.'

They stopped outside the eighteenth-century *maison de ville* in Rue Chauveau where Gillie had lived with six other nurses. The narrow alleyway remained at the side, but it was no longer dark and secretive. Now a Greek statue of Venus de Milo was artfully positioned at the end, and two cherry trees from the gardens either side had carpeted the ground with pink blossom. For a brief moment Gillie remembered Étienne kissing her to distract the German soldier, the heady rush of excitement. She remembered his hand around her waist.

She was diverted by her nephew tugging at her skirt.

'Can we get the ice cream, Tante Gillie?'

Gillie laughed and took his hand.

She pushed opened the door to the café and they went inside. Immediately the smell of cooking and cigarette smoke hit her and she wanted to leave. There were too many memories, too much sadness.

'Come on, Alfie, let's go.' She was about to turn around when the proprietor, a tall man of substantial girth and cropped hair, came out from behind a plastic curtain.

'Can I help you?'

'Do you sell ice cream, *monsieur*?' Alfie was speaking, his child's voice hesitant.

'We certainly do, the best in Paris.' He leant down and scrutinised Alfie. 'Especially for skinny little boys.'

Alfie automatically moved closer to his aunt, but the prospect of ice cream was too much for him. 'May we stay, Tante Gillie?'

Gillie looked around the café. Nothing had changed. The same chipped linoleum covered the floor. Even the posters were the same, one of the Eiffel Tower in springtime, another an advertisement for Gauloises cigarettes. Someone was drinking beer in the corner, but his face was hidden behind a copy of *Le Figaro*.

'So,' the proprietor said, winking at Alfie. 'You may sit at my best table. *Madame*, what can I get you?'

Gillie glanced at the identical tables.

'I'll have a *café noisette*, and my nephew here will have Coca-Cola and an ice cream with a large chocolate wafer.'

A short while later the man returned with a tray containing their order. Though his arms were thick and muscled, he set it down with surprising agility.

'Have you been here before?' he asked, scratching his head. 'You seem familiar.'

Gillie nodded. 'I used to come here during the war.'

'Ah – I remember, you're the nurse. I knew it. You are not like my usual customers.' His mouth opened, and he gasped in surprise. 'Well I'll be damned – you are Étienne's girl.'

Gillie looked anxiously at Alfie, but he was far too busy devouring his ice cream to be concerned about the conversation.

'You'll be forgiven for not recognising me – Marcel Ducre.' He jerked his head towards the table in the corner. 'But perhaps you will remember Geraud. He hasn't changed after all these years.'

At this, the man in the corner folded his newspaper and looked at Gillie. She immediately recognised the long thin face with the broken nose. She drew in her breath.

'Geraud,' she whispered. The man took this as his prompt and sauntered over.

'Of course, I can see it now – you are Étienne's girl.' Geraud's voice was low, without inflection. 'I wondered what had happened to you.' He eased his lean frame into the chair beside Gillie.

'You didn't seem to care at the time,' she countered, instantly regretting her words.

He looked at her thoughtfully. 'If I recall you were persistent, always asking questions.'

'I got nowhere. You all clammed up.'

'They were difficult days.' Geraud lit a cigarette. 'So much going on, no time to think, let alone placate a hysterical girl.'

Gillie could feel her anger bubbling beneath the surface. She glanced at Alfie who was spooning the last mouthful of ice cream into his mouth. 'Do you need to go to the cloakroom, *chéri*?' she asked.

He nodded and jumped down, running to the painted sign announcing the cloakroom facilities, and pushed open the door.

'Well, did you ever find out?' she asked when he had gone.

'*Non*,' he said, after a long pause.

Gillie wasn't going to give up, not after waiting so many years. 'I looked for him for months afterwards. I can only assume he died at Fresnes?'

'I'm afraid I don't know.'

Gillie looked into Geraud's pale eyes and she knew he was lying. She was now angry.

She gestured to Marcel who was hovering nearby. 'May I have the bill please?' she said, her voice cold.

'It's on the house, for old times' sake,' the proprietor stated.

'I insist,' Gillie countered.

'And I said definitely no. Think of it as a present to Étienne.'

Gillie hastily gathered up their belongings and stood up. When Alfie came back she took his hand. 'Time to go,' she said, pulling him towards the door.

'But Tante Gillie.'

'*Non, mon chéri*, we have to go, now.'

They were heading down the street when she could hear footsteps on the pavement behind them. She turned to see Geraud coming towards them.

'*D'accord*, so here is the telephone number of the café.' He pressed a napkin in her hand. 'Marcel will always take a message.' Then he was gone, his tall figure disappearing into the gloom.

Gillie drew Alfie closer.

'Is something wrong, Tante Gillie?' Alfie asked. 'You are shivering.'

'No, it's getting cold and we'll be late for the train.'

Two weeks later Gillie returned to Paris and the café in Rue Chauveau. When Marcel turned the sign on the door to 'closed' as she entered, her confidence faded.

'So you returned,' Geraud commented, scratching his nose.

'You gave me the number.'

'That was not meant to be an invitation, it was meant only to placate you.' Geraud was looking irritated as he sat down opposite her.

'I think you know more than you have been admitting,' Gillie blurted.

'And what exactly do you think that is?' Geraud asked, getting out the same crumpled packet of Gauloises.

Gillie hesitated. 'I always had the feeling that Étienne was betrayed; that's why everyone closed ranks. Now I want the truth.'

'And how are you going to get the truth fourteen years later?' Geraud queried, inhaling deeply.

'Possibly from you.' Gillie glared at the two men, but her legs were trembling.

Geraud looked at Marcel, who nodded imperceptibly.

'You don't give up do you?' He stubbed out his cigarette.

There was something about Geraud that Gillie found menacing. His quiet monotone voice belied an anger he was failing to hide.

'Please,' she begged. 'Just tell me what you know.'

Geraud leant closer. 'You must understand, what we have to tell you must never be disclosed.'

Gillie waited, her heart thumping in her chest.

'He was executed at Fresnes, *madame*, just as you suspected.'

Gillie dug her nails into her arm. 'I knew that must have been the case, of course, but to hear you say it...'

'He was betrayed and tortured. But he didn't give anything away.'

As she tried to digest Geraud's information, Marcel put a bottle of brandy on the table with a thump, and three glasses. Gillie swallowed hers in one, gasping as the liquid hit her throat. She was about to stand up when Geraud took her arm, gripping it tightly.

'One day the traitor will be found, of that I can assure you.' He was looking at her intently. 'Would you ever want to know?'

'*Oui, absolument*,' she confirmed.

She scribbled her address on the back of an envelope. 'It was good of you to tell me; the speculation is finally over.'

'Should anything happen, *madame*, we will be in touch.'

She took out some money, but Marcel pushed it away as he refilled her glass.

'Again, no charge, only a toast.' They raised their glasses. 'To Étienne.'

Gillie climbed on the train and sank into a seat in the corner.

So Étienne was dead. The years of wondering were over; finally she knew the truth. Of course, in her heart she had always known, but there had been a small nagging doubt that he had left her, walked out without saying goodbye. Now she knew that this wasn't the case: he had loved her, and he had died loving her. She bit her lip and stared from the window.

As they were nearing the station, she felt a weight lift from her shoulders. She had grieved for Étienne, longed for Étienne, now she could truly say goodbye.

Chapter Twenty

Sophie had been on the ward all day and was looking forward to getting outside into the remnants of the July evening. She was changing to go home when a nurse hurried down the corridor towards her.

'Doctor Bernot, I am afraid you are needed in *Services d'Urgence*. There has been a multiple pile-up on the N20, with several casualties, every doctor is on call.'

'*Bien sur.*' Sophie put her Métro pass away, her white coat back on and went downstairs.

As soon as the swing doors opened, a duty nurse ran up to her.

'*Je suis désolé*, Doctor Bernot, it is chaos down here. If you please, go to bed seven. A girl has just been admitted with concussion. She was knocked off her bicycle.'

'How old?' she asked.

'Sixteen.'

The girl was already in the cubicle when Sophie arrived and drew the blue curtain aside. 'What is your name?'

The girl looked up at her. 'Aimee.'

There was a large bruise on her forehead.

'So Aimee, where did you fall off your bicycle?'

'Somewhere near the Boulevard Saint Germain,' she paused, her brow wrinkling. 'I think that's where I was.'

Sophie took her pulse, then her temperature. She removed an instrument from a metal set of drawers.

'Aimee, this is an ophthalmoscope. It will shine a beam of light into the centre of your eye. It won't hurt, I promise.'

'It can't hurt more than my head, Doctor.' She smiled weakly. 'I didn't know they had lady doctors.'

'They don't normally, certainly not in France. I'm breaking the mould.'

Aimee laughed, then groaned, and put her right hand to her forehead. 'Good for you, Doctor.'

'I'm sure you'll be fine,' Sophie assured her, 'a small concussion. I want to keep you in overnight. But your arm...' She gently touched the girl's arm. Aimee winced.

'I believe it is broken.'

'Ahh,' the girl groaned. 'What about my ballet?'

'I'm afraid it will have to wait for a while.'

She signalled to the nurse. 'Take her down to the radiology department for an X-ray. She will obviously need a cast, so book it in, and when she is done, bring her back to the ward. We will keep her in for observation overnight.'

'Of course, Doctor.'

That night Sophie saw more patients that she could remember. Every time she thought she was finished, another came in. There was an unrelenting stream, with symptoms as simple as a pea up a child's nose, to an asthma attack. When a middle-aged man staggered in, with sweat covering his brow, Sophie was alarmed. She could smell Ricard on his breath.

'I need to see the Doctor in charge,' he announced. 'Now.'

'I am a Doctor, *monsieur.*'

'I mean a man, not a bloody nurse.'

'Sit down please, I need to listen to your chest.' The man slumped into the chair, his body trembling.

'Are you a diabetic, *monsieur*?' she questioned.

'I've taken my insulin. For God's sake, get someone experienced, not *une oie blanche*.'

'*Monsieur*, I am neither a goose nor am I naïve. As I am sure you are aware, the hospital is dealing with a high volume of cases tonight, so I am the only doctor in charge. If my diagnosis is correct you have hypoglycaemia, but I'm sure you know that. We need to test your blood sugar now.' She looked at the nurse. 'Please get me a sharp, and the testing kit.'

While the man swore under his breath, Sophie pricked his finger and checked the results. The man was now shivering uncontrollably. '*Monsieur*, we need to raise your blood sugar or you will go into a coma. Nurse, could you bring this gentleman some sugar cubes dissolved in water.' When she had gone, Sophie turned back to the patient. 'After you have finished this, we will check your blood in fifteen minutes' time. If all is well, we will let you go home, but if I may suggest *monsieur*, knowing your condition, you should drink less alcohol, and don't waste our time.'

She had just finished treating a girl with severe burns to her hand, when the same nurse hurried over.

'I know you are busy, Doctor, but you are needed. A young woman involved in the accident has just been brought in, and she is pregnant. Professor Devereaux requests that you take responsibility for the patient.'

Sophie hurried to the other side of the ward. Nurses were rushing to and fro, pushing saline drips to different beds, carrying units of blood, while behind the screens she could hear patients moaning. The professor came towards her.

'Doctor Bernot, the patient in cubicle three is bleeding heavily.

The baby needs to come out and fast. It is possible we will lose them both.'

'But I am not yet qualified to operate, I'm—'

The professor was already hurrying away for another emergency. 'Please see to her, she is yours, I'm afraid.'

'I will find someone,' she called after him, but he had disappeared into the melee.

Sophie grabbed a passing nurse's arm.

'Find Doctor Michaud,' she instructed, 'he is needed in surgery now.'

She went into the cubicle. Two nurses were holding swabs between the girl's legs. There was a large gash on her forehead and bruises beneath her eyes. Blood was gushing from her vagina. Sophie was almost sure that the impact of the crash had caused the placenta to detach from the uterine wall. The baby wouldn't be getting the oxygen or the nutrients it needed to survive. They had to get her to theatre fast. Professor Devereaux was correct; they could easily lose them both.

At that moment the nurse ran towards her. 'Doctor Michaud is on his way. Please start surgery without him.'

Before Sophie had time to ask, the porters arrived. They took hold of the trolley and ran down the corridor to theatre and the waiting anaesthetist. While the theatre nurse set up the transfusion, Sophie changed into scrubs. Doctor Michaud would be here in a moment, she thought, choosing her instrument from a gleaming metal tray. With a delicate stroke of the scalpel, she drew a line along the girl's abdomen and watched as the streak of red blood coloured the white skin. He will be here, she intoned, cutting through fat and muscle, the first peritoneum then the second, until she reached the uterine wall. She was completely focussed on the job in hand, and was preparing to make the cut, when Doctor Michaud arrived. In a seamless transition Sophie stood aside while the doctor made the last cut. At once blood gushed from the uterus. With level-headed professionalism, Doctor Michaud delivered the baby, passing it to the paediatrician who was standing nearby, then he removed the placenta. The bleeding immediately lessened. The line for the blood transfusion was already set up and blood was flowing into the patient's arm.

The doctor turned to Sophie. 'Thank you Doctor Bernot, I have to deal with another patient, please close.' And he was gone, hurrying from theatre. As Sophie stitched up the uterus, and the new blood circulated through the girl's body, her colour began to improve. From the other side of the operating theatre, to her enormous relief, she heard the baby cry.

When the new mother and baby were ensconced in special care, Sophie went to check on them. How peaceful the mother looked, how serene; the horrors of the last few hours erased by the life in her arms. For an instant Sophie pondered on the enormity of childbirth and the void left in her own heart after giving her son away.

The girl opened her eyes and tried to focus on Sophie.

'I recognise you, the woman doctor,' she murmured.

Sophie lifted her wrist to check her pulse, '*Oui*,' she smiled, 'and now you have a beautiful baby girl.'

'I will always be grateful,' she whispered, closing her eyes. At once the feeling of satisfaction made up for Sophie's loneliness, her exhaustion, the appalling hours, the terrible pay. Doctor Michaud's calm demeanour had been an inspiration, but he couldn't take all of the credit. She had been part of the operation. She had helped to save a life tonight, possibly two. There was a fine line between life and death and she had helped to prevent mother and child from crossing it.

'It is my pleasure,' she said, '*Bon nuit* and congratulations.' She left them together, took off her scrubs and returned to the ward.

Professor Devereaux was looking for her. 'You look exhausted, how many hours?'

'Eighteen,' Sophie murmured, looking down at her hands.

'Eighteen? Outrageous, I'm sending you home.' She looked up to see amusement in the professor's eyes. 'And you wanted to be a doctor? But I've heard it was a good result tonight; I have every faith in you, Doctor Bernot.'

The flat was quiet when she unlocked the door. The only sound was the clock ticking on the mantelpiece and the occasional car passing in the street outside. It was at moments like these that she missed her grandmother's presence most. Lamplight filtered through the net curtains and as she looked around the sitting room she realised how drab it was; unloved. The little campanula had died long ago, she had never replaced it, and the carpets were worn. She gazed at Max's picture hanging above the fireplace. Would he have been proud of her, especially today, she wondered. But of course she would never know. Her mind returned to her son. He would be climbing trees now, riding a bicycle. Did he paint like Max? She took the photograph of the laughing child with her brother's eyes from the mantelpiece. She might be in pain, but her son was not.

She climbed into bed and pulled the covers over her head. Her last thoughts as she fell asleep were of her grandmother, Max, and her little boy, safe in his bedroom at Pommard.

Chapter Twenty-One

Marcus Donadieu unpinned the drawings from the drafting board and rolled them into the cardboard tube. Grabbing his weekend bag he ran through the entrance hall of the Parisian office and jumped into the waiting cab, arriving at Orly Airport with only minutes to spare. By the time he got through customs and his passport was stamped, his forehead was damp with perspiration. His anxiety only lessened when he had a glass of wine in one hand, an architectural magazine in the other, and Orly Airport was a tiny speck below. Not only did he dislike flying, but in a few hours' time he would present his drawings for the project in Bloomsbury Square to the board. Hopefully they would like them – but in the case of Sir Humphrey, he couldn't be sure. The longer he had worked for him, the more exacting he became.

He went immediately to Bruton Street and took the lift to the fifth floor.

'If you would like to take a seat in the waiting room,' a smartly dressed girl, informed him, showing him the way.

He had been there for less than five minutes when she was back. 'You can go in now sir, they are ready for you,' she said.

Sebastian met him at the boardroom door and shook his

164

hand. 'Marcus, it's so good to see you. We can't wait to look at your proposals.'

Marcus smiled. Sebastian was charming and polite, always putting one at ease. He had matured so much in the last few years, very different from the exuberant young man he had first met. Now more measured, he was climbing the corporate ladder with lightning speed.

In the boardroom, the other partners murmured their greetings, including the handsome and articulate financial director, Robert Marston. After coffee and biscuits, Marcus unrolled the plans.

There was silence as Sir Humphrey and his team pored over them. It seemed the senior partner was enjoying the moment as he took off his glasses, and scrutinised the assembled company. Marcus winced as Sir Humphrey returned his gaze to the drawing, took a sharpened pencil from the table and jabbed it down on the immaculate drawing.

'I was wondering what you would come up with,' he said, making a large squiggle in the roof line. He looked up at Marcus. 'I do have my own comments of course, but first, Marcus, I'd like you to explain to the assembled company why you came to this conclusion.'

Marcus rubbed his forehead; this was the only part of his job that he disliked. For a second he thought of Charles encouraging him with a pithy remark. 'Sir Humphrey is a pompous little Englishman, you show him what for!' The E in English would have been drawn out, something that always made him laugh.

He cleared his throat.

'I know this project is not as large as some, but we all agree it is significant. With the Liverpool Victoria Friendly Society occupying the east side of Bloomsbury Square, and the Royal Pharmaceutical Society of Great Britain at the end of the row, we needed to make sure the development was both significant and that it fitted in with its surroundings. This left me with a conundrum. The prospective infill sits between two building styles, Georgian on the left and Victorian on the right. As you know my preference is for the simple Georgian style, uncluttered by fussiness. I like to bring elegance and restraint to my buildings, and I believe that is why you employ me.' He smiled at the assembled company. 'It seems that if I have a reputation, it is as the architect who tries to save as much as possible of the original, instead of the current trend of pulling it down. I may be old-fashioned, but it offends me to replace these beautiful buildings with concrete blocks.' There was a titter of agreement in the room.

'Hear, hear!' It was Sir Humphrey.

Marcus continued, his confidence returning. 'After talks with the notoriously difficult Metropolitan Borough of Holborn, they have accepted my proposals. Our infill, if you agree, will mirror the Georgian building on the left. However, in deference to you, Sir Humphrey, I have pushed the roof line higher. We may have one less floor than our Victorian neighbour, but we have more than compensated by the new higher ceilings and larger rooms, particularly suitable for its new use as a commercial building. In truth we have one full floor where the Georgian house next door only has a dormer.'

There was clapping in the room and Sir Humphrey laughed.

'Well done *monsieur*, you have entirely won me over. I like the look of this, and it is in keeping with the growing commercialisation of the area. The Council may be difficult, but they are not stupid where their pockets are concerned. Offices bring in much higher rates than houses. I for one am entirely happy with your proposal and I have nothing to add, for a change.' He grinned, his eyes crinkling with humour, and looked around the room. Peter Hamilton and Robert Marston nodded their approval, but Andrew Lovell spoke. 'I think you have hit upon the right tone entirely, Monsieur Donadieu, and as I said many years ago, I am happy to put my money on you.'

Marcus was taking a leisurely stroll through St James's Park, on his way to meet Sebastian for an early supper at Le Caprice. He loved London at this time of year, the leaves turning from green to red and gold, the first hint of autumn. He was wearing a light camel coat purchased from Aquascutum this very afternoon as a celebratory present to himself. He now felt entirely at ease.

'That was an impressive presentation,' Sebastian congratulated him as he arrived at the restaurant. 'Like the coat by the way.'

Marcus shrugged out of the coat and grinned at Sebastian. He gave it to the cloakroom attendant.

'I have to say your Sir Humphrey makes me nervous,' Marcus admitted, when they had finished their main course of rack of lamb with mint jelly.

'Don't worry, the older he is, the more cantankerous he gets. He is seventy-five for heaven's sake, it's time he retired.'

They both laughed, and Marcus called over the wine waiter.

'Another bottle of that delicious Montrachet.'

'Is that in deference to me?' Sebastian asked.

'The Côte de Beaune happens to produce some of the best wines in the world, but of course it's in deference to you.'

He smiled at Sebastian and for a moment he wished Charles could have known this mesmerising young man.

They finished supper and this time Marcus paid.

'I insist,' he said, getting out his wallet. 'You've always been so supportive of my work.'

'Who wouldn't be, you are so talented.' Sebastian looked at Marcus. 'But in case you didn't realise, you are also my friend.' He rose from the table and shook Marcus's hand. 'Forgive me, I'm for an early night. I'm seeing Alfie tomorrow.'

As Marcus walked from St James to the cobbled Soho streets, he wished he could have spent the rest of the evening talking to Sebastian. They had so much in common and a closeness had grown between them, but understandably Sebastian needed an early night. In the morning he would make his weekly journey to France to see his son.

London was humming with people. Groups were coming from the theatres, men and women were strolling arm in arm. A heavy feeling settled in his chest. He was always lonely.

He was cutting through a Soho alleyway when an entrance to a bar attracted him. Normally he would have avoided it, but tonight he was drawn towards the warm glow of lights coming from the interior.

A doorman let him in and he went to the bar. A jazz band was playing on the tiny stage, and cigarette smoke filled the air. He ordered a drink, then another. At different tables men were chatting together, enjoying themselves, leaving Marcus feeling empty and disheartened. Would he ever find a meaningful relationship, he wondered, or would he always be on his own?

He went to the cloakroom, stared into the mirror. His pale face looked back at him. What the hell am I doing here, he wondered.

As he washed his hands, memories from the distant past flicked into his mind. His mother was holding his hand on the beach at Deauville. Her dark hair hung to her shoulders and she was wearing a white dress sprigged with flowers. They had gone there for the day, walked along the boardwalk and had watched the rich and famous bathe in the sea.

'You could take your trousers off, *chérie*,' she had suggested. 'Put your toes in, I should imagine it's warm.'

He remembered being shy suddenly. 'No Maman, I can't.'

'Course you can.' Her laughter had been gentle, and she had leant down so that their faces were level. 'You are *mon petit chou*, my best boy, you know that don't you?'

The fact that she was her only boy was irrelevant. He felt truly loved. He had taken off his trousers, his socks and shoes, and he had run to the sea in his underpants, the sand scrunching between his toes. As the cold water hit him, he had turned back to her, gasping in delight. 'Come in, Maman, you must!'

She had peeled off her stockings and had waded in up to her knees, her skirts and petticoats dragging in the salty water. She was laughing, and she had never looked more beautiful. Afterwards they had lunch at one of the many restaurants on the quayside, and before they took the train back to Paris, she had bought him a tiny boat with miniature sails and a mast with a little French flag stuck on the top. He had put it on his mantelpiece at home.

Marcus dried his hands and the memory faded. He was on his way to fetch his coat when he turned back; he would have another drink for the road.

He had just ordered an Armagnac when a young man sat down beside him.

He had light brown hair and he was wearing trousers with a pleated waist and a silk shirt tucked inside. His hair was swept back from his face and Marcus could tell immediately that he was completely *à la mode*.

He put out his hand. 'I'm Giles. And you are?'

'Marcus.'

'Ah,' he smiled, 'a Frenchman. I went to Paris recently for the shows.'

Marcus looked a little perplexed.

'Sorry – fashion shows. I'm a designer you see. God, I love the city, every restaurant is so chic – and the bars! And of course there is little of that nonsense we have here. It's so liberated, and fun.'

Marcus began to laugh at the young man's exuberance; Giles was unlike anyone he had met before.

'Yes, Paris is wonderful, I agree. But Rouen, where I live, now that is better still.' He grinned. 'But a little smaller, I accept.'

Giles leaned in conspiratorially. 'So I have admitted I design dresses – what do you do, Marcus?'

'I'm an architect; I design houses!'

'We are the same, you and I,' Giles teased.

'Except that I know nothing about making dresses. And I daresay you know little about building houses.'

'Well then, Marcus, I'll have to come and visit you in Rouen and you will show me around.' He handed Marcus his card, and was trying to get the barman's attention, when a man in a green velvet jacket, sashayed across the room towards them. He kissed Giles on the cheek. 'Sorry I'm late darling, but the traffic was awful. If you want to be in time for dinner, we should run.'

Giles looked at Marcus apologetically and got down from the stool. 'Don't forget, I'll visit you in Rouen,' he exclaimed.

Marcus was finishing his drink when he overheard a conversation coming from a table nearby.

'Night old chap, I am going to give the bar a miss for a week or two. Rumour has it there will be another raid, and I don't want to be here if the old Bill arrives.'

The term 'old Bill' was new to Marcus, but he understood immediately and drained his glass. After collecting his coat he hurried outside and walked back to his hotel alone.

Chapter Twenty-Two

September 1958 came and went in a blur as Sophie and Georges worked around the clock completing their rotation through the medical specialties. As newly qualified doctors, they were currently based at the *Hôpital Cochin* in Paris. But whilst Georges had a life outside the hospital, Sophie did not. Her life consisted of the wards and the library: it was work, study and more work. She was having lunch in the canteen, her notes open in front of her, when she realised it was Valentine's Day. A card from Todd might have been nice, she thought, before returning to her revision with a sigh. When Georges plonked himself down opposite her, she folded a piece of paper and drew a large heart. 'For you,' she said, grinning. 'And now you can test me.' She pushed a sheaf of papers across the table and he made a face.

'Cupboard love, Sophie,' he declared. He skimmed her notes quickly. 'Not sure that I know much of this myself,' he muttered tucking into a bowl of soup.

'Well you should, you are impossible. Let me ask you some questions instead.' She grabbed the papers back. 'Here is a good one. How does cancer of the pancreas present to the patient?'

Georges thought for a moment. 'I know it can present with jaundice, but I can't think of anything else right now.'

'How can you have got to your ninth year of training without having this information in your head?'

'Easily,' he leant forward and tweaked her nose. 'I want to be an obstetrician, not an oncologist.'

'The maddening thing is you always get top marks.'

'It's because I'm a genius,' he grinned.

Sophie slapped his hand.

'You need a break,' Georges instructed a week later when Sophie met him in a café round the corner from the hospital. 'You look awful.'

'Thanks,' she muttered, running a hand through her hair, but for the first time she was not sure that she cared.

'Not sexy at all.'

Sophie grimaced and sent the remains of her croissant slicing across the table. 'Now that's mean.'

'I need to be mean,' Georges replied, removing the croissant from his white coat and popping it into this mouth. 'Take a break, Sophie. You will burn yourself out.'

'But I have to pass! I want to be a surgeon, for heaven's sake.'

'At the risk of sounding unkind, you are getting positively boring. Of course you have to pass, but you have no life at all. When was the last time you came out with me?'

'You have a girlfriend and I am sure she doesn't want me hanging onto your coat tails all the time.'

He laughed. '*Touché.*'

'Tell me,' Sophie asked, her head on the side, a smile twitching at her lips. 'Why Lydia? She is …' She paused, considering her words. 'She is very conservative.'

'Because I wanted a girlfriend who is everything you are not. First, she completely adores me.'

'So do I.'

'But not in that way. Second, she tells me that I am wonderful, and she wants to marry me and have babies, three at least.'

Sophie started to giggle.

'And you dearest, wonderful Sophie don't want me.'

'I do,' she laughed.

'Yes, but only as a friend. But I digress. Go Sophie, have a few days off, you are certainly owed the time. Take the boat train to England. Be a tourist, London would be fun at this time of year. Ask Todd to join you. He will take your mind off work. For God's sake take some time for yourself before you are ninety.'

The more Sophie thought about the idea, the more she warmed to it, and it would be nice to see Todd.

She remembered the moment he had come back into her life, standing outside her flat with enough cream roses to fill a florist shop. When she had first opened the door she was furious.

'What are you doing?' she had asked, unable to prevent the delicious scent from wafting into the hall.

'I went to the hospital to find you and found Georges instead,' Todd had said, putting on his most winning smile. He leant over to kiss her, but Sophie had moved away.

'Ouch that hurt,' he had said, a wounded expression on his handsome face.

'You haven't contacted me for months – what right have you to appear on my doorstep now?' Sophie put her hands on her hips and glared at him.

'I tried to contact you, Sophie, but immediately after I had returned home, I was despatched to South Vietnam to report on the referendum and Ngo Dinh Diem's new presidency.'

'You should have tried harder,' she had pouted, still holding firm.

'You have to believe me, I tried.' Todd rested his hand on the door jamb above Sophie's head and she could smell his aftershave and see his suntanned wrist.

'I am not sure that I do,' she had said, her expression prim.

'Have you read the newspapers, Sophie?'

'Of course I have,' she replied, jutting out her chin, knowing full well she rarely had a moment to glance at the headlines.

'Mark my words, Sophie, Vietnam is a tinder box. It is already unstable and with Ho Chi Minh leading the communists in the North, it will only be a matter of time before the situation could escalate to something unimaginable.' Todd had looked so earnest that Sophie had started to laugh.

'You come back here with a bunch of flowers and I admit a pretty good explanation and you expect me to take you back?'

'Yes please, Sophie,' he had said, scooping her into his arms, the flowers dropping to the floor.

Three years after their reunion they were still together. Though their relationship was tumultuous at times, it was also passionate. More importantly they got on well and they made each other laugh. They saw each other when they could, and to Sophie it now seemed the perfect arrangement.

'We have a very modern relationship,' she had said to him a few months after their reunion. 'We see each other when we want to, we have fun without the intensity and suffering. It works perfectly for both of us doesn't it, Todd?'

When he didn't immediately reply she had looked at him closely. 'You are not getting serious, are you, Todd?'

'Hell no,' he had replied.

Sophie followed Georges's advice and wrote to Todd. He was delighted with her plan.

'Great idea,' he responded. 'I am missing you, Sophie, and I need a break too.'

Sophie took the boat train from Paris to London. It was a mild October morning when she arrived, and the turning leaves were the perfect accessory to her rust swing coat. It was the best time of year to be in the capital city, she decided, walking through the streets, window shopping, seeing French impressionist paintings in the English galleries, running into the doorways of exclusive shops to escape the showers. And yes, Georges was right, she felt positively liberated. She had needed this break more than anything.

On the first evening she met Todd at Le Caprice in St James.

He ambled in carrying a briefcase and hugged her. 'Sorry I'm late, Sophie. My, you look gorgeous.'

'Thank you Todd,' she said, a wicked glint in her eye. 'And you are not so bad.' As the head waiter led them to their table, Sophie was aware of the glances of the male clientele. It was nice to feel glamorous for a change and out of her doctor's coat. The black satin dress with the plunging neckline was definitely a find. She sat down in the banquette seat and ran one delicate finger down the velvet-lined walls. 'This restaurant is extremely sophisticated, Monsieur Todd.'

'Just like you,' Todd remarked, and Sophie giggled and for a moment she looked more like a child, her eyes round with enthusiasm.

'My uncle once brought me here on my birthday just after the war.'

'He brought you all the way to London from America, just for your birthday?'

'He was good to us,' he explained. 'He didn't have kids of his own and he'd made a fortune in real estate, so we were the lucky recipients of his generosity.'

They were seated in the corner and the time sped by.

They had finished their coffee and Sophie was looking longingly at the last petits fours on the plate.

'Go on, take it,' Todd urged.

She popped it into her mouth. 'Delicious,' she sighed.

Todd opened his briefcase. 'And now my little Sophie, I have something to show you.' He drew out a periodical and put it face down on the table.

'It's a magazine,' she stated, looking a little disappointed.

'But not just any magazine. Do you remember I took a photo of you outside the hospital in your white coat?'

'Of course. It was just after you said you would do an article on me for *Time* magazine.' Her face changed. '*Mon Dieu*, you didn't?'

'I certainly did. I hope you don't mind?'

Sophie turned over the magazine and her face was staring back at her from the cover. She started to laugh. 'What will people say; *mes professeurs*?'

'It's very complimentary about your hospital and indeed your professors, so I can't see what's not to like about it. I have said your hospital is progressive and the teaching staff totally enlightened.'

'*Sophie Bernot forges the way for women in France,*' the caption read.

'Well, are you happy about it?' Todd asked, his face a little anxious.

'Let me read it first.' As Sophie found the page her face lit up. '"This young woman is breaking down boundaries, she is determined and capable and she is proving that a woman is as good as any man."' She put down the magazine and looked at Todd.

'You remembered.'

'Of course I did, Sophie. I remember everything that you say.' He put his hand over hers and as Sophie looked into his eyes, she believed she could fall in love with this man.

But she realised with a jolt, she needed to tell Todd that she had a son. She couldn't keep it from him any longer. If she wanted any future with Todd she owed him the truth.

*

The next day, after a brief stop at Liberty's, Sophie loitered in front of Hamleys, London's most celebrated toy shop. Did Alfie have a wigwam, she wondered, or a red leather football like Max? She was staring through the plate glass windows at an assortment of toys, when Todd tapped her on the arm.

'A penny for your thoughts? Or in your case, a centime.'

She looked up at him and while the crowds parted around them, she told him about Alfie.

'So you see, I couldn't tell you before because I was not sure if I trusted you after Île de Ré, but it's very different now,' she ended.

Todd's face was strained. 'I'm glad you've told me,' he said.

They had a drink in a pub, and an hour later, Todd's normal light-hearted humour had returned.

They were making their way down Bruton Street towards Hyde Park Corner when a plaque attached to the railings of a Georgian house caught Sophie's eye: Blackheath Holdings. The name was horribly familiar. She stopped for a moment, scrutinised the elegant building, until with a sickening flash it came to her: it was Sebastian's company. This was the building where he worked, maybe he was at his desk inside. It was purely coincidence, of course, but it unnerved her. She was on the brink of giving her love to Todd, but suddenly she could feel Sebastian's presence close by. She had been trying to push any thoughts of him to the back of her mind; now they flooded back.

'Is something wrong, Sophie?' Todd asked. 'You seem distracted.'

'No,' she replied unconvincingly, 'nothing is wrong.' But as they continued along the street, she scrutinised every face, and the occupants of every car that went by.

'Come on young lady, stop dreaming,' Todd quipped, and

Sophie pulled herself together. She was with Todd now. Sebastian was the past.

'We need some lunch.' He grabbed her hand and made for the sandwich bar on the corner of Berkeley Square. He grinned at the proprietor, a large woman wearing a floral pinafore.

'Do you have bagels, ma'am?'

'No sir, this is what we have.'

'Then I'll have two of those delicious-looking egg baps.'

She laughed. 'You're one of them Yankees.'

'I'm afraid I am, ma'am.'

Moments later armed with sandwiches, Coca-Cola and a bar of chocolate, they pushed open the gate into the gardens, flopping down on a bench opposite Alexander Munro's biblical depiction of the *Woman of Samaria*. Sophie studied the marble nude, the irony of the repentant sinner not lost on her.

While Sophie ate her sandwich, and tried to concentrate on Todd, Sebastian Ogilvie left his office to buy some lunch. He made his way to his usual sandwich bar on the corner of the square.

'Hello Gladys, the usual please.'

'Morning love, gorgeous as ever.'

'October is always glorious.'

'I wasn't talking about the weather!'

'Gladys, you'll break my heart one of these days.'

The woman laughed and put his sandwiches in a paper bag.

'You couldn't swap this?' She put a franc on the steel counter. 'My last customer gave me the wrong coin. Bloody foreigner.'

'For you, Gladys, anything.' He took the coin and smiled. 'It's French.'

Sebastian took his sandwiches and sauntered back towards his office. It was such a warm day he was tempted to go into the square. He glanced towards it; how lovely it looked, the weak sun emerging through the clouds. There were people on the park benches – a girl in a rust coat with dark hair. He looked at his watch. It was already two o'clock, and he had a backlog of work on his desk.

Sophie was having supper with Todd in their hotel, later that evening, when he put his hand on her arm. 'I have something to tell you, Sophie,' he said.

She put down her fork, wondering what was coming next.

'I never told you the reason I had to leave Paris in a hurry.'

Sophie knew something was wrong. She could see it in his eyes.

'The thing is Sophie, I'm married.'

'You're what?'

'We have been separated for over two years and I am trying to get my wife to agree to a divorce. I wanted to tell you, but the time was never right,' he explained.

'And children? Have you several of these as well?' Sophie asked, trying to remain calm.

'No Sophie, we could never have children, and tests have proved that it is my fault. I hope you'll forgive me for not telling you, but I didn't want to risk losing you. I thought you might leave. You see, I am falling in love with you, and I no longer want any secrets between us. But of course we both kept things back – you never told me about your son.'

Sophie looked at him, suddenly furious.

'How dare you compare your infidelity to my son. I didn't tell you about Alfie because I wished to protect him; you didn't tell me that you were married because you knew I would never have slept with you if you had. *Mon Dieu*, and to think I forgave you after Île de Ré, and I was right all the time.' She scraped back her chair. 'It will be better if you get your own room.'

179

Chapter Twenty-Three

Nineteen fifty-eight was drawing to a close and Sophie was working in obstetrics at *Hôpital La Salpêtrière*. It was no coincidence that Georges had applied for a training post nearby. Her brief holiday in London with Todd had left her confused and angry, but with more surgical exams looming and the pass rate to the next stage notoriously low, she had forced it out of her mind.

On New Year's Eve, she was one of only two junior doctors in the reference library. She was distracted from her books when Georges sauntered in and perched on the edge of her desk.

'Georges, I'm studying.' She looked up at him, trying not to smile.

'Nothing new in that.'

The young doctor in the desk three rows ahead tutted loudly.

Georges looked contrite. 'Are you coming out with us tonight?' he asked her in a loud whisper.

'I can't.'

'It's *Le Caveau des Lorientais* for heaven's sake; don't you want to see in the new decade with your friends?'

'Georges, of course I do, but how many times do I have to tell you, I can't afford to come.'

'But it is your favourite jazz club, and I'll pay for you anyway.'

'Don't be such an idiot, you know what I mean! Some of us have to work.'

The same doctor slammed down his books. 'Some of us can't work when you are making such a racket.' He stalked from the library, slamming the door behind him.

Georges giggled and slipped into the bench beside her. He put his arms around her. 'Oh Sophie, why do you still have this effect on me?'

'Ha,' she laughed. 'What would Lydia say to that?'

He looked sheepish. 'She thinks I'm a little in love with you.'

'And I know you have never been in love with me. You are my best friend. By the way, I'm applying for a residency in Dijon.'

'That's miles away.'

'I can't miss this opportunity. It would mean working under Professor Charpentier, the pioneering cardiothoracic surgeon. I wrote to him and he took the time to reply. He said I should definitely put myself up for the position, and he would support my application in any way that he could.'

'So it is obviously still the heart?'

'I am enjoying my stint in obstetrics, but the heart is still the dream.'

Georges raised his eyebrows to heaven. 'It seems I will have to find a residency in Dijon; someone needs to keep an eye on you. Isn't it fairly near Pommard by the way, and your son?'

'Is it?' Sophie ventured, burying her face in a book.

'Talking of dreams, is there really no chance of you coming tonight?'

She shook her head, 'I'm on call anyway.'

Sophie was engrossed in a paper on the future of heart and blood vessel operations, written by the influential Lebanese-American surgeon Dr Michael deBakey, when a nurse tapped her on the shoulder.

'I'm sorry to disturb you, Doctor Bernot, but a young woman has gone into labour and you are needed urgently in the maternity ward.'

Sophie packed up and stretched her tired muscles. It would undoubtedly be another long night. She ran along the corridor and crossed the courtyard. She was on her way to the unit when a well-dressed young man hurried towards her. She recognised him immediately as Hakim, the young Algerian husband of one of her patients. She had been looking after Nadia Abdelrahman until recently when, suspecting there might be complications with the pregnancy, she had referred her to Doctor Michaud.

'Ah Doctor Bernot, thank goodness. Nadia is in the delivery room with the midwife. Something is wrong and Doctor Michaud still hasn't arrived.'

'It's all right, Monsieur Abdelrahman, I'll take over until he gets here,' Sophie soothed.

As she walked down the corridor, she glanced at the slight man at her side. He was always courteous, but his dark eyes were never still.

On his wife's first appointment six months before, Sophie had learnt the reason why. They were in her consulting room. Nadia was sitting rigidly in the small upright chair, Hakim beside her.

'I see you have come a long way to see us,' Sophie had said, smiling gently as she had tried to put them at ease.

'We had to leave Algeria,' he had explained.

'The revolution?' Sophie asked.

Hakim looked at the floor.

'I am a doctor, Hakim, anything you tell me is in confidence.'

He hesitated as if making up his mind, then spoke quickly, his hands clasped together. 'Two of my wife's close relatives were wrongly accused of being members of the National Liberation

Front. They were tortured and shot by the French military. The killings have become indiscriminate. We had to get out.'

'I'm so sorry,' Sophie replied, remembering Todd's outrage at the situation in Algeria.

Hakim broke into her thoughts. 'My only concern now is for my wife, her mother who lives with us, and our young daughter.'

'I trust we are treating you well in France?'

Monsieur Abdelrahman raised his head so that their eyes met and for a moment they fixed on her. 'The colour of our skin doesn't make it easy for us.'

'I had hoped we had learnt our lesson from the last war,' Sophie apologised, feeling shame for her countrymen.

'Mankind will never learn,' he had said, shaking his head. And Sophie remembered the roundup of Jewish families in '42, their shameful incarceration in the Vélodrome d'Hiver, before they were despatched to the camps. Thomas, a boy from her class, had been amongst them and she had never seen him again.

'It is my hope that within the walls of this hospital, religion and race are irrelevant,' she murmured.

Throughout the conversation his wife had been sitting quietly, occasionally lifting her hand to pull her headscarf into place.

Sophie had opened Nadia's file and turned towards her. 'I have the medical details on your form, but I would like to know about you, Nadia.'

Nadia had looked surprised. 'Of course but ...'

'It helps me to understand you as a patient,' Sophie qualified.

Nadia had leant forward suddenly, the passive expression disappearing.

'You are fortunate to be a doctor. As a child I dreamt of being a nurse, but it is impossible in Algeria. Hakim has always treated me as an equal, but others are not so blessed.'

'It has been a struggle here too, a woman doctor, *quelle horreur*!' Sophie had laughed, throwing up her hands.

Nadia's shoulders visibly relaxed and a smiled crossed her face.

'It's true. At first, some patients reacted with disbelief. I remember one old man stating he would not be treated by a goose, or was it that he would rather be treated by a goose?' She giggled suddenly, and Nadia joined in.

'Well, I am grateful that you are looking after me,' Nadia said, when both women had composed themselves. 'As a Muslim woman it is better, you understand. This baby is so important, Doctor, for us it signifies a fresh start in our new country.'

Sophie smiled. 'Of course and I am honoured, but I must explain, Nadia, yours will be a trial labour. After your previous emergency caesarean in Algiers, it is quite possible that Doctor Michaud may need to intervene to take baby out. Don't worry, he is one of the finest obstetricians in France, so you are in safe hands.'

'*Je comprend*s.' Nadia replied.

'You could always train as a nurse in France,' Sophie added as an afterthought. 'It would be hard work, but achievable – after your children have grown a little.'

'That would not be possible.' Nadia bit her lip and looked at Hakim.

He smiled at her. 'You can tell Doctor Bernot. People should know what has happened in our country.'

Nadia took a deep breath. 'A ban was imposed on education for the entire native Algerian population.'

'Everyone?' Sophie queried, aghast.

Nadia nodded. 'I can read and so can Hakim, but all the skills you need to become a nurse?' Her voice trailed off. 'I think not.'

'But you are a clever woman,' Sophie encouraged.

'I can only read because Hakim's father was the chauffeur to a French diplomatic family. They included Hakim in their children's lessons.' She glanced at him with pride. 'He has now taught me. But there are other things I would like to do, Doctor,'

Nadia had said, leaning forward. 'You see, I was not confined indoors. Hakim took me into the streets to witness what was happening.'

It was if the floodgates of Nadia's soul had suddenly been opened. Her voice was filled with intensity.

'In Algeria the situation has gone beyond race; the French farmers are fighting to keep the land they took from the Algerians, who quite rightly want it back. There are factions fighting each other. It has become a civil war, and my family has been caught at the centre of it.' Tears welled suddenly in her dark eyes. 'There will be more bloodshed and violence until Algeria has gained independence from France.' She had looked down, all the energy leaving her.

Sophie looked at the girl in the brightly coloured scarf. She had thought her to be mild and submissive, but Nadia Abdel-rahman was passionate with a mind of her own.

That was six months ago, and in the intervening period Sophie had met Nadia's four-year-old daughter Yasemin and her sixty-year-old mother. They were a delightful family. She remembered Yasemin shaking her hand when they were introduced, her eyes shining in her heart-shaped face.

'Are you looking forward to a little brother or sister?' Sophie asked.

'Oh yes,' she had said, touching her mother's tummy. 'If he is a boy I want to call him Oussama. Do you like it?'

'Very much. But what does it mean?' Sophie had questioned Yasemin.

'Lion, because he will be like a lion, strong and bold.'

Sophie had been enchanted. 'Well that is a very good name,' she had replied.

She had seen Nadia at every appointment until the month

before, when she had concerns about Nadia's low estriol levels, and had alerted Doctor Michaud.

'I believe it would be better if you take over this patient. There is an indication of placental sulfatase deficiency. She may need a caesarean at thirty-eight weeks.' She had handed him the notes.

'Nadia Abdelrahman,' he had said, his eyebrows raised. 'Algerian, isn't she?'

Now, as Sophie continued down the corridor with Hakim, she was filled with a sense of foreboding. Why had the midwife waited until now to call her and where was Doctor Michaud?

'She still has three weeks to go, Doctor Bernot,' Hakim said, his dark eyes questioning. 'She will be all right and the baby?'

'It's probably nature's way of saying baby needs to come out. Let me examine her. I'm sure there is nothing to worry about,' Sophie reassured him.

The midwife was waiting for her.

'Her waters broke four hours ago with evidence of meconium in the amniotic fluid. The foetal heartbeat is falling rapidly, and the cervix is not dilating,' she clarified, passing Sophie the patient's notes.

'Why didn't you call me sooner?'

'We sent a porter with a message to Doctor Michaud's house, so it didn't seem necessary.'

'Perhaps that was for me to decide,' Sophie snapped, glancing at the midwife. 'So did Doctor Michaud receive the message?'

The midwife blushed. 'We assumed so at the time.'

Sophie was getting rattled. It was an error of judgement on the midwife's part. If the message hadn't been delivered into the consultant's hand, Sophie should have been informed immediately. The baby's first faeces, otherwise known as meconium, could block the airway on delivery, but it was also a sign of foetal distress.

'Has Doctor Michaud been in contact since?' she demanded, looking at the duty nurse.

'Not exactly. We can't get hold of him,' the nurse told her.

'But he needs to attend,' Sophie exclaimed.

The nurse looked embarrassed. 'We will send the porter again.'

Sophie could feel her frustration mounting. She had admiration for Doctor Michaud's talent, but not for his arrogance. His attitude towards Nadia Abdelrahman had been indifferent to say the least.

Sophie walked through the maternity ward into the delivery suite. The midwife followed her into a side room.

'Thank goodness you have come, Doctor Bernot.' Nadia looked up, her eyes frightened. 'The baby has stopped kicking. Is that normal?'

'Quite normal at this stage,' Sophie reassured her, 'but I need to examine you.' She knew she could not tell her the truth – it would only panic her.

Sophie felt the girl's abdomen to establish the baby's position, then taking out her fetoscope, she pushed it firmly against her swollen belly. As she listened to the weak and irregular heartbeat, she felt a jolt of alarm. She was taking Nadia's blood pressure when the young mother clutched her stomach and doubled up.

'Try and breathe through the contraction,' Sophie calmed her.

'Should we give her Oxytocin?' the midwife asked, hovering beside her.

Sophie shook her head and moved to the door. 'No, I don't want the cervix to dilate. She needs a caesarean section immediately. Call Doctor Michaud again, and please inform Monsieur Abdelrahman of the latest developments.'

A quarter of an hour later, when the gynaecologist still hadn't arrived, she went to the nurses' station.

'Any word from Doctor Michaud?'

'We have called his house several times; there is still no response,' a young nurse informed her, looking down at the floor.

'Is there something you are not telling me?' Sophie demanded, her panic rising.

'I heard one of the consultants mention a New Year's Eve party nearby,' she admitted, looking uncomfortable.

'The child's life is at risk. I suggest you find out the address of this party and send someone to bring him here, even if you have to use force,' she yelled.

In the cubicle the situation was rapidly deteriorating, the baby's heart rate was dropping dramatically. The midwife looked beseechingly at Sophie. 'Where is he?' she mouthed.

Nadia was weeping softly. 'Please help me, there is something wrong.'

Sophie was in an impossible dilemma. Nadia needed urgent surgery, but she was still not qualified to perform an unsupervised operation. Sophie was certain the cord was wrapped around the baby's neck and with each contraction this would tighten. Nadia and her baby would be in grave danger if she didn't intervene.

She listened with the fetoscope again. The situation was now dire.

'Instruct the duty anaesthetist and request theatre to be prepared,' she called to the nurse. 'I need to operate immediately.'

Sophie was on her way to theatre when Doctor Michaud hurried from the lift, a red carnation in the buttonhole of his pinstripe suit.

'I hope this is important,' he panted, glancing at his watch. 'And I really don't appreciate you sending a porter to fetch me.'

For an instant Sophie wanted to slap his pompous face. The porter had found him in a house in Rue le Brun, dancing with a woman who was definitely not his wife.

'We have been trying to reach you for hours. Nadia Abdel-rahman is your patient.'

'Her waters hadn't even broken when I left.'

'You left five hours ago, and the baby is now in severe distress. I hope we are not too late.'

Doctor Michaud's attitude changed immediately. He quickly scanned the notes, his face blanching. 'Continue to theatre, I'll go and change.'

Within a matter of moments, Sophie had entered theatre, Nadia had been anaesthetised, and a drape had been set up leaving only her abdomen exposed. Sophie glanced quickly at the theatre staff, all masked, all dressed in scrubs. She took a scalpel from the tray.

She had made the first incision when Doctor Michaud arrived.

What happened next would haunt Sophie for the rest of her life. As she had predicted, the cord was tightly wrapped around the baby's neck, denying any chance of oxygen. Inserting his finger to loosen the cord, the surgeon had lifted the child from his mother's womb, but the tiny body was already floppy and blue. He cut the cord, clamping it, and passed the baby boy to Sophie.

'Mother showing signs of a postpartum haemorrhage; I must stem the bleeding, concentrate on the child.'

Sophie went into immediate action. Using a suction device to clear the airways, she was filled with relief when the baby boy took his first shallow breath, but this quickly changed to dismay.

'We need to resuscitate now,' she called to the midwife, laying the limp, pale infant on the table.

Sophie would never forget the next ten minutes as she tried to revive him, chanting as she compressed his tiny chest.

'One, two, three, breath,' she repeated over and over again. 'Come on please. Oussama, you have to breathe.'

Finally the midwife took her arm. 'No more compressions. It is enough, Doctor Bernot. The baby is dead.'

'One more time,' she had said, pulling her arm free. As she

compressed the tiny chest she could feel everyone's eyes upon her.

'Enough now, Doctor Bernot.'

Sophie stepped back at last, her energy sapped. She watched as the midwife picked up the still baby and wrapped him in a blanket. That blanket should have held joy, she thought. It should have given the parents hope for a brighter future.

Sophie touched the baby's cheek. 'You didn't stand a chance, Oussama,' she whispered, holding back her tears.

'It is not your fault. You did everything you could,' the midwife stated in a bleak tone.

'I promised the parents that all would be well.'

When Doctor Michaud had arrested Nadia's bleeding, the crisis was finally over. But there was a sombre mood in theatre, a sense of failure.

'I'm so sorry,' Sophie whispered to Nadia's sleeping form. Then she left the room, rolled off the rubber gloves, took off her mask and surgical cap, and went to find Hakim.

He was pacing the corridor, his hands pushed deep into his pockets. As she walked towards him, a single thought whirled in her head: how do you explain to a parent that their child is dead?

He turned around and their eyes met. One glimpse told her that this sensitive troubled man already knew.

'Hakim, *je suis désolé*,' she murmured, touching his shoulder. 'Nadia is recovering, but your baby son did not survive.'

He nodded. 'How is my wife?' was all that he said.

'She has not yet come round. I will take you to her.'

As they walked along the linoleum floor, his quiet despair compounded her own misery, but it was his dignity that emphasised the enormity of the surgeon's neglect.

Nadia was waking from the anaesthetic as Sophie entered the recovery suite with Hakim.

'Her vitals are good,' a nurse informed her.

'Thank you. Leave us please,' Sophie requested. The staff were melting away as Doctor Michaud arrived. He looked first at Hakim and then at Nadia. He had changed into a pair of grey slacks beneath his white coat.

'I would suggest, Doctor, that I should be the one to deliver the news to Nadia,' Sophie said, her voice cold.

'Yes. Quite. I would agree with you,' he replied, his face showing his relief. 'Well, if you will excuse me. My condolences,' he said to Hakim and hurried from the room.

Sophie leant down towards Nadia, so that her mouth was near to her ear.

'I am so sorry Nadia, I have some terrible news, your baby is dead.'

As the girl struggled to focus, Hakim took her hand.

'My dearest love,' he whispered, 'we still have Yasemin.'

At once, Sophie felt like an intruder in their private moment. She excused herself, hurrying back to theatre. There was something she could do. She could bring the grieving couple their baby. They needed to say goodbye.

'Stop,' she shouted, reaching the theatre as the orderlies were about to remove the tiny body to the mortuary. 'I will take him.'

She picked up the lifeless form, laid him gently into the waiting crib and wheeled him back to the parents.

'Your baby boy, Oussama,' Sophie said, placing him in Nadia's arms.

The mother looked up at her with dazed eyes.

'Oussama,' she murmured. 'But he will never have a chance to be a lion, Doctor, because Allah has taken him.'

'He will always be your lion, Nadia,' Sophie whispered.

Nadia kissed his forehead, touching his rosebud mouth, then unwrapped the blanket to inspect his small but perfect body.

'He's beautiful,' she sighed, passing him to her husband. 'He looks just like you.'

Sophie left them, but at the door she paused to look back. It was a tableau of grief: mother, father and baby son.

It was not until much later as she unlocked her own front door, sank onto the sofa drained and exhausted, that her tears came. As she buried her face in the cushions, she questioned her ability to be a surgeon. What had happened tonight was a needless tragedy and she had been part of it. 'If only I had done something sooner,' she sobbed. 'I should have saved him.' As she lay there, memories she had suppressed for so long flooded back. She had given birth to a beautiful healthy boy. She remembered his first cry, the moment he was placed in her arms, the warmth of his tiny body, the overwhelming wonder and joy. He was alive, and yet she had given him away. Tonight this innocent child, born to expectant parents, was dead.

The church clock nearby struck twelve and she could hear celebrations in the street outside, reminding her that it was New Year's Day.

Chapter Twenty-Four

The drawing room was bathed in dappled February sunlight as Gillie opened the door.

'*Ma cherie*, it's you. You look nice,' her mother said vaguely as she arranged daffodils in a crystal vase. Strands of hair had escaped the pins and she had a faraway look in her eyes. 'I know it's months away, but your brother is taking Alfie to Cannes for the first week of August,' she informed her daughter. 'A week by the sea. *C'est amusant, n'est ce pas?*'

'But Maman, don't you remember, I have planned my summer holidays around our camping trip. Alfie is looking forward to it and so am I.'

Her mother took off her glasses and put them down on the grand piano.

'But darling,' she said, 'Alfie is his son.'

Gillie's fingers were strumming on the lid. 'And I'm not allowed to forget it. Who changed his nappies when he was a baby, and stayed up at night when he was teething? It is me who takes him to school and helps him with his homework. Yet when I have arranged to take him on holiday, it now seems I can't!'

She stormed from the room, slamming the door behind her.

Gathering the dogs she pulled on her gumboots, and was about to go outside when she caught sight of herself in the mirror. She was a ridiculous sight, she thought, grabbing a scarf. She was wearing her old school games shorts and a thick jersey that had shrunk years before, but she had been painting her bedroom and she couldn't be bothered to change. No one would see her anyway, it was only a stroll in the park to let off steam.

She was stomping up the meadow, Coco and Louis panting behind her, when a yapping ball of curly black fur pelted towards her. Before she knew it, the thing was humping Louis.

'Get off, you horrible little dog,' she shouted.

While trying to placate a poor confused Louis, she was unaware that a man was coming through the meadow towards her.

'*Pardonez-moi, mademoiselle.*'

She jumped and turned around to find a rather attractive man with sun-bleached hair laughing down at her.

'Hercule, get away, horrible dog. His behaviour is outrageous; my apologies.'

The heat rose in her face. 'Hercule? I hardly think the name is appropriate.' She felt stupid. Not only had she been rude, but she was wearing a ridiculous combination of clothes.

'It, or should I say he, is my mother's dog. She adores him.'

'I can't imagine why. And actually this land is private.'

'It is?' He raised an eyebrow.

She could tell the man was mocking her. She adjusted her jumper that was spattered with large blobs of yellow paint and glanced down. Her legs above her boots were pink and mottled. She was hardly in a position of authority looking like this.

'You'll find the right of way beyond the winery,' she said stiffly.

'Thank you, *mademoiselle*,' he grinned. 'And may I know the name of the woman whose dog Hercule has so deeply offended?'

She blushed redder still. 'Gillie Ogilvie,' she replied. 'And my family owns this land you are trespassing on.'

She was having supper in the dining room with her mother and grandmother when Marie-Claire put down her fork.

'A nice young man has moved into Les Volets Bleus, Gillie, and I've asked him for drinks tomorrow. You will be in, won't you?'

Gillie nearly choked. So that was why he was on their land.

'Really, Grand-mère?'

'He's the artist, Christophe Plaquet. His paintings are well thought of, I have heard.'

'Is everything all right?' Her mother could sense her discomfort.

'Yes Maman, everything is absolutely fine.'

Gillie finished her supper in silence. It was embarrassing, humiliating. Not only was Christophe Plaquet a well-known artist, but as he lived on the estate, he and his ridiculous dog were entitled to walk anywhere at all.

The following evening Gillie dressed with care. At least tonight she would look presentable. She put on a spotted red silk dress with a row of pearls and tied her hair in a band.

Christophe arrived promptly. 'Mademoiselle,' he leant over her hand. 'I prefer you in shorts,' he whispered so that only she could hear.

Gillie could feel her cheeks burning. Once again, he was making fun of her. Fortunately Alfie came in at that moment.

'Grand-mère says you are an artist. Will you teach me to paint?'

'I'm sure Monsieur Plaquet is very busy, Alfie,' Gillie interrupted.

Christophe bent down so that his face was level with Alfie's.

'I would be honoured,' he said. 'If your great-grandmother allows.'

'We'd be delighted, wouldn't we, Gillie?' Marie-Claire's eyes were sparkling; she was obviously enchanted by the handsome young man.

'Are you settling in well?' she enquired. 'I have always loved the cottage. I lived there with my husband for a while.'

'It is splendid, thank you. The shed in the garden is now my studio, but with the weather so mild, if it is possible I paint outside. The light here is extraordinary.'

The conversation continued with Gillie observing from the fireplace, her foot tapping the marble hearth.

'Can I come next Monday after school?' Alfie asked as he was leaving. 'It's Tante Gillie's day off and she always collects me.'

'You certainly may,' Christophe replied, formally shaking his hand. 'I shall be waiting, young man. But wrap up well and bring a hat.'

'Oh I shall,' the little boy replied.

Much later, Gillie retired to her room and pulled off her dress. Christophe Plaquet was arrogant and conceited, but he had charmed rest of the family. Perhaps he would prove *sympathique* on their next meeting. She would give him one more chance.

Monday came, and Alfie was no sooner in the car than he began to plague his aunt.

'You promised.'

'No, you demanded.'

'Please? I can run across the fields, you don't have to come with me.'

'And what would your father say about that?'

'Why is it that everyone treats me as a baby?'

'Because Alfie, you are not yet six!'

'It's my birthday very soon. Please Tante, I want to learn to paint and I liked him, really and truly.'

'All right, all right,' she acquiesced as she always did where Alfie was concerned. 'I'll take you, but we'll drop the car at home first and walk.'

Les Volets Bleus, as its name suggested, had violet blue shutters, and as Gillie opened the gate into the cobbled forecourt, she remembered living there as a young child. She had loved it then and it was just as pretty now. The roof was low pitched, over creamy stone walls. The roses and lavender that had filled the flower beds in the summer months had given way to a selection of pink and white hellebores, and clumps of daffodils were beginning to open in the grass. There was a small wrought-iron archway that led the eye to the oak front door.

Alfie was hopping from one leg to the other. 'Monsieur Plaquet,' he called.

'I'm here beyond the vegetables patch,' came the reply.

Alfie turned and ran down the narrow brick path beyond the vegetable garden to the square of grass where Christophe had set up his easel. Another smaller one was placed at its side.

'So Alfie, this is yours and the bigger one is mine. Just like the Three Bears – except there is not a middle easel for your Tante Gillie.'

Alfie giggled. 'And we are not going to sit on the easels and break them like the Three Bears, are we?'

'No, we are not.'

Gillie came up the path behind him. She felt awkward. 'Alfie wouldn't stop nagging me, so here we are,' she said.

'Well I am extremely glad he nagged you, I was rather hoping you were looking forward to coming,' he teased.

'Yes, I mean, no.' She felt her cheeks redden. 'Is this your painting?'

'Unless someone else has stolen in during the night and painted the same landscape, then yes I believe it is.'

Why did he always make her feel so stupid, she wondered, avoiding his gaze. She looked at the half-finished canvas. It was a landscape, and the hills and vineyards beyond the garden were painted in thick, swirling daubs. It was rather like a Van Gogh, she thought, looking at the churning clouds in the foreground, the cows munching on the grass; in fact it was utterly compelling.

'It's good,' she mumbled. Then she looked up and their eyes met. 'Very good.'

'That is praise indeed.'

She was walking back down the path when he called after her.

'There's no point leaving, go inside and pour yourself a coffee or drink a glass of wine. Please make yourself at home.'

Gillie hesitated, biting back a retort that it really was her home. 'All right, but don't let Alfie get too cold.'

At that moment the poodle trotted towards them.

'You will have to negotiate with Hercule first,' he smiled.

While Christophe and Alfie began their lesson in the garden, Gillie went inside.

The house was just as she remembered. The L-shaped kitchen led onto a light and spacious sitting room. A fire had been laid in the large stone fireplace and it now burned in the grate. The ceiling was supported by white-washed beams. Books were scattered over a large kilim ottoman, and bright cushions were lying on the cream sofas. These were obviously Christophe's additions.

She made herself a cup of tea and sank onto the sofa. She wasn't prying, she thought, idly picking up the books, but it was interesting to see what he read.

Jean-Paul Sartre, Gide, Balzac, and a small leather-bound volume of Jane Austen's *Pride and Prejudice*. Gillie smiled. Christophe Plaquet's taste was certainly eclectic. For a brief moment she could envisage the discussion they might have.

Sartre's theory of existentialism had always fascinated her. And what about *Pride and Prejudice*, a romantic novel written in English? Gillie realised she wished to know more about the artist.

When Christophe came in with Alfie, her nephew's face was beaming as he put his canvas on the ottoman in front of her.

'It's fine Tante Gillie, the paint is dry.' He poked his finger into the orange sun. 'See? Christophe said I would get better with practice. Do you like it?'

'The gentleman's name is Monsieur Plaquet and yes, I like it very much.'

'He said I could call him Christophe, didn't you?'

'I most certainly did,' the artist patted his young pupil on the head.

'He is a good pupil, very receptive.'

Gillie stood up. 'You've been most kind, but we really should go. Alfie has homework to do, haven't you, *mon cheri*.'

'I could always do it in the morning?' Alfie grimaced. 'I don't like homework, Christophe.'

'Who does?' he agreed.

'*Viens petit*,' Gillie took hold of his arm. 'Like it or not, it has to be done.'

She was about to march him from the room when Christophe picked up the open book.

'You can learn a lot about a person from the books they read. Do you like Jane Austen, Gillie?'

She paused, because she loved her novels passionately, but she wouldn't reveal that to Christophe.

'Her novels are an acquired taste,' she said with an enigmatic smile. They were going out through the picket gate into the meadow when he called after them.

'Monday next, same time?'

'Yes please, Christophe,' Alfie replied.

As Gillie lay in bed that night, she wondered about Christophe Plaquet. He was annoying, attractive, extremely talented and apparently famous. It was no use lying to herself, she liked him. But post-war France was full of unmarried women. He could have anyone he chose – why on earth would he consider her?

The Hotel-Dieu de Beaune was more than a place of work to Gillie. She knew every patient's name and their history. The long-term patients became her friends. Every morning she spoke to each in turn, but now she was distracted.

'How are you feeling today?' she asked Monsieur Dabry, an old retainer who would never leave the hospital.

'Much better for seeing you,' he replied. 'You look particularly radiant today, *mademoiselle*. A young man is on your mind perhaps?'

'Nonsense,' she replied, but she was smiling because it was true. For the first time in years she felt that wonderful fluttering and sense of anticipation. She couldn't wait to be at the cottage on Monday ... She checked herself. She must stop this nonsense now.

She made it through the week and picked Alfie up from school on Monday afternoon.

'You look nice,' Alfie exclaimed, his head on one side. 'Something is different about you, Tante Gillie.'

'No, it's not.'

'I'll ask Christophe, he'll know what it is.'

Gillie shook her head a little too vehemently. 'That's not a good idea.'

If Alfie had noticed, so would Christophe. Once again she would look a fool. But it was true, she had taken hours putting on one dress, discarding it, trying another. The final outcome was a pale blue cashmere jumper and a pretty flared skirt. This time rather than gumboots, she wore shoes and stockings that showed off her long legs. Now she wished she had just worn slacks.

When they arrived at the cottage, she passed Alfie his coat and bobble hat and he jumped from the car.

'Christophe,' he called, running through the gate.

The artist came towards them. 'My young pupil and his lovely aunt.'

'She looks pretty doesn't she, Christophe?'

'Extremely.'

'Don't be so silly,' Gillie interjected.

'I'm not.' Christophe was looking at her, one eyebrow raised. She was convinced he was mocking her again. Fortunately Hercule arrived at that moment, and jumped up at her, diffusing further embarrassment.

Christophe had set up the easels in the same place, but this time he had put a chair under an apple tree nearby. He had put two rugs on the back.

'I thought you might like to see the young artist at work,' he said to her, picking up the rug and putting it around her shoulders. 'There is another for Alfie; we can't have you or your nephew getting cold.'

For the next ten minutes she observed both the young artist and Christophe. It seemed he had a natural aptitude for teaching, and it was obvious that Alfie was inspired.

'When you start, don't be worried about the little details; you need to paint the shapes of the hills first, and then the details later.'

'Is my tree better, Christophe?'

'It is, but only suggest the leaves with feathery strokes.'

Gillie smiled; she had been wrong about him. She admired the way he was so patient and kind to Alfie and there was a modesty that she hadn't noticed before. She had to admit to herself that he was an unusually handsome man. His features were not perfect, his nose was a little crooked, but the laughter in his eyes made his whole face light up. As he was leaning over Alfie, helping him with his brushstrokes, his shirt sleeves rolled up, she noticed his long artistic fingers and the soft hair on his suntanned arms.

A month passed before Gillie plucked up the courage to invite him to dinner at the house.

'Alfie would love you to meet his father. He comes home at weekends – are you able to join us for dinner on Saturday?' she asked.

'I'm so sorry,' he replied. 'I have to be in Paris this weekend. My mother wishes to see her dog.'

'I quite understand.' She turned away, trying not to let the disappointment show in her face. 'Perhaps we can arrange another time.'

She walked back across the fields with Alfie, her face burning. What had she been thinking? It was awful, humiliating. And what a pathetic excuse – his mother wanted to see the dog. He could at least have tried to be more inventive.

The following Monday, she dropped Alfie off and sped away in the car. Her mother had agreed to collect him.

She was walking Coco and Louis up the drive when her mother returned with Alfie and slowed down.

'Christophe was sad not to see you,' Alfie shouted when the car drew up beside her. 'He gave me this for you.' He leant over his grandmother and passed an envelope through the open window. 'He said I was not to read it.' He started to giggle. 'I think Christophe loves Tante Gillie, Grand-mère. He looked very sad when she did not come today.'

'Really?' Liliane's eyes lit up. 'Ahhh, Gillie I hope so, he is *tres charmant.*'

'Nonsense, both of you.' Gillie walked on, but she felt like laughing and crying at the same moment.

When the car continued up the drive, she tore open the envelope and pulled out a hand-drawn card.

In haste, Mademoiselle Gillie. Hercule is disappointed not to have seen you today. I can only hope, for his sake, that it was a pressing engagement.

Gillie started to laugh. The sketch of Hercule with his paws over his ears and extremely downcast eyes was enchanting. Christophe was infuriating but funny and she liked him so very much.

This time Gillie did not have to wait until Monday. She was walking up the hill the following morning when she heard a voice calling her name. Christophe was coming through the gate of Les Volets Bleus with Hercule at his side.

He caught up with her.

'Every morning I have waited to see if you would come this way.'

'You have?'

'I think you are avoiding me and I am not sure why.'

'Why would I avoid you?' She strode on up the hill, refusing to look at him.

Christophe laughed. 'You see, Hercule is on a lead, so he is unable to fornicate with Louis.'

'That is silly, he just needs to behave.'

'Hercule gives you the word of a poodle.'

Gillie was now laughing. 'Unclip the wretched dog and you can walk with me.'

She slowed her pace and they continued through the gate at the top of the hill and along a track to the vineyards. As they wandered through the recently pruned vines, Gillie's face was animated.

'Adeline tells me that I am just like my grandmother; do you think that is the case?'

'I rather hope not.'

'Why?' Gillie looked affronted.

'Your grandmother is quite formidable.' He grinned.

Gillie shook her head. 'When you know her better you will realise that she is actually as soft as butter. But, of course, if you threatened her vines...'

'I will avoid that at all costs.'

Gillie's expression grew serious. 'The vines have always been her passion. Now of course there is little to see, but in September, when the Pinot Noir grapes transform from green to purple and are reaching maturity, they are so beautiful.'

Christophe was looking at her intently and she blushed.

'Go on,' he said after a pause.

'I was Alfie's age when she first brought me up here to check if we were ready to harvest. It was five in the morning. I'll never forget her plucking a grape and savouring the taste. "Hmph," she said. "Somewhere between sugar and acidity. They are ready to be picked."' Gillie glanced at Christophe. 'There is only a small window of opportunity, you see. If you leave it too long, the starlings descend and there is no harvest to pick.'

'You adore her, don't you?'

'Of course I do.'

As they ambled back down the hill, Christophe asked her about Sebastian and Alfie, and she told him how her nephew had arrived in Pommard.

'I can't tell you the whole story,' she said, 'but rightly or wrongly, Sebastian felt it better if Alfie didn't know everything.'

'Ah,' he said. 'I hope that is the right decision.'

'I hope so too. One day Alfie may be angry.'

'That is a possibility. If I was Alfie I would want to know.'

They walked on in silence, and at the end of the track he turned to her. 'Why aren't you married?' he asked. 'A beautiful woman like you must have fought off a hundred suitors?'

Gillie kicked at a clod of earth. 'There was someone,' she said at last. 'But he died in the war.'

'I'm so sorry. That is terrible, I shouldn't have pried.'

She met his gaze. 'I am glad you did. I only learnt recently what had happened to my friend; he was shot at Fresnes. And you, Christophe, what is your story?'

Christophe cleared his throat and looked away. When he turned back, his face was tense.

'A less noble one, I'm afraid,' he said at last, picking up a stone and spinning it across the dry ground. 'I was engaged to be married, but two months before the wedding, I found my future wife in bed with another man.' He laughed harshly. 'He was very rich, of course; he was also one of my benefactors!'

'That is awful.'

'In hindsight the marriage would not have lasted, but at the time it was a painful experience. It has made me wary.'

'So if I ask you to join us for dinner again, are you going to say no?' Gillie asked, a slight edge to her voice.

Christophe looked at her. 'Ah, could this be the reason you avoided me? My mother is unwell, that is why I have Hercule here, but every month we go to Paris to visit her. And yes, I would love to come if you were to ask me again,' he said, his good humour returned.

Though Gillie was concerned for Christophe's mother, she was also delighted by his words. Christophe had been telling her the truth, and not just avoiding her.

The following Saturday, Gillie laid the table while Adeline cooked a feast. Gillie could see Alfie and Sebastian through the French doors. They were playing boules on the terrace below.

'I'm beating Papa,' Alfie cried, running up the wide stone steps towards her.

'He most certainly is not,' Sebastian laughed.

'I am, I am,' Alfie giggled. 'Can I stay up for supper, Tante Gillie?'

'No, darling.'

'Please, the colonel is coming, and Christophe.'

'No Alfie, you will do as your aunt says.' Sebastian followed his son, lifting him onto his shoulders.

'May I have a drink of lemonade and some crisps?'

'After you have cleaned your teeth, you little monster? You can come down and see everyone, then bed. Now let's go and see what Adeline is cooking.'

'Don't you steal any supper,' Gillie admonished.

'We wouldn't dare,' Sebastian replied.

There was a festive atmosphere in the house as they waited in the drawing room for Christophe to arrive. Gillie was wearing a mint green dress with a low neckline and jade earrings to complement her green eyes. Her brown hair was tied back in a ponytail. The result, she decided looking in the mirror, was passable.

The colonel was chatting to her grandmother.

'So Gillie,' her grandmother said, turning to scrutinise her, 'a little make-up I see. She looks extremely attractive, doesn't she Aramis? Don't kick me Liliane, what have I said?'

'You must not embarrass your granddaughter.'

'Ahh I see. How stupid, I am usually so quick. Could this have something to do with the artist?' She held out her glass for Sebastian to fill. 'I shall behave – I give you my word, *ma cherie*.'

The colonel looked at her, his eyes twinkling with amusement. 'Marie-Claire, you must.'

'I promise, Aramis,' she replied demurely, and everyone laughed.

When there was a knock on the door, Alfie darted from the room, determined to be Adeline. He grabbed Christophe's hand and pulled him into the drawing room.

'Papa is longing to meet you. Papa, this is Christophe. He is going to make me an artist aren't you, Christophe?'

Christophe laughed. 'I shall certainly do my best.'

Sebastian shook his hand. 'I have heard great things about you,' he said. 'Thank you for being so kind to Alfie.'

'*Avec plaisir.* Your son is delightful.'

'He is a good boy, aren't you, Alfie?'

Alfie nodded. 'So can I stay up for supper?'

'Absolutely not,' Sebastian laughed.

Liliane had done the seating plan. She had put her daughter next to Christophe, with Sebastian opposite and Marie-Claire on the other side. The colonel was sitting at the end of the table next to Marie-Claire.

The first course came in, then another. Adeline had excelled herself: a delicate crab mousse was followed by finely sliced chicken breasts dusted with flour and thyme and sprinkled with lemon juice. The dessert was Adeline's celebrated white chocolate *brulée* with raspberries.

Christophe chatted to everyone, shamelessly flattering Marie-Claire and bringing light to the old woman's voice. Gillie watched his smile, the way he lifted his glass. He had an effortless grace and she was mesmerised. Occasionally he turned to her and it was as if she was the only person in the room.

'Tell me your favourite painting?' he asked, when Marie-Claire had moved her attention to Aramis.

'Here?' she asked. 'Or anywhere?'

'We shall start with this room.'

Gillie knew immediately. It was a portrait of one of her

ancestors and her large green eyes were filled with maternal love for the baby in her arms.

'Let me guess,' Christophe suggested. His eyes slowly travelled the room, past the landscapes of Venice, the two pastoral scenes by the Dutch master Cuyp, the biblical painting by Bassano, then returned to the portrait.

'That is the one,' he stated. 'She has the look of you; not as beautiful of course, or as well formed. She is a little under-developed in certain areas.'

Gillie could feel her cheeks redden. 'Shhh.'

'Why? No one is listening. Would you ever sit for me, Gillie?'

'What do you mean?'

'You know what I mean. I want to paint you.'

'How?'

Christophe laughed, and it was a rich deep laugh and when everyone turned to look at him, he grinned like a schoolboy. For an instant Gillie was reminded of Étienne. She shook her head at the fleeting flash of recognition. Christophe was as unlike her former lover as anyone could be; it was obviously a reflection of her own growing feelings towards him.

His eyes met hers then he turned to Marie-Claire. 'Would you mind if I painted your granddaughter?' he asked.

'Mind?' Marie-Claire raised a delicate eyebrow. 'From all that Alfie tells me, you are *un génie*, so I'd be delighted, young man.'

'You are impossible,' Gillie whispered afterwards.

'But you haven't answered my question,' he replied.

When the guests had gone, Liliane and Marie-Claire retired for the night, while Sebastian and Gillie remained in the draw-ing room.

'You are taken with Christophe, aren't you?' Sebastian poured himself a cognac and sat down on the gilded *fauteuil*.

Gillie blushed. 'I hope you approve.'

'Since when would you take any notice of my opinion? But, yes, he seems thoroughly decent.'

'That sounds so English.'

'We are half-English, and I work there, remember.'

Gillie sat down beside him, her expression serious. 'I do care what you think, especially now.'

'Well then, dearest Gillie, he seems a good man. I just hope he is honourable.'

'I'm so afraid of being hurt, Sebastian.'

'But if you don't take a chance ...' Sebastian put his arm around his sister's shoulders and she leant against him. 'In life you have to take risks.'

'They don't always end well.'

'No, but that is life. Don't forget, I have had my share of heartbreak. But I am glad because without it I wouldn't have Alfie, and he is everything. But now I'm for my bed.' He kissed her cheek and stood up. 'But if I were a betting man, I would say he is smitten, and so he should be.'

Chapter Twenty-Five

Sebastian had left work early for a dentist's appointment in St James's. After yet another filling and a lecture from the dentist about fizzy drinks and chocolate, he went to the library.

There was a book he wanted: the new Nevil Shute, *The Rainbow and the Rose*. He was a fan of Shute's insightful, well-written adventures, and apparently this novel was no exception.

He found the book easily, wedged between a copy of plays by George Bernard Shaw and a novel by the Belgium writer, Georges Simenon. He opened the cover with the thrill of anticipation. Books were his enjoyment and a diversion when he was away from his son. Recently he had toyed with the idea of resigning from his job in London and returning to France, but the truth was he loved the work and his associates. So the weekly journeys to France continued, along with his solitary life.

He took the book to the counter and was looking in his wallet for his library card, when a girl's voice interrupted his thoughts.

'You'll like it, well at least I think you will. It's good.'

He looked up. 'Thank you,' he said smiling. And then he wasn't sure whether he was smiling because of the girl's comment or the girl herself. The first thing that struck him was the orange streak in her mid-brown hair. Then he noticed her eyes – green outlined with black coal, and her large hoop earrings.

She put her head on one side and started to quote from a poem.

'*When colour goes home into the eyes*
And lights that shine are shut again
With dancing girls and sweet birds' cries
Behind the gateways of the brain;
And that no-place which gave the birth, shall close
The rainbow and the rose.'

She reached the end of the verse and grinned. 'It's by the poet Rupert Brooke.'

Sebastian looked a bit vacant.

'The book's title!' She started to laugh, and it was a glorious laugh, wicked and irreverent.

'Sorry, that was rude,' she said, when she had stopped.

But Sebastian could see she wasn't sorry at all. She took the book from him and stamped it with a thump. He noticed her hands, slightly bony with long fingers.

He put the book in his briefcase.

'Three weeks,' she said as he was doing up the catch.

'Three weeks?'

'Before I have to stamp overdue on your card.'

Sebastian could see she was teasing him, but he could think of no witty reply.

'See you, then,' he said. 'In three weeks' time.'

When he was outside on the pavement he cursed himself. He had sounded pathetic and gauche. What the hell was wrong with him?

The following evening he was in the pub, when Robert dropped into the bench beside him, a beer in his hand.

'Sorry, late again.'

'No problem.'

'So what did you want to tell me?'

'It's about a girl, actually.'

Roberts eyes lit up. 'Where did you meet her?'

'When I say I've met her, we've had a brief conversation, that's all.'

'Come on, you're being elusive.'

Sebastian started to laugh. 'OK, so she works in the library, she said the book I took out was good.'

'That's all?'

Sebastian nodded.

Robert started to laugh. 'Well, is the book good?'

'It is rather. She's very unconventional. She has this orange stripe in her hair, and she spouts poetry.'

'She sounds perfect.'

Sebastian put down his empty glass. 'Anyone would be perfect to you. You are so desperate for me to have a wife.'

'Bring her to supper, Giulietta would love to meet her.'

'I think it's a little soon! Maybe I should take her for a drink first!'

The following Monday, Sebastian returned to the library. To his disappointment there was a different woman at the desk. He had returned the book and was just leaving when he bumped into the woman he was looking for. She was balancing a tray in one hand with a shopping bag in the other.

'Oh, it's you,' she smiled. 'Did you finish the book? You must have enjoyed it if you read it so quickly.'

'It was exceptional, thank you, but I have a question.'

'Yes?' There was a query in the girl's eyes and Sebastian couldn't help noticing that her legs, in a skirt that stopped short at her knees, were long like her hands.

'Would you like to come for a drink one evening?'

'Why not?' she laughed. 'When?'

*

Sebastian was pretending to read the newspaper as he waited for Amelia, but every so often, he glanced towards the door. It was a wet April evening and the panelled bar was packed. Office boys, secretaries, men from the city all crowded into the smoky room. When Amelia arrived and slipped into the wooden bench beside him, he realised to his horror that his newspaper was upside down.

She put her head on one side and tried to read the print, then she started to laugh.

'Umm,' he said, shaking his head. 'Not the best impression.'

'I disagree,' she giggled again.

'On that note and to hide my embarrassment I shall depart to the bar and buy you a drink. When I come back we can pretend this never happened.'

'A glass of Dubonnet and lemonade,' she requested with a grin.

'That sounds interesting, I'll try one too,' he said.

'So,' she said when he had returned, with two glasses and a bowl of peanuts, 'what next?'

Sebastian looked perplexed.

'What book are you going to read next?'

'I am rather hoping that you will advise me.'

One drink turned into three and Sebastian learnt that Amelia had recently finished her degree in English Literature at Cambridge.

'I was able to immerse myself in the subject I love, in unique libraries, in the most beautiful city. It was a rare privilege, Sebastian.'

'I felt the same at Oxford.'

'Ah, but you don't have the Pepys Library at Oxford. Imagine one of the most famous diarists in the world, recording history three hundred years ago. He recorded the Plague, the Fire of London – it's all there. His description is so vivid. It's as if it happened yesterday. Listen to this quote, Sebastian. It is so immediate.

'"This day much against my will, I did in Drury Lane see two or three houses marked with a red cross upon the doors."' Amelia leant towards him, her face passionate. 'I can actually feel his distress, can't you?'

'It is certainly compelling,' Sebastian agreed. 'Will you take me if I promise to show you the Bodleian Library? I believe it is a hundred years older than your Pepys Library, give or take a year or two!' There followed a healthy debate on the superiority of Oxford versus Cambridge, until they accepted that each university had its own merits.

'My job in the London Library is only a stepping stone. I want to get into the world of publishing, but my ultimate aim is to be an author.' Amelia was fiddling with her earring as she concentrated. 'I probably won't be a Virginia Woolf but I'd like to make my mark. Think, how wonderful it would be to see your own book on the library shelf!'

Sebastian couldn't really think of it, but he could think of Amelia. He liked her green eyes that she fixed on him intently and the ridiculous stripe in her hair. Even her boots that stopped above the ankle worn with red woolly tights were attractive. She had an outrageous quality and was totally individual. For the first time since Sophie, he began to have feelings for a girl.

When he returned back to his flat he had an urge to tell his sister about Amelia. He was delighted when she picked up the telephone.

'I think I've met someone,' he said immediately.

'Really?' Gillie sounded pleased, but not as excited as he expected.

'Tell me about her,' she continued.

'Well she works in the London Library, so she is obviously bookish – but funny, too. She is also extremely attractive.'

'I'd love to meet her, but perhaps not just yet.'

'Of course – I need to get to know her better.'

'Sebastian,' Gillie broke in, 'I'm so sorry, but I was literally about to telephone you. Grand-mère is unwell. As you know she has been coughing, but absolutely refused to see the doctor, now she has difficulty breathing. I am kicking myself because I am convinced she has pneumonia.'

'Oh God, and there I was rambling on.'

'Don't be silly, I'm thrilled for you.'

'I'm coming home,' Sebastian declared. 'I'll book my ticket immediately.'

'Wait until the doctor has been. We will know more then.'

Sebastian was with clients the following afternoon when his meeting was interrupted by Cheryl.

'Sorry, Mister Ogilvie,' she urged. 'Your mother needs to speak to you, she says it is important.'

Sebastian excused himself and rushed to the phone.

'Sorry darling, Gillie was right, it is pneumonia.' His mother's voice was stilted, as if she had been crying. 'I wouldn't worry you if it wasn't serious. It's happened so quickly and has taken us all by surprise.'

'I don't think I'll get a flight today, but I'll come tomorrow,' he said.

He flew to Paris the following afternoon and took the train to Beaune where Gillie was waiting for him.

'Is she really bad?' he asked.

'She's was asking for you and Pierre; she never asks for anyone.'

Pierre was sitting by the bed reading to Marie-Claire who lay propped against her pillows when he entered. Her gaunt face confirmed his fears.

'I hope you're feigning all of this,' Sebastian quipped, trying to control his emotions.

She shrugged. 'Always teasing your grand-mère.' She turned her head and with frail fingers patted Pierre's hand. 'What a joy to have all my family here at once; you would think this was a special occasion.'

'When I am with you, it is definitely a special occasion,' Pierre said, getting up. He brushed his hand across his eyes and hugged Sebastian.

'Lovely to see you my boy, I will leave you two together, but don't tire her.'

Sebastian shook his head and their eyes met, their grief shared.

After the door had closed, Sebastian perched on the edge of the bed and held her hand.

'*Ecoutez-moi.*' His grandmother pushed herself up in the bed, pausing for a moment to catch her breath. She fixed her rheumy gaze on her nephew.

'Soon the estate will be yours. It takes good management and cunning to hang onto it. I know you will carry on this tradition.'

'Don't worry yourself, Grand-mère.'

She held up her hand. 'Hush. I have said this before, but I need to say it again. Be firm, but more importantly, be fair. The world is changing, many of the young are moving to the cities. Encourage them to stay here.' She lay back on the pillows and closed her eyes.

'But Grand-mère, you don't need to tell me this because you are going to get better.'

Marie-Claire shook her head. 'This time, my dearest Sebastian, all the pills and potions in the world won't cure me. But please, don't grieve, I have had a fulfilling life, and a wonderful family. But I'm old for heaven's sake.' She started suddenly, her eyes flicking open. 'Don't be too soft with Alfie. Your son has a strong will that needs channelling in the right direction.'

Sebastian chuckled, his eyes shining with unshed tears. 'He has obviously inherited his great grandmother's spirit.'

Marie-Claire smiled. 'I certainly hope so. Now, go to the drawer in my dressing table, right-hand side. There is something I want you to have.'

Sebastian opened the drawer and took out a dark green box, trimmed with gold.

'Your grandfather's watch. You never knew him, but he was a good man. It's a Patek Philippe, rather valuable actually. One day you will pass it on to Alfie.'

Sebastian took it from the drawer and handed it to his grandmother.

'I want to put it on your wrist,' she said. 'But you may need to help me as my fingers no longer work as they should.'

Together they managed the crocodile strap.

She held his hand for a moment. 'I hope this will always remind you how much you have meant to me. Look after your mother. Gillie will need your support too. I do hope she marries that nice young artist.'

Sebastian stood up and kissed her forehead. 'Thank you, I shall treasure the watch and wear it with pride.' He was at the door when he went back to her and put his arms around her. 'Maman and Gillie are bringing you some of Adeline's famous broth.'

That evening Sebastian and Gillie walked through the vineyards together.

When they reached the top of a rise, they stood in silence and looked down over the terracotta roof tiles, towards the church tower and the distant hillsides beyond. There was a sense of permanence in the landscape, a sense of calm, which belied Burgundy's turbulent history.

'How will we manage without her?' Sebastian questioned.

'I'm not sure,' Gillie murmured, her voice bleak. 'She gave me this bracelet yesterday. She knows how much how I loved it as a child.' She drew back her coat to reveal the elegant art-deco diamond bracelet on her wrist. 'Not sure that it is appropriate for wearing to work, but I'll never take it off.'

'You will start a new fashion,' Sebastian smiled. 'And I have Grandfather's watch. She thought of everything, didn't she. Oh Gillie, it makes me so sad.'

Gillie tucked her arm through his. 'Let's try not to think about that now, *cheri*; she is still a force of nature, an integral part of our lives.'

'And when it does happen,' Sebastian murmured, 'we will support each other as we always do.'

They started to walk back down the hill and were nearing the house when Sebastian spoke again.

'Something happened yesterday, Gillie, and I am not sure what to think.'

Gillie glanced at her brother; he had an intense look in his eyes.

'I called in at the office on my way to the airport. Robert had a copy of *Time* magazine on his desk left by an American client. Guess whose face was on the front cover?'

'I have no idea,' Gillie said, drawing away from him, but she did have her suspicions.

'It was Sophie, larger than life. She kept to it, I'll give her that. "*Young Parisian Doctor Breaking the Boundaries.*"' Sebastian's jaw was clenched as he spoke, then he turned to Gillie. 'But I was furious with myself for the emotions it brought up.'

Gillie felt her throat tighten with guilt. She was in touch with Sophie without him knowing. Sophie had put her in an impossible situation, and one that was hard to disentangle, but she needed to tell him now. Her brother should know.

'I was so angry Gillie; this is the woman who had abandoned her son!'

'There is something you should know,' Gillie started to say, but Sebastian had gone, striding away from her, his hands buried in his pockets.

As Sebastian entered the house, his chest was pounding; all he could think of was the moment in the office the day before, when he had seen her face on the front piece of the magazine.

'Are you all right, old chap?' Robert had asked, alarmed at his friend's agonised expression.

'It's her,' Sebastian had gasped, picking up the magazine and pointing to the photograph, 'Alfie's mother.'

'Good Lord!' Robert had exclaimed.

'Bloody woman coming back into my life, like this.'

'She hasn't come back into your life, Sebastian, she has been interviewed by *Time* magazine, that's all.'

'What should I do?'

'Absolutely nothing,' Robert retorted. 'Read the article inside on Guy Singer's extraordinary skyscraper in downtown Manhattan, then throw the magazine away. It is quite a feat of innovation by the way.' Robert had got up and put his arm around Sebastian's shoulder. 'So sorry about your grandmother, I know how much she means to you. And I'm not being callous, but you have to understand, Alfie's mother is in the past and it is far better to keep it that way.' As Sebastian was about to close the door, he had called after him, 'Now don't go forgetting that gorgeous librarian.'

Sebastian had read the editorial on the aeroplane, his thoughts in turmoil. Sophie was training to be a heart surgeon in Paris, and would be one of the first women specialists in France. For a moment he was proud of her, she had fulfilled her dream. But Robert was right, he now had a charming eminently suitable girlfriend. He had put all thoughts of Sophie behind him and he must not open the door.

Sebastian shook his head, coming back to the present. He would change and go and see his grandmother. How he needed her wise council, her humour.

He entered her room and tiptoed over to the bed. She squeezed his hand.

'I love you my darling boy,' she whispered, 'but now it is the moment for me to talk to my priest.'

'Goodnight my dearest Grand-mère,' he said. 'I will go and fetch Pierre.'

They took it in turns to sit with Marie-Claire through the night. The next morning she was noticeably weaker, her hands and feet were very cold. She could take sips of water, but any movement exhausted her. It was time for Alfie to say goodbye. Sebastian brought him in with his aunt and he tried to be brave. 'Night night, Memé G,' he said for the very last time.

'Please be a good boy and remain as wonderful as you are,' she said, letting his little hand go. As he was led away his shoulders were shaking.

Having said her goodbyes Marie-Claire visibly relaxed, drifting in and out of sleep. When the porcelain clock chimed six she opened her eyes and requested the last rites.

As Pierre anointed her, he noticed her breathing was more irregular, the gaps between each breath becoming longer. At that moment, his role changed from being a priest to that of her son. After gathering the rest of the family together by her bedside, with Liliane holding her hand, she died an hour later supported in his arms.

Chapter Twenty-Six

The large church in Pommard was packed for the funeral of
Marie-Claire de Villienne. Under normal circumstances the two
hundred and fifty seats would be half full, but today every pew
was filled to capacity, and at least fifty people had to stand at the
back. There were farmers with their families, growers, labourers,
friends. There was even an aged American army veteran, who
had been her student at the temporary university in Beaune, set
up at the end of the First World War. In her long life, Marie-
Claire had touched so many people's hearts.

She had left few instructions, but one of them was clear:

'I would like a party to celebrate my life, it is not a time to
mourn. Please, no black, I have always hated it.'

Liliane had done the flowers and the scent of early sweet
peas and peonies filled the air. This time, Jean had raided his
garden gladly; they were flowers for Marie-Claire de Villienne,
his mentor, his employer and his friend.

As Pierre stepped into the pulpit and looked at the sea of
faces in front him, he breathed deeply. He had presided over
many funerals before, but the sheer force of his grief had taken
him by surprise. His beloved mother Marie-Claire was a woman
before her time.

His father had died when he was thirteen, but as an officer

in the French army, he had rarely been at home. Until Liliane's marriage to Jasper, it had been just the three of them. Marie-Claire had not only read to them, but she had joined in their imaginary games involving the characters in the stories. She had taught them to swim in the lake, disciplined them in the art of fencing. In fact, she had taken on the role of mother and father and she had given them a wonderful, carefree childhood.

He remembered riding with her through the vineyards on one of his visits home, listening to anecdotes told in her melodious voice. 'Now that was a marvellous year,' she had said, her eyes lighting up as she described the harvest of 1929. 'But of course 1937 was the truly outstanding year.'

As they trotted along, she had recounted how they had hidden their wine for the duration of the war. 'Do you see, Pierre, the cave?' She pointed to the entrance of an ancient cave in the hillside. 'That is where we stored the best barrels. When they were safely inside, we bricked up the entrance and rolled a huge boulder in front of it. Every man in the village helped, including the plough horses of course. Jean's father was in charge in those days, and like his son he enjoyed a good story. It became the village secret, it was marvellous.' She had laughed suddenly; a warm, infectious laugh. 'We bottled the residue we normally gave to the pigs and stored those in the racks for the Boches to find. I even had to share one with an officer. It was quite disgusting. They certainly didn't get the better of us.' She had turned to Pierre, her face lit with excitement. 'Oh Pierre, the war may have been ghastly, but our little secret was such fun.' Then she had spurred on her horse and they had cantered back to the house.

As Pierre opened his prayer book and traced his finger down the page, he remembered their parting words before she died.

'You and your sister have been the greatest joy in my life,' she had told him. 'I could not have wished for a better and more loving son.'

'And you,' he had said taking her fragile hand, kissing it gently, 'gave everything to us.'

She had tutted softly. 'My sadness is that you lost your one chance of personal happiness, when you have given so much to others. But I am proud of your devotion to the church. Now, you must let me go my dearest Pierre, it is my turn to meet your God.'

Pierre raised his eyes to meet the congregation. 'We are here to celebrate the life of Marie-Claire de Villienes, mother, wife, grandmother, vintner, and the heart of our family.'

After a moving dedication given by the colonel, who at times had to pause to regain his equilibrium, the mourners returned to the house for a reception in the courtyard outside the beautiful vaulted winery. While waiters moved discreetly through the assembled company serving drinks, men in blazers and women in light dresses mingled in the April sunshine. At some point during the afternoon, Liliane ushered her guests into the cool and dimly lit interior of the winery, and Sebastian stepped onto a podium at the front.

'Welcome,' he began. 'My grandmother was an exceptional woman. Most of you, indeed probably all of you, have witnessed her humour, her charm and her indomitable will. How many times have you seen her achieve the impossible? She guarded her wine almost as fiercely as she has guarded her family, and it is entirely due to this extraordinary woman that the vineyards are flourishing. It is testament to her popularity that there are so many of you here today. If she were with us, she would insist that you were not here to mourn, but here to celebrate a life well lived.' He raised his glass. 'To Marie-Claire de Villienne.'

The crowd raised their glasses and toasted the remarkable woman they all loved.

'My grandmother gave me strict instructions to open only the best burgundy today and to keep the wine flowing.'

There was laughter from the gathering. Sebastian stepped down and went to his mother's side.

'I can see many of Maman's traits in you,' she said. 'Don't you agree, Pierre?'

Pierre smiled. 'He has her will and her vision.'

'Thank you, Uncle. I have learnt so much from my family, especially from you.'

'But you are also your own person,' he replied. 'I have watched you grow from a sensitive boy to a gifted young man. The estate is in the best of hands.'

When Sebastian had left in search of the colonel, Liliane and Pierre walked outside. Liliane's stoic demeanour collapsed as soon as they were out of view of the guests.

'I can't bear it, Pierre, she has always been here, and now ... I wasn't prepared for this. Of course I should be, she was old, but she seemed ageless.'

'We are never prepared for it,' Pierre sighed. 'But just think of our mother as a gift we have had, not one that we have lost.'

'I'll try,' she said, pulling out a handkerchief and wiping her eyes. 'Do you remember the times she had to scold me for some prank or other.'

'Remember, how could I forget?' Pierre laughed. 'You dyed her favourite grey mare's tail pink if I recall, and another time, you taught your pony to come up the steps and into the hall; unfortunately it ate Maman's flower arrangement.'

Liliane laughed. 'She pretended to be cross, but I think she was secretly proud of me.'

'Probably.'

'Perhaps now is the time for Sebastian to return to France, permanently,' Liliane said, her voice growing stronger.

'It must be his decision,' Pierre replied.

They wandered towards the lake and as a flight of ducks glided towards them, their feet skimming the still water, Liliane took her brother's arm. 'Today you are not a priest, you are my brother, so I can ask you this. Did you ever want to run the estate? To take up the reins?'

Pierre looked at her for a moment, weighing up the possibilities. Should he tell her that he had once loved a woman deeply, passionately; he had wanted to bring her here as his wife. Should he reveal that the thought of having children with her had kept him going through one of the most terrifying periods of the Great War. He slowly shook his head.

'No, my dearest sister, I gave myself to God.'

Sebastian found the colonel sitting on an upturned barrel at the other end of the winery where the barrels were stored.

'I used to help your grandmother with the harvest,' he said looking up at Sebastian, his blue eyes bleary. 'My wife was long dead of course, and your grandfather. We always got a little tipsy during the festivities at the end.'

Sebastian sat down beside him.

'I've never told anyone before, but I have always loved her,' he confided in a hushed tone.

'I know,' Sebastian replied.

'Really?' the old man was surprised. 'I thought I was discreet.'

'Always discreet,' Sebastian smiled.

While Sebastian consoled the colonel, Gillie and Christophe wandered into the small private garden at the side of the house. It was enclosed by a high yew hedge planted by Marie-Claire.

'It's my little retreat,' the old woman had announced. 'No visitors are allowed.' Visitors, however, did not mean children. She would take her children, grandchildren and then great-grandchild to play within the verdant green walls. Soon a chicken hutch was installed, housing five *Poule de Marans*, and the children's favourite pastime was collecting the chocolate brown eggs. Each successive generation had listened to her stories, some from her imagination, others from an old copy of *Grimm's Fairy Tales*, but all told from the stone bench where Christophe and Gillie were now seated.

'Thank you for coming to the funeral,' Gillie said, leaning against him.

'Your grandmother was a special woman,' Christophe murmured into her hair. 'I had grown extremely fond of her. I know you will miss her, Gillie, but she would not want you to be sad. Think of her as just a step away from you.'

'I'd like to believe that.'

'Then you must.'

'Are you religious?' She sat up and looked at him.

'I believe in God if that is what you mean, but I don't like what is done in the name of religion.'

'Christophe Plaquet, I learn more about you each day.'

Christophe's smile was gentle. 'There is a lot more to me than you realise, Gillienne.'

'When I first saw you, you made me so mad.'

'And now?' he asked.

'I think you know the answer to that,' she smiled.

Christophe was leaving later that evening, when he collected a cardboard tube from the hall table. He gave it to Gillie.

'This is for you my love,' he said. 'To remind yourself that your grandmother is only a step away.'

Gillie opened the tube and pulled out a roll of art paper. It was a charcoal sketch of her grandmother. Not only was it a very good likeness, Christophe had captured her wry humour and her spirit.

She had tears in her eyes as she kissed him. 'Thank you, Christophe, it means everything,' she said.

*

Sebastian had resumed his London commute and life had returned to some sort of normality, but to the family, the Chateau Villienne seemed empty without Marie-Claire. Alfie continued his painting lessons with Christophe. They gave him something to look forward to.

'It's horrid and quiet,' he said, painting big black clouds in the sky.

'Why clouds?' Christophe had asked him. 'It's a lovely day.'

'Because it doesn't feel lovely, Christophe. I have an unhappy feeling here.'

He patted his chest and Christophe smiled.

'That means your grandmother is in your heart,' he said. 'I'll tell you what, today we shall paint everything black: black houses, black cats, black flowers.'

'Black sheep?' Alfie interjected.

'Yes, black sheep too.'

For the next half an hour great daubs of black paint took shape on Alfie's canvas.

'There,' he said putting down his brush. 'Done.'

'Excellent. Let's go inside and find your aunt. We will have a cup of tea.'

'I don't drink tea, Christophe.'

'Silly me,' Christophe grinned. 'Of course you don't. Let's see what I have in the cupboard.'

Soon Christophe, Gillie and Alfie were having apple juice and biscuits around the kitchen table.

They walked back across the meadows together, Alfie throwing sticks for Hercule.

'That was so very thoughtful,' Gillie said, holding onto his hand.

'Poor little chap needed some distraction.'

'We both do,' she sniffed. 'Nothing is the same without my grandmother's presence.'

'We are here for a short time, and then we go. Be grateful for the time you had with her. Pose for me Gillie, that will be a distraction.'

She looked at him. 'What kind of pose?'

Christophe laughed. 'Much as I would love you to take your clothes off, I mean a head and shoulders portrait.'

'I didn't think anything else,' she blushed. Even now, Christophe could manage to make her feel uncomfortable.

'Well, will you? You have such an interesting face.'

'What sort of interesting?'

'You have high cheekbones, with wide eyes, and your mouth is probably a little too large, but the combination of your features works well together.'

Gillie started to laugh. 'Well, I asked for that. When shall we start?'

'Tomorrow evening? I'll cook you supper afterwards.'

Gillie wore a simple shift dress that buttoned down the front, and flat pumps. As she looked at herself in the mirror, she imagined Christophe's hands on her shoulders, his lips caressing the nape of her neck. She carefully applied a dab of lipstick and a little mascara. It would have to do, she thought as she walked across the meadow, her embroidered summer bag over her shoulder. The fluttering of nerves that had started as she dressed were now taking over, but she had to remain composed. Any hope of this was derailed when Christophe strode from the house to meet her.

'My muse,' he said, smiling.

'Hardly.'

'Definitely.' He was looking at her, one eyebrow raised.

'Will I do?' she asked, feeling awkward.

'Come inside and we'll see.' He sat her on a chair on a small podium and stood in front of her assessing her.

'Sorry,' he said, 'but I want your shoulders bare. You agreed, remember.'

She unbuttoned the top of her dress revealing her neck.

'No, that won't do. Go into my bedroom, there is a dressing gown hanging on the back of the door. Remember to take off your brassiere.'

Gillie went into the bedroom. *Why did I agree to this?* she thought as she unclipped the strap. She slipped on the paisley robe, noticing the faint smell of amber and lavender that clung to the silk.

Edith Piaf was playing on the record player as she returned and climbed back onto the podium.

'This will make you relax,' he said putting a glass of wine in her hand.

'You like "*Je ne regrette rien*", I assume?'

Gillie nodded and held her breath as Christophe gently removed the robe from her shoulders.

'Why would you want to hide from me?'

'I don't,' she stuttered, taking a gulp of wine.

As she finished the glass, a warm feeling replaced her nerves. Christophe arranged her hair, his fingers touching her skin. She shivered involuntarily.

'Sorry, cold fingers,' he said, but it wasn't the cold; she wanted him to touch her again.

'Now you look truly beautiful,' he said, standing backwards, his head on one side, and Gillie smiled, for he was only the second man in her life who had made her feel beautiful.

For the next hour Christophe concentrated on his painting. She was leaning against the cushion, her head thrown back, her lips slightly parted.

'So,' he said, 'enough for one day. Now you can go and put your clothes back on.'

'May I see?'

'Absolutely not,' he said, laughing. 'That is entirely against the rules. But I will make you supper, like I promised.'

Gillie had never been cooked for by a man. Étienne made the occasional baguette filled with black market salami, but she had done all of the cooking on the gas ring in the flat kitchen, with whatever ingredients were available at the time. As she watched Christophe dice the mushrooms and beat eggs to make an omelette, she felt a wave of longing. She had to pull herself together, she thought, taking another sip of wine.

The omelette was followed by cheese, fresh bread and strawberries. As Christophe walked her home afterwards, Gillie realised she did not want to go. If he had asked her, she would have gladly stayed with him, slept with him, discarded every bit of clothing.

Gillie sat for him the following week, and for two weeks after that. Still he had made no advances.

'He obviously doesn't like me,' she whispered to herself, as she arrived home after the fourth sitting, tears of humiliation stinging her eyes. That night she dreamt of Christophe. She could feel his hair brushing against her face, her mouth parting beneath his, his body against her. The dream was so vivid, that when she woke up, she was filled with longing.

On the fifth sitting Christophe came up to the podium until he was standing in front of her.

'So,' he said. 'Do you want to see it?' He turned the easel around and she gasped.

The woman in the painting was not her, it couldn't be. This woman had golden lights in her brown hair and her green eyes were open with invitation. Her creamy white skin was luminous, the dressing gown just covering the top of her breasts.

'It's . . .' She didn't know what to say.

'I will tell you about the woman in the painting,' he said, putting his hands on the collar of her dressing down. 'She is the most sexy, beautiful creature I have ever met. And the extraordinary thing is, she doesn't know it.'

'Me?' she asked at last.

'You.' Christophe pulled her towards him and slipped the gown from her shoulders burying his face in her soft skin. He released her for a moment and went to the gramophone, chose a record and put it on.

Erik Satie's 'Once Upon a Time in Paris' drifted across the room.

Gillie stood in front of him while he undid the silk tie from her waist. 'I have dreamt of seeing all of you,' he said, tracing his finger from her neck right down to her stomach. 'I just wanted to wait until the painting was finished.'

With that, Gillie allowed a smile to cross her face as she tilted her face to kiss him.

The following morning Gillie crept through the back door and into the kitchen of the Chateau de Villienne. It was at six o'clock, and she would be in good time to take Alfie to school.

'Hush,' she giggled when Louis and Coco leapt up to greet her. 'It's too early for a walk.'

Slipping up the back stairs, she tiptoed quickly past her mother's bedroom. The wireless was playing, and the door was ajar. She caught a brief glimpse of Liliane sitting in her favourite chair by the window. The newspaper was open in her lap and she was doing the crossword from the day before.

As Gillie ran the hot water and put her toe in the bath, there was a lightness in her body and a feeling of joy. Everything had changed, the world felt different, she felt different. She leant backwards, replaying every moment of the night. Although she had believed herself to be in love with Étienne, their encounters were brief and hurried. They were moments snatched in a period of great danger. Their lovemaking was frantic and desperate, always knowing each moment could be their last.

This atmosphere of trepidation left little time for romance. But with Christophe there was all the time in the world and they explored each other slowly and tenderly. It was so different to anything she had experienced before.

Chapter Twenty-Seven

April 1959

Marie-Claire had been a constant in Sebastian's life and he missed her dreadfully. Even during the war, her letters had arrived in England with surprising regularity. Now she was gone, and it seemed his drive had gone with her. He was in his flat one evening after work, a letter from his grandmother open on the desk in front of him. He could remember the exact moment in June 1944 when he had received it. He had just finished breakfast at his school in Yorkshire, and Wednesday was post day. Grabbing the cream envelope from the hall table he had rushed up to his dormitory, tearing it open.

> *Mon cher Sebastian,*
> *We have just heard that your father has been wounded but he is alive. His injuries are not life-threatening apparently, but we shall know more very soon. As I write, your mother is driving down to the hospital in Normandy having acquired some petrol from one of our guests!* – 'guest' was their code for the German officers billeted at the chateau – *We will let you know just as soon as we have any news. But try not to worry dearest boy, he will be all right I am sure of it.*

Anyway keep safe, be good and when you see that horrid uncle of yours in his equally horrid house, be sure to play a trick on him. That will keep your spirits up!

Fondest love

Grand-mère

As Sebastian put the envelope back in his desk, he recalled the flurry of letters that had arrived in the following weeks, from both his mother and his grandmother, but it was his grandmother's coded letters that had made him smile.

Adeline continues to produce the most delicious feasts for our guests, in the way only Adeline can. This was also a code for the Germans getting the worst cuts of meat, if of course they had any. *Last week your mother instructed Adeline to use a generous amount of starch on the Captain's sheets! He told us he had the most uncomfortable night – I can't imagine why.*

How Sebastian missed her; but she wouldn't want him to grieve, she would want him to get on with his life.

He grimaced, returning to the present. He had been getting on with his life, until Sophie's photograph had appeared on the front of the magazine. Why after all this time had it unsettled him? Why could he think of little else? On this occasion he hadn't travelled to France to find her, instead he had picked up the telephone.

'You are the tenth man claiming to be the doctor's relative,' Todd's assistant had said, answering the long-distance call. 'Sorry we can't give you access to any private information.'

Sebastian had thanked her and was about to put down the receiver when her tone had changed. 'One moment,' she had said. 'You can leave a message for Mr Dexter and I will make sure he gets it. It was his editorial, but he is also the doctor's boyfriend; he may be happy to help.'

Sebastian's disappointment was mixed with relief. Sophie had moved on and so had he. He would contact Amelia, make up for his neglect and take her out to dinner if she agreed.

He dialled the number and a stranger picked up the phone. 'Is Amelia there?' he asked.

'Who can I say is calling?'

'Sebastian,' he replied. He could hear an intake of breath from the girl at the other end, then a pause and her muffled voice as she covered the mouthpiece with her hand.

'It's the bloody Frenchman. Do you want me to get rid of him?'

'It's all right, I'll speak to him.' At last Amelia came to the phone.

'Hello, I thought you had dropped off the planet.'

'I am so sorry.'

'You stood me up. The theatre, remember? I waited in the foyer for you, it was most embarrassing.'

'Oh my God, I had completely forgotten,' Sebastian apologised, appalled. 'My grandmother was dying, and I went straight back to France.'

'Oh.' There was a pause on the other end of the line. 'I'm so sorry to hear about your grandmother.'

'You have to believe me, in the panic it completely slipped my mind. Can I make it up to you?'

'Probably not.'

'Not even a quick drink?' he begged.

He could hear the girl who had answered the phone in the background.

'Tell him to bugger off.'

Then he heard Amelia's giggle. 'Sorry, I expect you caught that.'

'I did actually.'

'All right – I suppose a drink won't hurt. The Red Lion, Duke of York Street, near the library, six thirty tomorrow.'

Her voice was suddenly concerned. 'So did she die? Your grandmother?'

'Yes, Amelia, I am afraid she did.'

Sebastian was waiting at a table near the door when Amelia arrived. She was wearing tartan slacks and a black polo neck jersey. She looked enchanting, Sebastian thought, waving at her.

'Hello.' She settled into the bench opposite.

'What would you like to drink?'

'A glass of wine.'

By the end of the evening, Amelia seemed to be enjoying herself.

'I'm not going to ask you in,' she said, when he dropped her off at her flat. 'Susan doesn't like you very much.'

'I sort of got that.'

She grinned, and the smile lit up her face. 'Can you blame her?' She twiddled with a piece of orange hair. 'Anyway, look, I've been invited to watch this new singer recording an album at Abbey Road Studios next Wednesday. Cliff Richard, I think his name is. Do you want to come?'

Amelia and Sebastian saw each other whenever they could. Sebastian found her refreshing. She was honest, funny and entirely individual, her wardrobe was occasionally traditional, but more often completely eccentric. She delighted Robert and Giulietta when they invited her for supper.

'So,' Giulietta had asked, after putting the first course on the table. 'I hear you are going to be a writer, but first a librarian?'

'I dream of being a writer,' Amelia had replied, putting down her fork. 'So what better way to begin than being surrounded by books. When the library is empty I can read. Your great Italian poet and philosopher Leopardi is my latest adventure.'

'He is?' Giulietta was leaning forward, a wicked smile on her face. 'So here is a wonderful quote: "*Children find everything in nothing; men find nothing in everything!*"'

The two girls started to giggle, and Robert glanced at Sebastian.

'I see you two are now going to gang up on us men.'

'Of course,' Giulietta replied.

The two men had grinned at each other. It was obvious the girls would become friends.

Sebastian was about to say goodbye when he drew his friend aside. 'You are about to get an invitation to Chamonix for my 30th birthday in June,' he said in a hushed tone. 'It was my grandmother's idea, I'll explain another time.'

'Sounds exciting.'

'But there is something else, Robert: at last I am going to attempt Mont Blanc. Marcus Donadieu is coming. No chance you could join us, I suppose?'

Robert's face was wistful. 'I'd adore to, you know that, but with very little help with the children, I'm afraid I can't be away for so long. We will of course come for your birthday.'

'What about a training expedition in the Brecon Beacons next weekend?' Sebastian asked, a winning expression on his face.

'I might get away with that,' Robert laughed.

'Amelia is perfect for you,' Robert said at work the following day. 'She is captivating and that streak in her hair is outrageous.'

'It is rather.' Sebastian looked up from a set of plans he was working on. 'She's so refreshing, and I agree the stripe in her hair is crazy, but I love it. I wish she could have met my grandmother. They would have chatted for hours.'

'Are you asking her to Chamonix?' Robert queried, collecting some photocopying from the large Xerox machine in the corner of the office.

'You don't think asking her to my birthday party sends the wrong signals?'

'It depends what your intentions are.'

Sebastian put down his pencil. 'I like her, Robert, truly, but something is always holding me back.'

'You mean someone?'

'I suppose so. I know it's mad, but sometimes I have these dreams, they are as clear as anything, Sophie is with me, we are a family.'

'I thought you were angry with her.'

'When I saw her face on the magazine cover, I was, but now...? I just can't seem to let her go entirely. Does that make sense?'

'Be grateful to her for Alfie, but for God's sake forget her. She has caused you enough pain and you must move on with your life.' He picked up a file from his desk, adding the new paperwork. 'I'll see you later, Sebastian, I have a meeting with our accountants at noon. Oh and by the way I can come with you to the Brecon Beacons next weekend. A bit of endurance training will be a welcome change from children's homework on a Saturday morning.'

'Fantastic,' Sebastian grinned. 'Alfie is staying with a little boy from school, so it's perfect timing for me.'

After Robert had gone, Sebastian scribbled some notes and set off for Bethnal Green in the east end of London. This large project involved close cooperation between his firm, Blackheath Holdings, the London County Council and the Metropolitan Borough Council. It went beyond the normal involvement of regional and local authorities because politically it was close to their idealistic aims. On this occasion they were using a well-known firm of English architects and in a short time, the first six-storey apartment block would be finished. Another two were in the pipeline for the following year. Sebastian's desire was not only to provide well-built housing for the working classes, but the two-acre plot would offer green space outside, and attractive communal areas within the buildings themselves. He was determined that the increasing problem of isolation in many of the high-rise blocks would be avoided.

As he walked from the tube, past the remaining bombed-out buildings and temporary prefabricated houses, he hoped that before too long, the last of these would be swept away and the residents of Bethnal Green would have housing to be proud of.

He arrived at the site, put on his hard hat and climbed the ladder to the second floor to meet Elliot, his foreman.

'Morning boss,' Elliot beamed, coming through the windowless shell towards him. 'Plenty of breeze blowing today.' Elliott was one of the first post-war immigrants to arrive from Jamaica on board the *Empire Windrush*. His father had been a carpenter and he had passed his ability to his son. Elliot had done an apprenticeship with the construction company Taylor Woodrow, widening his skills, before moving as foreman to Blackheath Holdings. His ability had put paid to any prejudice against him.

Sebastian pulled his jacket closer. 'You are right there, Elliot,' he said. 'It certainly doesn't feel like the end of April.'

'The windows arrived yesterday.' Elliot scratched the end of his nose. 'The men are unpacking them now.'

'That's late. I hope you gave the supplier a talking-to.'

'I did, sir, a resounding reprimand, but if we had used wood...'

Sebastian laughed. 'That's the carpenter in you. Aluminium is more practical, and your windows will never need painting.'

'Yes boss,' he said, a smile on his face. 'Whatever you say.'

After inspecting the cavity walls, Sebastian went through his schedule. The apartments were going to have central heating and each flat would have its own bathroom. The level of comfort in Chamberlain Court would hopefully be beyond the tenants' expectations.

He left the building site and returned to Bruton Street, looking forward to seeing Amelia at the end of the day.

They had arranged to meet outside the cinema, to see the Hitchcock thriller everyone was still talking about. *Vertigo* was a year old and he still hadn't seen it. As Amelia walked towards him, Sebastian had to suppress a grin. She reminded him of his favourite childhood cartoon character, Bambi, with her long legs and fragile build.

'Hello,' she kissed his cheek, pulling off her newsboy hat so that her long hair tumbled out.

'Hello you,' he said. 'Let's go inside.' An hour later Amelia was still beguiling him. One moment she was leaning forward, glued to the screen, the next she was burying her head in his shoulders, shaking with terror. This frightening film was definitely a good idea, he thought with a smile.

Afterwards they went out to dinner in a little French restaurant in Piccadilly and another hour flew by. They discussed poetry, authors, architects. Amelia kept him amused with stories from her time at Cambridge and more recent anecdotes from her job at the library.

'It's often the most famous authors who are the worst,' she said, scrunching up her nose in the way that she did when she was thinking. 'I was called Stripey, last week. I mean, Stripey, who the hell did she think she was?'

'Well I am beginning to care for Stripey rather a lot,' Sebastian confessed, taking her hand over the table. 'And I actually like the name.'

'Well, I don't,' she giggled, drinking her glass of champagne. 'I need a superior, bookish name. Stripey Stormont doesn't actually have a very good ring to it.' She put down her glass. 'Do you really like me, Sebastian?' she asked, her eyes suddenly serious. 'I mean, you are so damn attractive and I'm just me.'

'You are beautiful, Amelia, and yes I mean it.'

'You won't hurt me, will you?'

'Why would I hurt you?'

'I really minded when you stood me up.'

'You know it was a mistake, but I promise I won't do it again.'

They were leaving the restaurant when he caught her hand. 'Well who was it, I'm intrigued!'

She looked at him perplexed.

'The author who called you Stripey?'

'Oh, I can't tell you that,' she giggled.

'Spoilsport!' he smiled.

As Sebastian dropped her at the door of her flat, and kissed her on the lips, he couldn't wait to see her again.

Numerous dates later, Amelia arrived at his flat with a carrier bag of shopping in one hand and a bundle of books in the other. She put them down on the counter.

'So,' she said, pulling out an assortment of lentils, pulses and vegetables that made Sebastian's heart sink. 'Let's hope cooking is the way to a man's heart.'

He put his hands about her slender waist. 'We'll have to see about that.'

'Not now you won't,' she laughed, pushing him away from her.

Sebastian was smiling as he uncorked a bottle of wine. Since Amelia had come into his life, a few feminine touches had been added to the drawing room. Brightly coloured cushions now scattered the grey Heal's sofa, and a bunch of anemones filled a vase on the windowsill. The two Giacometti sculptures of a man and woman had been moved to stand on the modern walnut sideboard. His mother Liliane had found the elongated figures in Paris shortly after the war. She had visited the sculptor's studio and had been intrigued not only by the shambolic sculptor with the mass of dark hair, and clothes spattered with paint, plaster, even bits of paper, but also by his studio where he had created magic amongst the debris of rubbish that littered every surface. The sculptures were Sebastian's pride and joy, but he had to admit their new placing suited them admirably.

'You're clever,' he had said, stroking Amelia's neck as he surveyed the open-plan room. 'Though I liked my suitably masculine and sophisticated flat before, it is more welcoming now.'

They had supper that night with candles burning on the table and as he ate Amelia's lentil stew, followed by apple crumble, he smiled to himself. This was the third time he had sampled Amelia's cooking, and it didn't get better. Though she was a wonderful girl, she definitely wasn't a chef.

As he helped her to clear up afterwards, he came to a decision. He would ask her to marry him before they went to Chamonix. Amelia was bright, sweet, Alfie had liked her when he had met her – they had certainly bonded over her vegetarianism. He groaned to himself; meat would be banned from their table and what would Adeline say about that! He hadn't made love to her yet, not because he didn't want to – when he thought of her small pointed breasts with pale nipples and her delicious long legs, he was filled with desire – but each time they came near, she had stopped him.

'Not yet,' she had said with a small smile, and Sebastian had been left in no doubt of what 'not yet' meant.

Without doubt Amelia Stormont would make him a good wife and she would be a great mother to Alfie. She was the sort of girl who would run Chateau Villienne superbly, and she could write her novels from anywhere in the world. There was in fact only one person who may not appreciate the arrival of a bookworm vegetarian and that was Adeline.

The week before they were due to go to Chamonix, Sebastian took Amelia out to dinner at his favourite restaurant, Kettner's in Soho. They were halfway through the main course of asparagus risotto when Sebastian put down his knife. 'I've got it!' he exclaimed.

'Got what, Sebastian?'

'Botticelli's *Venus*.'

'Now you are being obtuse.'

'You, Amelia Stormont, are Venus.'

Amelia smiled, her eyes lighting up. 'The goddess Venus, blown by the west wind, Zephyr to the shore of her homeland Kithera. Well I am extremely flattered. Apart from the fact that she is as naked as the day she was born, she is extremely beautiful.'

'Let's go and see her,' Sebastian suggested. 'And I can prove it to you.'

'You want to take me to Italy?'

'I certainly do.'

'I would love that, Sebastian, I've always wanted to go there.'

'Then it's settled.'

Amelia looked up, her eyes teasing. 'I suppose you will want me to be naked on a shell to make the final analysis.'

'Definitely,' Sebastian declared.

Sebastian finished the last of his risotto with a smile on his face. Amelia was definitely going to keep him on his toes for the rest of his life. She was well read, bright and beautiful. Alfie would definitely grow to love her. He could feel the small box in his pocket. He would give her the ring tonight, ask her to be his wife.

It was not the ring his mother had sent him; for some reason Marie-Claire's didn't seem appropriate. Perhaps it was too old-fashioned, he thought, or perhaps there was another reason.

They had finished dinner and were having coffee when he put the box on the table.

'I have something I want to ask you,' he said.

She looked at the box and back at Sebastian.

'The thing is, Amelia "Stripey" Stormont, I've grown rather fond of you.'

'Yes?'

'Well, very fond actually.'

'Go on, Sebastian.'

She was leaning forward staring at the box. 'Are you about to get down on one knee or something?'

'In here?'

Amelia was looking at him with a mixture of humour and adoration but for some reason, the joy had gone out of the moment. This was not the time for flippancy; this was the most important question of his life.

'Amelia Stormont, would you do me the honour of becoming my wife?'

'Of course I will,' she replied. Sebastian opened the box, took the solitaire from its velvet bed, and slipped it onto her finger.

'It's beautiful,' she exclaimed, and the waiter stopped at their table with a bottle of champagne. While the other diners clapped and cheered, and his future bride flung her delicate arms around his neck, Sebastian felt separated from the excitement. He didn't feel the heady rush of elation that he had hoped for.

Chapter Twenty-Eight

Alfie continued his painting classes with Christophe, and Gillie continued with her sittings. But in May the portrait seemed no nearer to completion.

When Liliane enquired about the time it was taking, Gillie had an answer.

'He is a perfectionist, Maman; he was not happy with the first attempt, so he has started again.'

It was a small but necessary lie, enabling her to continue the affair without her mother's knowledge. When she finally had the courage to confess, both Liliane and Sebastian laughed.

'For heaven's sake, Gillienne,' her mother said. 'I may be vague, but a blind man could see how smitten you are.'

'How smitten they both are,' Sebastian interjected. 'I am delighted for you, Gillie, he seems a thoroughly good man.'

'He is,' Gillie said happily, a secret smile on her face as she relived the moments when their behaviour had been far from good.

'So what next?' Liliane asked.

'Oh Maman, I don't know, so please don't ask.'

But Gillie longed to know; she was in love with Christophe and she wanted to marry him. One day Sebastian would run the estate and her involvement with Alfie would lessen as he grew up. She wanted children of her own: Christophe's children.

One Monday, after a sudden deluge of rain temporarily adjourned Alfie's painting lesson in their usual spot under the cherry tree, they ran inside, carrying their canvases.

'We'll finish our session in the shed,' Christophe said, kissing Gillie's cheek. He unlocked a drawer beside the bed, taking out the shed key. 'We may be a while. Alfie is in the middle of a masterpiece and I don't want to stop now.'

Gillie made herself a cup of tea, picked up some magazines and returned to the bedroom. Sitting down on the bed she recalled their lovemaking the night before. Christophe was definitely an excellent tutor, she thought, remembering the exquisite moments of passion.

She put down her cup and watched with dismay as some of the liquid ran into the slightly open drawer. She mopped at it with her handkerchief, took out a wallet, a notebook and several old cards. She was wiping the inside cover of the notebook when she noticed the photographs in a compartment inside. She dithered. They were private, none of her business. But before she could change her mind, she found herself rifling through the notebook. There was a photograph of an older woman with elegant features, his mother she assumed, and another of a beautiful woman with thick fair hair. She must be his old fiancée, she thought with a twinge of jealousy, wondering if he was still in contact with her. When she looked at the photograph underneath, she froze with shock. Her own face stared back from the image. Standing beside her with his arm draped around her shoulder was Étienne. She remembered it being taken by a friend when they were walking by the Seine, just the week before he had disappeared.

It was as if someone had punched her in the stomach. What

was the photograph doing in Christophe's drawer fourteen years after Étienne had disappeared from her life?

She gathered her things and was running to the door, when something made her go back. Christophe couldn't know that she had found them; at all cost he must never find out.

When she was satisfied that everything was as it should be, she scribbled a note.

Had to get back, Christophe, something has come up. Please can you bring Alfie home.

Running through the meadow she reached the house and hurtled up to her room, locking the door behind her. Her mind was racing as she scrabbled for a scenario that made some kind of sense.

'Oh my God,' she groaned, standing with her back to the door. Slowly her legs gave way and she slid to the floor. Had Christophe known all along about her relationship with Étienne? What was he doing on their estate? Had he come here to find her? Perhaps he was the one who had cost Étienne his life. She rocked to and fro, the different possibilities whirling in her head. One thing was certain, she could no longer trust him. As the light faded, Gillie wept for Étienne and for herself and the future that was no longer possible.

Chapter Twenty-Nine

Christophe noticed Gillie had gone before he even came inside. The house looked different without her; it felt empty as soon as he opened the door.

'Your aunt seems to have left,' he said to Alfie, picking up the hastily scribbled note. 'Are we in trouble, do you think?'

'Of course not, Christophe,' he replied. But Christophe wasn't so sure. He took Alfie home and returned to the house with a sense of foreboding. Something was wrong, he was sure of it. It didn't take long to find out.

He was changing in his bedroom when he noticed the tiny piece of cardboard lying on the floor, and the drawer imperceptibly ajar. The cardboard was a small trick he had learnt in the war. He opened the drawer. There was a tiny brown stain on the edge. He sighed. So Gillie had spilt her tea and opened the drawer. He pulled out the notebook. To the unskilled eye it was just as it had been, but not to Christophe. Gillie had opened the notebook and she must have seen the photograph inside.

His heart lurched. Everything he had carefully disguised was now exposed.

*

Gillie was running downstairs when Liliane came from the study, a wine list in her hand.

'Gillie,' she called.

'Not now, Maman.'

'Yes, now.'

Something snapped in Gillie. She turned around and marched back to her mother.

'What do you want?'

Liliane dropped the wine list on table and put her arms around her daughter. 'Something's wrong isn't it, *ma cherie?*'

Gillie froze. Her mother's indifference was easier to cope with than this sudden empathy.

'Come, let's go and sit down. Has something happened with Christophe?'

'Why are you taking an interest now, after all these years?'

Liliane was shocked by her words. 'I am always interested, tell me please.'

Gillie could see the sincerity in her mother's face. It wasn't that she didn't love Liliane, but in the past her mother never seemed to have had time for her. She was always too busy running the house, the winery, being there for Sebastian. There it was in the open: she was jealous of her brother. As she looked at the compassion in her grey eyes, she felt herself dissolve – for much of her life she had been overlooked in favour of Sebastian. At school she had worked hard, achieved good results, but somehow, they went unnoticed. For six months before the war, while she worked as a nurse in Paris, her mother was in England with Sebastian. When Étienne had disappeared, her mother hadn't even known he existed, and now all these years later she was concerned.

Liliane led her through to the library. 'Sit,' she pointed to the sofa.

Gillie obediently sat, her mother beside her.

'Now you need to tell me.' Liliane lifted her hand and put a stray curl behind Gillie's ear, then with a touch light as a feather she stroked her cheek. 'Has he been unfaithful?'

Gillie shook her head. 'No Maman, it's far more complicated. It's a very long story.'

'Well my darling, I shall listen.'

'Weren't you on your way to the winery?'

'I was, but if customers arrive, Adeline can deal with them. Start from the very beginning.'

Gillie swallowed. She could feel all her defences slipping, all the walls she had built over the years, crumbling. 'Really?'

Her mother nodded, and Gillie told her about her chance meeting with Étienne in a dark passageway in Paris. She conveyed the excitement and danger that had suddenly entered her life, the passion and the devastation when it had all ended. She told her about her recent expedition to the circus with Alfie, and the impulse that took her back to the American Hospital, and the café she had frequented with Étienne.

'They recognised me after all these years,' she said, looking up at her mother. 'The owner Monsieur Ducre, and Étienne's friend, Geraud. They finally told me the truth.'

'It must have been awful for you,' Liliane murmured. 'Why didn't you mention this before?'

'Because you never asked about my life.'

Liliane felt sick. Her daughter was correct; she had been so busy looking after her ailing husband and helping Marie-Claire to run the estate that somehow she had overlooked her own child.

'*Ma cherie*, I am so sorry. You seemed so self-sufficient and organised, I didn't think you wanted me to interfere. I was obviously wrong.'

'You were wrong,' Gillie said, 'but you are asking me now.'

Liliane took her daughter's hand. 'Please, I want to hear everything.'

'It was the not knowing that was awful,' Gillie continued. 'I had no idea if he was dead or alive. To be told the truth at last was shocking, but it was also liberating, Maman.'

'What has this to do with Christophe?' her mother asked, taking her handkerchief from her pocket and wiping a tear from her daughter's eye.

'I found a photograph in his drawer. I didn't mean to look. It was of Étienne and me.'

'That is extraordinary, but there may be a perfectly feasible explanation.'

'Don't you see, it means he came here under false pretences. He knew about me. He wasn't some casual artist looking for a country retreat, he lied to me, Maman, from the start. He used me.'

'*Mon Dieu*! What do you intend to do now?' Liliane's brow wrinkled in dismay. 'Of course Christophe can't stay here.'

'I'm going to find Geraud, he may know more about Christophe. Would you come with me, Maman?'

As Gillie looked at her mother, she could see her eyes were focussed, full of energy. For the first time Gillie could see her as she had been as a young girl: inquisitive, longing for adventure. Her grandmother's stories about her wayward daughter were obviously true.

'Of course I will. We will go to this café in Rue Chauveau together,' Liliane declared. As Gillie rested against her, breathing in the scent of lilies and garden flowers, some of the trauma of the previous hours dissipated. She felt loved, cared for; the burden of her knowledge less powerful now it was shared.

Liliane jumped in the car and drove out through the front gates. Half a mile later she turned onto a track that led directly to Les Volets Bleus. She had taken the dogs and her shotgun just in case. When she stepped from the car, she knew immediately she had come too late. The house was empty, with signs of a recent departure. There were washed dishes on the draining board, waste paper and old paint tubes in the bin. She put the china away and emptied the bin, examining the contents in turn. But there was nothing that would lead them to Christophe.

She was about to leave when she saw a stack of canvases in the corner of the room, obviously abandoned in the artist's haste to get away.

She went through the pile, but they were pristine. When she came to the last and turned it over, a portrait of her daughter stared back at her. But it was not the Gillie she knew; this girl was sensual and bold, her eyes gazing directly from the canvas. For a moment Liliane was shocked, not by the beautiful girl in front of her, but by the realisation that she didn't know this young woman at all. She sat down on the sofa and propped the painting on a wooden chair. Gillie had been focussed as a child, getting on with school and life with a quiet determination. It was always her younger child, Sebastian, who seemed to need her more. It had obviously been her oversight.

Liliane took the canvas home and hid it in her bedroom cupboard. She picked Alfie up from school, and afterwards, the three of them ate the supper that Adeline had prepared.

For once Adeline didn't pry. 'I've made you your favourite pudding, Mademoiselle Gillie,' was all that she said, putting the *crème renversée* on the table in front of them.

Gillie looked up at her. 'Thank you, Adeline, that is very kind.'

Later that evening Liliane gave Alfie his bath.

'Christophe has gone to Paris for a while,' she explained, washing the soap from his back.

'Why, Grand-mère?'

'Because, young man, he has work to do, but I'm sure he'll be back soon.' It was a lie obviously, but she had always felt protective where Alfie was concerned. As she wrapped him in a towel, Gillie's words went around in her head. *Why are you taking an interest now, after all these years?*

She would make it up to her daughter, if it was not too late.

The following day Liliane left Adeline in charge of the house and Adeline's husband in charge of the winery.

'I hope you don't mind looking after the two o'clock appointment, Jean, a wine merchant from London? I need to be away for the day.'

'It would be a pleasure, *madame*,' he replied, brushing the dust from his shirt and running his hand over the growth of stubble on his chin. 'But first perhaps, I should change.'

Liliane smiled as she walked away. Jean's dark eyes could not disguise his delight. Not only would he avoid a day working in the garden, but he could spend the entire afternoon tasting his favourite wines.

Gillie had already rung the café, without success, but they decided to go to Paris regardless. From Gare de Lyon, they took a taxi straight to Rue Chauveau, but the café was closed. When Gillie peered through the glazed door, the tables and chairs were stacked together. There was definitely no one there.

'I'm sorry, *ma cherie*, this is very disappointing,' Liliane consoled her.

Gillie bit her lip. 'Perhaps it's better this way. I'm not sure if I could face Geraud tonight, he hates all my questions.'

Liliane hugged her daughter and at once the floodgates opened.

'I thought it was different this time, that Christophe actually liked me,' Gillie sobbed. 'Am I so unlovable?'

'Don't be so silly, you are beautiful. Think of it this way, my love – it might just be a mystery waiting to be solved, rather than this horrid charade.'

Gillie pulled a handkerchief from her pocket. 'No Maman, the whole thing was a sham.'

'Well then,' Liliane's face was grim. 'If I ever get my hands on Christophe, I will certainly give him a piece of my mind.'

When Gillie had wiped her eyes, she showed her mother the alleyway.

'So this is where it all started with Étienne?' Liliane asked.

'It is, Maman.' Gillie brightened a little. 'And that was my room.' They looked up and a light was on in the bedroom on the top floor.

Liliane smoothed her daughter's hair. 'Trust me, my love, someone wonderful is out there just waiting to meet you. You will be happy again. First, however, we are going to go to my favourite hotel for dinner, Le Meurice in Rue de Rivoli.'

'Are you sure?' Gillie questioned as the taxi stopped outside the discreetly sumptuous exterior.

'Entirely sure. Your father used to bring me here when he wanted to spoil me. Now I want to spoil you.' She took her hand. 'I will never let you down again, I promise.'

They took the last train back to Beaune, and though they were still speculating about Christophe, and Gillie's questions had not been answered, they had spent the happiest time together in years. As Gillie leant back against the seat, the lights of Paris flashing past the window, she was filled with conflicting emotions. There was distress at losing the man she given her love to, and hurt at his duplicity, but there was also a sense of gratitude. Her mother had been there when she needed her most.

It was Friday night, a week after Liliane's trip to Paris with her daughter, and Sebastian had just got home. He was playing snakes and ladders with Alfie in the study when Liliane joined them.

'I have asked the colonel for supper tomorrow, if you don't mind?' he said to his mother.

'Of course,' Liliane replied. 'I'll confirm with Adeline.'

Alfie looked up from the board. 'And I'm going to see Amelia again next weekend aren't I, Papa?'

'When I come back, she will be with me,' he smiled.

The following evening the colonel arrived in time for a quick game of draughts with Alfie before bed.

'Off you go, young man,' Sebastian said, when Adeline banged her gong.

'Can't you take me up?'

'As long as there are no delaying tactics! Now be off with you,' he grinned.

After supper, when the women had gone to bed, Sebastian poured the colonel a glass of port from a crystal decanter.

'Are you bearing up?' he asked.

'Sort of, Sebastian. If I am being honest, I miss the old girl more than you could imagine. She was a bolt from the blue, you know; I fell in love with her the moment I set eyes on her at a dance in the village hall. She was so beautiful. Your great-grandfather scuppered it, I'm afraid. Thought I wasn't good enough for his daughter.'

'I know all about bolts from the blue,' Sebastian murmured.

'You mean Alfie's mother – pretty little thing.'

'Was she upset to leave her son?' Sebastian asked, leaning forward in his chair.

'I should say so, I had to go and fetch her nice friend Georges from the car... I can't remember his surname. He had to support her out of the house she was in such a state.'

'I see.' Sebastian shook his head. 'What did he look like, this Georges fellow?'

'Dark shaggy hair, decent chap.'

A memory stirred at the back of Sebastian's mind. 'Was he her boyfriend?' he asked.

'No, he seemed more like a brother. I remember thinking he was a good friend to have around. Talking of pretty little things, Gillie tells me you have met the one, and you are engaged.'

'We haven't formally announced it yet, but she is coming next weekend. You'll be joining us for supper I hope?'

'I look forward to that enormously, Sebastian. Take a word of guidance from an old man. Look to the future, you can't dwell on lost love.'

'I'll try, Colonel,' Sebastian said, remembering his trip to Paris in search of Sophie and his bitter disappointment afterwards. And now years later he had found out that Georges had just been a friend all along.

Chapter Thirty

Sophie had applied and successfully competed in front of an appointment committee for the medical residency in The Dijon Bourgogne Université Hospital. Here she would finish her training in cardiothoracic surgery.

On a warm Saturday in May at precisely ten forty-five, she was waiting at the airport barrier for Todd. A wry smile crossed her face as she searched for him in the crowd. After their breakup in London she had vowed she would never see him again, but at least five letters and several bunches of flowers later, she had finally relented, and they had met at the Café de Flore in St-Germain-des-Prés.

'I'm sorry I didn't tell you about the marriage bit,' he had said, crumbling his brioche. 'You have to understand that I was scared of losing you.'

'You did lose me,' she retorted.

'So you see I was right. But I have been asking Pamela for a divorce for years. We are not happy, Sophie, she wants kids and I can't give them to her.' His normally relaxed face had been anguished and Sophie had put her hand over his, stilling his fingers.

'And I didn't tell you about Alfie; we were both wrong, Todd.

257

So yes, of course I forgive you, but I suggest we try to be a bit more honest with each other.'

'Agreed,' Todd had said, his face lighting up.

Sophie had put her finger to his lips. 'But let's not speak of the marriage thing, Todd, or indeed my son – let's just enjoy the time we spend together.'

During the following weeks Todd had been attentive and kind, and though Sophie was still extremely attracted to him and she adored his humour and quick wit, she realised she could never love him in the way she had loved Sebastian.

Sophie felt a slight jolt in her stomach as she saw Todd coming towards her. There was something about his walk, his long legs striding across the tarmac, that was extremely sexy, she mused. And the casual way he wore his clothes betrayed his nationality. Todd Dexter could never, ever be French.

'Hi sweetheart,' he said, kissing her mouth. 'I kinda missed you.'

'Well, you have had a long time to miss me,' she laughed, accepting the package he handed her.

'I know, but my bosses have to agree to my proposals.'

'So what is your assignment now?'

'The De Gaulle effect, but this time it wasn't difficult to persuade them.'

'Come on then,' Sophie said, linking her arm through his. 'Let me take you to my new flat.'

After dropping off his luggage, they walked to the covered food market, Les Halles, in the centre of Dijon. While Sophie flitted from one stall to another, inspecting the fish, fresh that day, the tiny edible woodland mushrooms, the fruit, Todd went in search of their lunch.

'This way, Todd.' Sophie caught up with him. 'You must

meet Jules.' She took his hand and dragged him towards a large counter where every possible cheese was displayed with artistry.

'*Bonjour*, Mademoiselle Sophie,' the farmer grinned, rubbing the side of his nose with his index finger, before turning his attention to Todd. 'Now *monsieur*, you will sample *Époisses de Bourgogne.*' He took a spoon from the marble counter and scooped out some of the creamy cheese from a small wooden box. 'If you like it, you will buy the box; if not I will give it to Mademoiselle Sophie – you will win either way!'

Todd beamed as he put it into his mouth. 'Gee, you don't get this in New York.'

As they left the stall with the *Époisse*s and a slice of camembert, Sophie looked up at him.

'You Americans can do some things, but you will never compete with our food.'

'Insult accepted,' he smiled.

Armed with cheese, French bread and fruit, they headed to the *Parc de la Colombiere* where they found a shaded area of trees. Sophie sat at the base of a large hornbeam and arranged her cotton skirt beneath her legs while she set out the food. Todd lay back in the grass watching her.

'I think you need to open your present now,' he instructed.

Sophie opened the brown wrapping paper, and a negligee of the finest silk slipped into her hands. It had a very low back that would only just cover her bottom and an equally suggestive front.

'It's beautiful ... what there is of it,' she quipped. 'Thank you, Todd.' She leant over to kiss him and he caught hold of her hand.

'I want to see you in it,' he said, his voice husky. 'I want to take it off you.'

Sophie looked away, troubled by the intensity in Todd's eyes.

Later, when the slip of silk lay abandoned on the floor and Todd was sleeping, Sophie got out of bed and went to the window. She adored Todd, and she now accepted his marriage in the same way that he had accepted her son. Perhaps if she had truly loved him, she would have minded more.

They spent three days together. While she worked at the hospital, Todd went into the streets, stopping people at will, questioning them on their new president. They had supper together, made with ingredients they bought at the market. He watched her as she filleted a sole.

'I can see why you are a good surgeon,' he remarked as she skilfully put the bones to one side.

'Practice with a knife,' she said with a smile.

'Do you love it, Sophie, is it still all you ever wanted? Surgery, that is?'

'I do,' she replied. 'When everything goes as it should. Unfortunately I have never achieved the degree of objectivity you need to become a great surgeon. I get too involved with my patients.'

'Surely you should be involved.'

'Up to a point. If you become too upset when a patient dies, it can affect your judgement, even your practice. It's the children who get to me most. When I was doing a placement at the Hôpital Saint Louis, there was a little boy dying of cancer. He was undertaking a course of the new chemotherapy. It's such a powerful drug, the poor child lost his beautiful curly hair. I couldn't bear it. We would stick needles into him and he never complained. Near the end he asked me when he would go to the angels. I wasn't sure how to answer him, but he put his tiny little hand on my arm. It's all right Doctor, he said. I'm not afraid. There will be no more pain when I am with the angels.'

Sophie bit her lip and looked away. 'Sorry, I mustn't be maudlin. There is of course the other side of the coin when you make sick people better. That gives you the best feeling in the world. But enough of me,' Sophie turned on the taps, washing her hands in the warm water, 'how is your editorial going?'

'There is so much to talk about, France is buzzing with activity. You have a new Constitution, the Fifth Republic has replaced the Fourth, and you have de Gaulle. He has achieved so much in such a short time, but I mustn't bore you.'

'Go on please,' Sophie begged. 'I am always buried in medical books or working. It's shocking but I really don't know what is going on in my own country.'

Sophie cleared the plates and put a bowl of fruit on the table. Todd peeled a pear and Sophie watched his hands, strong and supple.

'For one, you are experiencing rapid economic growth, accompanied by a huge investment in housing for the masses. Offices are being built and de Gaulle's Minister of Culture Andre Malraux is overseeing the rehabilitation of historic neighbourhoods in the centre of Paris. Did you know a new urban plan has been adopted in the City? Higher buildings will be permitted. There will be high-rise flats, offices. Your skyline will soon be rivalling New York! The plans for the new business district at La Défense are moving ahead. De Gaulle is a genius, just the man to bring France back from economic ruin.'

'It hasn't been that bad,' Sophie interjected, looking across at him.

'It's not been great, but it's hardly surprising after all those years of occupation. It took the heart out of Paris.' Todd was leaning forward, his elbows on the table, his eyes shining with passion.

'Since the end of the Second World War you have had a series of ineffective prime ministers, social and political unrest and the Indochina war that has cost the lives of one hundred thousand French soldiers. Tunisia and Morocco, your former protectorates, have received their independence, more colonies will follow. And at last you have someone in charge who will hopefully put an end to the Algerian crisis. As you know, I strongly believe they should gain their independence.'

'I had an Algerian patient, Nadia Abdelrahman.' Sophie paused, remembering Nadia's account of events in Algeria and France and ran her fingers over Todd's hand. 'They fled Algeria, expecting to be safe here, but France was not the refuge they hoped for.'

'There have been rumours of torture – pro-independence activists have disappeared. I would love to delve into it, but I will leave that for another day.'

'Please take my advice and don't voice your opinions too openly, it could be dangerous.' She touched his face. 'You're a good man, Todd.'

'I dislike injustice, Sophie. Did you know that your media is censored? Atrocities are being committed by French troops and few are brave enough to speak out.'

'I don't want to find out that you have disappeared,' Sophie warned him.

'I'm a Yank, I need to write about it, the world needs to know. But at least de Gaulle believes the Algerians have the right to determine their own future.'

They were clearing supper away when another argument started. Todd was drying up the plates.

'Thank God you now have a bathroom. Your flat in Paris was basic to say the least.'

'It was all my grandmother could afford,' she said stiffly.

'Don't be touchy, honey.'

'Touchy! You have just insulted me and my family and don't call me honey. My name is Sophie in case you have forgotten.'

Todd was standing with his back to the sink, his face hard.

'What is wrong with you for Christ's sake?'

'I don't want to be with you when you are like this,' she cried.

'Come on, Sophie, snap out of it. Don't spoil a lovely evening.'

'Todd, you may have had a wife until very recently ... in fact, what am I talking about, you are still married, so don't you dare talk to me like that, you are not my husband.'

Todd threw down the tea towel. 'If that's how you feel about it, I'll leave now.' He took something from his pocket and slammed it on the table.

'This is what I was going to ask you, Sophie, the reason that I wanted to come to France and write about de Gaulle. Pamela is thinking of granting me a divorce. I was going to propose.'

He gathered his clothes from the bedroom, throwing them into his leather holdall and went to the door. 'I'm going back to Paris, I think it's better this way.' He picked up the box, and shut the door behind him.

Sophie remained at the table long after he had gone. Todd was going to ask her to marry him and she had missed yet another opportunity for happiness. She put her head in her hands, but the tears of a devastated woman failed to come. She was sad, but she realised now that she wasn't ready to marry him. As she got ready for bed, a wry smile twitched at the edge of her mouth. It was typical of Todd to ask for her hand before he was legally free.

Chapter Thirty-One

It was late May and Sophie was on her way to America. As the plane flew through the night, she knew that at this moment in her training, her focus should be centred on achieving her goals, not on Todd. Her goals did not necessarily include, however, being propelled through the air in a metal container at ten thousand feet.

She remembered finding Todd sitting outside the door of her flat three days after their argument, a sheepish grin on his face, and a large bottle of Chanel No. 5 packaged in his lap. 'I couldn't keep away, Sophie. I'm sorry, I should never have said those things.'

'They were unforgivable.'

'I know, and I haven't been able to sleep since. May I come in?'

'I suppose so, but we need to have a serious talk.'

Todd was standing at the window of the small sitting room, staring into the distance when she had handed him a martini.

'Is this the end of us?' he had asked, turning back to her, his normally carefree face strained.

'No, I don't think so, but I am not sure where we are going.'

'I thought we were good together?'

'We have been, but I wonder sometimes if we can make each other happy.'

'It's Alfie's father, isn't it? I always believed I was the third wheel in an old love.'

Sophie hesitated for a moment, a range of emotions crossing her face. 'There is no one else,' she assured him.

'One day I would like to marry you so we can grow old together.'

Sophie laughed. 'But Todd, you are still married.'

'What if I was free?'

Sophie stroked his cheek. 'I do love you, but I am not sure if that is enough?'

He put his arm around her waist. 'You mean a great deal to me, Sophie Bernot. We will work this out, I promise.' He had grinned suddenly. 'Just in case you were going to ask me to stay, I have to get back to Paris to wrap up this editorial. I'll see you as soon as I can.' He had put the bottle of scent on the coffee table, leaving without another word.

Sophie had fixed herself another cocktail, turning on the gramophone to listen to *La Bohème*. After her third martini, feeling more than a little tipsy, she had thrown herself onto her bed fully clothed, while her favourite aria reached its crescendo. Todd was a good man, a man of integrity. Something she had admired from the moment she had met him. It also helped that he was handsome, intelligent, and he made her laugh. But there was still something missing. Why couldn't she love him completely? She had not been honest with herself. Todd was right; at the back of her mind and in her heart there was always Sebastian, the father of her son.

As the dawn light filtered through the aeroplane blinds, the image of a small boy came into her mind. She pulled a photograph from her bag. Alfie was carrying a football, a cheeky smile on his heart-shaped face. His shorts were crumpled and two baby teeth were missing at the front. 'How adorable he is,' she whispered touching the photograph, remembering the hours she had spent looking for a suitable present at a toy shop in Boulevard St-Germain. In the end she had bought him a football and though he would never know who had given it to him, she at least had the photograph.

She was having breakfast when the plane was rocked by a fresh wave of turbulence, forcing all personal thoughts aside. She gripped the armrests, her nails digging into the blue leather.

'Are you all right, ma'am?' An air hostess was leaning over her.

'Thank you, I suppose I am.'

'I assume it's your first time?'

'If I have anything to do with it, my last,' her smiled wobbled. An operating theatre with all its challenges was preferable any day to this contraption in the sky.

The woman put a hand on her arm. 'I can assure you flying is as safe as crossing the road.'

'Then you haven't crossed any roads in Paris,' Sophie muttered beneath her breath. She looked into the air hostess's kind face. *Je suis ridicule, pardon mademoiselle.*'

'Everyone is a little apprehensive to start with. You'll come to love it,' the young woman smiled.

Half an hour later, to Sophie's relief, the plane descended through the clouds and touched down at LaGuardia Airport in New York, but it was over an hour before she passed through customs. An official from the hospital was waiting for her at the barrier.

'Doctor Bernot, hope your flight was OK? Doctor Eppel asked me to meet you from the plane, you being a woman in a strange city.'

Sophie wasn't sure whether to be angry or amused. She was twenty-six for heaven's sake, not a child.

'Thank you, my flight was fine,' she replied. 'But I had to

assure your customs officials I was neither a communist nor a spy.'

The man coughed. 'There's a little paranoia in the US today.'

'I'd say it was more than a little.'

'But you could be a communist doctor,' he smiled.

After being dropped at her hotel, Sophie went straight to bed. She had flown halfway across the world to see the heart–lung machine, and she wasn't going to waste a moment of her stay. To see the extraordinary life-saving machine in action was something she had wanted from the moment Professor Manon had told his students about the new phenomenon. Now, six years later, Professor Charpentier had persuaded the hospital in Dijon to sponsor her trip. He had shown her the letter he had put in front of the board.

'It is the young and dedicated physicians who are the future of medicine. Doctor Bernot is just such an example. It is our duty to make sure they are familiar with the latest technology.' Doctor Charpentier had made the dream become a reality, and now the day had come at last.

She had a quick breakfast and went straight to the hospital. It was modern and sleek, with glass walls and gleaming floors.

'Doctor Eppel is expecting me,' she said to one of the girls on reception.

The girl looked down her list. 'I'll call his secretary immediately.' She picked up the phone.

Moments later, a tall, elegant brunette, wearing a pencil skirt and twin set, was coming down the hall towards her.

'Come this way please, Doctor Eppel is delighted that you have come to witness him in surgery.'

'I'm looking forward to it very much,' Sophie assured her.

'The doctor is at the heart of innovation, excuse the pun.' She laughed, showing perfect white teeth. 'And we are extremely fortunate to have one of the first heart–lung machines in our hospital.'

While the secretary fetched her a coffee, Sophie glanced around the luxuriously furnished room. It was unlike any surgeon's office in Dijon or Paris, she reflected, wondering if this applied to his salary too. When Doctor Eppel entered the room in an expensive tailored suit, and immaculate hair, her suspicions were confirmed.

'How wonderful that you have travelled all this way to see us,' he said, in a smart Bostonian accent. He shook her by the hand and Sophie couldn't help noticing his finely manicured nails.

'We're operating in half an hour, but I imagine you wish to see our new baby first, so you can understand how it works. If you change into scrubs, I'll meet you here in five.' Sophie's face went blank, she was good at languages, but flippancy was beyond her capabilities.

'Sorry, Doctor Bernot – a silly expression. Our baby is the new heart–lung machine.'

Doctor Eppel was less intimidating in scrubs, Sophie decided as she followed him to theatre. He held open the door and they went inside.

He drew her towards the cardiopulmonary bypass pump. 'It may look like a stainless-steel drinks cabinet but trust me, this machine saves lives.' Any flippancy had gone; he was now a dedicated surgeon, passionate about his work. 'This amazing pump can take on the role of the heart and lungs during cardiac surgery,' he continued, his face inordinately proud. 'It has a rotating arm which propels the blood forward by compressing the plastic tubing. Included in the circuit is an oxygenator in which thin rotating discs expose the blood to oxygen, so that the blood changes colour and becomes redder. These are the two constituents: the pump and the oxygenator. By providing an artificial circulation, the heart can be isolated, opened, and the problem dealt with.

'But here is the question, Doctor Bernot, how do we protect the heart during this period? We cool the patient, thus reducing its oxygen requirements. In addition to the pump and oxygenator, it has a heat exchanger, so that the blood can be cooled and later rewarmed. It's all in the same circuit.' He patted the machine proprietorially.

'The operation we have this morning is fairly routine: our middle-aged patient needs a new valve. I will keep you abreast of the procedure if the situation allows it.'

'Thank you.' Sophie could feel her anticipation building.

As the team entered, and the unconscious man was wheeled into theatre, Sophie moved to the side. She watched intently as Doctor Eppel hooked the oscillating saw around the manubrium at the top of the sternum, and drew it down, cutting through the bone. Using a retractor he divided the two halves of the ribcage to reveal the heart.

'We will now put in the tubes,' he instructed, accepting a needle and thread from the scrubs nurse without looking up. 'The patient has already been heparinised to prevent clotting,' he explained. 'We will reverse the effects afterwards.'

As he deftly sewed the tubes, using two pursestring sutures to secure them into the superior and inferior venae cavae, he continued his commentary. 'I will now connect these to the machine. I will use the same suture in the aorta prior to insertion of the arterial catheter, this of course returns the blood. Once I have made sure all the air has been excluded, I will give instructions to my excellent pump operator Felix to go on bypass.'

There was silence in the theatre as Doctor Eppel finished the sutures and Sophie could hardly breathe. This was what she had crossed half the world to see. This was the moment she had been waiting for.

'Felix, are we ready to go?' he asked.

'Flow is adequate and providing enough circulation,' Felix replied.

The machine had now started. The surgeon clamped the aorta and made a transverse incision to expose the diseased and narrowed valve.

'Come forward, Doctor Bernot,' he offered, his eyes never leaving the patient. 'You may wish to observe the calcification on the three cusps.' Sophie came closer.

'I will now excise the aortic valve itself.' He deftly cut out the valve and inserted an artificial valve, stitching it in place with multiple sutures. He closed the aorta and removed the clamp.

'With the blood supply restored to the heart, we will rewarm our patient to normal temperature.'

Sophie knew the moment things started to change. The heart was not contracting as it should. It was disorganised, a writhing mass of muscle.

'Defibrillator,' the surgeon instructed, his brow furrowed above his mask.

A single shot with the pads and the rhythm was restored. But though the heart was beating normally, the tension remained. Sophie moved back and out of the way.

'Patient still bleeding,' Doctor Eppel instructed. 'Has the heparin been neutralised?'

'It has,' the anaesthetist replied, his face showing concern.

'There is more bleeding than I would like. Please give more protamine and send samples to the lab.'

Despite the intervention, the bleeding continued. The tension in the theatre amplified, the surgeon's anxiety palpable.

'We need the remaining blood from the heart–lung machine – transfuse immediately,' he instructed. 'We need to keep up with the loss.' But it was hopeless, the blood wasn't clotting, and it kept on flowing. Though the surgeon's voice was level, Sophie could sense his desperation.

'Please send an urgent message to donors, we need them now. Doctor Bernot, if you could organise the collection.'

Grateful to be of use, Sophie hurried from theatre. In a short time six donors had arrived.

'Your response has been magnificent, thank you,' she said, inserting the needles into their veins. 'I am hoping your contribution will save our patient's life.'

With the blood collected she hurried back to theatre, but she could tell it was over, the moment she opened the door.

There was silence in the room, and a feeling of hopelessness hung in the air. Doctor Eppel pulled off his mask. 'Doctor Bernot, thank you for your efforts but the blood loss was too great. We have lost the battle, I'm afraid.'

Sophie had witnessed death many times, but never like this. The expectations had been high, success never in doubt, but it had ended in disaster. She left theatre, walked past the nurses' station, conscious of their shocked eyes upon her. She could see the patient's wife being comforted by Doctor Eppel. She sighed; at least she hadn't been the one to break the news.

'Doctor Bernot.' Sophie was on her way to the canteen when Doctor Eppel caught up with her. 'Will you come into my office?'

He had changed into his suit, but he was no longer suave and immaculate. There was a look of utter fatigue on his face.

'I am sorry...' He swallowed. 'We are not meant to feel like this, but I do. Every time I lose a patient, I want to know if I could have done it better, whether it was my fault. Did I take risks with someone's life? You see, Doctor Bernot, the patient could have lived for another couple of years. If I had given him the option, what he would have preferred, what would his answer have been?'

He put his elbows on his desk and cradled his head in his hands. 'Sometimes I think I am too enthusiastic. We have made so many steps, but we are not there yet.'

Sophie cleared her throat. 'If you don't take a chance now, how will we ever get to the point when these operations are routine? You believed you could give the patient more than two years, you believed you could give him life. He would have taken that chance. I would.'

He looked up at her. 'So much wisdom in such a young doctor.'

She shrugged her shoulders, thinking of Hakim and Nadia Abdelrahman. 'I have seen a little of life.'

Sophie was about to leave when he spoke again. His eyes had regained their intensity. 'We must find a cause for this bleeding, Doctor Bernot! We owe it to these patients to organise research to make this surgery safer. But we need the answers now!'

Sophie wasn't sure what to say. The senior consultant had let her into his confidence and she felt honoured, but at the same time a little overwhelmed. She considered her words.

'I have no doubt that you will find the answers,' she replied. 'Despite the outcome, your commitment has been an inspiration.'

He smiled wryly. 'This hasn't been a great recommendation for the heart–lung machine, but this is my first failure. Tomorrow I am operating again. I would like you to assist me. Hopefully we will do better next time.'

'I fly back to Dijon tomorrow evening, but I would be honoured to assist you beforehand. Thank you for having faith in me, Doctor Eppel.'

Chapter Thirty-Two

Sophie was back in Dijon and fully occupied with her own patients in the cardiology department and with assisting in theatre. This morning it was the closure of a patent ductus arteriosus which she had picked up a month earlier. The child had come into the outpatient's clinic with acute tonsillitis and after listening to her chest, the doctor had telephoned her department.

'You are right to have referred her,' Sophie had confirmed, listening to the continuous murmur.

She was on her way to the operating theatre, when Dominique, the head nurse on the ward, called out to her. 'There's a letter for you, Doctor.'

She collected the envelope and hurried to scrubs, putting it into the pocket of her white coat.

Fifteen minutes later, the team of Professor Charpentier, Sophie and three nurses were waiting in theatre as the unconscious eight-year-old girl was wheeled in, the anaesthetist following behind.

As Sophie glanced at the child, her blonde curls drawn back from her pale face, she was fully aware that she had an equal duty to all the patients, young and old. Her sentiments should be the same, but this poor little girl looked tiny on the table and so vulnerable.

She looked up to find the professor smiling at her.

'Let's see if we can give this little one back her life,' he said.

As he selected a scalpel, Sophie realised how lucky she was to work under this magnificent man. He was not only a brilliant surgeon, but he was also compassionate and enlightened.

'You will have to stand up for yourself,' he had told her when she first came to the hospital, 'because you will meet chauvinism and even injustice within these walls, but I know a strong young woman like you can deal with it. The world is changing, Sophie, and you will be part of that change.'

Sophie had seen that first incision a hundred times and even made it herself, but she still held her breath as he incised the left chest, using a retractor to separate the tiny ribs. She was now watching his every move, no longer conscious of the child's age, only aware of the miracle of anatomy and the mastery of Professor Charpentier.

Having retracted the lung he exposed the area beneath the aortic arch to reveal the communication between the aorta and the artery to the lung.

'This is the vessel that should have closed at birth to become a fibrous cord,' he instructed Sophie, his eyes never leaving the site. 'And this is the communication we must close. But at this point we must be more than careful. The nerve that supplies the larynx lies nearby and is easily damaged. We don't want to leave the child with a hoarse voice for the rest of her life.'

He put out his hand and the theatre nurse handed him some angled forceps. He passed the forceps behind the ductus, and Sophie felt herself tense. If the vessel was torn, the consequences could be dire. But the professor made this difficult procedure look simple, as he deftly passed beneath the ductus to grasp the silk ligature, then tied it around the tiny vessel.

'Doctor Bernot.' He briefly raised his eyes. 'I would suggest you feel at the site to confirm that there is no longer any

274

vibration, and if you agree, then I suggest that you take it from here.'

As Sophie stitched up the little girl, she truly understood the purpose behind her ambition to become a surgeon. It was to enable a child like this to live a full life.

After she had washed and changed back into her white coat, she pulled the letter from her pocket. She recognised the writing and tore it open, a smile on her face. It was from Georges.

Ma chère Sophie,
I have news. I know you will be happy for me, at least I
hope you will be. Lydia has agreed to marry me. I really can't
imagine why, I am as you know terrible husband material.
But I am actually really excited. I wish you could be my best
man, but that might be a little difficult!!
My love to you always
Georges.

PS I have applied for a short residency in Dijon – six months
only, because the wedding is planned for December. I will let
you know if I get it.

Sophie was happy for him, of course she was. Why then did she feel like crying? It seemed her best friend, the man who she relied on for support, who had always picked her up when she was at her lowest ebb, would feature less in her life. She hoped she would still see him, but it would most likely include Lydia. It just wouldn't be the same.

She folded the letter and put it back in the envelope. She was being selfish. She would write immediately and tell him she was overjoyed. She grimaced; now that really was a lie. In six months' time, her dearest friend who had always been there for her would belong to someone else.

Chapter Thirty-Three

June arrived and it was time for Marie-Claire's parting gift to her grandson. She had left some money in an envelope to pay for a celebration for his 30th birthday.

'*To my deep regret*,' she had written in the accompanying letter. '*I will not be with you my darling boy, so I have put this sum of money aside. Spend it all, have fun and raise a glass of our finest champagne to your grandmother.*

Always

Marie-Claire

On the thirteenth of the month, the family and a few good friends gathered at the Hotel des Lacs in Chamonix. Sebastian and Marcus had arrived earlier for three day's training on Monc Blanc, before their intended climb.

'Forgive us for being late,' Giulietta apologised to Sebastian as they entered the dining room. 'We never seem to get anywhere on time.'

'Perhaps it has something to do with your three young children and a fourth on the way?' Sebastian teased in hushed tones.

'It's all his fault,' Giulietta looked accusingly at Robert.

'Babies or being late?' Sebastian queried, looking innocent.

'I had nothing to do with either,' Robert grinned.

Pierre gave grace and when everyone was seated, he said a few words.

'The last time I saw you all was at my dear mother Marie-Claire's funeral. It was her wish ... no, it was her command, that we should be together today.' He smiled at everyone and raised his glass.

'I would like to make a toast to my late mother and to my nephew Sebastian on his thirtieth birthday. But there is another toast due this evening, one that would have delighted her. Sebastian is to marry the lovely Amelia.' He turned to them. 'I wish you both a long and happy life together.'

When the clapping had died down, he resumed his speech. 'This time is precious,' he said, casting his eyes around the table, lingering on each guest in turn. 'When I return to Vézelay it will be to silence. Dear friends, you have given me so much to think about in my hours of contemplation. It has been a pleasure to be with you all, especially on this auspicious occasion. Sebastian, Marcus, I wish you *bon voyage*. If I were a younger man I would insist on coming with you. Be safe on your journey to the summit of Mont Blanc.' He raised his glass once again. 'To Sebastian and Marcus. To every success on your mountain adventure.'

'You are as fit as any of us – why don't you join us?' Sebastian suggested.

Pierre smiled. 'No, dear boy, I have done my time in the mountains.'

Liliane sipped her wine and glanced around the festive room. There were vases of flowers down the centre of the table, interspersed with large pillar candles. At each place setting there was a brightly coloured cracker. She remembered making them with Gillie as the evenings lengthened, sticking jewels and glitter onto the crêpe paper, reminiscing about Marie-Claire, conjecturing about Christophe. Not only had it been cathartic, but their understanding of each other had deepened.

Her eyes lingered on Sebastian. He was chatting to his friends, his arm thrown around Amelia's shoulder. She was looking up at him whilst fiddling with her funny fringe. She was undoubtedly a charming girl and would be the perfect wife, but Liliane hoped she would make her son truly happy. She had caught the occasional wistful expression on Sebastian's face and it crossed her mind that he may be remembering the mother of his child.

Tomorrow he would leave with Marcus to climb Mont Blanc. Though she respected his wish for a challenge, she had doubts about the adventure and had suggested that it was a little foolhardy. She recollected the news coverage of two young men who had perished on the mountain only three years before. They had waited ten days to be rescued, before finally losing their lives. The rescue attempts had been blighted by a series of catastrophes and poor decisions. It was a moment of national shame.

'Do you have to go?' she had asked her son only the day before.

'Mother,' he had said putting his arm around her, 'stop worrying and if you are thinking of the Vincedon and Henri affair, that was in December, this is June. We are not foolish, we will be fine, I promise you.' She pushed the concerns from her mind; this was a party, not the time for her pointless anxieties.

Pierre caught her eye and smiled reassuringly. Once again he knew what she was thinking. He was dressed in a dark suit and immaculate white shirt; the only outward sign of his ministry was a cross around his neck. He was still so handsome, she thought, still vital. She tried to remember the first signs of his turning to God but failed. She could only remember the kind and sensitive young man who had always looked after her. How her girlfriends had loved him, always coming to the house in the hope of seeing him. Though he had been oblivious to their charms, he had always been courteous. He had been such a catch. She sighed; time had flown, it seemed like yesterday when she was young and carefree, and now…

She watched as the girls chatted together across the table.

'What is it about men?' Giulietta was saying. 'Robert is cross that he can't climb the mountain, but he has to be back at work the day after tomorrow. They are just big boys.'

'I agree with you,' Gillie intervened. 'They are always trying to prove something to themselves, I'm not sure why.'

Amelia had pulled away from Sebastian and was leaning forward.

'Tarzan,' she stated.

'What?' Gillie giggled.

'You asked why men had to prove themselves. They feel they have to be manly and heroic just like Tarzan.' She blushed a deep red suddenly, and the three girls burst into laughter.

Liliane smiled; everyone had warmed to Amelia, she was spirited with an irreverent sense of humour. She was a refreshing change from the more conventional girls and she was reminded of herself at that age.

She was distracted from her thoughts by Alfie, who stood up and coughed. Everyone turned towards him.

'Papa,' he said, his little face flushed with excitement. 'I have something for you.' He disappeared beneath the table, reappearing with a large painting. 'Here you are, Papa, it's got the house, and the dogs and everyone. Even Adeline. That's me in the front, so you won't be lonely when you are in London.' Sebastian started to clap. 'I'm not finished yet, Papa,' he declared, and everyone laughed. 'Christophe helped me to begin the painting, but then he had to go away. I would have put you in, Uncle Pierre, but you were not at home so I couldn't have made a real likeness, if you see what I mean.'

'I see entirely what you mean,' Pierre smiled, and Sebastian picked up his son and hugged him close.

'Thank you, Alfie darling,' he said his voice cracking. 'It is the most perfect present and I will treasure it always.'

Liliane caught her daughter's eye.

'You look so pretty in that dress,' she mouthed.

Gillie smiled across the table, remembering her mother offering her the floral chiffon dress with the sweetheart neckline, a few weeks before.

'You must have it, *ma cherie*, it will be perfect for Sebastian's party,' Liliane had insisted, and when Gillie had protested she had stopped her. 'Really darling, it will look wonderful on you, I am far too old. Go and fetch it from my wardrobe now.'

As Gillie had rootled through her mother's dresses she had come across the canvas. She had known what it was immediately, and as she turned it around and stared at the bold and sensual painting, she had felt the pain and loss all over again. Her mother had arrived at that moment. 'I had forgotten it was here. I am so sorry.'

'It's all right,' Gillie had replied, sinking into her mother's arms, but it wasn't all right, it was all wrong, and as the memories of Christophe had resurfaced she tried to brush them away. Whatever anyone had suggested to the contrary, his disappearance was an admission of his guilt – it was the only possible explanation. She was brought back to the present when Robert dropped into the empty chair beside her.

'Did you ever have any luck finding out about your friend?'

'Étienne? I did actually,' she said, fiddling with her glass. 'It was what I had been expecting all these years, but it still came as an awful shock. He was shot at Fresnes.'

'Gillie, I am so sorry.'

Gillie shook her head, 'It's strange but after my initial distress, it was actually a relief to finally know the truth. But I now have another problem. Have you five minutes?'

'Of course.' Robert filled up Gillie's glass and his own.

While Gillie explained her current predicament, Robert sat quietly making the occasional comment.

'Before you write Christophe off completely,' he said at last, 'remember things are so often not what they seem. The offer still stands. I will be glad to help in any way that I can.'

Chapter Thirty-Four

Sebastian kissed his mother's forehead.

'Goodnight, Maman. You won't see us in the morning so thank you for a wonderful birthday.'

Liliane took his face in her hands. 'You be careful, you haven't done a climb like this without a guide before.'

Sebastian laughed. 'I wouldn't do it if there was any danger involved.' He winked at Marcus who grinned back at his friend.

He went next to Giulietta, taking both her hands. 'Thank you for coming all this way.'

'We wouldn't have missed this for the world,' she said. 'You are Roberto's dearest friend.'

After saying goodbye to the rest of the assembled company, he went to his son. 'Look after the family, Alfie.'

Alfie puffed out his small chest. 'I will, Papa.'

In the lobby Sebastian turned to his sister. 'Are you sure you don't mind driving us to Courmayeur?'

'Mind?' she laughed. 'Getting up at five, of course I do, but it's your birthday.'

Sebastian hugged her. 'You're the best.' They walked up the stairs arm in arm. 'Any further news on Christophe? Do you want me to kill him for you?' he asked when they reached the landing.

'If I remember correctly, you offered to kill the politician too.'

'Did I?' he laughed.

Gillie sighed. 'I am no nearer to solving the puzzle, but Robert has offered to help me.'

'You know I'll do anything I can, but with his past expertise, Robert is your man.'

The rest of the family and friends had long departed for their bedrooms when Sebastian tiptoed into Amelia's room.

'Everyone loves you,' he said, kissing her shoulder.

'But do you love me, Sebastian?'

'You know I do,' he said.

She put her hands on his chest and looked into his eyes.

'Please be careful and come back in one piece. I would actually like to become your wife.'

Sebastian picked up her chin and kissed her lips. 'I am so lucky to be loved. Of course I'll be careful. It is June, sweetheart, Mont Blanc will be like a walk in the park!'

'Are you sure?'

'I'm sure, now take that silly nightie off.'

Sebastian, Marcus and Gillie met each other at six o'clock the following morning at the bottom of the stairs.

Dawn was breaking, and it was drizzling as the two men lugged their kit to the car.

'That was a great evening,' Marcus said, with a yawn.

'And it was also the last decent meal we'll have for a while,' Sebastian sighed, opening the boot. He lobbed a small cardboard box to Marcus. 'Except of course for our packed lunch, compliments of the chef here.'

Marcus caught it and grinned happily. 'And the last decent night's sleep. So I ask myself, why do we do this at all?'

'Because,' Sebastian stated, 'it's the most exciting thing either of us has done in a very long time.'

Gillie took the long but only logical route from Chamonix to Courmayeur. Crossing the border into Switzerland and the small town of Martigny in the Lower Valais, they continued their slow, circuitous journey up the mountains gaining altitude all the way. They at last reached the Great St Bernard Pass linking Switzerland to Italy.

'One day I hope there will be a tunnel,' Gillie grumbled, negotiating the perilous mountain road in poor visibility. Either side of them were the remnants of high banks of late spring snow.

They were at Aosta by noon and Courmayeur an hour later. Gillie stopped the car at Val Veny and helped them to unload.

'This is for you,' Sebastian said, passing her an envelope. 'It gives you our route, and a rough indication of timing, just in case.'

'Just be safe,' she hugged him quickly then returned to the car. 'Bye Marcus,' she called. 'Have fun and see you in a couple of days.'

After they had finished sorting their gear, Sebastian studied his map then tucked it into the inside pocket of his jacket. He gave a ski pole to Marcus, keeping one for himself, and throwing their rucksacks over their shoulders, they started on their way.

'Sure you want to go all the way to the top?' Sebastian challenged. 'You can still change your mind.'

'Me?' Marcus replied. 'Never. Trust me, the weather will clear.' He sniffed optimistically.

'Let's see if we can make the Lac du Miage by two,' Sebastian suggested.

They set off at a brisk pace, their boots crunching on the gravel. By the time they reached the moraine of the Glacier du Miage, the sun had broken through the clouds, and was shining on a small lake, the turquoise waters shimmering in the barren, rocky outcrop.

Sebastian lifted his face to the sun. 'I've waited so long for this, Marcus, and now we are here.'

Marcus laughed. 'And for you, even the weather has changed.'

After a quick stop for lunch, they rolled their thick cotton jackets into their rucksacks and picked up their kit. They were ascending the moraine of the glacier, and had lapsed into silence, each man enjoying the splendour of his surroundings, when Sebastian's thoughts drifted to Amelia. Their lovemaking the previous night had been both tender and passionate. She had given herself to him entirely. He smiled for a moment remembering the sight of her as he left, innocent and beguiling in sleep, but as he picked his way upwards, over boulders and ice, his mind inadvertently turned to another walk, another time, and a girl on a mountain in a red jacket. He cursed inwardly. He mustn't think of her, he couldn't let a figure from the past ruin everything.

When the trail entered a mountain valley that was filled with the glacier, they strapped their crampons over their heavy leather boots. The temperature had dropped, and the challenging part was about to begin.

They were now surrounded by rock walls, several hundred metres high. On the southwest side they rose to the Aiguille de Tré la Tête, and the northeast side to the Brouillard Ridge, then upwards towards the summit of Mont Blanc.

It was quiet in the valley, the eerie silence broken only by the sound of their crampons crunching. There were no people, no birds, no wind, nothing but rocks, ice and sky and the occasional gunshot crack of seracs and rocks crashing above them.

Four kilometres into the valley, at the point where the Glacier du Mont Blanc and the Glacier du Dome came together on one side, with another small glacier on the other, Sebastian sat down on a boulder and studied the route. Marcus grabbed the opportunity to take out his camera. As the shutter opened and closed, he called to his friend.

'Up there, look Sebastian.'

As Sebastian followed his gaze, he saw the ibex standing on the ridge above them, motionless, inquisitive, his curving horn lit by the afternoon sun. He put away the map and released the rope coil from his back. He threw one end to his friend.

After they had roped themselves together, they crossed the glacier above the ice fall, and progressed slowly to the rock on the other side. From there they followed markings up the ridge. The air was getting thinner and they were climbing now. Sometimes they found an old steel cable to hang onto, or a rusty ladder attached to the mountain by a sagging piece of wire.

At seven o'clock that evening, they reached their destination for the night, the Refuge Gonella on the Aiguilles Grises. Sebastian took his altimeter from his jacket; they were three thousand and seventy-one metres high.

The sun was low in the sky, and the mountain tops were an iridescent orange against a backdrop of blue. Though tired and hungry, Marcus took a new roll of film from his rucksack and fed it into the spool. As he focused his lens on the Glacier du Dome towards the Bosses ridge, he felt excitement in the pit of his stomach. It was the route they would take in a few hours' time.

After making up a fire, they had supper at the cabin's rough wooden table.

'Climbing makes you realise that you can never dominate nature,' Sebastian mused, wiping a crust of bread round his plate.

Marcus nodded. 'As I watched the light shift over the mountains, I realised that for all our sophistication, we are insignificant. The ibex stared at us as if we were intruders in his world.'

Sebastian smiled. 'Arrogance, conceit; neither has a place

286

up here. Climbing isn't about success or ambition, it is about comradeship and attempting the unknown.'

'And beauty, Sebastian. This evening, watching the sky, the colours, pinks, blues and purples. Seeing nature like this. It has to be worth it.' Marcus grinned, his face a little strained. 'Of course you have to be prepared for anything the elements throw at you.'

Sebastian laughed. 'Don't worry, Marcus, we will be absolutely fine.'

They slept for four hours and at just after midnight they refilled their water bottles and packed up their kit. Pushing open the refuge door, they paused for a moment to look up at the stars.

'They seem so near,' Sebastian murmured.

'As if you could reach out your hands and touch them,' Marcus concurred.

Then they turned on their head torches and scrambled down to the Glacier du Dome. The snow was good and the conditions perfect, but it was dark and freezing cold.

'All well?' Sebastian shouted.

'Headache,' Marcus mouthed, pointing to his temples. Sebastian waited while he drank some water and they continued on their way.

They had been going for two hours, climbing up rockfaces, traversing glaciers with Sebastian in the lead. Each moment that passed, he was acutely aware of the danger. They were on their own on the mountain. At any moment the ice could give way, or an avalanche could descend.

They were negotiating an ice fall on the upper section of the glacier, when Marcus slipped. Sebastian could hear his scream, followed by the swish of his body as it was carried away down the slope. His reaction was immediate. 'Axe,' he yelled, digging his crampons into the ice and throwing his weight backwards.

He could see the headlamp bobbing below. Seconds later, the rope jerked violently around his shoulders as Marcus came to a halt.

'All good,' his friend shouted. But as Marcus trudged slowly towards him, holding onto his axe, the stark reality hit Sebastian. There was only a fine line between success and failure – often the difference between life and death.

It was five a.m. when they arrived at Col des Aiguilles Grises. The wind was blowing fiercely over the ridge and they were bitterly cold. They could see the comforting lights of Les Houches in the valley below.

'Last chance to go down?' Sebastian questioned, stamping his feet to warm them. Marcus shook his head.

They continued north on the ridge, scrambling over rocks and boulders as they followed the spur, stopping occasionally to get out their flasks. Dawn was breaking when they finally arrived at the Piton des Italiens with eight hundred metres still to go. Here the ridge split into two and Sebastian took out his compass. After studying the contours of the mountain, he took the right-hand turn to Mont Blanc. At times they walked, but where the ice was exposed, they straddled the narrow ridge and pulled themselves along, anchoring themselves to the mountain with their axe, but their progress became slower still as the wind howled around them. Time had no meaning for Sebastian. He couldn't even remember his last thought. His steps were mechanical, repetitive; sometimes he forgot he was walking at all.

When the ridge became too narrow they crossed to the northern side. From there it was ice-climbing, using the front points of their crampons chopping with their axes, to traverse a slope that was at least sixty degrees. At last they reached Col du Dome where the Italian and French routes met. The sun was rising, turning the sky from violet to blue. Sebastian grinned at Marcus. 'Nearly there, *mon ami*. We are through the worst.'

When they reached the Refuge Vallot, Marcus was panting heavily. 'It's the altitude,' he gasped, 'so little oxygen.'

'Perhaps we should call it a day,' Sebastian suggested.

'I'm a little light-headed, that's all.' But as they ascended the Bosses ridge, he could only take a few steps at a time.

'You really want to go on?'

Marcus nodded his head. 'Fuck off, I'm trying to survive.'

The ridge was narrow and very exposed, demanding all their concentration, and every ounce of their flagging energy. Putting one foot in front of the other was an effort and they had to force themselves to go on. Finally, seven and a half hours after leaving the Gonella refuge, they reached the summit and were standing on the top of the highest peak in Europe at an altitude of four thousand eight hundred and eight metres high.

'We'll celebrate later,' Sebastian shouted to Marcus, scanning the vast sea of mountain tops that stretched as far as the eye could see. But despite their achievement, he felt little of the expected elation. Instead, as the wind tore at his jacket, he felt a twinge of alarm. He wiped the first flakes of snow from his goggles and pointed down the mountain with his pole.

'First a photograph,' Marcus yelled in reply.

Sebastian slapped his gloved hands together and grinned into the lens.

They started the descent of the Bosses Ridge. Clouds were scudding across sky, hiding their view of the valley below. What had been difficult on the way up seemed almost impossible now. By the time they reached the bottom of the ridge, it was snowing hard and visibility was poor, and both men were tired and extremely cold. Marcus's breathing was ragged as they pushed their way into the Vallot hut.

'Tea?' Sebastian asked, masking his anxiety. He had done

several summer climbs before, but the weather had never closed in like this. He lit the small stove and made tea for Marcus, adding five spoonfuls of sugar. He needed to get his friend off the mountain, he was not in good shape.

'No time for a rest,' he instructed, 'we must get you down.'

As Sebastian opened the door, it was dragged away by the wind. There was a mighty crack as it crashed back against the hut wall. He grabbed Marcus by the arm and they staggered outside. It took both their weight to close the door.

They had started the descent of the Grand Plateau and were just beneath the Col du Dome when they heard a noise that sent a wave of terror through both of them. The 'whumph' was a clear indication that the snowpack was fracturing and starting to slide.

'Avalanche!' Sebastian yelled.

'Get the hell out of here,' Marcus screamed, as the sliding, cracking snow began to move, and a plume of snow smoke rose in the air. The noise was deafening, building to a crescendo as the snow hurtled towards them. They had no time to get rid of their kit. Marcus was flipped over and over. He came to a halt a hundred metres down. He lay stunned and winded, buried to his waist, but alive. While he dug himself out, scooping at the compacted snow, the avalanche had gathered momentum and was continuing its thunderous journey down the mountain, devouring everything in its way. Panic built in his chest – there was no sign of his friend. He started to yell but Sebastian didn't respond. He scanned the path of the avalanche, looked upwards, then down below. He realised with terrible certainty that Sebastian was probably buried beneath metres of snow.

Chapter Thirty-Five

As the wall of snow ploughed into Sebastian, he automatically crossed his arms, as he had been trained to do. His only hope in an avalanche was to protect his chest cavity and create a small pocket of air. Seconds later, the snow had compacted, and his body was encased in what felt like a concrete tomb. Snow was invading his nose, his ears, he couldn't move. It was pitch dark and he wanted to scream. He was suffocating. Panic threatened to overwhelm him, but he had to remain calm. He had to conserve his energy and his breath. While his mind was whirring he held onto the thought that Marcus would be looking for him. Marcus would find him before he ran out of air. Then he realised with horrible clarity that Marcus might be trapped too. Sebastian could feel his heart pounding. He couldn't give up hope. Marcus was out there somewhere, searching for him. All his energy must go into survival, he wouldn't countenance failure. He tried to wriggle a toe inside his boot, but was the boot above him or below, was he upside down? He had lost all sense of orientation. There was only one way to find out. He could feel a trickle of warm urine running down his leg. He was the right way round.

*

As the snow continued to fall on the grey world, Marcus could find no sign of Sebastian. No rucksack, no axe, no pole, nothing to suggest he was alive. The avalanche had stopped, and quiet had returned to the mountainside, a deathly hush of heavy white. He rubbed at his goggles, but it was still a white empty world.

He began to dig for the rope like a man possessed.

'Please God,' he prayed. 'Let Sebastian still be attached to the other end.' When he found the rope buried quite near to the surface, he felt a glimmer of hope. It would lead him to Sebastian. He was conscious of the seconds ticking by. Each one counted. He wouldn't allow Sebastian to die. Sweat froze on his brow, he couldn't brush it away. He was nearing the end of the cord, when it dove down into the snow. Marcus knew he was almost there.

'I'm coming for you, Sebastian,' he shouted.

He was scrabbling like a dog, scooping at the snow, but he had to do it faster. He had to save his friend. It was then that he saw a strand of ice-covered hair.

'Oh my God,' he cried. 'Hold on, Sebastian, I'm here.'

Sebastian could no longer breathe. His thoughts had lost all rational meaning: Sophie was standing on the mountainside, Alfie was there, and his mother. They were calling to him, waiting for him. There was a sensation above him, or was it below him? He was no longer sure. He let himself drift away.

Suddenly he was being pulled and there was a terrible pain in his shoulder. He gasped and opened his eyes.

Sebastian lay in the snow, his body shaking.

'I thought that was it,' he whispered. 'I thought I was going to die.'

'But you didn't.' Marcus pulled a sleeping bag from his ruck-sack and wrapped it around him. He took out his water bottle and held it to his lips. When Sebastian tried to sit up, pain sliced through his shoulder. He touched his leg and winced.

'Just rest,' Marcus soothed.

When minutes later, Sebastian attempted to stand, he fell backwards in the snow.

'How the hell am I going to get down?' he gasped, tears of frustration pricking at his eyes.

'You have one leg, one arm and me!' Marcus encouraged.

'You're joking, right?'

'No.'

'Thank you, Marcus, but I'm fucked either way.'

'The Refuge des Grands Mulets should be open. We'll get help.'

'I'll never make it to the refuge.'

'You will, but first I'll look for your kit.'

Marcus had found his axe in the moraine nearby and his pole further down. He returned to Sebastian and tried to help him up, but Sebastian crumpled.

'You need to put some weight on your leg.'

'It's agony,' he gasped.

Marcus rolled back his trouser leg and felt for damage.

'There are no signs of a major fracture. Come on, you have to get up.' He handed him his pole and Sebastian tried again. On the third attempt with Marcus, supporting him, he struggled to his feet and limped forward, using his stick in one hand and his axe in the other. At each cautious step, pain shot through his leg, causing him to gasp.

Marcus was now in the lead. Though their progress down the Grand Plateau was slow and laborious, he pushed Sebastian on. When the gradient permitted, Sebastian slid on his backside in the snow.

Throughout the long trek towards the refuge, stumbling over rocks, wading through snowfields and navigating crevasses,

Marcus shouted words of encouragement, but while the snow blew sideways, stinging at their faces like ball bearings, his words were whipped away in the wind.

Setting a compass bearing for Pitschner rock, they continued on down, but as visibility declined further, their progress became slower still. With Marcus in the lead, he became the marker for Sebastian. He was treading cautiously, on the lookout for depressions or shadows in the snow, fully aware that as temperatures rose, the snow was more perilous. There would be a thousand dangers beneath.

Through the dense whiteout, Sebastian searched for the contour of Pitschner rock looming ahead of them. It was another marker to guide them, another obstacle to manoeuvre around. They were traversing the area between the two glaciers when it happened. One moment Marcus was reassuring his friend, the next he was yelling as the weakened snow bridge collapsed, and he fell into the crevasse below.

Roaring with pain, Sebastian dug his crampons into the ice and threw himself backwards, but joined by a rope to Marcus, he was dragged relentlessly towards the edge. A thud followed, then silence. The rope slackened.

Sebastian crawled forward and looked into the gloom below. 'Marcus!' he screamed, fear smothering rational thought. 'Marcus!' On a ledge about twenty feet below he could make out a still form.

He tried to pull on the rope but with an injured shoulder, there was no strength in his arms.

He was unable to belay from the top and Marcus was dead or unconscious below. Paralysed by anger and frustration, he lay on his front, his tears melting the snow. Pulling himself together, he realised their current situation was impossible. If he lowered himself down, neither of them would get out, they would die together in the crevasse. He lifted his head when he heard Marcus groan.

'I need to know if you have broken anything,' he called, scrabbling to his knees.

'Everything hurts,' came the muffled reply.

Sebastian fought to keep his voice level. 'I'll get you out.'

'We both know you can't help me. You have to go down alone.' Marcus turned his head, his voice barely audible.

'I can't leave you.'

'If you don't, we'll both die. Get the hell out of here and bring back a team,' he rasped.

With their predicament now dire, Sebastian accepted that it was their only chance.

'Get into the sleeping bag if you can,' he instructed, keeping his voice calm. 'You have the stove and provisions, enough to keep you going until I return.' He untied the rope that bound them together and with shaking hands he released the buckle on his rucksack. Every movement was excruciating, every action made him swear. Taking enough water and chocolate for his journey down, he attached the rucksack to the rope and lowered it over the edge.

'Come back soon.'

'I'll be back with help,' Sebastian assured him. 'Trust me, Marcus.'

'I do,' he whispered. But Sebastian couldn't hear.

Sebastian found Marcus's pole and planted it in the snow. He prayed it would still be visible on his return.

Sebastian limped on in the direction of the refuge, but without Marcus ahead as a marker, he was on his own with only a compass to guide him. Exhausted, he continued on down, talking to himself as he negotiated a crevasse or a bank of snow. As he neared the place where the refuge should be, his optimism rose. He visualised a team waiting, a warm fire, he could almost smell the food. Snow was falling, he could only see a few feet ahead. The refuge was just in front of him, it had to be. But it wasn't there. He lumbered on, one painful step at a time, stopping occasionally to wipe his goggles as he peered into the white landscape. When half an hour later, there was still no sign of the refuge he pulled his altimeter from his jacket and rubbed at the glass. The refuge was at an altitude of 2951 metres. It appeared he was approximately one hundred metres below it! A wail rose in his throat.

'Fuck,' he yelled, 'fuck,' and threw down his pole. Overwhelmed with despair, he crumpled to his knees, every nerve in his body screaming with pain. Pulling himself together, he considered the options. With snow whipping and spinning around him, there was no question of going back up the mountain to try and find the refuge, he would have to continue on down.

He pulled off his gloves and with icy fingers, he struggled to set a new bearing on his compass. It would pass through La Jonction to the edge of the glacier. From there he would reach dry land and take the short path to the Gîte à Balmat. With his route planned, he stood up, breathed deeply and scrambled on. Occasionally he tripped and fell, cursing obscenities, but he pushed himself on, he had one goal in mind, he had to get help and return to his friend.

Forty-five minutes later, Sebastian scrambled onto the rocks at Montagne de la Côte. Though the pain was unrelenting, the snow had changed to sleet and visibility was clearer. In the half-light he could see the gîte ahead of him. His lurching gait quickened. He finally reached the steps and pulled himself up, but as he pushed his weight against the door, he was met with resistance. He pushed again, it was locked. He groaned, sinking onto a step. He should have checked to see if the season had started, but what difference would it have made? He knew they would have done the climb either way.

The trail across the Montagne de la Côte threw up endless obstacles testing every inch of his resolve. The route seemed interminable through forests and barren trail. The smallest movement of his shoulder sent shockwaves through his body. Removing his crampons made him scream. He concentrated on taking one step at a time, keeping his head down, just ploughing on, forcing himself to think of anything but the pain. A lone eagle's cry broke his mood. He envisaged his son waiting for him at the hotel. He had to get back to him. He had to save Marcus.

Marcus lay on the ledge. One moment he was lucid, the next he was confused. His head throbbed, his pelvis hurt, he was fearfully cold. As he looked upwards beyond the ice walls, to the patch of sky beyond, he knew this would be the end, he would never leave the mountain. This would be his tomb.

How ironic; for so much of his life he had longed to come out of the shadows, wanted people to accept him as he was, and when he had finally found true friendship, his life was being snatched away. But at least he had experienced the warmth that he had known as a young child.

Sebastian would get back to Alfie, he was sure of it now. He could see them together, playing in the sunshine. He thought of his own mother, remembered the day by the sea, splashing in the waves, and her laughter as she lifted him up and swung him around. His lids became heavy. He couldn't reflect any more, the past was there as it always had been; some occasions were just too painful to endure.

It was dark when Sebastian reached the Chalet du Glacier des Bossons and banged on the door.

A window opened above him. 'Do you know what time it is?' It was a man's angry voice.

'I need help.'

Seconds later he could hear footsteps on the stairs, the door opening.

Sebastian's vision was coming and going. There was a man in front of him who seemed to be swaying.

'My friend … a crevasse above Pitschner rock,' he garbled.

At once his head felt light and the world went black.

The man caught him as he fell.

When Sebastian came to, he was propped on a settle beside a fire. Two men were watching him.

'Your friend is on the mountain?' The younger of the two questioned, his freckled forehead wrinkled in concern.

Sebastian tried to get up, but his legs buckled. 'We must go to him,' he urged. 'We need to leave now.'

'You are not fit for anywhere except the hospital,' the older man, Monsieur Vinet said, putting a warm mug of soup to his lips. 'You'll be a danger to yourself and everyone else. It is a miracle you managed to get down on your own.'

'No, don't you understand, we have to find him.'

'After fifty years of living and working these mountains, trust me, I do understand,' he stated. 'Mountain Rescue will find your friend. You will go to the hospital.'

Persuading Monsieur Vinet to take him back to the hotel so that he could alert his family and not the hospital, wasted minutes of valuable time.

Shaking his bald head, Monsieur Vinet went to fetch an ancient Jeep from a shed beside the chalet. As the vehicle jolted and lurched over the rutted mountain track, Sebastian bit his lip to prevent his screams.

It was eleven o'clock in the evening when Monsieur Vinet supported Sebastian into the hotel foyer. He collapsed into a chair.

'Please call Mountain Rescue,' he urged the tired-looking receptionist. 'And wake Madame Ogilvie.'

Soon the entire family was assembled in the entrance hall.

'Papa, you're hurt.' Alfie rushed to Sebastian and flung himself into his arms. As Sebastian shrieked in pain, the child leapt backwards, his face stricken.

'It's all right, Alfie. I'm a little bruised that's all.'

Gillie tried to steer him away, but he wouldn't be moved.

'But he's hurt, aren't you, Papa. I'm not leaving and where's Marcus?'

'Alfie, you can see I am safe. Back to bed, young man, while I talk to Uncle Pierre.'

'Come on, darling, let's take you upstairs.' Liliane, wearing a silk dressing gown, took her grandson's hand.

'You'll come and say goodnight, Papa?'

'Of course.'

While the child was led reluctantly away, Pierre knelt down by Sebastian.

'I assume Marcus is still on the mountain?' he asked.

'A snow bridge collapsed, he's injured. We have to help him, Pierre.'

'First you need to help me pinpoint the location.'

Sebastian's eyes were heavy. He mustn't let them close.

Pierre removed the map from his nephew's pocket and spread it on a table beside him.

'Show me where,' he said, taking out a pen.

Sebastian tried to study the map, but his lids were drooping. 'Near the refuge des Grands Mulets,' he muttered.

'Here?'

He tried to focus on the map, but the print was coming and going. 'Beyond Pitschner rock, down a bit.'

Pierre moved the pen.

'Yes, yes there. Go to the right. Stop. That's it. No more than fifty metres from the rock.'

'Positive?'

Sebastian was struggling to stay awake. 'Yes, I'm sure.'

As Pierre marked an X on the map, Sebastian's body sagged forward.

'I planted his pole,' he murmured, but the weather... You must find him, Pierre.'

Chapter Thirty-Six

The doors swung open and in a blast of cold air, the leader of the Chamonix organisation of professional guides strode into the foyer. He nodded at Monsieur Vinet and went straight to Sebastian.

'How many are left on the mountain, *monsieur*?'

'Only one,' Sebastian's voice was rasping with fatigue. 'But he is injured and trapped in a crevasse. It's marked on the map.'

The guide took a pair of glasses from the pocket of his jacket. 'I need you to describe specific features of the landscape.'

Pierre spread the map on a table. 'This is the spot my nephew has identified.'

Sebastian's head was lolling forward. He looked up. 'There's no time to lose. Please send a helicopter and get together a team.'

'No helicopters, I'm afraid. The disaster of three years ago put paid to that, but I will take a team at first light.'

'First light?' Sebastian forced himself to concentrate.

'I'm afraid the conditions at the moment are too dangerous; I cannot risk the lives of my men.'

'But that may be too late,' Sebastian whispered.

The guide's face softened. 'Your friend will be out of the storm.'

The guide turned to Liliane, who was now dressed in outdoor clothes. 'We need to get this young man to hospital. Madame, I'm sure you will wish to accompany your son.'

When the door had closed on the ambulance, Monsieur Vinet went to the Jeep. Pierre, wearing a jumper over his pyjamas, ran into the rain after him.

'Do you know anyone who would help me?' he asked. 'I intend to go up now.'

Monsieur Vinet, looked at him hard, assessing him. 'You on a mountain at night, in this weather, are you mad?'

'I've climbed a lot in my youth. I'm fit, trust me I'm quite capable.'

'Leave it to the rescue team. They have the equipment, they will go in the morning.'

Pierre's jaw was clenched as he looked beyond Monsieur Vinet towards the distant skyline. He had promised Sebastian; the morning was too late.

'I'm going now.'

'Agh!' Monsieur Vinet shook his head. 'I've rescued many men from the mountain: stupid, inexperienced men. We risk our lives trying to save them.'

'I will pay you well,' Pierre urged.

He laughed harshly. 'I wouldn't take your money, but I can't let you die. I'll help you. Get dressed in your warmest clothes, then I'll find you some kit.'

Before they left the Chalet du Glacier des Bossons, Monsieur Vinet dragged an old sledge to the front of the house. 'This will be our stretcher,' he stated. 'I have used it many times.'

There were three of them following the trail to the glacier, Monsieur Vinet, his son Olivier, and Pierre.

As Pierre strode behind them, he felt strangely liberated. His senses were heightened. He could hear his boots crunching on the shale, the wind rushing through the trees. He could smell the scent of forest and wet pine.

A cloud scudded across the sky, shrouding the moon like a gauze veil. Somewhere in the darkness an owl hooted. As Pierre looked upwards marvelling at the beauty of creation, he prayed they would get to Marcus in time. Surely God would grant him that. Perhaps by saving Marcus, he would save himself and the shadow left by Fleur's death would be lifted at last.

They reached the glacier at two o'clock.

'So you really are fit,' Monsieur Vinet commented with a wry smile. 'And now I discover you are a man of God. I would never have been so bold.'

'That is why I didn't tell you,' Pierre chuckled. 'Take an abbot on a hike at night over perilous terrain? You would never have agreed.'

They were strapping on their crampons for their trek across the glacier, when Monsieur Vinet spoke again.

'The glacier is a thing of great beauty,' he said, his voice tinged with regret, 'but I have noticed that the spring and summer melts are much heavier. I fear these beautiful rivers of ice will soon start to shrink and it is my belief that Man has played a part in this.' He prodded at the ice with the toe of his boot and turned to Pierre, his face grim. 'With their atomic bombs and chemical warfare, Man will destroy the planet, and what will God think of that?'

'Unfortunately we are responsible for our own destiny,' Pierre replied, 'but I am hoping the planet will be safe for a while.'

'Possibly, Father, but if we don't do something to stop this stupidity, who knows.'

Pierre gazed into the darkness. Monsieur Vinet was probably right. The human race was culpable, but not Monsieur Vinet. He had agreed to help a stranger. He was one of God's men.

It was dark when Marcus woke. He switched on the torch and as the beam illuminated the pillars of ice that stretched above him, he trembled with fear. The two-foot wide ledge was all that was keeping him alive. Despite the sleeping bag wrapped around him, hypothermia would soon set in, he would lose consciousness and he would fall. Inch by inch he pulled the rucksack towards him and drew out the stove, but his hands were shaking, and he couldn't light the match. Forcing himself to remain calm, he looked at his surroundings. In any other situation, the sparkling cave of ice stalactites would have been beautiful, a fantasy world, but this was no fantasy. It was a lonely way to die.

Though the trek across the glacier was treacherous, Pierre wasn't afraid; the dangers seemed little in comparison to those he had known in the past. They moved across the ice, listening, watching, roped together as a team. No one spoke but there was a silent bond between them. The three men were equal in the eyes of God, there was no hierarchy, they were merely brothers relying on each other for their safety.

With each step, Pierre felt nearer to Fleur. Alfie's christening was the last time he had allowed himself the luxury of thinking about her, but now as a silver crescent moon peeped through the blustery sky, he remembered her coming to him in the moonlight, her white skin glowing. He could almost feel the warmth of her body in his arms, the smell of jasmine in her hair. 'Fleur,' he whispered. My beautiful Fleur. He wondered if this would be his last moon, the last flake of wet snow to touch his cheeks. He felt a shudder deep inside his body, beneath his ribs, at his very core. Was God calling him?

They were nearing the spot Sebastian had marked on the map, but there was no sign of a pole.

Monsieur Vinet raised his hand and turned to Pierre. 'With your direct access to God, I suggest it is up to you.'

For ten minutes they searched, called, but with no reply. When they believed they had failed, and the pole was buried beneath the snow, Pierre cried out.

'Over there. It may be nothing at all.'

Monsieur Vinet moved closer, cautious, alert.

'*Mon dieu,*' he exclaimed. '*Ici.*'

Taking out a spade, he dug until the entrance to the crevasse was clear. He called Marcus's name but there was no reply.

Pierre arrived behind him. He lay down and leant over the edge. Shining his torch deep into the crevasse he could see the still body of Marcus curled on the ledge.

'Hammer in two pitons at the top and I'll abseil down,' Monsieur Vinet instructed his son.

'No. I'll go,' Pierre declared.

The climber looked at him in astonishment. 'You?'

Pierre nodded. 'I asked you to help me. This is beyond your call of duty. It is my responsibility. I promised my nephew.'

'You have no experience.'

'Indeed I have, and as you have observed, I am not as feeble as I seem. I insist.'

A look of understanding passed between the two men. 'Well then, it is agreed.'

Monsieur Vinet made a harness for Pierre and after attaching another rope with a bowline knot, he smiled.

'You are a brave man, *monsieur*. It is an honour to know you.'

'And you too, Monsieur Vinet.'

After two ice pitons had been hammered into the ice, a carabiner clipped in, and the rope attached to the 'krab' with a knotted loop, Monsieur Vinet tugged at the knot. 'This should hold.'

Pierre nodded. 'Thank you and God bless.'

As he lowered himself into the crevasse he could feel the rope rasping on the ice. Down he went and further down, until he reached the ledge.

He inched his way along the ice, refusing to look into the gaping void beneath. 'Dear God,' he prayed. 'Please let him be alive.' Where the ledge became wider he crawled along it until he came to Marcus. The young man's face was discoloured and swollen, his eyes were closed. He knelt down and felt for a pulse. It was faint, but his prayers were answered as Marcus opened his eyes.

'You have come back for me,' he murmured.

'Sebastian got down the mountain and I have returned for you. Do you remember me, Marcus, Sebastian's uncle?'

'The priest?'

'Yes, the priest,' Pierre smiled.

'And my name?'

'Pierre de Villienne.'

'Well then, we have established that your brain is working.'

Half an hour later, when Marcus was rehydrated and warmed by the little camping stove, Pierre asked him to move. Marcus responded first with his feet then with his arms.

'Can you lift your head?'

Slowly with Pierre supporting his shoulders he was able to sit.

'It's my pelvis,' he groaned.

'Your body will mend, but we need to get you out of here. Will you send down the ropes,' he called to Monsieur Vinet.

'Coming down,' came the reply.

Pierre made a harness for Marcus and attached him with another bowline knot. 'You are going to need every ounce of your resilience. This will not be easy, Marcus, but remember I am here, always.' He remembered Fleur saying the same words to the young soldier on the day they had first met. This time the young man would live.

'We are ready,' he called.

'Ready,' came the reply. Slowly, Marcus was levered up the crevasse. When he cried out in pain, Pierre gave words of reassurance from below. 'God is with you. Look upwards, always upwards.' Inch by inch, Marcus's bruised and injured body was hauled up the uneven walls, moving from darkness into the arc of torchlight. As Marcus reached the top and was hauled over the edge, Pierre felt the years of guilt and misery slip from his shoulders.

Whatever had happened in the past, God had forgiven him. He had done something truly good.

It was his turn now. Harnessed to the rockface, he started to climb. Hand above hand, finding a foothold here and ledge there. He remembered climbing with Jasper. They were young then, agile and brave. He was no longer young, but the feeling of exhilaration was the same. He was nearing the surface when the sensation in his hands changed. Something was wrong, but he was not sure why.

He could see Monsieur Vinet's tense face staring down at him. 'We need to hurry Father, and we must move right back to get a firmer foothold. We're going to pull you in.' Pierre could feel the comforting wrench in his chest as they took up the slack. Only seconds now and he would reach the surface.

He was only a metre from the top when he realised there would be no way out. He could see the ice walls fracturing, the remains of the snow bridge collapsing. He could hear Monsieur Vinet cry out, but as Pierre looked upwards, there was no panic in his heart. He saw the moon shining above him, and heard the wind blowing. His last thoughts as the ice came crashing towards him were of Fleur.

Chapter Thirty-Seven

As soon as the ambulance arrived at the hospital Liliane knew her brother would never come home. Before they had even opened the door, the fear in her stomach told her that Pierre was gone.

'He's dead, isn't he?' she said, her voice flat.

Monsieur Vinet nodded. 'Your brother died saving Marcus. He is a hero, *madame*.'

Liliane collapsed to her knees on the wet ground, oblivious to the medical orderlies who carried Marcus from the ambulance, oblivious to everyone. 'Pierre, my dearest Pierre,' she sobbed.

Monsieur Vinet, who had witnessed such grief before, helped her to her feet.

'In the short time I was with the abbot, I recognised he was the greatest of men. Living on the edge of the mountain, I have seen acts of courage in my time, but never have I seen someone willingly give his life in this way.'

When Marcus opened his eyes, Gillie was standing at the end of his bed talking to the consultant.

'Any longer in the crevasse and the consequences would have been very different.'

'He's lucky to be alive,' Gillie agreed.

'I am amazed how little damage there is. A couple of ribs are broken but fortunately not displaced. I've taped them up, but I don't need to tell you, he must be careful. His hip is fractured, here,' he was holding up X-rays for Gillie, and she was studying them carefully.

'As you can see, the break is in the upper part of the bone near the hip joint area. It is only a short crack and doesn't require surgery. We will start physical therapy immediately, and we will provide an exercise programme to continue in Pommard. Monsieur Ogilvie's X-rays are being sent straight to Dijon.'

Marcus was confused. Why were they talking about Pommard? He would be returning to Rouen just as soon as he was discharged.

The consultant left, and Gillie came to his side.

'You're awake.' She was smiling down at him.

'How is Sebastian?' he asked, memories of the perilous climb flooding back.

'He's going to be fine; it will take a month or two because he has a broken fibula and they had to pin his shoulder. He is a bit battered, but he will make a full recovery. He is being taken to the hospital in Dijon first thing in the morning.'

Relief flooded Marcus; his friend was safe, but not Pierre.

'And your uncle?' he looked away, fighting back his tears. 'Have they found him?'

'They will never find him,' Gillie murmured. 'He will stay there on the mountain.'

Marcus cleared his throat. 'He saved my life, Gillie, I am so sorry.'

Gillie bit her lip. 'Of course he did, that's just like my uncle. One day, when we are both feeling a little stronger, we will speak about it, but perhaps not now.' Her voice broke and she walked to the window and stared outside.

'I have left Alfie with my brother,' she said at last. 'I am going to look in on them. Sebastian has suggested that while he is in hospital in Dijon, you should consider convalescing with us at Pommard. We would be glad of your company, what do you think?'

Marcus looked at her and nodded. 'If you are certain ... I would love to. Thank you, Gillie.'

Alfie was curled on his father's hospital bed reading when Amelia arrived. She leant down and kissed the young boy's forehead.

'Shhh,' she whispered. 'It's a surprise.'

Alfie nodded, his eyes solemn, then she kissed Sebastian's mouth.

'You've come,' he murmured.

'Of course I have,' Amelia smiled gently. 'The library has given me compassionate leave. Now, Alfie, what has your father done to himself?'

Alfie ticked off a long list on his fingers. 'He has a broken fibula, a pinned shoulder, lots of bruising, a nasty gash on his cheek,' Alfie pointed to the taped cut on his father's face, 'and he has to wear a sling for at least six weeks.'

'Poor Papa,' Amelia said, ruffling Alfie's hair. 'Soon he will be home.'

'Unfortunately I am being sent to the hospital in Dijon for a few days, but you will all be able to visit me every day.' Sebastian grimaced as fresh pain shot though his shoulder.

'But I thought you were coming home now,' Alfie burst out.

'The doctors need to be sure Papa is absolutely better before he comes home,' Amelia reassured him. 'Would you like it if I stayed with you at Pommard, Alfie? It would be such fun and I could read you stories every night.'

Alfie brightened immediately. 'Uncle Robert has ordered me a new book. *Five Get into Trouble*. They go on a camping trip and Dick gets kidnapped, but it shouldn't have been him. We can start with that if you like.'

'Goodness, that sounds exciting, I'd like that very much.'

When Alfie had gone to the cafeteria for hot chocolate with his aunt, Amelia dragged a chair from the corner and sat down.

'I am sorry,' she said softly. 'It must be so hard for you.'

Sebastian cleared his throat.

'The climb was my idea and it cost my uncle his life. Alfie thinks he has returned to the monastery, but I can't tell him the truth; not yet. He will be completely devastated; first his great grandmother, and now Pierre.'

'Children are more resilient than we think,' Amelia responded. 'He will get through this.'

'But Alfie has lost too many people in his life.' Sebastian plucked at the cotton sling. 'I was irresponsible, Amelia. My uncle is dead, and Alfie could have lost me.'

Chapter Thirty-Eight

Marcus and Sebastian left the hospital in Chamonix on the same day, but while Marcus went to Pommard with Gillie, Sebastian travelled by ambulance to Dijon University Hospital.

For Marcus it was a strange experience. After so many years of living on his own, he was now in the midst of a busy household. Adeline fussed over him, cooking special dishes for him, while Gillie supervised his physical therapy in the private garden, pushing him harder each day. She seemed to enjoy his company. One morning when he had finished his exercises and they were sitting on Marie-Claire's bench, she opened up about Christophe.

'I loved him, Marcus, and now...' She threw a handful of corn to the hens. 'I will find out what it was all about, but at the moment I can't bear to think about it.'

Marcus was rarely alone, leaving him little time to dwell on the accident. Every morning Alfie flitted into his room armed with a chess board, cajoling him to play, or he would enlist his help with his latest model aeroplane. Marcus was a willing accomplice and delighted in these childhood pursuits.

He showed Alfie how to build a medieval fortress using cardboard and glue, and they spent hours cutting out the battlements, making towers, a keep, even a gatehouse and a drawbridge. When the impressive structure was finished, they set to with paints, both clad in matching green overalls.

Alfie was always inquisitive, forever inquiring. 'What was the keep for, Marcus?' he asked.

'It was a strong, safe building inside the castle, the last resort where the people could go if the castle walls were breached.'

'What does breached mean, Marcus?'

Marcus loved the questions and relished answering them. He even made Alfie a rocket using soda syphon cartridges, to the raised eyebrows of Alfie's grandmother. He hadn't been so happy in years.

His hostess was always gracious, but he could sense that she was reserved around him. He was obviously a constant reminder that he was alive while her brother was dead.

'It was a bad day when the abbot died,' Adeline had announced on his first morning, putting a plate of eggs in front of him. '*Madame* is never going to get over it, they were so close.'

'It was my fault, he was rescuing me,' Marcus had uttered staring at the eggs, no longer hungry.

'It wouldn't have made no difference who it was, you or anyone else, he would have still given his life. You should hear of his exploits during the Great War, going into no man's land to carry the injured to safety. He was a true angel of God,' she explained.

As Marcus reflected on her words, he remembered Pierre climbing down into the crevasse when he had all but given up hope, praying with him until he was ready to be taken up. He had continued to encourage and reassure him, as inch by inch he was pulled towards the surface. Pierre de Villienne had given him the impetus to fight to stay alive.

Amelia was as good as her word. She read to Alfie, made up games and played with him. Marcus would watch them from his deckchair as they walked through the meadow towards the lake,

Amelia carrying a rug and books, her skirts floating around her legs, their heads together as they talked. Sometimes they would run around waving their arms pretending to be aeroplanes before throwing themselves down beside Marcus, and Alfie would fall asleep with Amelia stroking his flushed little face.

Amelia's thoughtfulness encompassed Marcus too. She always enquired about his health and asked if he needed anything. Their conversations covered an eclectic range of topics, from architecture to design and even fashion. When he showed her a photograph of his apartment, her face lit up.

'Oh it's beautiful,' she gasped. 'One day will you show it to me?'

'Of course, I would love to,' he replied. And it was true, he would be proud to show Amelia because he knew her interest was genuine. He found her enchanting, and he believed she would be the perfect mother to Alfie.

On most evenings, a small band would set off for the hospital in Dijon, leaving Adeline in charge of Marcus. On these occasions he did not wish to intrude.

'I can't presume on your hospitality any longer,' he protested to Gillie. 'I need to get back to work in Rouen.'

Gillie tutted. 'Does your firm value you?' she asked.

'I'd like to think so,' he replied.

'Then I suggest you stop being silly, you can hardly walk, so you are hardly well enough to return to work. We love having you here and I have watched you with Alfie, he adores you. It would be churlish to leave,' she smiled.

'Just another few days, then I have to return to my desk. I will get behind on my projects and I am working on something rather interesting at the moment.'

'Tell me,' Gillie urged, sitting on a chair in the library beside him.

He described his latest project, converting an old Parisian wallpaper factory in the tenth *arrondissement* into a block of flats.

'We have preserved the industrial feel, Gillie,' he said, his face animated. 'And the living rooms, I believe you would love them. Huge windows in every apartment, and on the top floor, the glass ceilings are seven metres high.'

'It sounds perfect, just the sort of apartment I would dream of. I was beginning to hope there was a future with Christophe; maybe we could have lived in Paris. Now of course it will never happen.' She sighed, her shoulders sagging.

'You have to be positive in life, dear Gillie.'

'But I would love to share my life with someone.'

Marcus looked at her and smiled ruefully. 'Wouldn't we all.'

'But it's not the same for a man, Marcus, the clock is ticking for me, you ...' She stopped. 'Oh, I think I have been a little tactless.'

Marcus looked her in the eye. 'It is not easy, Gillie, I would to love be as most men are, but I am different.'

'You are a very dear man,' Gillie took his hand.

On the eve of his departure for Rouen, Marcus took a taxi to the hospital.

'So good to see you.' Marcus limped across the ward towards his friend.

'Can't even shake your hand, sorry,' Sebastian indicated his shoulder, 'but I'm allowed outside, special treat,' he grinned, 'for good behaviour.'

They were sitting on recliners in the evening sunshine, their walking sticks discarded nearby. Marcus recounted how he had been beaten by Sebastian's son at almost every card game imaginable.

'He is very determined, you know.'

'Just like his mother.' Sebastian was looking at him, his eyes thoughtful. 'You never knew her, but he grows more like her each day.'

'Tell me?' Marcus asked, intrigued, because Sebastian had never mentioned her before.

'Apart from being extremely attractive, she was vibrant, inquisitive, and yes, she was so determined. She would get this look, and you knew that nothing was going to stop her. Alfie is the same. And her smile, it would light up her entire face, and you wanted to be part of it, part of her. There was very little I could do to stop myself falling in love with her.'

'But why isn't she with you now?'

'Ambition, I suppose. And I am not sure if she ever really loved me.' His face looked bleak. 'Anyway, enough of Alfie's mother, apparently there is talk of you leaving us.'

'However much I adore being with your family, I do have an office to run,' Marcus smiled. 'Reluctantly, I will leave tomorrow.'

Throughout the afternoon, neither mentioned their time on the mountain; it was as yet too painful for both of them. But as the taxi drove Marcus back to Pommard, he imagined their nightmares were shared.

Sophie was in the cafeteria when she overheard the nurses talking.

'Have you seen the man in ward seven, he is very handsome, such blue eyes.'

Why did the nurses have to gossip so, Sophie thought, irritated? It was somehow wrong.

'*Mais oui*, but he also has a chateau in Pommard, and a beautiful girlfriend – he is out of your league.'

Pommard? Sophie gulped her coffee. It couldn't be Sebastian, surely? She put the remains of her lunch on the trolley and went to the nurses' station. She picked up the patient list, her hands shaking. Sebastian Ogilvie – the name hit her like a thump to her stomach. It was obviously an injury. He was in a side room in the orthopaedic ward.

It was Friday night and Sebastian had been in the hospital for ten days. He wanted to go home to be with Alfie and Amelia.

The old maritime explorer, Monsieur Cartier, was stamping through the passages, shouting to get the topsail down, until a nurse gently took him back to bed. Sebastian could hear a clang in the distance, then silence. Lights moved across the glass panel separating his small room from the ward. He closed his eyes, but the pain in his shoulder kept him awake. He had just managed to doze when the medicine trolley stopped outside his door.

'*En as-tu marre?*' It was the pretty nurse Eve.

'*Merci*, I'm fine,' he whispered.

'You don't look particularly fine to me.' She stuck a thermometer beneath his tongue.

'Temperature is normal, but I have just the thing for a good night's sleep. Would you like a suppository or a pill, *monsieur*?'

'Pill please,' Sebastian instantly replied, disliking the French preference for inserting every drug they could up the backside. Eve chuckled, gave him a pill with a glass of water and sorted out his bed. 'I'll get the doctor to come and look at you. You can never be too sure.'

The trolley had gone, rattling away down the corridor and after half an hour of trying to get comfortable, Sebastian had at last fallen asleep, but he was once again living his nightmare: he couldn't breathe, he was suffocating. He was buried beneath the snow. He woke with a start, sweating. In the half-light he thought he could see a young woman with a red jacket looking down on him, she was smiling. 'Sophie?' he whispered, through a haze of drugs. But the woman above him was a doctor in a white coat. He struggled to sit up. She was reading the clipboard at the end of the bed.

'Sebastian,' was all she said.

For a moment they looked at each other. Sebastian remembered the small gap in her front teeth, her high cheekbones and gamine face. There was something about her smile that had once bewitched him, and her eyes. Her hair was shorter and was cut in a simple bob that stopped at her chin, but apart from the doctor's white coat, she looked the same.

'Sophie,' the name sounded stiff and strange on his tongue. 'What are you doing here?' he croaked.

'I could ask you the same,' she smiled, 'but I have your notes. You always said you would climb Mont Blanc.'

'But it didn't end well,' he said.

Sophie looked at him, her eyebrow raised, and Sebastian resisted the impulse to touch the small frown on her forehead, run his hand through her hair.

'I thought you had become a doctor in Paris?'

'So you have been following me?'

Sebastian laughed. 'That is what you said the first time we met.' He paused, the pain in his shoulder forgotten as he studied her. 'I saw the editorial in *Time* magazine.'

'Ah, that. I actually knew you were here. I heard one of my colleagues talking about the patient from Pommard – actually it was the nurses in the canteen,' she grinned.

'So you were following me.'

'You could say that.' She sat down on the edge of the bed and looked at him.

'Tell me about Alfie?' she begged.

'There is too much to tell, but he is my life.' Sebastian's eyes softened.

'There is not a day that goes by when I don't think about him,'

Sophie said, choking on her words. 'I have been so tempted to contact you, to implore you to let me see him.'

'I would never have stopped you.'

'I believed it was better for Alfie.'

For a moment the old resentment and anger bubbled inside Sebastian.

'How can you know what is better for Alfie? You gave him away.'

'You are correct, Sebastian. I had given up all right when I left him with you. But I truly believed it was best for my son.'

'Our son,' he corrected her.

She stood up and brushed her eyes with the back of her hand. 'Now Sebastian, I will take your blood pressure and your temperature. A few more days here and your specialist will let you go home.'

As she was leaving, Sebastian caught her arm. 'Will you come again tomorrow?'

'I will be back on the cardiology ward, it's in a different building. But yes, I will come after I have finished.'

'I will wait for you,' he said.

The following afternoon, his mother came to see him with Amelia and Alfie. Once again, Sebastian wanted to go outside. While he talked to Liliane, Amelia took off her shoes and ran through the grass, chased by a grubby, small boy. When she picked him up and swung him round, her white cotton skirts floating about her, the sun shone through her hair.

'There is something ethereal in her beauty,' Liliane observed.

'You're right,' Sebastian agreed.

'Alfie seems to like her.'

Sebastian paused for a moment. Where were the ready words extolling her beauty and her qualities? Because there was no doubt Amelia was beautiful and she was kind and intelligent; the perfect mother for Alfie – or was she? Did Alfie really like her, could he love her? He shook his head in frustration. Of course he could. These doubts were new and disturbing. Seeing Sophie after all this time had unsettled him.

'He has grown very fond of her,' he said.

His mother had taken Amelia and Alfie back to Pommard, leaving Sebastian alone with his thoughts. Would Sophie return, he wondered, or was her appearance the previous night just a dream. As the clock in the passage outside struck nine, he could feel his chest tightening. Would she come?

He flipped through a magazine, trying to distract himself, but his thoughts kept returning to Sophie. It would be another hour before he saw her shadow through the opaque glass panel. The next second, she was standing by his bed.

'I thought I'd never see you again.' He spoke softly, his eyes never leaving her face. 'And now like this ...'

'Do you want to talk about the accident?' she asked.

'My uncle was killed on the mountain,' he stated, choking back his emotion. 'He was saving my friend.'

'I'm so sorry.' She put her hand over his, and he flinched, the sensation was so powerful.

'You must think we were stupid. Two foolhardy young men who thought they owned the world.'

'I think all young men with dreams of conquering the mountains are rash, but it is not going to stop them. I understand what it is to have dreams.'

For three nights she came to the ward. There was anger occasionally, and confusion, but Sophie tried her best to explain.

'You have to understand, I wanted my son to have everything that I did not – most of all, a family. My childhood was lonely, Sebastian. My grandmother did her best, but so much of my time was spent alone. When she died I believed there was no

320

option; if there had been another way, trust me I would have taken it, but I could never beg you to help us, Sebastian.'

'Beg me? Don't you see I would have married you, Sophie?'

'But your family, they would never have sanctioned it.'

Sebastian laughed harshly. 'How could you possibly know that? Don't you see you could have had it all? You could have been with your son in the formative years of his life and you could have continued with your medicine.'

Sophie looked at him, emotion welling in her chest. 'I didn't know.'

'Well, perhaps you should have asked.'

She turned away, a tear escaping. 'If only, Sebastian.'

'If only what?' He caught hold of her arm; he could feel the touch of her skin beneath his fingers, the frisson between them.

Sophie hesitated. 'If I hadn't been a stupid and naïve young woman, then perhaps things would have been different.'

'And now?' he asked, forgetting about Amelia, about everything but the woman beside him.

'And now it is obviously too late for both of us.'

She was leaving, when she stopped at the door. 'Could I see Alfie? Not of course if it makes things difficult, I understand your sentiments entirely.' The words came out in a rush and she was biting her lip in the way Sebastian remembered.

He thought for a moment. The last thing he wanted was to disrupt his son's life, particularly now.

He could see tears pricking in Sophie's eyes.

'Of course, but at this moment in time, you will be a good friend from the past, not his mother. I hope you understand.'

She nodded, her cheeks flushed.

'There is something else you should know.' Sebastian drew in his breath. He couldn't bear to tell her, but he had to. 'I am engaged to be married.'

'I see.' Sophie leant against the door post. 'Congratulations, Sebastian, you deserve to be happy.' She lowered her head but not before Sebastian caught a glimmer of pain in her eyes.

'Amelia is staying with my mother in Pommard. She will be coming to the hospital at three tomorrow.'

'And Alfie?'

'He will be coming too.'

Sophie hesitated, then she straightened her shoulders and looked Sebastian in the eye. 'I would be glad to meet Amelia, if it means I will see my son.'

When Amelia and Alfie arrived, Sebastian took some coins from his bedside cabinet.

'What would you say to a bar of chocolate, Alfie?'

'Yes please, Papa,' Alfie jumped about the room.

'You know the nice lady in the café at the end of the passage. Do you think you can manage to go there on your own?'

'Of course I can.'

Amelia watched from the doorway as he skipped along the corridor.

Sebastian propped himself up against the pillows, a shadow of stubble on his chin. 'Amelia, there is something I need to tell you and I am not quite sure how to put it.'

Amelia's eyes widened with concern. 'Is something wrong?'

'No, nothing wrong. But you might find it difficult. Alfie's mother is working here in this hospital.'

'I see. When did you find out?' she said at last, her voice flat.

'Not until yesterday. I thought she was training in Paris. But now it seems she wants to see Alfie.'

Amelia remained silent, digesting this new information.

'I hope you can find it in your heart to accept this?'

'Will you tell Alfie she is his mother?'

'Not yet,' he replied. 'After we are married, when we are all settled as a family, we can tell him together.'

At that moment Alfie came bursting in the door waving his bar of chocolate.

The following afternoon at the allotted time, Sophie was doing the ward rounds, trailed by several students. 'I need to see the patient in side room three,' she smiled at the students. 'I believe he wishes to speak to me in private, so please will you find our old friend Monsieur Cartier. Question him about his recent expedition to Madagascar.'

While the students went in search of Monsieur Cartier who once again had left his bed, Sophie made her way to the side ward. Her legs felt weak and she could feel perspiration break on her forehead. She paused outside the room, counted to three, then she opened the door.

Alfie was reading to his father. He looked up as she came in. She stared at him for a moment, completely unable to move, her heart in her mouth. Her son was the image of Max.

'Are you all right, doctor?' It was the little boy's voice.

She cleared her throat. She had to remain calm, she couldn't break down, it would frighten the child.

'*Oui,*' she said at last, her voice trembling.

'Alfie, *mon cheri,*' Sebastian gave his son a little shove, 'this is a friend of mine, Doctor Sophie Bernot.'

Alfie got off the bed and came towards her. He put out his hand to shake and it took all of Sophie's strength not to sweep him into her arms.

'I think I would like to be a doctor when I grow up, or a vet or a conservationist. Anyway I think it is a very important job.'

'Hello Alfie,' Sophie said, feeling his warm little hand in her own.

'I wanted to be a circus artist when I was little,' he continued.

'But I went to the circus with Tante Gillie and the tigers were in cages. I am of the opinion all animals should be free.'

'I agree with you,' Sophie said at last, her equilibrium returning as she scrutinised every feature of his earnest face. 'When I was a little girl, our neighbour had a cage in the garden with two squirrels inside. One night I opened the door.'

'What happened to them?'

'They scampered out as fast as their little legs would carry them. I used to watch them running around in the trees afterwards. I put out food and they would come into our garden, put their faces against the back door. I was convinced they were thanking me, but it could have been the nuts.'

Their conversation was interrupted by a tall, extremely beautiful woman with green eyes who hovered in the doorway.

Sebastian looked flustered.

'Amelia, may I introduce you to Doctor Sophie Bernot.'

Sophie let herself into her flat and went straight to the kitchen to open a bottle of wine. Her hands were shaking as she poured herself a large glass. Sebastian had said she could have had it all, but he was about to marry Amelia Stormont, and everything was over. All her secret hopes and dreams, that one day he would come back to her, had gone. And now she had seen her son, and he was exactly as she had imagined. He had Max's heart-shaped face, his impish smile. Max had wanted to save the world and so did Alfie. She went into the sitting room, sat down on the leather sofa and put her head in her hands. Every day of every year she had imagined him, and now she wanted to be with him as a mother should be, always. She had been such a fool; how could she have given him up?

She could see Amelia's perfect face and the eccentric stripe in her hair. It would have been easier if she had been rude or arrogant, or even dull, then she could have hated her. But she was courteous and beautiful and terribly tall!! She put the glass on the floor, slopping the contents, and as the dark stain spread across the pale carpet, tears spilled down her face. How could she have let Sebastian go?

She realised suddenly that she truly loved him. Nothing had changed since the day she had left him.

When Sophie didn't come to the ward that night, Sebastian limped to the window overlooking the road, pulled up the blinds and opened it wide.

There was something comforting about the sound of traffic, the occasional laughter as people returned from the bars. It was normal, and he needed normality. His mind unwittingly returned to his last encounter with his uncle and his urgent request. '*You must find him, Pierre.*'

Sebastian had made light of his mother's fears, and now her brother was dead. He was engaged to quirky and gorgeous Amelia, but Sophie had returned to his life muddling everything. He groaned; he didn't deserve Amelia, in fact he didn't deserve anything at all.

He returned to bed, tossing and turning, until the dawn light filtered through the blinds, and at last he fell asleep.

Sophie came to see Sebastian one last time before he was discharged.

'So?' she smiled in the way that she did, but he recognised the sadness in her eyes. 'Are you going to allow me to see Alfie in the future?'

Sebastian paused. 'My sister and my mother are coming to collect me. I would like them to meet you, if you don't mind.'

'You mean you want them to vet me?'

'Of course not … But as you can imagine, they were not very well disposed towards you.'

'I understand, of course I do.' Sophie looked down at her hands, her lip trembling, and Sebastian wanted to take her in his arms.

'Your mother must hate me.'

'Not hate exactly, but I think it would be good if you were at least introduced.'

Sophie was apprehensive as she waited in the foyer. It was quite obvious Sebastian had no idea of her communication with his sister. He would undoubtedly be furious and that was the last thing she wanted, not now when she was begging access to see her son. Her hands started to shake as she caught a glimpse of them coming towards her. Though Gillie and her mother had dark hair, they had Sebastian's bone structure and the same look of assurance that only generations of affluence could bring.

'Maman,' Sebastian limped up to Sophie, 'this is Alfie's mother, Doctor Bernot.' Sophie went towards her. She could see Liliane's eyes widen.

'Sebastian has just told us,' Liliane said, hesitating before she shook Sophie's proffered hand.

'I am sure you despise me, and rightly so,' Sophie blurted out. 'I just want you to know that although I gave up my son, it was the most difficult decision of my life.'

'I don't understand how a mother could abandon her child, no matter the circumstances.' Liliane's voice was cold and level.

'I accept everything you say. I'm just asking if you will all allow me to see Alfie occasionally. I will not intrude, I assure you; he doesn't even have to know I am his mother.'

During the conversation, Gillie looked on feeling uncomfortable. It was true she had deceived both Sebastian and Liliane. It was also true that Sophie had never deserved her compassion, but as she looked at the girl in front of her, she could see why Sebastian had fallen in love with her. Even in her misery she was dignified, but there was much more. She was not conventionally beautiful like Amelia, but she had an extraordinary presence with a vibrancy that radiated from her. She was distracted from her thoughts when her mother turned to Sebastian.

'It can only be your decision,' she said.

'I believe it is important for Alfie to know his mother,' Sebastian confirmed.

Liliane raised her eyes to meet Sophie's. 'If Sebastian is happy for you to see Alfie, then I have no objection to you visiting Pommard.'

When they had gone, Sophie dragged herself back to her tiny office and closed the door. She had done a twelve-hour shift and she was now on call. As she lowered her head to the desk her thoughts were confused. She was able to see her son – it was more than she could have hoped for, and yet she was coming as a friend. She should be happy but she was not. She had lost Sebastian for ever and she couldn't hold her son in the way that a mother should. As exhaustion overwhelmed her, she closed her eyes. She would have just a few moments' rest.

She was awoken an hour later when a nurse knocked on her door.

Chapter Thirty-Nine

Georges, who was now working in obstetrics at the Dijon Bourgogne Université Hospital, offered to drive Sophie to Pommard to see her son, but she declined.

'No, dearest Georges,' she said, as they sat in their usual bar. 'This time I should go on my own.'

'I was right all along Sophie,' Georges declared, skewering an olive. 'You took the residency here because of Alfie.' He looked at her thoughtfully. 'And to be near Sebastian of course, and I came here because of you.'

'You are right about Alfie, not about Sebastian,' she said, her face flushed. 'And as for you, in a moment you are heading back to Paris and a lifetime of slavery!'

'You are a baggage, Sophie Bernot,' he grinned.

'I worry about you, Sophie,' he said, when the bowl of olives was empty, and he had ordered another. 'At the risk of sounding clichéd, you will get your fingers burnt, *ma cherie*.'

'Georges, it's too late for that.' She squeezed his hand. 'Anyway, you must stop worrying about me. When you get married I will have to manage on my own.'

The following day Sophie took a taxi to Pommard and asked the driver to let her out at the end of the drive. As she walked up the tree-lined avenue, she remembered the last time she had come here, the day she had given up her son. As the agonising memory hit her, she paused for a moment, gazing at the landscape of vineyards and golden meadows, and the beautiful house with large sash windows. Was Alfie's room behind one of those windows, she wondered. Did he look out over the gravelled courtyard to the scenery beyond? She could see him kicking a football by a fountain. Was it the ball she had given him? He put it down and ran towards her.

'I'm glad you have come because Adeline has made her special tarts. We only have them if there are guests.'

'That's very considerate of her,' Sophie replied, feeling her lips twitch in amusement.

'I liked seeing you in the hospital, Papa did too. He is going back to London next week. Amelia is staying a bit longer to organise everything.'

'Ah, the wedding you mean?'

Alfie nodded. 'Papa says all his friends will want to see his beautiful bride.'

Sophie tried to keep her voice level. 'She is very pretty.'

Alfie looked at her, his head on one side. 'You are too. I think a wedding will make Grand-mère happy. She has been so sad since my Uncle Pierre died.' He scrunched up his nose. 'Papa didn't tell me for three weeks and I was so upset.'

'I imagine he wanted to protect you, Alfie. It was too much in one go for a little boy.'

'I'm not that little, I am going to be seven in six months' time. Do you want to have tea? I wasn't allowed to touch the tarts until you arrived.'

Gillie joined them in the study.

'My mother and Amelia send their apologies for not being here, but they are shopping in Beaune.'

'Oh, I quite understand,' Sophie countered, her face relaxing.

'Alfie is becoming an accomplished chess player. Do you play chess, Sophie?' Gillie asked.

'I'm afraid I don't.'

'Would you like me to teach you?' Alfie was tucking into a strawberry tart with gusto. 'Marcus, that is Papa's friend, who he went climbing with, taught me some good moves. And we made a castle. I can show you that too.'

'Yes please, Alfie, but if your aunt doesn't mind, I have brought you a present and I would love to see if we can make it fly.'

'Fly?' Alfie's eyes were round.

Sophie drew something large and blue from a carrier bag.

'A kite?' Alfie jumped up and took the proffered gift, examining every detail. 'I have always wanted one, thank you. Can I try it out now?'

As Alfie ran into the garden with the kite, Sophie wiped her hands on a small linen napkin. She smiled at Gillie.

'Thank you for writing to me over the years, I think I would have gone mad not knowing about him.'

'Well you shouldn't have left him in …' Gillie shook her head. 'Sorry, you had your reasons.'

'At the time I didn't know what else to do.'

'Sebastian still isn't aware we have been in contact, and I would rather we kept it that way.'

'Of course.' Sophie glanced out of the window; she could see her son in the meadow. She stood up. 'Would you forgive me if I went to find Alfie.'

'This is a brilliant kite, thank you, Doctor,' Alfie said when she caught up with him.

'It might help if there was a little wind, shall we go and find some?'

They walked up a hill behind Pommard together, Alfie holding his kite.

'You are out of breath,' Sophie observed.

'It's a big hill,' Alfie laughed.

There was a light breeze and for a glorious hour they took it in turns to run with the kite and let it go. As the kite dipped and dived, Sophie watched her son's face. She had never been so happy.

Alfie walked back with her down the drive. 'Will you come again?' he asked.

'If you would like me to,' Sophie replied.

Three weeks later Sophie returned to Pommard, and despite her reservations, Gillie's opinion started to change.

'I am a nurse,' she told her during another break for tea. 'At the mediaeval Hospices de Beaune, but you are about to qualify as a heart surgeon.'

'In another year I will be able to operate without supervision,' Sophie replied, choosing a small blueberry pastry made by Adeline and putting it on her plate. 'It's exciting, everything I have worked for and yet...'

'It can't have been easy as a woman,' Gillie countered.

'Every day patients tell me they would rather be treated by a man.' She smiled at Gillie, her eyes a little wistful. 'It is an incredible career, Gillie, but it has come at a great cost.'

Their eyes met and Gillie understood what Sophie was trying to say.

'Well, I am sure you can make it up to Alfie now.'

'I'd like to try, if your family will let me,' she said.

As Sophie walked back down the drive an hour later, with Alfie trotting at her side, Gillie watched them. They looked so right together, and though she still found it hard to forgive her for giving up her child, Sophie had obviously regretted her actions ever since. Yes, she conceded, smiling wryly, she was warming to Sophie Bernot.

Sophie's visits continued, and in late September she met Gillie in Beaune. She waited in the car while Gillie collected Alfie from school. All the way home he chattered in the back, and seemed delighted to see her.

'My teacher Madame Sully – we call her Madame Surly behind her back because she is always cross – gave me lines today, Doctor Sophie.' He rolled his eyes and Sophie wanted to laugh, but she kept a straight face.

'Why?' Gillie asked. 'That's not good, Alfie.'

'But Tante Gillie, I didn't mean to get ink on my textbook, it just came off the end of my pen.'

Gillie glanced in her rear-view mirror. The little boy's hands – and even his knees – were covered with blotches of ink.

'Alfie,' she scolded, shaking her head. 'Perhaps if you are good, Doctor Sophie will sit with you while you do your homework and those wretched lines.'

'So you are enjoying working at our hospital in Dijon?' Gillie asked, while Alfie ran upstairs to change. 'It's a long way from Paris.'

'*Mais oui*, it is beautiful. Paris is so busy, too much noise. Why is it that drivers, usually men, sit on their car horns? It was actually quieter during the war, no petrol for the masses.' She smiled ruefully and the two women found themselves opening up to each other.

'At the beginning of the war, I was working at the American Hospital in Paris, but I couldn't bear to stay after my friend died,' Gillie revealed with a catch in her voice.

'I understand,' Sophie murmured. 'I lost my parents and my brother.'

'Oh no,' Gillie gasped. 'I'm so sorry. That's truly awful.'

'We all lost loved ones back then.'

They were quiet for a moment until Gillie blurted, 'do you have a boyfriend, Sophie?'

Sophie laughed, and the solemn mood was broken. 'Sort of, though we have a strange relationship. Todd is an American investigative journalist.'

'Ah – he wrote the editorial in *Time* magazine.' Gillie smiled in relief. Sophie would be no threat to Amelia.

'His job takes him all over the world and I often don't see him for weeks, but it seems to work for us. And what about you, Gillie?'

Gillie found herself telling Sophie about Christophe. 'I'm going to find him, Sophie,' she ended. 'If it's the last thing I do.'

'Well, if you ever need help,' Sophie turned towards her, 'Todd would be your man.'

'I'll remember that, thank you,' Gillie replied.

At that moment Alfie returned to the bench where they were sitting, and tugged at Sophie's hand.

'Would you like to come to the lake, Doctor Sophie?' he asked.

She jumped to her feet. 'I'd love to, young man.' As they went through the wrought-iron gate into the meadow, she looked back at Gillie, her eyes shining.

When they reached the lake, Alfie pointed out the ducks. He had names for them all.

'That's Mimi,' he said, 'and there is Monsieur Porcy, because he is a little fat.' He giggled, showing dimples in his cheeks and Sophie was enchanted.

The visits to Pommard were the highlight of her month. Each time Sophie said goodbye to Alfie, she counted the days until she would see him again.

By an unspoken agreement with the family, she came to the house when Sebastian wasn't there.

On one occasion Amelia offered to drive her back to Dijon.

'It will save the taxi having to wait,' she said, smiling at her, 'and you can tell me some interesting hospital anecdotes on the way.'

Sophie looked a little perplexed.

'I'm going to be a writer,' she qualified. 'And I need some good plots, not of course that I expect you to break any confidences.'

'Well then,' Sophie replied. 'I am sure I can think of a few.'

As they drove through the narrow country lanes, Sophie regaled Amelia with stories of hospital life.

'I'm so impressed by your career,' Amelia declared, as they drew near to Dijon.

'You're a warrior, battling to save lives in a world of men.'

Sophie laughed and the more she knew Amelia, the more she liked her. She would never try to stand in her way.

'I couldn't be a doctor,' she laughed, wrinkling up her nose. 'Actually Sophie, the only thing I was ever really good at was telling stories.'

'And I could never do that,' Sophie replied.

Amelia grinned. 'At the moment, however, it's all shopping and planning, and I don't seem to have the time.'

'I can think of worse things to do,' Sophie murmured.

They had entered the hospital gates and Sophie was about to climb from the car, when Amelia spoke. 'I admire you, Sophie, truly I do.' She paused, gathering herself together, then her words came out in a rush. 'I know this may sound silly, but would you like to come to the wedding? I know Alfie would love it.'

Sophie bit her lip. Amelia was one of the nicest people she had met. It was hardly surprising that Sebastian was in love with her.

She chose her words carefully.

'Thank you. I am honoured, truly I am, but I am not sure if I should. It is your day, your time, and I don't want to be in the way.'

'Really?'

'Really, Amelia.'

The engine was running when Sophie put her head back through the open window. 'Sebastian is so lucky to have found you, and for my part, Alfie couldn't be in better hands.'

Chapter Forty

Autumn came, and Gillie returned to work, leaving Amelia in charge of Alfie.

'I love my nephew beyond anything, but you are going to be his stepmother; it's time for me to stand aside,' she had said, hugging Amelia. 'I will always be his aunt, but this will give you a chance to build up your own relationship with Alfie.'

When Amelia had protested, she had smiled. 'Truly, it's right. Besides, it's time I went back to work. Just know I am only a telephone call away.'

She had given Amelia a list of useful telephone numbers: the dentist, the doctor, the hospital in Beaune. 'In an emergency take him to Dijon University Hospital,' she had advised. 'And don't forget Friday is his half day from school, you collect him at twelve.'

Amelia placed the list in a special folder she had created for Alfie, with his name on the front.

'Of course you can always ask Adeline,' Gillie suggested. 'She will even get over the fact that you are a vegetarian if you make her feel needed.'

Amelia followed her advice, and over the next few weeks was happy to defer to Adeline on everyday matters.

It was not long before Adeline was cooking special treats for Amelia.

'I have made you a delicious vegetable cassoulet,' she said, bringing it steaming into the dining room for Sunday lunch, and depositing it onto the sideboard with a flourish.

'Vegetable cassoulet?' Sebastian groaned. 'No *roti de boeuf*?'

'*Non*, Monsieur Sebastian, not a single slaughtered cow is in this recipe.'

At this Alfie giggled into his napkin. 'Poor Papa, he is out-numbered.'

'But there is his favourite *tarte au citron meringuée pour dessert*.' Adeline smiled.

On the thirteenth of November, Sophie was behind the nurses' station in the cardiology ward. She had a strong black coffee in one hand and a croissant in the other as she looked at the board. It was going to be a busy day, but any exhaustion she may have felt was quickly replaced by excitement. She would be assisting a new cardiac surgeon, Professor Duchaine. She ran her eye down his list of patients, deposited the rest of her croissant in the bin, washed her hands and went to the ward. An eighteen-year-old boy was propped up in bed, his chest heaving as he tried to catch his breath.

'Is my operation still this morning?' he gasped.

'It is, and I will be the assisting surgeon to Professor Duchaine.'

'Am I going to be all right?'

'Nicolas, you are in the most capable hands – Professor Duchaine is famous for his success in this operation. He will look after you, I promise. I can see from your chart the nurse has done the observations, so after you have put on this embar-rassing gown, you will be taken down to theatre.'

'What happens then?' he asked suddenly.

'Once you are downstairs, your notes will be handed to the

theatre staff. They will check your wristband again and ask you any other details from your medical records. Then the anaesthetist will put a mask on your face and you won't feel a thing. When you wake up it will be over, and more importantly you will be well.'

'That's not what I mean. I'd like to know what you are going to do to my heart.'

Sophie was taken aback. 'You really want to know?'

'Yes,' he said, his brown eyes apprehensive, but she could see he was trying to act like a man.

Sophie glanced at her watch. 'I made notes after the last operation. I'll show them to you if you like.'

Nicolas nodded. 'Please.'

Sophie smiled at him. 'The young woman he last performed this operation on is completely fine. She has so much energy she has taken up bicycling and fencing. She wants to do absolutely everything.'

Nicolas's face brightened. 'Will I be able to play football again?'

'I am sure you will,' Sophie assured him.

Having retrieved the notes from her tiny office she hurried back to the bed.

'You see this diagram: the mitral valve lies between the left atrium and the left ventricle, the pumping chamber, here,' she pointed with her pen. 'The valve allows blood to flow into the left ventricle, but in your case, possibly due to an infection when you were younger, the valve is narrowed and forming an obstruction. This leads to back pressure and congestion of the lungs, which causes you to be short of breath. Today the professor will split the valve and enlarge it. You will have an impressive scar, but it will fade to a thin, white line. Does that answer your question?'

'It does, sort of.' He smiled weakly. '*Merci*, doctor.'

*

On the same Friday in November, when the apples were rotting on the ground, Alfie took out his kite after returning from school.

'Come on, Alfie, the grass is wet and your shoes will be ruined,' Amelia protested, walking down the steps into the formal garden at the front of the house. She leant against the pillar that separated the garden from the meadow.

'Lunch is ready and you know what Adeline is like if we are late.' Amelia glanced at the house, expecting to hear Adeline's voice scolding them.

'Just one more go, Amelia,' Alfie begged.

She watched as he ran through the grass letting out the line. The wind was taking the blue kite upwards, until it was bobbing about in the sky, the tail streaming behind. 'Look Amelia,' he cried. 'Look.'

Suddenly Alfie plummeted face first into the grass. It was Amelia's turn to run. She threw herself down in the grass beside him. 'Alfie,' she cried, turning him over, lifting his head as she tried to rouse him, 'Alfie, my dear little boy.' When he remained unresponsive, she lifted him up and staggered towards the house. Adeline watching from the kitchen window, yelled at her husband who was drinking his espresso. 'Jean, go quickly, it's Alfie.'

Jean was out of the house and down the steps in a flash. He took the limp child from Amelia.

'We need to get him to the hospital,' Amelia gasped. 'We need to ... Oh my God what is wrong with him?'

Minutes later they were in the car, while Adeline stayed behind with instructions to alert the family.

'University Hospital, Dijon,' Amelia yelled from the back seat, cradling Alfie in her lap, as the car roared down the drive.

When they pulled up outside the front of the hospital, while Jean cared for Alfie, Amelia jumped out and charged into the reception. 'We need the emergency doctor now, someone fetch him please. Seven-year-old child, unconscious in the car.' She pointed to the door just as Jean came through it carrying Alfie.

'Get someone.' She was shouting now. 'On second thoughts a doctor who works here, find Doctor Sophie Bernot.'

Nicolas was coming round in recovery and Professor Duchaine was in a hurry to leave for a conference in Paris.

'The operation has gone well and I'm happy to leave the patient in your care,' he said to Sophie. 'Forgive me my dear for abandoning you, but I have to face the appalling traffic.'

'No problem at all,' Sophie reassured him. 'I hope you get there in time.'

She was checking Nicolas's blood pressure when a nurse hurried towards her.

'An unconscious little boy – seven years old, has just been brought in by a woman who asked for you specifically. He is being assessed now.'

'Where?'

'Emergency Admissions Unit.'

Sophie felt her legs go weak. She knew in the pit of her stomach it was her little boy. She started to run.

Sophie tore open the cubicle curtain. Her son was lying on the table. He was barely conscious and was struggling to breathe. The on-duty doctor was listening to his chest, while Amelia held onto his hand.

'I've called for the cardiologist,' he informed her, removing the stethoscope from Alfie's chest. 'The heartbeat is irregular, his skin clammy, he can hardly breathe. Classic signs of heart failure.'

Sophie pulled back the blanket. Alfie's legs and tummy were swollen, and his nails were blue. There was a blue tinge to his lips.

'Atrial septal defect, I'm sure of it.' Sophie was talking to herself. *That would explain the shortness of breath when we went up the hill*, she thought.

She looked at the doctor. 'Yes, I agree with you. Get me a portable X-ray and the echocardiogram,' she instructed the nurse who was hovering in the cubicle.

'*Oui Doctor.*'

'And nurse, please find Professor Charpentier. Inform him we have a probable ASD, with the need for immediate surgery. The patient is my son.' She scribbled a note on a piece of paper. 'Take this to him. There is no time to get him to a hospital with a heart–lung machine. We have to do the surgery now.'

'Another thing,' she called after her. 'Please find Doctor Georges Thibault, request he comes to theatre three.'

While Alfie was taken to theatre, a pale and distraught Amelia was escorted by a nurse to the waiting room. She was about to go outside for some air when Liliane and Gillie arrived.

'Tell me everything,' Alfie's grandmother said, taking Amelia's hands.

Half an hour later Amelia was in the hospital garden. She sat down on a bench, got up, paced the gravelled paths and sat down again. She had run through the scenario a hundred times – Alfie's limp little body in the grass, the weight of him as she ran to the house, the nightmare drive to the hospital and her relief when Sophie had entered the cubicle. In a split second, the woman she knew had changed to a surgeon fully in charge of the situation.

As Amelia pushed open the glass doors to the hospital foyer, she was unaware of the nurses, doctors and porters hurrying around her; she was deaf to the noise. Instead her eyes were fixed on a portrait of the Saviour, hanging on the wall. 'Please let his mother save him,' she prayed.

*

Sophie was now in theatre, surrounded by a team of nurses, house-officers, Claude the anaesthetist and Georges.

'The atrial septal defect must have gone undiagnosed for years,' she explained to the team. 'It has led to pulmonary hypertension and this has produced his current condition. The only treatment, in spite of the danger, is to repair the hole now.'

'The nearest heart–lung machine is in Paris,' Claude protested. 'So what are we supposed to do?'

'I am about to explain.'

She called one of the orderlies. 'I need a tin bath filled with ice and cold water. If we haven't enough ice, get more from the canteen.'

As the orderlies were despatched to get the bath, she turned back to Claude. 'I have heard about a technique used on a child in the United States – we will use the same method now.'

'This is madness.'

'Please, there is no other alternative, so here is the plan. We will cool the body to thirty degrees centigrade, slow the heart right down so the tissues of the body and brain don't require as much oxygen. That's how hibernating animals survive.'

'This child is not a hibernating animal,' the anaesthetist interjected.

'No, Claude, he is my son! And don't say I shouldn't be operating because I am fully aware of that. Professor Charpentier will take over as soon as he arrives.'

'*Mon dieu*,' Claude pulled down his mask.

'I can do this, Claude. It's been proven the brain can survive without a circulation for up to nine minutes without damage, providing the body temperature is thirty degrees. It was originally trialled in Minnesota on a girl, younger than my son, cooled with a special blanket. The surgeons had enough time to get in and sew up the hole. I need that extra time. They had a cooling blanket, we don't. The patient survived using this technique, it's our only option.'

Claude nodded. 'I would suggest only a moderate sedation.'

'Agreed.'

The anaesthetist put the mask over Alfie's face, and he was quickly asleep. The ice arrived, and he was lowered into the bath.

When his body had cooled to thirty degrees centigrade, she instructed Georges and a house officer to lift him onto the table.

While the nurse secured a green drape over his body, leaving only his chest and abdomen exposed, Sophie gave her instructions.

'Georges, you monitor his temperature, and you Nurse, count down the time.' Georges met her gaze.

'You can do it,' he murmured, and at once she had the courage to go on.

The nurse took out her stopwatch. '*Oui, Doctor.*'

As Sophie drew the scalpel down her son's chest, she could feel everyone's eyes on her. Using an electrocautery she cut through the layer of fat onto the bone and cauterised the blood vessels. It was then the nurse passed her the saw. She breathed deeply and turned the switch to 'on'. At that moment Professor Charpentier arrived. He glanced at the bath.

'I see you have improvised. The Minnesota case, I believe.' He took the saw and Sophie stepped to the side. Suddenly Sophie was an onlooker and her fear flooded back. As the professor lowered the noisy blade, cutting from Alfie's sternum, she winced. When he cranked open his chest with a small metal retractor, her fingernails dug into her arm.

'Claude?' Professor Charpentier's voice broke the silence.

'Yes, Professor, the heart is still beating, but slowly as requested by Doctor Bernot.'

'Clamp!' He put out his hand and a nurse put a clamp into it.

He clamped the vessels, bringing blood back to the heart and with a downward slice of the blade, he made an incision in the heart itself, exposing the hole.

'Suture,' he instructed the nurse. A threaded needle was put in his waiting hand.

'Four minutes left.' The nurse called out the time.

As he sewed up the hole in the septum, Sophie's eyes were glued to his hands. She was biting her lip as the seconds ticked by. She no longer had any control of what was happening to Alfie.

'Three minutes left.'

'Now to sew up the incision in the heart itself.' His stitches were flying in and out of the heart muscle. He had just tied the knot when the nurse signalled he had thirty seconds left. He removed the clamps enabling blood to re-enter the heart.

He looked at Sophie.

'Nearly finished,' he said. 'Now we need to get the heart contracting properly.' He was calm but Sophie could tell he was concerned. The heart was failing to beat and time was running out.

Sophie could feel the panic build in her chest. This was the dread of any surgeon.

'Defibrillator,' the professor instructed. 'Now.' The atmosphere in theatre had changed. Sophie started to pray, images of the fateful operation with Doctor Eppel fresh in her mind.

The nurse passed him the two pads. Sophie bit her lip as he applied them directly to the heart.

'Deliver the shock.' There was silence in the room. For a moment the heart stopped. 'Come on, Alfie,' she prayed, 'come on.'

Suddenly his heart kicked into life.

The mood in theatre changed as Alfie's heart commenced to beat in a stable rhythm. Sophie could feel the relief of her peers as the circulation re-established.

'Let's close him up,' the professor said, and she struggled not to cry.

The professor was stitching up her son's chest when he looked up at her and smiled.

'That was quick thinking, Doctor Bernot. Your son would not have reached Paris.'

Sophie nodded, unable to speak.

'Wrap him in warm blankets,' he instructed the nursing staff, 'quickly now.'

The nurses did as they were told, and as Alfie's body temperature slowly rose to normal, his skin colour changed. The blue around his lips disappeared.

He is going to survive. Sophie rejoiced inwardly and, totally ignoring protocol, she flung her arms around the professor's neck.

'Thank you, thank you, Professor, for giving me back my son.' She turned to Claude. 'And thank you for supporting this procedure.'

Sophie found Amelia hunched on a bench in the corridor, chewing her fingernails.

'Tell me,' she blurted, jumping up, her face ashen.

Sophie's face broke into an exhausted smile. 'He is fine, he is going to be fine. We will monitor him continuously, but we mended his heart in time.'

She was glancing at her watch when Liliane and Gillie hurried into the room.

'He's fine,' Sophie repeated, 'but if you will excuse me I will go to him now.'

Half an hour later Sophie went into her office and closed the door. It was over. Alfie had survived. But it could have been so very different. She could feel emotion well from the pit of

345

her stomach. Her shoulders started to shake. Alfie had been operated on in a most unconventional way but, thank God, his life had been saved.

Chapter Forty-One

It was dark when Liliane, Amelia and Gillie were taken to a side room by the theatre, where they were able to view Alfie for the first time through the glass partition. Liliane's knuckles were white as she gripped onto the wooden ledge. Alfie looked so tiny and isolated amidst the huge banks of equipment.

'It's all right, Madame Ogilvie,' the specialist nurse assured her. 'I know it looks a little alarming, but this equipment is for your grandson's safety. Doctor Michaud is just going to check the arterial line now.'

'There are so many tubes, I couldn't tell one from another,' Liliane murmured, her brow wrinkled in concern.

'It's the tiny line that goes into the radial artery in the wrist. It monitors the pulse and measures the blood pressure,' she explained. 'Don't worry, there will always someone with Alfie until he leaves for the ward.'

'Thank you for reassuring me,' Liliane said. 'You've been very kind.'

'It breaks my heart to see Alfie like this.' Amelia sighed, pressing her face closer to the glass. 'Awful.'

'But his colour is already better,' the nurse affirmed. 'And we are keeping him on the ventilator until morning, so he can hopefully get some rest. The dear little boy is going to be fine.'

The following morning Liliane and Gillie were waiting outside the side room when Sophie arrived.

'I am afraid you will only be able to see him for a maximum of five minutes,' she instructed, handing each of them a gown, protective shoes and a mask. 'You will have to put these on as we can't risk infection.'

Sophie took them inside and while Alfie slept, she explained to Liliane the purposes of the tubes. 'We believe the more you know about the equipment, the less daunting it is.'

Liliane was trying her best to understand.

'The tube coming from his chest,' Sophie clarified, 'is to drain the residual blood and fluid; the other is an intravenous catheter that will deliver fluids and important medication.'

'He must be in so much pain,' Liliane murmured.

'With drugs we can keep him drowsy and mostly pain-free, and we monitor him all the time. Children are remarkably resilient,' she confirmed.

They were going towards the lift when Gillie drew Sophie aside. 'How could I have missed this? I'm a nurse for heaven's sake. I keep trying to remember if there were any indications, anything that should have pointed to this. At his sports day he was a little breathless, but he had just been in running a race.'

'He was panting when we took his kite up the hill,' Sophie interjected. 'I should have realised something was amiss. There is no point blaming yourself. It really isn't your fault. I have seen several children where the symptoms do not become evident until they are older. Anyway, there is only one important thing, Gillie; Alfie's heart has been repaired.'

Sebastian arrived at Dijon Station late the following morning. He jumped from the carriage and ran down the platform towards Gillie.

She hugged him quickly. 'Alfie is a little woozy and quite sore, but thank goodness Sophie got to him in time. She said she would wait for you in the hospital foyer.'

When Sebastian first saw Alfie through the plate glass window, he caught hold of Sophie's arm.

'My God,' he whispered. 'My poor little boy, he looks so fragile.'

'He is actually remarkably strong and he is fighting back, Sebastian. Now go and see our son.'

Alfie must have sensed his father's presence when he came into the room because he opened his eyes.

'Hello, little man. Papa had to get dressed in a very funny gown, but it is me, I promise.' Sebastian stroked his pale forehead.

'Papa,' he whispered. 'I was waiting for you.' He tried to sit up but flopped back against the pillows.

'It hurts,' he cried, scrunching his face in distress.

'What a brave soldier,' Sebastian murmured, breathing in the scent of Alfie's hair, but also the lingering smell of antiseptic.

'Rabbit hurts too, but nice Doctor Bernot has bandaged his chest.'

Sebastian took Alfie's soft toy from the bed and spoke to it gently.

'Poor Rabbit, I hope you get better soon.' The rabbit's long ears flopped forward so that he looked particularly woeful.

'Will you please tell Alfie I have had a big think while on the aeroplane.'

'Rabbit wants to know what about?' Alfie said, his eyes focussing at the prospect of his favourite game.

'If Rabbit agrees, Papa is going to give up his job in London and live at Pommard.'

'Rabbit is happy, Papa,' mumbled Alfie, and closed his eyes.

When Sebastian came out, Sophie was waiting for him. He followed her to her office and hovered in the doorway.

'I think you had better use my chair,' she instructed.

Sebastian sank down, while Sophie perched on the edge of her desk, holding a file.

'I promise it's not as bad as it looks, Sebastian,' she assured him, trying to sound in charge of her emotions.

'I would give anything for it to be me lying in that bed, and not Alfie.'

'Of course you would,' Sophie replied, wishing that Sebastian would hold her, so that she could dissolve in his arms. She paused for a moment, trying to regain her equilibrium. She had to be professional.

'The operation was a success, he will make a full recovery.'

Sebastian looked up at her, his blue eyes filled with shock. 'You give me your word, Sophie?'

'I do, Sebastian.' She pulled her eyes away, taking refuge in her medical knowledge. 'All the equipment, the tubes, they are to keep him stable; remember he has had major surgery. Anyway, now to the business of recovery.' She took a leaflet from the file. 'I will explain everything but take this home to refresh yourself. The hole in his septum is now repaired, but his recovery will be a long and delicate process. The first phase will take six to eight weeks and that means plenty of rest. When he comes home, please make allowances for Alfie, at times he will be tired and a little irritable – hardly surprising. There will be no major exercise, running, jumping, putting his arms above his head. He mustn't do anything that could cause him to fall. Basically use your common sense.' She started to write some notes, but gave up because her hands were shaking. 'No swimming in the lake,' she continued. 'The water could cause infection to his wound. If I don't see you again before you return to London, these are the things your family will need to look out for.'

'I'm not returning to London.'

Sophie met his gaze.

'I can't. Not now, not after this. I want to be with my son every single moment of every day. This has been a big lesson, I need to prioritise my life.'

'Of course you want to be with him.' She looked down at the floor. 'We would all love to be with him,' she whispered.

You had your chance, Sebastian thought, biting back the words.

Sophie returned to her notes but couldn't find her place. 'Sorry,' she muttered. 'Where were we?'

'You were about to tell me what to do when Alfie comes home in three weeks' time.'

'Yes, of course,' Sophie coughed. 'He is a little boy and will want to be normal, but you must all be vigilant. You must watch out for any oozing from the wound, but it should be healing nicely by then.' She looked up. 'Don't hesitate to contact a doctor if his temperature should rise significantly.'

Sebastian nodded.

'If he complains of itching or numbness, it is all part of the healing process. As far as exercise is concerned, he can get dressed but stand for only fifteen minutes at a time. A good diet, emotional support with lots of rest and he will soon be fit as anything. I think that is it.' Sophie put her notes back in the file and stood up.

'He could have died,' Sebastian said.

'Yes, but he didn't.' Sophie was standing in front of him, he was so close she could see smell his aftershave. Why couldn't she tell him she loved Alfie so much that it hurt, and she was dying inside because she couldn't be with her son every moment of the day. Why couldn't she tell Sebastian that she loved him, that she always had. Sophie looked at her watch. 'Forgive me, Sebastian, but I must continue on my rounds.'

*

351

Sebastian stayed at Alfie's bedside through the night and only returned to Pommard the following morning. Amelia was working when he came into the library. She got up from the desk and ran towards him, throwing herself into his arms.

'I've missed you so much, and all this...'

Sebastian held her for a moment knowing he should be thrilled and comforted to see her. She was his fiancée, the woman he adored, but at this moment, his thoughts kept returning to Sophie.

'I am so sorry you had to deal with everything without me,' he said, feeling her slim body in his arms. 'Thank God you asked for Sophie.'

'Gillie told me I should go to her if anything went wrong with Alfie,' Amelia explained.

'That was good advice,' he said, trying not to think of the distress on Sophie's face just an hour before.

Amelia drew backwards. 'Poor little boy. How is he? I was only allowed to see him through the glass.'

'Very sleepy and sore, but Rabbit was thrilled with my proposal.'

'And what is that?' she asked, looking at him from beneath her lashes.

'What would you say to living in France, Amelia, making Pommard your home?'

'I am happy to be wherever you are,' she said, her eyes lighting up. 'It would certainly be the best thing for Alfie. He really misses you during the week and so do I.'

'You are always so understanding. I don't deserve you, Amelia.'

'You do, if you love me?'

Sebastian wanted to reply but the words didn't come. Of course he loved her, this was mad. So why couldn't he say it?

'Are you working on the book?' he asked, trying to distract her, noticing the jumble of paper on the desk.

Amelia nodded, picking up the foolscap paper. 'I started my novel. I had to do something to keep myself from going mad.'

'Well then, tell me about it.'

'Now?'

'Yes, right now.'

Amelia hesitated. 'Well if you really want to know, it's about a young girl, in war-torn London. I have begun to map out the story and this is the perfect place to write. I can't wait to move here, darling.'

'I'm so glad,' he said, but he felt like a fraud, because there was a heavy feeling in his stomach.

She looked up at him. 'I was actually worrying about returning to work. I couldn't bear to leave Alfie for long, not now.'

'It's settled then.'

'But I will have to go back to London first, just for a little while.' Amelia ran her hand down his gaunt cheek. 'The library have been so understanding but I need to return to explain the situation and hand in my notice.'

'When will you go?' Sebastian asked, afraid that if she left he would be more vulnerable, more at risk of giving in to his feelings for Sophie.

'In a few days I think. It will give you time to concentrate on Alfie.' She paused for a moment. 'Will you manage without me?' she asked, a flicker of concern in her eyes. 'I mean, I don't have to go.'

'Depends how long you are away.' Sebastian picked up a strand of her hair.

'A few weeks at the most. I will have to break it to my parents and reassure them that France is not so very far from Kent.' She kissed Sebastian's cheek. 'I'll be back as soon as I have packed up my life in London.'

Chapter Forty-Two

It was two weeks after Alfie's surgery and he was now back in the children's ward. Rabbit was doing his best impersonation of Adeline chasing Jean with a rolling pin, when the little boy's eyes brightened.

'Doctor Sophie is coming, Papa.'

Sebastian put the soft toy in his pocket, with only the Rabbit's head peeping out, and turned around to face Sophie. For a moment they stared at each other. 'It seems you are always looking after my family,' he murmured.

'That is my job,' she replied.

She unbuttoned Alfie's pyjama top and Sebastian grimaced. The sight of his son's little torso encased in white bandages still had the power to shock him.

'So how is my young patient?' she asked, taking her stethoscope from her neck. 'I need a listen to your important new chest.'

'You mustn't make me laugh, Doctor, because it hurts.'

'Well then, I shall be most serious and cross.'

'No, not cross,' Alfie pleaded.

After a moment Sophie looked up. 'That sounds quite the best heart I have ever heard.'

'Are you going to listen to Rabbit's too?'

'Of course I am, but I can see he is hiding in Papa's pocket.' As Sophie took the rabbit from Sebastian, their hands touched. Sophie flinched, and drew away. 'Well, Mister Rabbit, your heart is recovering very quickly, so we can take your bandage off tomorrow,' she said, avoiding Sebastian's eyes.

'But Rabbit says he likes the bandage,' Alfie commented.

'Then he can keep it on as long as it doesn't get dirty. You know how rabbits like to dig holes.'

Sebastian watched the exchange with an extraordinary mix of emotions. The doctor talking to her son was not the young girl he had once known. This woman was compassionate and mature. She was the surgeon who had helped to save his son's life. No, it was *their* son's life, and Alfie had no idea this woman was his mother.

'So young man,' Sophie said when she had finished. 'I have ordered ice cream for your lunch tomorrow, followed by an omelette.'

'Oooh yes please Doctor, but may I have the omelette first?'

'Really, you are a most unusual child.'

Sebastian quickly became a fixture on the wards. While other family members and friends restricted their visits to the evening, Sebastian was on his own with Alfie during the day. With special dispensation from Doctor Bernot, he arrived at nine, armed with newspapers, books for Alfie, and games.

'Please don't call me Monsieur Ogilvie,' he urged the nurses. 'We hate formality don't we, Alfie?'

'And Rabbit is not Monsieur Rabbit,' Alfie giggled.

Before long, all the hospital staff had complied and Sebastian was even included in the hospital lunch.

'We can't have you bringing in baguettes, putting crumbs over our nice clean floor,' Nurse Renee stated, a smile on her plump face. 'So today it is *saucisses et purée de pommes de terre* followed by *crème glacée*. Is that to your liking?'

'Entirely,' he had replied.

Everyone was captivated by Alfie.

'I have brought you a present,' Nurse Renee informed him one morning, hiding something behind her back. '*Tintin in Tibet*. But perhaps Papa does not approve of comics?'

'Papa will definitely read it too,' Sebastian laughed.

For a moment she looked stern. 'I have to give you a bed bath first.'

'Papa or me?' Alfie giggled, and the nurse blushed puce.

'You imp,' she laughed, tickling his foot.

'I hate bed baths,' he squealed.

'Well then, no comic.' She was halfway down the ward waving the comic in the air, when Alfie called after her. 'All right, Nurse Renee, bed bath first.'

To his dismay, Sebastian found himself counting the hours until ward rounds, and the moment when he would hear Sophie's distinctive footstep in the corridor outside.

It seemed Alfie felt the same.

On his penultimate day in hospital, Sophie held the soft toy to her son's cheek. 'Rabbit gives you a kiss from Doctor Bernot.'

'Why doesn't Doctor Bernot give me a kiss?' Alfie asked.

Sophie laughed and put her face close to Alfie's. '*Bien sur, mon petit chou.*'

Sebastian could hear her intake of breath as she stepped back.

'Have I made you unhappy, Doctor Sophie?' Alfie asked, tugging at her sleeve.

'You could never ever make me unhappy,' she replied. Afterwards she stumbled into the cloakroom and leant against the sink. For three weeks she had treated him, watched over him, and loved him. How could she let him go? In saving his life she had tied herself to her son with an indivisible bond. But Alfie didn't know he was her son, he didn't know that she had followed every step of his life from afar.

She bit her lip, tasted blood on her tongue. And what about his father, what about Sebastian? She had watched him too, the way he smiled, the way he cared for Alfie. He was everything she was not. He was honourable and loyal. He would never have given his son away. And now it was too late. She had her chance, but it was gone.

Sophie was doing her rounds the following morning, when she came to Alfie's bed.

'So,' she said, putting a thermometer beneath Alfie's tongue, 'how is my little soldier today?'

Alfie shook his head, pointing to the thermometer.

'Silly me!' Sophie laughed. 'You can't speak with this in your mouth.' She took the thermometer out and shook it down. 'Quite normal. You'll be flying your kite again in a few weeks' time.'

She was about to leave when she felt his hand on her arm.

'Do you have children, Doctor?' he asked.

Sophie touched his nose with her index finger. 'I do,' she said at last. 'I have a little boy and he is very special, just like you.'

'He is lucky.' Alfie sighed. 'He has a kind Maman. My mother had to leave us.'

Sophie trembled. She couldn't allow this to go on, she had to tell him, she could no longer live with the deception. Of course Sebastian was right to protect his son, but she was Alfie's mother.

She had imagined the scenario a thousand times. She would sit Alfie on her lap and explain how there was once a lady who wished to dedicate her life to helping sick people. Her decision would involve her making a very difficult choice. Though she loved her own little boy beyond anything, she had to allow him to live with his papa, who had a wonderful family and a secure home. The lady knew it would be a happy place for any child to grow up. The conversation wouldn't be easy, but it would be the truth. She would ask Sebastian if she could tell him soon.

Sebastian arrived early, his arms filled with presents.

He handed Nurse Renee a box of fragrant lavender soaps and a card from both of them.

'Ah, *merci*,' she sighed, sniffing the soap, and kissing Alfie on both cheeks. 'Now be a good little boy and do what Papa and *mademoiselle* Amelia say, do you promise me?'

'I promise you,' Alfie replied.

In fact there was a gift for anyone involved with Alfie's care. Last came Sophie. Sebastian had chosen a delicate floral scent from a shop in Beaune. He had tried to conjure up the scent she was wearing when they had been together in the mountains.

Alfie gave it to her. 'This is from Papa and me.'

Sophie dabbed some on her neck. 'It's lovely,' she smiled, her eyes a little bright, and Sebastian breathed deeply. He would keep the scent of her in his mind.

'And if it is all right with your papa,' Sophie said, carefully replacing the stopper, 'I have something for you, Alfie.'

'What is it, Doctor Sophie?'

'Give me your wrist.' She took a little pouch from her pocket.

'This was mine as a child, Alfie. It was a present from my brother and it was very precious to me.' As Alfie stared at the luminous dials, his face lit up.

'Mémé G gave Papa a watch that was old and precious, now I have one too. Thank you, Doctor Sophie.' He threw his arms around Sophie and hugged her.

Sophie handed Sebastian a file. 'These are Alfie's notes. Be sure to give them to the local doctor in Beaune. Gillie will obviously listen to his heart every day, but I would advise her to keep on checking the wound.' Sophie rushed through her prepared speech. 'I think that's all, but if you are concerned you know where I am.' She put her hands in the pockets of her white coat and was about to turn around.

'Are you sad that I am leaving?' Alfie asked.

'Of course.'

'Rabbit says thank you for mending his chest.'

'Tell Rabbit it has been the greatest pleasure,' Sophie replied. She kissed her son's forehead and hurried from the ward.

Sebastian followed Sophie to her office and knocked on the door. She was sitting with her back to him.

'You can come and see him any time,' he said gently. 'You know that, Sophie.'

'I do, of course, but it's not the same. In the hospital I have looked after him, been near him. Now he is going home and...' She stood up, her face averted. 'And he doesn't even know who I am.'

'We will remedy that soon, I promise you, we just have to pick the right moment. Alfie has been through so much, I am not sure he is ready.'

Tears were slipping unchecked down her cheeks and her mouth was trembling. 'I understand, but I so want to be his mother....'

Sebastian couldn't help himself; he moved towards her and put his arms around her. 'It's all right, my love,' he murmured, 'everything will be fine.'

'But it won't be, I've ruined everything.'

Before he had time to think, Sebastian had pressed his lips against her hair, holding her close. He dropped his arms in confusion and stepped back. He was engaged to be married, what was he thinking of?

'Forgive me,' he said, his voice gruff. 'I need to go.'

'Of course you do,' she replied, her voice shaking.

Sebastian walked from the room leaving Sophie behind.

Chapter Forty-Three

Alfie was at last back in his own bedroom in Pommard. Even the short journey home had exhausted him, and though he was doing his best to stay awake, his eyelids were fluttering closed. Sebastian put down the book. *Five on a Treasure Island* would wait for another day. As he leant down and kissed his son's forehead, he was filled with emotion. Alfie meant more to him than anything in the world and he could have lost him. This ebullient, captivating little boy could have died. He had tidied Alfie's sheets and was putting Rabbit in his arms when he saw a letter poking from beneath his pillow. He drew it out and went to the window.

Dearest Alfie,
You have been such a brave young man these last three weeks
– in fact you have been the best patient in this entire hospital.
We have stuck so many needles into you and given you such
horrid medicines and you have taken everything without a
word of complaint. I am so proud of you mon cheri, and I
will come and see you very, very soon.
Take care precious child and do what Daddy and Amelia
say. I shall miss you.
Lots and lots of love,
Doctor Sophie

Sebastian held the letter to his chest; the writing was just as he remembered from the climbing book. It was familiar to him; Sophie was familiar to him. He remembered holding her in his arms in the hospital and he realised at once that he must face up to the truth. He could never marry Amelia. However ideal she was, however kind, she wasn't ideal for him. It wasn't fair to her; she deserved someone who could give her all of their love, someone better than him. It was staring him in the face: he was still in love with Sophie. He had to travel to London immediately to break off his engagement, before Amelia made her arrangements to return.

His mother and Gillie were waiting for him in the dining room when he came down. Adeline had a knowing look on her face.

'Trouble is brewing, *madame*,' she said, putting a bowl of soup in front of Liliane. 'I've known your boy since he was in short trousers and you can't fool me.'

'Do you mind not talking about me, Adeline, as if I'm not here,' Sebastian admonished.

'Huh,' she tutted. 'I'm right though, aren't I?' She stalked from the room and shut the door.

Liliane looked at him. 'So?' she asked.

'I'm afraid it's true. Would you mind looking after Alfie? I need to go to London first thing in the morning. I'll be back Tuesday.'

Gillie and Liliane glanced at each other.

'Amelia is wonderful, she would be the perfect wife and mother, but I can't go through with the marriage, Maman. And before you ask me, it is my fault entirely.'

'I assume this has something to do with Doctor Bernot?' Liliane asked, her voice strained.

Sebastian nodded. 'But Sophie has nothing to do with my decision. She has no idea. I realise it would be wrong to marry

Amelia, unfair on her, when I am still in love with the mother of my child.'

'You are right to go; don't worry, we will look after Alfie. You will probably break the girl's heart, but better now than later, I suppose.'

'Poor Amelia,' Gillie sighed.

Sebastian changed at his flat in London and drove straight to Kent, where Amelia was waiting for him. She was swaddled in a duffel coat, the hood pulled over her hair, as she ran down the drive towards him.

'How is Alfie?' she asked, throwing herself into his arms.

'He is doing really well,' he replied, 'we have built two model aeroplanes and he is starting on a castle. He is unstoppable.'

'I can't wait to see him. I've really missed the dear little boy, and you of course,' she said, taking his arm and leading him into the garden.

As Amelia chattered on, Sebastian drew in his breath. He dreaded the pain he was about to inflict, but he couldn't leave it any longer.

'I've been showing Mummy my photographs of Pommard,' she said, pushing back the hood. 'Apparently you have a particularly rare species of *Pulsatilla vulgaris* in the meadow. In case you didn't know it's a pasqueflower. My parents would love to come to France the week before the wedding if that is all right.'

Sebastian turned towards her, stopping her. 'Darling, there's something I need to say. I have to talk to you.'

Amelia looked like a gazelle about to take flight. 'Why?' she asked, her hand flying to her mouth.

Sebastian paused for a moment trying to find the right words that wouldn't completely destroy her. But of course he would, they were about to be married for heaven's sake. She had even been to Paris with his mother to choose the dress. Guilt surged through him as he tried to keep his voice even.

'I'm so terribly sorry, Amelia, I don't know how to say this, but I can't go through with our marriage. With Alfie's operation, everything that's happened. I'm just not ready.'

'Oh my God,' she uttered, her eyes round with horror. 'It's Sophie, isn't it? I thought I could trust you, and her for that matter. I even asked her to the wedding.'

'No, Amelia. It's not Sophie, it's me. Something has changed, and it isn't fair to marry you feeling like this.'

Amelia started to cry, her beautiful face blotchy with tears.

Sebastian went towards her, but she pushed him away. 'Don't. Don't you dare touch me,' she screamed, stumbling towards the house.

'I am so sorry. I wish with all my heart this hadn't happened, but it has, and it would be wrong to pretend otherwise.'

Amelia stopped and faced him, brushing her hand across her eyes. 'What am I going to tell everyone?'

'Tell them that I am a shit, tell them anything you like. I am just so sorry, darling. You don't deserve this.'

'No, I don't deserve this, and you *are* a shit! My flatmates never liked you. I wish I had listened to them!'

She started to walk away from him. Then she turned around and pulled off her diamond engagement ring, her lip trembling.

'Take it,' she threw the ring at him and backed away as it hit the gravel. 'Don't you ever come near me again.' Then she was gone, running into the house.

Chapter Forty-Four

When Sebastian returned to Pommard, Alfie's godfather, Robert Marston, came with him. They arrived at six o'clock in the evening and while Sebastian hurtled up the stairs to his son, Robert lingered in the hallway with Liliane.

'It is kind of you to have me to stay, Madame Ogilvie,' he said, hanging his coat in the hall cupboard. 'I wanted to see my godson and if I am honest, Sebastian needed a friend.'

'Thank you, Robert,' she replied. 'I admit we are all a little emotional at the moment, and I for one am completely exhausted.' She gazed through the window, a distant look in her eyes. 'All a bit much,' she sighed.

Robert frowned. 'I am so sorry.'

Liliane shook her head and focussed on Robert. 'And how is Giulietta? I am sure the children must keep you both so busy.'

Robert gave a rueful smile. 'With three children and a baby due in six weeks' time, life is eventful, but her mother is staying until after the baby is born.'

'Well then, it's so good of you to spare the time. I know Sebastian appreciates it enormously.'

'If you will excuse me I will go to him now.' Robert pulled a box from his bag. 'And I have this very important present for Alfie!'

After a serious discussion with Alfie about Rabbit's operation, and having handed over his present with a promise to build the Airfix Supermarine Swift jet fighter in the morning, Robert went to join Gillie in the drawing room. She was throwing some logs on the fire when he entered.

'Are you bearing up, Gillie?' he asked, kissing her cheek.

'Me? I'm OK, Robert, it's the rest of the family that is in turmoil at the moment. Drink?'

They were sitting on the sofa having an aperitif, when Robert asked her if she had ever resolved the question of Christophe.

'I haven't,' she said, looking at him over the rim of her glass. 'All this has rather taken my mind off it.'

'Of course.'

'But if you ever had the time I would love to talk to you about it. I won't bore you now, it's the last thing you want to hear after a long journey.'

'Please do,' he said. 'And you would never bore me, Gillie. Remember – my exciting past has been relegated to the cup-board. All I can think about now is keeping the partners at work in check and which of my children has a disgustingly runny nose.'

As Gillie ran through the sequence of events, she realised that the enigma of Christophe had to be resolved. It had been a tumultuous year and her concentration had been focussed on her family, but thoughts of Christophe had persistently niggled at her, churning around in her mind. Last thing at night and when she woke in the morning, the question was there. Why had he come to Pommard, and if it was to find her, why had he left so suddenly? Both Robert and her mother had suggested there might be a plausible explanation, but in any event, she needed to find out.

'So, you see,' she finished, looking at Robert, 'I must know the truth.'

'I can help you, Gillie,' he said. 'I am still in touch with some of the intelligence chaps in my old department. There are also one or two bods from Special Operations Executive, who I could approach to ask around.'

Gillie stood up and went to the fireplace. She turned around, her face lit with intensity. 'Robert, that is so kind, and though I appreciate your offer of help enormously, I really need to unravel what I can. It's been going on too long.'

'Of course, Gillie I quite understand – this is your quest to follow. But you always know where I am if you need me.'

Gillie smiled suddenly. 'Perhaps you will tell me where to begin?'

Robert lit up a cigarette and crossed his long legs.

'Firstly,' he said, letting the smoke out through his mouth, 'you need to find anyone near to Christophe: friends, associates. Talk to them, Gillie. You must learn anything you can about him, build up a picture of the man. Was he really capable of betraying Étienne to the Gestapo? And, of course, what he was doing in Pommard? Has it ever occurred to you that he might think you had betrayed Étienne?'

'Me? Why on earth?'

'Just a thought,' Robert mused.

Gillie raised her eyebrows.

'You might have to employ a local with the correct skills to do some of the legwork for you. You can hardly turn up at his place of work, wherever that is.'

Gillie laughed. 'That would be a bit of a giveaway.'

'Good luck, and don't forget Gillie – if you get stuck call me.'

'I promise,' Gillie vowed.

Gillie travelled to Paris the following week, and went by Métro straight to Bernheim-Jeune, one of the oldest art galleries in Paris.

'Can you help me?' she enquired of a woman in a sophisticated black dress and high-heeled shoes. 'Do you know the work of Christophe Plaquet?'

The assistant gave a polite smile. '*Mais oui* of course, we actually have one of his paintings in the showroom. Do come this way.'

As Gillie stood in front of the canvas, she had to stop herself from feeling proud. Christophe had used her – he could even be a traitor – but she had to admit, looking at the vibrant colours and the strong brushwork, he was a fine artist.

'Are you interested, *Madame*? His paintings are still fairly reasonable, but with his growing acclaim, they are sure to go up. This would be a sound investment.'

'I am considering it.' Gillie affected to scrutinise the painting. 'Yes, his technique is excellent,' she declared, beginning to enjoy herself. 'Perhaps you could you tell me a little more about the artist? Where he comes from, where his studio is located? I would like to see the artist at work.'

At once the woman's demeanour changed. She drew herself up to her full height, and it seemed to Gillie that her nostrils flared. 'I am afraid we do not divulge this information, *Madame*.'

Undeterred at the rebuff, Gillie took the Métro to the Left Bank and wandered the streets inhabited by artists, dealers and ateliers.

As luck would have it, at the fifth shop she visited, on the Rue Cardinal Lemoyne, the owner, an eccentric elderly gentleman with a shock of white hair, seemed delighted to have someone to talk to, irrespective of sales.

'You see that painting,' he pointed to a small farmyard scene

368

by Pissarro, 'that came with me when I fled to England at the beginning of the war. We returned together in '48. I could never sell it, beautiful isn't it?'

'Enchanting,' Gillie agreed, following him through the small gallery where every wall was covered with paintings.

'I was lucky,' he revealed, taking off his spectacles and wiping the lenses with a cloth, 'I sent the rest of my collection in front of me. Those of my associates who managed to escape with their lives lost so many of their possessions. My dear friend Paul Rosenberg is still trying to recover several important treasures, but at least he got out.' He shrugged his shoulders. 'Anyway, enough of me, *mademoiselle*. I can tell you have come here for something in particular.'

'Actually,' Gillie said, 'I have come here because of someone, an artist. I was told by the gallery opposite that you deal in the work of Christophe Plaquet – but I must be honest, I want to find out about him, not buy a painting. I am so sorry.'

'My dear, you have listened so kindly to an old gentleman rambling on – of course I will you tell you about Monsieur Plaquet.' He rubbed his nose with his finger, then looked at Gillie.

'Well, *mademoiselle*, if you can tell a gentleman by the way he treats his mother, then Christophe Plaquet is a gentleman. They come here occasionally together, and he is solicitous and kind. As to his timekeeping, not so brilliant, but you can't dismiss a man for that. But you should visit his studio to see his latest work – I'm sure he would be delighted to know that such a charming woman is interested in his art.'

An hour later Gillie was on the train back to Beaune with an address for Christophe, a brochure showing his latest work, and a dear little watercolour by an up and coming artist she had purchased from the delightful old gentleman.

That night, after propping her latest purchase against the

dressing-table mirror, she scrutinised the postcard containing the address.

Christophe's studio was in his mother's apartment in the sixth arrondissement, Saint-Germain-des-Prés. But Robert was right, she could hardly go there herself. She frowned at her reflection. Knowing Christophe, he would probably think she was chasing him. And if he was a traitor, she mused, he would hardly admit anything to her. No, she needed someone to go in her place. They would have to be discreet and used to digging out the truth. There was only one person she could think of that was eminently suitable: Sophie's boyfriend. The more she thought about it, the more it made sense. A journalist would instinctively ask all the right questions. She would ask Sophie if he would consider a private investigation. As she tried to sleep, the old man's complimentary words about Christophe played in her mind. How she hoped they were true.

The following morning Gillie drove to the hospital in Dijon.

'Alfie's doing well,' Gillie assured Sophie, as she hurried through the swing doors towards her. 'But it's something else. You mentioned that your friend was an investigative journalist?'

Sophie nodded.

'Do you think you can persuade him to do something for me? I will pay him of course.'

Over coffee in a café around the corner from the hospital, the two women discussed the idea. The following evening Gillie received a call from Todd Dexter.

'You are lucky I'm in Paris at the moment on an assignment,' he said. 'If you want to meet me, shall we say one o'clock tomorrow, La Closerie des Lilas in Boulevard du Montparnasse? Do you know it?'

'I certainly do,' Gillie replied.

*

Gillie noticed Todd immediately at the table in the corner. As Sophie had said, he looked every inch of an American.

'So Gillie,' he said, shaking her hand. 'You had better tell me what this is all about.'

Gillie sat down and took a deep breath. 'What do you want to hear?'

Todd pulled out a battered notepad. 'Tell me everything.'

She spoke quietly for twenty minutes, but it seemed like an hour. She told him about Étienne, the café in Rue Chauveau, Geraud and Monsieur Ducre. She revealed the one undoubtable fact: Christophe had known who she was before he came to Pommard. All the while Todd scribbled notes.

'Shorthand,' he explained, snapping the pad closed. 'My own version, so don't worry, no one else would understand. It seems we need to find out what's going on. There may be a very simple explanation and your guy is in the clear.'

'He is obviously not my guy,' Gillie said, digging the middle out of a piece of bread. 'And I very much doubt he is in the clear.'

'We'll see.' He smiled at Gillie and she believed if the mystery were to be solved, the attractive American in the seat opposite would have a better chance than anyone.

'Why do you think Christophe came to Pommard after all this time?' she asked.

'That is what we are going to find out.'

They were standing beneath the small awning leading onto the street, when Gillie took two black and white photographs from her bag. 'I nearly forgot to give you these,' she said, handing them to Todd. 'The first is Étienne, and the other is Christophe. Next time I am in Paris, I will go back to the café in Rue Chauveau.'

Todd's expression changed. 'Let me see what I dig up, before you go rushing into a hornet's nest.'

Gillie raised a delicate eyebrow and smiled. 'I'm a big girl now, I am sure I will be fine.'

Gillie's steps were hurried as she made her way to the Métro, her bag clutched beneath her arm. It had been a satisfying meeting and Todd was the perfect man for the job, but it seemed he was also the ideal man for Sophie. Should she tell her brother that the woman he loved was clearly not free?

It had cost Todd his badge to a press conference with Brigitte Bardot to borrow the Delahaye convertible from his friend, but despite the fact that Simone de Beauvoir had described her as the *first and most liberated woman in post-war France*,' and the conference had been on his radar for weeks, he still believed it was worth it. He loved the feeling of the open road and it gave him time to think. As his fingers strummed the steering wheel in time to Bob Wilbur playing his saxophone on the radio, his thoughts turned to Gillie. Her tale of lies and deceit had definitely intrigued him. He had always had an enquiring mind, and loved the thrill of chasing a story, but he prided himself in finding a different angle and rooting out the facts. Here was an intelligent and beautiful woman, trying to solve a mystery that had begun during the war. The only evidence were two black and white images, one particularly faded. It was definitely something he could get his teeth into. He had always been writing other people's stories, but this would be different; he now knew the protagonist, it was closer, more personal, and she was connected to Sophie. He sighed as he changed gear and accelerated down a long, straight road. Why was it that he minded so much about Sophie? Of course she was sexy, but she was stubborn too. Something about her had got under his skin from the moment they had met. There was a vulnerability about her that he had never expected. It had been hard not to fall in love with her. But he knew in his gut she would never be truly his. He would have been happy to settle for second best, hoping this would change, but in his heart, he realised he needed to set her free. When he had challenged Sophie about the father of her child she had denied her feelings of course, but he had seen her face. It was quite clear to him she was still in love with Sebastian. If there was a remote chance Sebastian felt the same, he should not stand in their way. And then of course there was the child to consider. Todd gritted his teeth and stared through the windscreen. How he would have loved children, but it was not to be. Now he would do the right thing for both of them. He shook his head, amazed by his own altruism and turned up the radio. He was about to do the most important and unselfish thing in his life and he should feel good about it. But all he was left with was a dull ache in his chest.

Todd arrived just as Sophie was changing her clothes. He threw his bag on the floor and lay down on the bed, watching her. He needed to keep to his resolve, but he had always loved these intimate moments when Sophie was completely unaware of the effect she had on him.

'So you will solve the mystery of Christophe Plaquet?' she asked, putting on a blue silk dress, with a flared skirt. She glanced in the mirror, smoothing her hands over her hips.

'I imagine so.' Todd leapt off the bed and zipped up the back, his hands lingering on her shoulders. 'But my darling little doctor, we need to talk.'

She turned around, and for once his face was serious.

'You know I love you, Sophie, but that's not enough for you. I have to let you go.'

Sophie's face was still; there was no amazement in her eyes, just acceptance.

'And you are not even going to fight for me, are you my love?'

'Todd, I …' Sophie stammered, but the words dried up in her mouth.

'If you had protested even a little,' Todd interrupted her, 'then I would have known that you cared. But sweetheart, you are in love with Sebastian. I've known it for a long time, but I selfishly thought I could make you happy. And you are not going to deny it, are you?'

'I love you, really I do, but ...' she shrugged, tears slipping down her face and Todd held her in his arms.

'It's all right, my Sophie,' he breathed into her hair, his own eyes smarting, 'it's all right.'

'But it's not,' she looked up at him. 'I have made such a mess of everything.'

Todd lifted her chin and looked into her eyes. 'Sophie, you must tell Sebastian that you love him.'

'But he is engaged to be married, Todd.'

'He still needs to know, otherwise you'll always regret it. If you are meant to be with Sebastian, life has a way of making things work out.'

Sophie's eyes were glimmering with tears. 'Do you think so?' she said at last, and this was the confirmation Todd needed.

'I do, Sophie,' he said, knowing he had made the right decision. For one last time his arms went around her, wishing it could have been him that she loved. 'This Sebastian may not be admitting his feelings to himself, but you have to give him a chance.' He kissed her gently on the lips. 'Now, if you'll forgive me, I think I'd better go.'

'Will you keep in touch? she asked, unable to let go of his arm.

He broke away. 'Not for a while, darling. I shall throw myself into the mystery of Christophe Plaquet, then I shall accept the offer to go back to South Vietnam. The first US soldiers have been killed and they will need some good reporting.' He gave a wry smile. 'Nothing like a danger zone to mend a broken heart. But one day, *ma petite* doctor, who knows.'

Chapter Forty-Five

Sophie watched the door close on Todd and sank to the floor. Why couldn't she love him enough? What was wrong with her? Todd was everything she could possibly want – he was kind, intelligent, handsome – and she had let him walk away. One word from her and he would have stayed. Yes, they had often argued, but they had always made up in the end. And they had always had fun. She remembered an evening at a jazz club in Paris. After listening to their favourite musicians, they had left in the rain. How they had laughed as they ran down the streets and turned up at his hotel, soaked and bedraggled, with water in their shoes. Afterwards, they had made passionate love and had finished the evening sitting in front of the fire eating bread and cheese with a bottle of wine.

His words played in her mind, *I selfishly thought I could make you happy.* 'Oh Todd,' she cried, 'if only I could accept your love.'

As she pulled herself to her feet, she recalled in vivid detail standing on the threshold of her brother's room. What had happened that day had sealed his fate and her own. Though she didn't understand it at the time, she had carried the guilt since then. She felt unworthy to be loved.

After splashing her face with water, she went downstairs to the communal telephone. The only person who would truly understand was Georges. He was now back in Paris and she missed him every day. She dialled the number, recalling with a certain amount of self-pity his wedding to Lydia. How handsome he had looked, waiting for his bride in the front pew of the large church in Paris, his dark hair for once tamed, a large grin of happiness on his dear face.

He picked up the phone immediately.

'Georges!'

'*Ma cherie*, is everything all right?' he asked, concern in his voice.

'No it's not, Todd has just left me, Sebastian is getting married in precisely one month's time, and you're not here. I'm feeling utterly miserable.'

She could hear muffled talking in the background and Lydia's sleepy voice. 'Go next door, Georges, she obviously needs to talk to you.'

He picked up the extension. '*Ma pauvre petite*,' he said, letting her cry.

'What is wrong with me, Georges?'

'You're in love with the father of your child, so not much apart from that,' he affirmed.

'But Sebastian is about to be married and it's all hopeless.'

'Perhaps a little hopeless,' he agreed.

After half an hour of chatting with her friend, Sophie felt marginally better.

'I love you Georges,' she said, feeling unusually sentimental. 'Only platonically of course, because you are married.'

'*Moi aussi, ma cherie*.'

Two days after his break-up with Sophie, Todd was on his way to an address in the sixth arrondissement, Saint-Germain-des-Prés. As he made his way through the maze of cobbled streets, he refused to dwell on his disappointment. Instead he imagined the authors and artists over the centuries, who had congregated in the many cafés and galleries, haggling over books, paintings, discussing the meaning of life.

At a large and elegant stone building, he rang the bell to apartment two. The door opened, and he took the flight of stairs.

'Can I help you?' A maid opened the door.

'If it is possible I would like to speak to Madame Plaquet. My name is Todd Dexter, I work for *Time* magazine.' He handed her his card.

'She is not here, I'm afraid.'

'Please tell *madame* that I'm doing an editorial on the intellectuals and artists who have inhabited this area. I would be so grateful if I could call again tomorrow.' Todd winked at the maid, who tidied her cap in a fluster.

'*Madame* will be at home in the morning, if it pleases you to come back then.'

Todd returned the following morning. The maid immediately opened the door.

'*Bonjour jolie demoiselle,*' he said in his best French.

The maid blushed. 'She is expecting you. You may wait in the drawing room.'

As Todd waited for Madame Plaquet to arrive, he looked around the elegant room. It was furnished with immaculate taste. Silk curtains hung at the tall windows and Aubusson rugs covered the polished floor. Sconces and gilded mirrors hung from the walls amongst a variety of paintings. There were old masters from another age, several impressionist paintings, at least one by Monet. But there was one that stood apart. From his recent research, the sweeping brushstrokes and vibrant colour belonged to the hand of the artist, Christophe Plaquet.

When a refined middle-aged woman wearing a Chanel tweed dress from their latest collection walked towards him, he felt a twinge of excitement. He knew he was on the trail.

She held out her hand. 'Monsieur Dexter, it seems you are interested in the distinguished inhabitants of Saint-Germain-des Prés. As you are of course aware, there have been many. But first I am sure you would like a coffee, Americano I assume?' she said with a smile. The maid, who had obviously been hovering outside the door, came in immediately.

'Will you take a spoonful of sugar, *monsieur*?'

Todd kept a straight face. The girl was looking at him from beneath her eyelashes, she was definitely flirting.

'I have a sweet tooth, *merci beaucoup mademoiselle*.'

He spent a stimulating half an hour with Madame Plaquet, taking notes about the inhabitants of the area, past and present. In fact he *would* write the editorial, he decided. The charming Madame Plaquet had an inexhaustible knowledge, and he disliked misleading her.

'You see that painting, Todd, if I may call you that?' she smiled. 'Can you guess who it is by?'

Todd looked at the small townscape, knowing full well it was Monet. 'Renoir?' he queried.

Madame Plaquet laughed but it was a warm, friendly laugh, not patronising at all.

'*Actually* it is one of two that I own by Monet. Beautiful, is it not?'

'It is indeed,' Todd murmured.

'Of course Renoir lived in this little part of Paris too. Our famous café Les Deux Magots has hosted them all. Sartre still goes there, but it is now filled with tourists.' She shrugged her slim shoulders. 'You must have visited?'

'Indeed *madame*, many of my editorials have been written there. I have always hoped that if I work in such elevated surroundings, some literary genius will rub off on me.' He grinned at her over the porcelain cup.

'You are funny, Monsieur Todd.'

They had been talking for at least half an hour before Todd channelled the conversation to her son.

'That painting,' he said, pointing to the landscape. 'It is superb.'

'By my son,' she said. 'You may have heard of him, Christophe Plaquet?'

They walked over to admire the work, and Todd was struck again by the landscape of vineyards and trees with a large house in the foreground. He also found Madame Plaquet's pride in her son's work touching.

He was leaving the flat with another appointment fixed for the following day, when a dog bounded down the corridor towards him. It was a black poodle. He leant down and scratched his ears.

'Ah, Hercule seems to have taken to you,' she said.

The next morning, Gillie, dressed in slacks, her cream coat and a beret, travelled to Paris on the morning train. She had made contact with Geraud and would meet him at the café in Rue Chauveau. Afterwards she would join Todd at a cellar club in Rue Dauphine, Le Tabou.

Todd took the stairs to the apartment two at a time, determined that today he would uncover the truth. He was shown into the drawing room, where he spent a pleasant fifteen minutes examining the paintings anew.

'*Pardon*, Monsieur Todd,' Madame Plaquet apologised, coming towards him, but instead of the sprightly, elegant woman he had encountered only the day before, today she looked frail.

'I am feeling a little under the weather,' she said, pushing a strand of limp hair from her face.

'I should go. Forgive me, *madame*.'

'Please,' she indicated the chair opposite. 'Won't you sit down? I need a little distraction.'

Todd poured coffee for them both, noticing how the old woman's hands shook as she lifted the cup; the grey pallor of her lips. She looked up sharply, catching his expression of concern.

'Cancer, I'm afraid,' she stated. 'Six months at the most. My son Christophe has come back to live with me – he is such a good boy. Ah, here is my little Hercule.'

While the dog sat at her feet staring at the plate of biscuits, Todd was faced with a dilemma. How could he rake up the past, potentially exposing Christophe, and destroy his dying mother?

'Christophe gets cross with me,' she said, interrupting his thoughts, 'but today we shall get away with a little indiscretion.' She smiled wickedly and broke half a biscuit for Hercule. 'Would you like to see my son's latest painting? It is in the dining room. *C'est tres charmant.*'

She took his arm and led him along the corridor. They arrived at a large dining room with grey panelled walls. A crystal chandelier hung on a silk-covered chain. On the sideboard, a miniature easel was set up, holding the portrait of a young boy.

'He has been teaching this child to paint,' she explained. 'Alfie is his name. Enchanting, wouldn't you agree?'

Todd nodded, unable to speak. He had a strange feeling in the pit of his stomach. Something was wrong, and he wasn't sure why. The painting was more than charming, it was painted with feeling. The child was Sophie's son, Alfie, and the artist obviously cared deeply for him.

Todd was about to leave, having spent another enlightening but also troubled hour with Madame Plaquet. He had found his concentration wandering.

'Are you quite well, Monsieur Todd?' Madame Plaquet had asked when he had fallen silent.

'Forgive me, I am digesting all this information,' he had replied. He was at the door when she touched his arm.

'*Un moment*, I have a photograph I would like to show you of my son, no my two sons.' She disappeared along the corridor once more, her heels clacking on the parquet floor and returned carrying a large photograph in a silver frame. There was something poignant about the way she cradled the photograph against her chest that alerted Todd.

She handed it to him. He had seen the faces in the photographs only a short while before.

'My two sons,' she said. 'Christophe and Étienne. Tragically, Étienne was killed during the war.'

Todd ran down the stairs and into the street, his thoughts going around in circles as he processed this latest development. Étienne was Christophe's brother. He certainly wasn't expecting that. Obviously neither was Gillie, but how could she have guessed – there was absolutely no resemblance between the two men. He kicked at an empty can of Coca-Cola, sending it skittering across the pavement. Gillie had got it all wrong of course, Christophe would never have betrayed his brother, but he was still missing something. What was Christophe doing in Pommard after all these years? Why was he watching Gillie? And who had told him she was there? He stopped in his tracks.

Geraud knew Gillie lived in Pommard. She was meeting him in Rue Chauveau this very afternoon.

He turned around and went back the way he had come. He would probably incur the wrath of Madame Plaquet, and of her son, but for Gillie's safety he must reveal the truth.

Marcel was sweeping the pavement, and Geraud was smoking a cigarette, when Gillie arrived at the café in Rue Chauveau. He ground the stub beneath the heal of his shoe and opened the door. 'You go first,' he instructed, ushering her inside the otherwise empty café.

Indicating a table away from the window, he turned the key in the lock. 'You obviously got my message,' Gillie enquired, trying to keep her voice steady.

'We are here, aren't we,' he replied.

The men scraped their chairs closer to Gillie.

'So, *mademoiselle*, what do you want this time?' Geraud's voice was cold. 'We have told you what happened to your lover.'

'I have some new information.' Gillie paused to give weight to her words. 'There is a possibility that I know who informed on Étienne.'

'*Madame*, you are meddling in affairs that do not concern you,' he growled.

As he leant forward, his face almost touching Gillie's, she could smell the Gauloises on his breath.

'I am only trying to help,' she stuttered.

'I'll tell you what happens when you poke around in other people's business? People get stopped, accidents can happen,' he spat. 'Isn't that right, Marcel?'

Gillie could feel herself trembling as she faced the two men.

'You should keep your nose out of this.' Marcel thumped the table with his hefty fist.

Todd was once again in Madame Plaquet's elegant flat, but this time there were no cups of coffee, no light conversation.

'My sincere apologies, *madame*, but I need to speak to your son.'

Madame Plaquet looked bewildered. 'I'm not sure I understand.'

'Maman, who is this? What the hell is going on?' A man strode down the corridor towards them.

Todd recognised him from the photograph. 'I'm a friend

of Gillienne Ogilvie, we need to go to the café in the Rue Chauveau immediately. I think she is in danger, I'll explain on the way.'

Christophe blanched, a range of emotions crossing his face.

'Maman, please excuse us, we are in a hurry. I'll tell you everything when I get back.' He turned to Todd. 'My car is outside, and I know a shortcut.'

While Todd recounted the story, Christophe hurtled through the streets of Paris in his battered blue Citroën, bombarding Todd with questions, while jumping several red lights, and going the wrong way down a street. Luckily they arrived intact at the Rue Chauveau. As the car screeched to a halt outside the café, both men leapt out and Christophe hammered on the door.

'Geraud, let me in.'

There was silence.

'Let me in, it's Christophe, I'm with a friend,' he shouted, pounding even harder.

The door opened, and Christophe pushed past Geraud.

Gillie flew to Todd. 'Thank God you are here,' she said.

'What do you think you are playing at, Geraud?' Christophe yelled.

'We didn't touch her, she just needed a bit of a fright. She has been nosing around.'

Christophe shook his head. 'You imbeciles, she was trying to help.'

At that moment Gillie marched over to Christophe.

'You bastard,' she hissed.

'That's a nice welcome,' he grinned.

Gillie looked at him furiously. 'Why did you come to Pommard? And what did you hope to gain by finding me? It's my guess that you were a collaborator and you could have had

383

something to do with Étienne's death?' Gillie finally ran out of steam, her face flushed. She looked at Todd for support.

'My dearest Gillie, you have it all wrong,' Christophe put his hand on her arm, but she shook it away.

'You're a criminal and a coward,' she exclaimed.

At this Todd interjected. 'I think you need to listen to him, Gillie. I have found out that he is none of these things.'

'Well, what is he then?'

'I'm Étienne's brother.' Christophe said the words quietly so that Gillie could hardly hear.

'You're what?'

'He was my brother,' he repeated.

For a moment she was stunned. 'That's not possible, I would have known. You look nothing like him.'

'He wouldn't have told you he had a brother, Gillie,' Christophe confirmed. 'You know how it was in those times.'

After her initial amazement Gillie was angry again. 'But why did you come to Pommard?' she threw at him.

Christophe looked a little sheepish. 'All these years I've been obsessed with finding who betrayed my brother. Your name only came up recently. Please forgive me, but I thought it could be you.'

'Are you mad? All that time you accepted my mother's hospitality. You even came to my grandmother's funeral for heaven's sake. And to think I was taken in by you.'

Geraud, who had been watching the proceedings with increasing aggravation, banged his chair on the floor. Everyone turned to him.

'What is all this about, Christophe? You obviously know this girl?'

'Of course I know her, only someone as rash and idiotic as Gillienne Ogilvie would come here on their own. I probably should have told you, but I went to Pommard to look around.

384

I can assure you, Gillie was never responsible for my brother's death.'

'How dare you call me idiotic,' Gillie spluttered.

'All right – not idiotic, just rash. We are part of a network, trying to flush out war criminals and collaborators. Many of them are still at large. Geraud is part of the team, but you have been meddling and getting in the way. You are lucky that you didn't end up incarcerated somewhere cold and unpleasant,' he quipped.

'I was about to be, I'm sure of it,' Gillie complained.

'I doubt they would have resorted to throwing you in the Seine,' Christophe winked at Geraud to lighten the atmosphere in the room.

'But you lied to me,' Gillie countered. 'You pretended you knew nothing about my past and then you just left.'

'I'm sorry, I had to go. How could I explain that I had been spying on you? I was convinced you would never forgive me for the deception.' He smiled wryly, 'And looking at you I was obviously correct!'

'You are damned right,' she retorted, her eyes blazing.

'But there is another thing, Gillie… Falling in love with my brother's girlfriend was never part of the plan.'

Her mouth dropped open as his words sunk in. 'Did you really fall in love with me?' she questioned.

'Of course I did. I knew you couldn't have done anything to harm anyone, but I could hardly confide in you!'

At this point Todd, who had been following the exchange with bafflement, started to laugh.

'Geez, this will make a bloody good story. You couldn't make it up if you tried.'

Marcel scratched his head and walked toward the cellar. 'I am a little confused, but in this situation, there is only one answer – I shall open a bottle of my finest red wine.'

Chapter Forty-Six

In the spring of 1960, three months after the incident in Rue Chevau, Christophe made an appointment to see Liliane.

'If the house is still empty,' he said, smoothing the pockets of his new linen jacket, 'and you do not consider me an entirely unsuitable tenant, then I would love to return to Les Volets Bleus.'

'Should I have any doubt as to your suitability?' Liliane asked, fixing her eyes on him. She would not let him get away with his duplicity entirely. He had, after all, deceived her daughter.

'Probably,' he replied, returning her gaze. 'I am an artist, for one thing, and they are known to be pretty dubious characters.'

'A good one, however.'

'Merci Madame.'

'Do you paint all young ladies in a state of undress?' she asked innocently.

For once Christophe was lost for words. 'I ... I am not sure what to say.'

'I removed the painting and brought it up to the house for safekeeping. Shall I return it to you?' Liliane's lips twitched. 'It's a good likeness by the way.'

'That would be very kind.' Christophe was beginning to relax; there was another side to Gillie's mother he had not seen before.

'If you agree to the renewal of my tenancy, I would like to bring my mother here for a while. I believe you would find each other stimulating company.'

'I would like to meet her, and yes, I will renew your lease. But I have to add that if you hurt my daughter again I will personally take my revenge.'

'I have no intention of hurting your daughter. I am in love with her,' he said.

'Well then, you have nothing to worry about,' she replied with a smile.

Alfie was delighted with the news that Christophe had returned and insisted on accompanying his aunt to the house. They were walking slowly through the meadow, with the now ancient Coco and Louis ambling behind, when Hercule started to bark. The next moment the poodle had scrabbled over the top of the gate and had charged at Louis, attaching himself to his leg.

Alfie started to giggle. 'That's rude.'

'You really are a disgusting little dog,' Gillie admonished.

At that moment Christophe appeared in the doorway. 'Agh Hercule, why do you always shame me?' he said.

Chapter Forty-Seven

It was six months after Alfie's operation and a glorious Sunday in May. Sebastian was resting in the garden, with Coco and Louis panting in the shade nearby. Through half-closed eyes he could see a mist of insects hovering over the fountain. A swallow dipped, tipping his wings in the stone basin, shaking the water through its feathers in an almost imperceptible motion. In the meadow just below the garden wall, Jean was cutting the grass on his new tractor. Sebastian could hear the low throbbing of the engine and he could imagine Jean's satisfied smile. Making hay was preferable any day to getting on his knees in the flower beds.

Sebastian made himself some tea and went upstairs to Alfie's room. Model aeroplanes hung from the ceiling, and a toy train wound its way through an undulating scenery of forests and hills. In the corner, on a rectangular table, wooden cows and chickens that had belonged to Sebastian's father still inhabited the farmyard.

Sebastian sat down on Alfie's bed and ran his hand through his son's silky hair.

'Hello Papa,' Alfie murmured. 'Is Doctor Sophie coming to see me soon?'

'I am sure she will,' he replied.

Alfie sat bolt upright and pulled a sheet of paper from his bedside table. 'Can you read this Papa and send it?'

Sebastian took the letter.

Dear Doctor Sophie,
Thank you for mending my poorly heart. I am doing very
well and I am now back at school. I saw your picture in the
newspaper. There was a story of how you put me in a bath of
ice.
   I'd like to see you, I think Papa would too.
   Love Alfie

Sebastian couldn't help smiling. 'Yes, I'll send it, Alfie, my darling little boy.'

Two weeks after the letter had been sent, Sophie arrived at the station in Beaune. Gillie was waiting in the car.

'How is Alfie?' It was always her first question to Gillie.

'He's missed your bedtime stories.'

'I felt it was better for Amelia if I kept away for a while.'

Gillie glanced at Sophie, then drove on towards Pommard. She stopped the car on the gravel. 'Alfie is meant to be having a rest, but I expect he has been waiting at the window.'

Sure enough, they looked up and saw a little face at the circular window at the top of the stairs. After a quick wave he disappeared.

'He will have been counting the moments until your arrival on his new watch. He never takes it off, by the way.'

Sophie's eyes softened. 'Do you think Sebastian will let me speak to Alfie today?' she asked. 'You know, about being his mother?'

'Sebastian's friend Marcus Donadieu is coming to see Alfie. They developed quite a bond while he was staying here. Perhaps it would be better if you tell him when there are fewer distractions.'

'I quite understand.' Sophie looked away, but not before Gillie had seen the disappointment in her eyes.

'Be patient,' she advised. 'Everything will turn out well, you'll see.'

She opened the gate to let Sophie through. 'Thank you. Todd was magnificent, by the way. He really helped me find out the truth. Christophe came here thinking I had betrayed Étienne and I thought it was him.' She laughed, her joy palpable.

'How is Christophe now?'

'I am forgiving him slowly,' she grinned.

'I'm so pleased Todd was able to help you.' Sophie hesitated. 'He's a wonderful man, but...' She looked at the ground, kicking at the gravel with the toe of her shoe. 'The thing is, Gillie, we are no longer together.'

'Todd didn't tell me,' Gillie chewed her lip. 'Actually Amelia is...' She stopped as her mother came down the steps towards them.

'Alfie is on his way down,' Liliane said.

Sophie was sitting on the library sofa when Alfie rushed in and threw himself onto her lap. For an instant time stood still: the pale wooden bookcases filled with an assortment of leatherbound books, the roses overflowing from a large blue and white vase, the scent of lavender drifting through the muslin curtains were as much a part of that moment, as her son in her arms. She held him away from her.

'Alfie.' She said the word softly.

He looked at her, his head one side, and she was able to count his freckles one by one, see the tiny white line on his forehead, the result of falling off a slide as a small child. She was able to build up a picture of her son's life in the intervening years.

'So,' she said at last, 'shall we inspect that scar?'

'Why didn't you come and inspect it before?'

'Because your Aunt Gillie was looking after you, and she is a nurse after all.'

Sophie tucked in Alfie's shirt and looked through the open window. A man was walking up the drive. It would be Sebastian's friend Marcus, she assumed. But as he came nearer, a pulse began to beat in her temple. Despite a slight limp, there was a familiarity about the way he carried himself. His slender frame and the upright swing of his shoulders stirred a distant memory. She moved closer. The way the man's hair fell across his face before he brushed it away evoked a recollection of a long-ago game. She could see herself running through trees in the Bois de Boulogne, being caught up and swung round by her brother.

She lifted Alfie from the sofa. 'Go and find your father, *mon cheri*, I'll be back in a moment.' In a trance she walked through the French doors and waited at the top of the steps. Her knuckles were white as she gripped onto the wrought-iron railing.

The man was coming towards her. He was climbing the wide stone steps.

'Is Madame Ogilvie here?' he asked.

'It's me, Sophie.' Her voice sounded strange in her ears.

The man stopped. 'Sophie?' He shook his head, his dark eyes bemused. '*Sacre bleu*, it can't be.'

Marcus Donadieu stared at the woman on the steps. She was not the child he had once known, but her features were the same: slanting blue eyes, tilted nose. The voice was less girlish, but it was Sophie's voice.

She moved towards him, confusion etched into her face. 'Why didn't you come and find me? Why, Max? Grand-mère and I looked for you. We went to every hospital in Paris, every shelter, but you never came.'

'I couldn't.'

'You're alive.' She let out a sob. 'And for years you let me think you were dead.'

'It's a long story.'

'You have to believe me when I entered your bedroom, I didn't know what I was seeing, I thought...' She hesitated, afraid to go on. 'Will you tell me what happened after I was sent away? I need to know what I had done.'

Marcus took a deep breath and looked her in the eye. 'Father banished me, he told me that I could never come back and as for my friend, he died working in the mines. You betrayed me, Sophie, how could I find you after that?'

'But you must have known our parents were killed.'

'Not for a long time, and by then it was too late. I had a different identity and a different life.'

Sophie felt the years slip away and she was a young girl once more, running along the corridor to her brother's bedroom, her glorious future mapped out for her.

'I won, Max, I won the prize,' she cried and threw open the door.

She had stopped on the threshold transfixed, unable to move. Her brother was naked and pinned to the wall. He was making strange noises and a man was standing with his back to her, pushing against him. She had found it curious that her brother wasn't screaming. Sweat glistened on their bodies and Max's fists were curled into a tight ball. She wanted to cry out, but no sound came. As the two men swivelled to face her, she turned and fled, dropping the bar of chocolate, stumbling into the hallway, running along the passage through the front door. She had not stopped running until she reached the metal stairs to her father's office.

'You must come quickly,' she had cried. 'Someone is killing Max.'

Sophie sank down onto the stone step, remembering the aftermath of her revelation, and her father's face as he picked up an iron bar. 'You stay here,' he had yelled, but she had followed anyway.

They reached the house just as the man she recognised as a friend of Max's had fled across the cobbles. She had shut her ears to her father's fury.

'I'll kill you, be sure that I will.'

She remembered her confusion. The man was supposed to be her brother's best friend; she didn't understand at all.

Marcus sat down on the step next to her.

'I didn't recognise what I had seen until much later,' Sophie whispered. 'Only then did I realise what I had done, and I was so ashamed.'

She looked up at him, her face pale. 'I have spent my life believing you were dead with no way of making it up to you. I thought someone was hurting you. I had to get Papa. I wanted to save you. I didn't understand.'

Max took her in his arms and she sobbed against his chest.

'Will you forgive me now?' she asked.

Sophie was leaning against Marcus when Sebastian came in.

He took a step backwards, his face blanching. 'It appears you two know each other.'

'We do,' Sophie said, her face lit with happiness.

'Am I missing something?' Sebastian asked, an edge to his voice.

Sophie hesitated. 'You won't believe this, but Max, or should I say Marcus, is my brother. And I thought he was dead, Sebastian.'

Sebastian shook his head, the tension at once leaving his face. 'Is there anything else you need to tell me, Sophie?'

'Not at the moment,' she looked at him and their eyes met.

'I'm sure you will find something,' he said, with a wry smile. 'I will explain everything, I promise.'

'Will you walk with me, Max?' Sophie asked.

Max hesitated; his life had been blighted by his sister's betrayal. Could he forgive her in a heartbeat, forget the shame, the years of misery? He felt his resolve hardening, but when he looked at his sister's pleading face, he could remember her as a small child. How she had loved him, looked up to him; she had told the truth, she would never have knowingly betrayed him. She was an innocent, she would not have understood. He took a step forward, now was the time to let go of the past and look forward to a future with his sister.

'I would like that,' he replied.

In consideration of Marcus's injuries, they walked slowly through the meadow, stopping occasionally so that he could catch his breath.

'It's my ribs,' he explained. 'They are occasionally a little painful.'

'To say nothing of your femur,' she said with a gentle smile.

They stopped by the lake and Sophie put her arm through her brother's. 'To think all these years I thought you were dead,' she murmured. 'I can't quite believe it.'

She looked up at the trees, black silhouettes against the luminous sky, their reflections mirrored in the still water. They were the first trees she had seen since the extraordinary revelation. It was the first sunset, glowing purple, orange and red. The world looked so different now her brother had returned. A flight of ducks flew into land, gliding onto the surface and the air was thick with the smell of honeysuckle.

'It's astonishing,' Marcus mused looking around him, 'so much beauty. And you,' he chuckled. 'Where has the skinny girl with plaits gone?'

'She grew up.'

'How our parents would have loved your success. They would have been so proud of you. They always believed in you, but a surgeon for heaven's sake! What about your personal happiness, you are not married?'

Sophie shook her head, her chest tight. She could remember her grandmother encouraging her to marry Sebastian.

She drew in her breath. 'There is something else you should know.'

He was looking at her, his eyes questioning.

'Alfie is my son.'

'Alfie...?' Marcus paused, unable to say anything. He pulled a large linen handkerchief from his pocket. 'Sorry,' he croaked, 'this is all a little too much for one day.'

As they meandered through the meadow, Sophie told Marcus how she had come to know his friend.

'I had returned to Chamonix to say goodbye to you,' Sophie revealed, her eyes never leaving his face. 'I needed to let you go. I met Sebastian on my way to glacier d'Argentière, we spent three days together and Alfie was the result.'

'I am sure fate has a hand in this too, Sophie,' Marcus mused when he was able to talk. 'You should know it was me who encouraged him to go to Chamonix. I said he should walk through the woods to the bottom of the glacier, I'm not sure why.'

He rubbed his forehead, a gesture Sophie remembered so well. 'Perhaps our meeting again is the abbot's doing, or God's. You know Pierre gave his life for me.'

Sophie nodded. 'I never met him, but he was obviously an extraordinary man.'

*

As the sun dipped below the horizon, Marcus looked beyond Sophie into the distance. But he was no longer seeing the gentle landscape of vineyards dotting the hillside, and terracotta rooftops, instead there was a giant ice cliff above him as inch by inch the abbot hauled him to the surface. He could hear his comforting words echoing through the chasm. *'When all this is over, come and visit me at Vézelay, my son, for in the abbey you will find the quiet path to stilling the heart and knowing God.'* In that brief time, the abbot had understood his frailties, his insecurity and mental pain, and now he was gone.

'Pierre wanted me to visit him at Vézelay,' he uttered, his face bleak.

'Then you must. Go to Vézelay,' she murmured, 'just as he suggested, and if you agree, I will come with you. We can light candles for the abbot and for our parents. I know given time they would have understood. Can you find it in your heart to forgive them now?'

As they neared the house Marcus caught her hand, a smile spreading over his face. 'So, Alfie is my nephew. That darling little boy is my blood. When I stayed here after the accident I thought there was a bond between us, he has my mind. I was always good at card games, but Alfie! And chess, did you know he plays a fine game?'

Sophie squeezed his hand gently. 'He has always reminded me of you.'

Later that evening, while Sophie was upstairs reading a story to Alfie, Sebastian broke open a bottle of champagne.

'I think this in order,' he exclaimed.

Liliane arrived from her office to see what the fuss was about, with Gillie following closely behind.

'So,' Sebastian said, raising a glass, 'you are Alfie's uncle. That means we are sort of related.'

Marcus had a foolish grin on his face. 'I suppose it means that we are.' Sebastian grasped Marcus's hand. 'Welcome to the family,' he said.

Chapter Forty-Eight

Sebastian picked up a half-empty glass and went into the library. He could see the impression where Sophie had been on the green sofa and caught the last lingering waft of her scent. She had come back into his life like a whirlwind, disrupting his emotions, his stability and his life.

He sank back against the cushions. He'd intended to tell Sophie at once that his wedding was no longer taking place, but she had just been reunited with the brother she'd thought was lost; tonight was not the time. His carefully chosen words would have to wait for another day. He drained his glass. What did he hope to achieve, anyway? Sophie was in a relationship with Todd, and now she had Marcus. There was no place for him.

Later he went to the winery. It was here, in the quiet, vaulted cellars amongst the wooden barrels and wine racks, that he was able to think clearly. He pulled out a bottle, replaced it, then another. These wines had been maturing. Some were excellent, others less so, all made as the years had continued their endless roll. As he wiped the dust from a bottle and read the label 1815, a faint smile crossed his face. It was produced in the same year as the Battle of Waterloo. How many hearts had been broken in the intervening years, how many lives lost? His existence was just a fragment in time. But this was his fragment. If he had any chance of happiness it would mean fighting for Sophie, and he realised he was prepared to do so until his last breath.

Chapter Forty-Nine

Sophie was surprised that Sebastian had requested her presence at a family lunch at Pommard the following day. As she walked into the courtyard at the front of the house, she found the table had been set beneath the trees, covered with a white linen cloth. In between the elegant silver candelabra, bunches of wild flowers picked by Alfie were placed in jam jars, and tiny dishes were filled with curls of yellow butter. As everyone took their places she watched Alfie's happy little face. So this was what it was like to be part of a large family. Whatever else she had done in her life, she had done the right thing by her son.

When everyone was seated, Liliane stood up and smiled at the assembled company.

'It is my turn to say a few words,' she began. 'It has been an extraordinary year, but with the exception of the death of my dearest brother, we have so much to be grateful for. I would like to raise my glass to absent friends, my mother and Pierre. There are other people I would like to mention, our guest Marcus and our resident surgeon, Sophie, whose quick thinking saved my grandson's life.' She raised her glass to Sophie.

'To Christophe, who has returned to Les Volets Bleus and

into my daughter's good books.' At this, Christophe looked at Gillie, a question in his eyes.

'We would also like to welcome Madame Plaquet. I hope you are enjoying your stay.'

Madame Plaquet raised a frail but elegant hand. 'Enormously,' she said.

'Lastly, and most importantly, to our dearest little warrior, Alfie.'

'What about me?' Sebastian asked, and everyone laughed.

'And you, *mon cheri*.'

Adeline had excelled herself and produced a superb lunch. Green beans sprinkled with lemon were followed by lamb cooked slowly on the spit and dauphinoise potatoes. A *patisserie* followed, served with wild strawberries and fresh cream. A good house burgundy was brought to the table by Jean.

When offered a glass, he accepted, of course.

'I'll take two – one for me and one for *la belle femme*, if you don't mind!'

As the afternoon drifted on, and the conversation and quiet laughter continued, Gillie rose to her feet.

'I have something to add,' she announced, and all heads swivelled towards her. 'Since we are no longer holding a wedding at the house, and the caterers are booked, and the guests invited, shall we hold a celebration of life instead?'

'Sebastian isn't getting married?' Sophie gasped.

'No wedding,' Gillie smiled. 'I promised you things would turn out well in the end.'

Sebastian moved places with the colonel and sat down beside Sophie. 'I wanted to tell you yesterday,' he explained.

'Why aren't you getting married to Amelia?' Sophie blurted, when she had finally regained her composure.

'How could I, when I was in love with someone else? Despite

the fact that the woman I adore is with some jumped-up American journalist.'

'Todd is not jumped up,' Sophie retaliated, a wide grin crossing her face. 'And as a matter of fact, I am no longer with him.'

'You are not?'

'No, I am not.'

'Well then, you had better come with me.' Sebastian got up from the table and Sophie followed, disappearing into Marie-Claire's garden. The moment they were secure from inquisitive eyes behind the high yew hedges, Sebastian took her in his arms.

'You are not getting away from me this time, Doctor Bernot,' he murmured.

'I'm not sure that I want to,' she replied.

Much later when they had returned to the table amidst clapping from the family, Sebastian went to his son.

'Will you come with me for a little walk, Alfie, I have a story to tell you.'

Alfie jumped up. 'Yes please Papa, I love stories.' He skipped along beside his father.

Sebastian was opening the wrought-iron gate to the meadow when he looked back and caught Sophie's eye. For a moment he held her gaze, Sophie nodded, then he walked on.

He wandered with Alfie to the lake and as Mimi proudly escorted her ten ducklings across the water, he put his arm around his son's shoulders.

'Shall I begin?' he murmured.

'Will I like it?' Alfie asked, leaning against him.

'I believe that you will,' he said.

'Well, let me see, just over eight years ago I went on a short holiday to Chamonix…'

When he had finished, Alfie tucked his hand into his father's.

'Will you marry Doctor Sophie now, instead of Amelia?' he asked.

'Let's go and find your mother and see what she thinks,' Sebastian replied.

Epilogue

Sophie reappeared from the cloakroom, smoothing the jacket of her blue Schiaparelli suit. She had no sooner sat down at her table when the waiter, Armand, appeared at her side.

'Would *madame* like some more champagne? I believe your husband has arrived.'

'Thank you, Armand,' she said, her laughter bubbling to the surface.

'You have been very patient, and it seems at last you are right. We shall have a half bottle of the Krug Grande Cuvée,' she replied.

As Sophie glanced across the room, she could see her husband Sebastian striding through the Café Angelina towards her.

He leant down and kissed her cheek. 'You are still quite the most beautiful woman here,' he whispered.

'And you,' she replied, 'are not only the best husband, but also the most convincing fibber in the world. You are also late.' She glanced at her watch.

'I am so sorry, *ma cherie* – our grandchildren wouldn't let me leave. But you must have been happy.' He tapped the scrapbook that was open at the photographs of their wedding day. 'Look at that lovely bride.'

'I admit, I was allowing myself a little reminiscence. That was such a gorgeous dress,' Sophie sighed. 'I remember your mother marching me off to Givenchy. We had such fun, Sebastian. I still miss her.'

'Of course you do.'

'And look at Alfie! Do you remember him throwing the confetti?'

'If I recall, he put some of the rose petals down Adeline's front and she was very cross,' Sebastian laughed.

'I'd forgotten that,' Sophie giggled.

'And now your dear little boy is fifty-three, and if I'm not mistaken, that is him coming through the door.'

Sophie smiled with pride as her son wound his way through the tables. He was nearly as good-looking as his father, his dark hair flecked with grey.

'Maman, I got the day off work to surprise you, ahead of the awards ceremony tonight.'

She squeezed his arm. 'I'm a little nervous, if I'm honest.'

'Well, you shouldn't be.' He eased his tall frame into a chair. 'Everyone will be there. My entire family, and of course Gillie and the boys. Christophe has flown in especially from his retrospective exhibition in London. None of us would miss this for the world.'

'And the twins?'

'Sylvie is coming with her tribe, and I am afraid we will have to endure Dominic's bossy wife. How could you have let him marry her, Maman?'

'I could never control your brother and sister,' she smiled. 'And Georges?' she asked.

'Definitely Georges,' Alfie confirmed.

Sophie's eyes softened. 'But not Max. How I wish he were here.'

Sebastian put his hand over hers. 'He had a long and happy life.'

Alfie leant towards her. 'He would have been proud of you, Maman.'

'The first woman to receive a lifetime achievement award for cardiothoracic surgery,' declared Sebastian. 'That's a pretty extraordinary accomplishment in anyone's book.' He lifted his wife's hand and held it to his lips. 'And I am so proud of you, my beloved doctor.'

'We all are,' Alfie reiterated.

'Well,' Sophie paused, remembering the events from over sixty years before. 'When I was small child, I made a promise that one day I would mend faulty hearts.'

'And you have kept your promise,' said Sebastian, 'to yourself and to the world.'

Acknowledgements

This novel would not have been possible without the extra-ordinary knowledge and patience of pioneering heart surgeon David Watson MBE FRCS, who helped me to create an authentic atmosphere for my heart surgeon, Sophie Bernot. I was lucky enough to be in the presence of someone who had actually operated in the 1950s and 1960s, in a period of ground-breaking innovation, and whose career took him to the pinnacle of medical heights. He still advises to this day.

After surgical training in London at Barts, Royal London and Royal Brompton, he went to Leeds to help in the development in the new specialty of cardiac surgery.

He was one of the first surgeons to use Profound Hypother-mia in the treatment of Congenital Heart Disease. He created a research unit which made significant contributions to the evolution of the biological heart valve.

He was the Founder and Past President of Heart Research UK. For the last year David has checked my work and double-checked it for technical mistakes. He has patiently listened to my questions and answered every one. He has suggested medical scenarios that would work in the context of the day and he has corrected any mistakes that I made. I have loved every moment of my time being tutored by this fascinating and eloquent man.

Thank you David.

Last year, I went with my husband on an extended trip through France. I needed to find towns and villages for my characters. I found the beautiful Chateau de Villette in Poil, Burgundy, just out of the wine region. With the charming owners Coen and Catherine Stork's consent, I shamelessly moved their house to Pommard near Beaune and used it for my main character, Sebastian's ancestral home. Afterwards we went to Chamonix, where I visited the celebrated climber and artist, Andy Parkin at his studio. To my eternal gratitude, he helped a complete stranger understand the dangers and complexities of climbing. He drew maps of my character Sebastian's possible route up Mont Blanc, and he described where he could come to grief on the way down. We discussed avalanches and other hazards that the mountains can throw at you. Thank you Andy for checking and double-checking my ascent and descent of Mont Blanc, and for making sure the equipment used was accurate for the period. Thank you for your prompt replies when yet another email arrived.

Andy Parkin began his climbing career in the Peak District and then the rest of the UK before visiting Zermatt and Chamonix where he made many prized first ascents. He climbed in Alaska and Pakistan but in 1984, after a serious climbing accident in Switzerland, he threw himself into his other love, painting and sculpture. For the next few years while body and mind healed he sculpted works made out of debris found on his precious mountains, making pieces which reflected his beliefs that we need to be creative as regards to our approach to our planet.

He returned to climbing and made difficult ascents all over

the world, solo climbing being his big love. He became involved with Community Action Nepal created by Doug Scott and together they attempted the famous Makalu and K2. He began teaching at the deaf school in Baharbise, north of Kathmandu, towards the Tibetan border in 2009, and is proud that some of his ex-students have now become teachers and artists.

My thanks go to the wonderful late Teddy Faure Walker. During a period of extreme illness he gave up some of his precious time to write an account of his amazing adventures climbing Mont Blanc while serving in the Second Battalion Coldstream Guards. The clarity of his descriptions inspired and excited me and set me on my own journey to Mont Blanc. I will be forever grateful.

Thanks also to Chantal Gave, the most charming and elegant Parisian, who offered not only to read my novel, but to critique it through the eyes of a French woman. She then invited me to visit her in Paris, and to my eternal gratitude, she took me to every destination necessary to give colour and depth to my story. Over coffee in some of Paris's celebrated cafés, she told me what a French woman would say and what they certainly would not. She corrected details that I could never have known.

Thank you also to Nicola Finlay for your patience and eagle eye. I could not have done this without you. Also the wonderful Elise Smith, Pink Jack, Fleur Parker and Lauren Garnham. To my gorgeous daughter Clementine Coram James, who persevered through every version of the draft. To Eddie Coram James, an exquisite wordsmith, Henry Coram James, Emily Ryder, in fact my entire wonderful family for being so patient when I ask them to listen to snippets of the book! Thank you to Katya Marks, my gorgeous niece and medical student, who provided details of her course and indeed many aspects of student life. To my dear friends, Jo Frank, Louise Harwood and Caro Sanderson, for always being on hand to listen and give suggestions. To Keith Beslauer who generously showed me footage of his experiences during an avalanche when one member of his party actually lost his life. And to Dominic Hughes for introducing me to this brave man. To Patrick de Pelet, for double-checking all the French used in the novel. Thanks must go to my wonderful and patient husband, who took me on a tour of France last summer. Together we found locations and settings for each of my characters. Thank you for spending hours with me on Google Earth and for retaining your sense of humour most of the time. My thanks go to my wonderful agent Matilda Forbes Watson and her assistant Alina Flint, so much has gone on behind the scenes and you have been incredible. And of course to Clare Hey at Orion, my amazing editor, and Olivia Barber, her editorial assistant. I have been so lucky and I want to thank each and every one of you.